India Marion Monroe had long ago given up the idea that working in a coffee shop was stimulating...

These days, she had no reason to giggle about six shots of espresso in a drink; too many men liked to leer when they ordered a "sex-shot." The second most annoying thing about being a barista in an occupation that had dozens, she simply had to roll her eyes when they thought they were being funny or original.

The honor of most annoying thing, however, she reserved for the type of person at her window right now: A pretentious coffee lover, who thought that the more they modified their drink, the more cultured a human being they were. Usually from Seattle, they were the bane of her existence, if not her tip jar. Indeed, she didn't know what bothered her more about the whole thing: that they honestly thought they could taste the difference or that she honestly had learned to remember all that verbiage when it came out of their mouths.

Returning to the window, she looked out, batted her eyes, glanced at their license plate, and got to work: "Washington tags? Welcome to Surfland! Thank you for ordering a half one-and-a-half percent milk, half soy, half caf/decaf, no foam, sugar-free vanilla latte, with one Splenda, one sugar and served at 165 degrees. Can I grind you anything else?"

She was disgusted, he was disgusting, and she didn't have a choice.

Also by Barton Grover Howe

The Surfland Novels:
Beach Slapped
The Beach is Back

Surfland Day Trips (Short Novels):
Parrot Eyes Lost

Humor Collections:
Flying Starfish of Death: A Beach Slapped Humor Collection, 2008
Addicted to Foo-Foos: A Beach Slapped Humor Collection, 2009
Cats with Thumbs: A Beach Slapped Humor Collection, 2010
Mermaid—The Other White Meat: A Beach Slapped Humor Collection, 2011

The Beach is Back

A Surfland Novel

BARTON GROVER HOWE

To Kris and Dean,
Thanks for giving me a
reason to believe anything is possible.

— Barton

BGH Publishing
Lincoln City, Oregon
www.BartonGroverHowe.com

THE BEACH IS BACK

Acknowledgements

This book was largely written during
Spring Break 2012: The Week of Hell.
I am in debt to those who helped me survive it:

My wife, Allyson, and daughter, Nola:
Who went to see the in-laws for a week
so Daddy could be anti-social and angry all on his own.

Mother Nature and La Niña:
Who were kind enough to make it the
wettest March on the Oregon coast in nearly a century,
ensuring that it seemed nothing like actual spring.

The folks of Beachin' Pizza:
(I plan to use this as a book title someday...)
Who fed me at the beginning and the end of the week —
and especially Erin and Soleil, who made me cookies.

The Beach is Back

A Surfland Novel

Chapter 1

Jackson Poe

TUESDAY

"Seriously: In what universe is having Sylvester Stallone hanging naked over my cheesy sticks a good idea?"

A question meant to be asked to no one in particular, Jackson Poe knew his friend Rip Rockford would have an answer anyway — and Rip did not disappoint. "Oh, I don't know, Stallone is pretty cheesy. And I'd have to imagine he's got quite a—"

"Do not finish that sentence."

As was their nature, the long-time friends had found something to debate about as they grabbed an afternoon latte — this time the nature of kitsch. Poe hated just about all of it, and Rip found very little of it he didn't. Although even Rip had to admit Sylvester Stallone's wax and naked body-double from "Demolition Man" in dozens of Planet Hollywoods had been a little much. Not that he would admit this to Poe.

"Let's ask the barista," Rip said, goading Poe on. "Kinkel, what do you think of a naked Stallone hovering over your food?"

"I think," Kinkel said, only partly refusing to be pulled in, "that my drinks make enough people sick."

Neither Poe nor Rip had a response to that. It was unfortunate public knowledge that since Kinkel McGuire had started working at Bendovren Coffee, a number of his customers had wound up throwing up in a number of public places. As one of the customers had been the local health inspector for Surfland, Oregon, and the "place" had been on the editor of the local paper, things couldn't get much worse for Kinkel.

Breaking the awkward silence, Kinkel pushed three drinks across the counter. "That comes to $11.85, health insurance not included."

Dropping a five-dollar bill in the tip jar before a clearly surprised Kinkel, Poe simply smiled and said, "Hey, not every drink of yours makes people sick. And since one of them's going to that uptight pain-in-the-ass over there in the back corner, I'll just assume if one's bad, it's his."

Starting to walk across the coffee shop with two of the drinks, Poe felt a slight nudge in his ribs as Rip spoke: "You're a good person. But should you really be rewarding him for getting vomit all over your ex? I thought you still liked her."

"I do, but she's OK with what happened — mostly. You'll notice she buried it on page four. She knows how hard it's been to keep this place open; she didn't want to make it worse," Poe said, a small grin now coming to his face. "Besides, Aly broke up with me..."

Whatever else either of them might have said, however, was quickly drowned out by an increasingly loud conversation coming from the back corner.

"PLEEN! THA eh TAH-buh!"

"It is not terrible; it's inspired!"

"'Ah WAH-fuh Play Tuh BAH'? TAH BUH!"

Poe had to agree, "A Water-Ful Place to Be," was about as lame and generic a tourism slogan as he'd heard in a long time. The "inspired" genius of the latest Executive Director of Surfland Tourism, Plink Blayton, Poe hadn't met a single person who liked it — including Dick Yelpers, President of the Surfland Tourism Advisory Board, who continued to express his opposition.

"'WAH-fuh Play Tuh BAH'?" repeated Dick, now very much living up to his nickname, "Yelling Yelpers": "EV-ay-wah hah WAH-uh!"

Every eye was now on the back corner. Between the volume and Dick's speech impediment from a tragic super-heated pizza accident, it was nearly impossible to ignore the conversation. One which Plink acted like he'd never heard before, even though he had dozens of times.

"Again, not everyone has water; Arizona doesn't, Nevada doesn't, all those angry people in the Middle East don't; that's why they're pissed all the time," he said. "But Surfland does: We're seven miles of public beaches on the Pacific Ocean with a three-mile long lake right on the other side of Highway 101."

Poe now shaking his head at Plink's ability to somehow boil problems in the Middle East down to something that served his narrow purpose, Poe tried to bring some sanity — and volume control — back to the coffee shop.

"Gentlemen, while I'm sure this discussion is fascinating for the six-hundredth time, you invited me here, remember? So, perhaps it's time we move on. That, and the only thing that's keeping me from killing you, Plink, is that my hands are each holding a cup of coffee."

"I thought that's what I was here for," Rip said. "You said asshole mitigation was a legitimate business expense."

Indignant, Plink began to raise his voice again. "Poe, you have no right to call us—"

Cutting him off, Poe made every effort to be sincere. "Not 'us,' Plink. Just you, and since I'm the one holding a steaming cup of 180 degree liquid conspicuously near your groin, you should probably be nicer to me. Besides, you hired me, remember?"

Forced to admit both of these statements were true, Plink tried to take control of the conversation again. "Just make sure you give me the right cup of coffee; they brew me my own special blend here."

"Of that, I have no doubt," Poe said, setting down the coffee and quickly speaking again before Plink could react. "And trust me, I have no desire to drink that black-tar Splenda-laden swill you call coffee. Yours is right—"

Before Poe could finish, however, the entire shop seemed to shudder on its foundation. Nothing huge, but enough to get Poe's attention: "Was that an earthquake?"

"Oh, for Gods sake, Poe," Plink said, as he grabbed his cup of coffee. "So what if it was? It's the coast of Oregon; we have those. You're the one who wanted to get started. Let's start."

Conceding Plink had a point — that bothered Poe as much as the earthquake — Poe absent-mindedly grabbed his coffee and knocked back a huge swallow before getting down to business. He almost wished he hadn't; Kinkel's brewed abomination tasted nothing like Poe's normal cup of coffee.

"OK, Plink," Poe said, finally choking down his drink, "you need to have all the press releases done in time for me to proofread by Thursday morning. That way, I've got plenty of time to check them before Friday's—"

Before Poe could finish his sentence, however, he felt his chest and lungs began to tighten, feeling almost as if they were on fire. Stumbling forward, he crashed into Plink, sending both of their coffees spilling onto the floor, where Poe quickly found himself lying in them. A sticky feeling crawling up his back, he found himself looking up at his companions and a gathering crowd, who were now looking down at him.

"CAH NY-WAH-WAH! CAH NY-WAH-WAH!" Dick yelled.

"Oh, great," Kinkel moaned. "Now I killed guy. I wonder if they're hiring at the mall."

"Poe! Poe! Can you hear me? Help is on its way!" Rip told him.

"Nice, Poe," Plink whined. "You spilled my coffee. If you think you're being paid for this, you're wrong."

Reality starting to fade, Poe was bothered by three things: One: It was very possible he was going to die. Two: The last words he would hear on this Earth would be the plaintive bitching of Plink Blayton. And three: That —

"Poe!" Rip screamed at him, now starting to compress Poe's chest. "The paramedics will be here in three minutes! Hold on!"

OK, maybe it was back to two things — thank God Rip was there. And with his last conscious breath, he whispered his final regret: "Worst. Latte. Ever."

Chapter 2
Ryan Nordin

Where was Q when you needed him?

In the James Bond movies, 007 had Q to build all his gadgets and make sure everything worked. Ryan Norcross had only himself to do such research and design work, and as he fiddled with the alternator in his car for what seemed like the 80th time today, he wished his movie heroes were more than just fictional characters. Not that Q and Bond were the only differences between fiction and reality.

Bond always seemed to have the latest model of Aston Martin; Ryan had a 1962 Alpine Sunbeam convertible that he'd found on Craigslist. Bond had unlimited capital to pursue his goals, while Ryan just had the money he made working at his parents' coffee shop, Bendovren Coffee. Bond had a high-tech workshop to access, Ryan just had his garage, and lately not even that; covering for his parents at the coffee shop all the time, he was forced to do most of his work in the dirt lot behind the shop.

Bond had amazing good looks — no matter who was playing him. Ryan was Ryan: a normal junior in high school of average height and weight with a head of wavy black hair that definitely wasn't MI-6 issue. Bond had Moneypenny and a whole host of beautiful women, while Ryan had... Well, maybe there he had Bond beat.

"Ryan, get your head out of that engine," said a dulcet voice from behind the steering wheel. "I'm going to try to start it up, and I'd really hate to kill you in the midst of making something that's supposed to kill someone."

Stepping back from the car, Ryan looked in his driver's seat to see the only person besides himself he'd ever let sit there: Indy Monroe. A fellow gear head and James Bond movie freak, she had been his best friend ever since they'd met at Surfland's Harrison High School, the local 7-12 combined junior high/high school. Four years later and two years after her graduation they remained happily so.

"Don't make me regret giving you a key," he told her. "We've been working on this thing since eight this morning. You blow it up, you owe me all that time back."

"First of all, it's not a Lotus Esprit; one mistake isn't going to blow it up," she said, throwing back at him one of their favorite Bond scenes. "And don't you for one minute tell me about your time; I'm the one who's been out here all day on my day off. You're just my coffee monkey."

Frustratingly, Ryan had to admit it was true. It was supposed to be his day off as well, but with his parents out of town for the last three weeks, there was no such thing as time away from the family business. He didn't blame them; taking care of his sister after her accident had to come first.

So Ryan worked — a lot, squeezing in time with his car and Indy wherever he could. Today that seemed to mean wearing ruts into the ground running back and forth to the shop. He'd spent most of the day helping Kinkel with the occasional rushes of customers as well as trying to teach him how to make a decent espresso drink. It didn't seem to be working.

"He always uses too many beans, and he doesn't grind them enough," Ryan complained to Indy. "And he doesn't always wash his hands between drinks. I don't know, maybe that's why people keep getting sick."

"Look at the bright side: At least you don't own a Mexican restaurant; a bean problem there could be fatal," she said, her voice starting to take on a darker tone. "And don't even talk about not grinding enough. My boss says there's no such thing."

Wincing, Ryan regretted even bringing up the word, as it was a sore spot for both of them. At one time, Indy had worked for Ryan's parents. But as the economy crashed, so did Indy's hours, paycheck and tips. Virtually the sole support for her and her Mom, she'd had no choice but to find another job. That it was at a coffee shop called "Grind Me Hard Coffee" was horrifying to both of them, on so many levels.

Focusing on the car again, neither said a word. Each of them continued to check and recheck their work until finally Indy turned the key in the ignition. The engine rumbled to life.

Ryan smiled; whoever had done most of the work, the job was nearly done. Deciding that enough time had passed to make conversation comfortable again, Ryan used the suavest man in the universe to jump-start the mood: "Do you expect me to talk?"

Smiling, Indy knew just what to say: "'No, Mr. Bond. I expect you to die!'

"*Goldfinger*, Very nice," she said. "Now let's see if something else from that classic can come to life today, shall we?"

Ever since purchasing the car, Ryan had been spending his time and money converting it into "James Bond's car." It was no Aston Martin, but it was British, and for the moment that was good enough. For someone who already had a fake Walther PPK and an empty bottle of '69 Bollinger champagne, it was the ultimate creation.

His first step had been installing revolving license plates, one each from Germany, England and Oregon, the latter considerably trimmed. Not exactly legal, the Surfland police seemed content to let him get away with it since his parents owned the only coffee shop in town where they never had to worry about baristas spitting into their drinks. (That was another thing Bond had on Ryan: One had a license to kill, the other barely had a license to drive his car around town.)

Next, he'd fashioned spinner hubcaps that doubled as tire slashers. Definitely not street legal in their original form, he'd replaced the slashers with spray-painted slices of a Nerf football, almost cutting off his middle finger off installing them. On the upside, it was a particularly fun injury to show the many people who didn't understand his near-neurotic passion for James Bond.

Last week he'd put a secret control mechanism into the console between the front seats. Accessed by pressing a hidden button near the parking brake, the lid sprung open to reveal six silver switches. All of them were inactive — until today. For today was to be his greatest achievement: The (simulated) ejector seat from the Aston Martin DB-5 in *Goldfinger*. Another invention that would never be street legal, he'd fashioned his own compromise: tiny fireworks under the seat would explode and push the seat up about a foot. Not designed to actually move the rider anywhere out of the car, it at the very least would give them one hell of a surprise.

And now it was ready. Smiling, Ryan tried to imagine who he'd give a ride to first. Maybe Kinkel; he had a good sense of humor, and he owed Ryan. Right before Indy had to quit, Ryan's parents had given Kinkel a job after Kinkel got caught jamming his nipple into one of those machines that smashes pennies into souvenirs.

"I think it's ready, Indy," Ryan said. "Just one more thing to check; I'm not really sure how many fireworks I should put under there; I just want a lot of smoke, you know?"

"You want me to look at it? My dad used do a lot of pyrotechnics down in Hollywood," Indy said, a bit of regret in her voice. "He never worked on a Bond movie, but he did some cool stuff..."

Once again, reality brought silence to their day of fun; Indy's dad had been largely unemployed for years. And as he was fearful of leaving California in case a last-minute job requiring special effects came up, she hadn't seen him in nearly 11 months. Quietly, she walked up behind Ryan, who was now bent over the seat, his lower body sticking out of the open door.

"Sorry," she said. "I get kind of moody sometimes... Damn James Cameron! You should put the fireworks under his seat — without the seat," she said now laughing and bringing herself out of her mood.

"We still on for the fundraiser Friday?" she asked. "My Mom really appreciates you doing that. "With everything you and your parents are going through, she figured you'd have to cancel."

"No problem; I know your creepoid boss sure as hell isn't going to do it," he said, turning to look at her. "What my parents are going through is temporary. Your mom—"

BOOM!

In the days to come, Ryan would learn he had used far too many fireworks under the seat. Where he had just wanted to produce smoke, he had instead packed enough of what was essentially a micro-explosive to blow the seat completely out of the car. Had he not turned to talk to Indy, the very aptly named ejector seat likely would have killed him, instead of just knocking his senses into next week.

That was in the future, however. Now, there was just the partial return to the land of coherence, the recognition that he was lying on the ground with his ears ringing, and the realization that he had no idea what the hell had just happened. How long it took him to even notice Indy was lying on the ground next to him, he had no idea.

"Was that an earthquake?" he asked her. Not hearing an answer, he wondered if he had gone deaf. Hearing his own voice, however, he came to realize she was unconscious, too.

Now worried more about his friend than himself, he struggled to get to his feet, only to crash to the ground once more. Fighting unsuccessfully the urge not to pass out again, he simultaneously wondered who would call the ambulance — and why was it already here?

Chapter 3
Pete Polanski

"I'm telling you, Aly: There was no earthquake," Pete Polanski said over the phone in his most exasperated tone. "Trust me on this; I'm standing here with a dozen firefighters, every one of whom is trained to respond to every disaster imaginable, and not one of us felt an earthquake."

"Pete, I'm telling you: The whole newspaper building shook."

"That's what you said when Billy Nerker took out your awning."

"He hit the building, Pete," Aly said, now starting to get a bit annoyed herself.

"Exactly. But it wasn't an earthquake, was it?" Pete said. "Look, my point is, whatever it was, it was localized. For instance, look across the street: Are people running out of the coffee shop?"

"No, but that could just mean Kinkel's not working."

"Aly Oliviera, that is not very nice."

"Someone threw up on me, Pete. I don't have to be nice."

"Now, Aly, don't tell me that's the first time someone's thrown something vile on you," he said, now starting to disarm her frustration. "You're the editor of the Surfland Siren: Everyone hates you."

"The feeling's mutual," she said, now laughing herself. "Fine, just tell me if you hear anything else, OK?"

"No problem. And expect a press release from me by tomorrow morning about this mess in front of me..."

As the Public Information Officer for Surfland Fire & Rescue, it was Pete's job to field calls from the media and get information out to them. Whether that was answering calls about potential earthquakes or getting the facts out about a fire at a local restaurant, it was his job to talk to people like Aly. The fact that she was his friend, well, that just made it more fun.

Nevertheless, if Aly had called even half an hour earlier he wouldn't have had time to talk to her. A blaze had consumed Mermaid in Oregon, a popular dining spot for locals and tourists alike. All that remained was the giant 10,000-gallon aquarium where girls in faux fins had been swimming for 15 years.

Uniquely Oregon, they swam with cold-water fishes, not tropical ones, picking over an actual piece of an old lumber schooner instead of fake pirate ships. Having just had dinner there last week, Pete couldn't help but start to reminisce; he had no idea a redhead could look so good in a dry suit.

Must be the valves, he thought. They placed 'em right where —

And just like everything else today, his swim down memory lane was interrupted as his phone rang again. A very familiar — and increasingly bothersome — number showing on the screen.

"Aly: It. Was. Not. An. Earthquake. What do I need to do to explain that?"

"Nothing, smart ass," she said, allowing him his exasperation. "But maybe you can explain why there's a car seat sitting in the middle of Billy Nerker's windshield out back in my parking lot?"

Pete had to admit that was a new one. "You sure you didn't put it there? I've seen the way he treats you. I was there when he stood on a barstool at Bo's Crab and Anvil, banged a mallet on the crossbeams, and screamed to everyone you were a 'flaming homo-sapiens.' Tell me he hasn't pissed you off."

"Yes he has, and no I didn't, though I am pleased to note that Karma's a bitch." Aly said.

"Great," Pete said, getting the conversation back on topic, "you didn't mangle Billy's truck. But assuming the seat's not on fire, you should probably call the police," Pete said, his curiosity not outweighing the fact he had a potential crime scene in front of him. Whatever had taken out the restaurant had been quick, too quick, in his experience.

"OK, I'll give the cops a buzz — and Billy's insurance company. I've got 'em on speed dial, after all—" Aly said before stopping. "Uh, Pete... I think Kinkel is working."

"Why is that? Billy just throw up on you?"

"No. There's an ambulance pulling up in front of Bendovren Coffee across the street."

Telling her he'd get back to her as soon as possible, Pete hung up on Aly and gave the on-scene captain at Bendovren Coffee a call. Within minutes Pete became aware that there were two different scenes in play: an apparent heart attack inside and two unconscious teenagers out back in the parking lot. All were on the way to the hospital and expected to make a full recovery, information that was all the more valued when he was told who the victims were.

This time, he'd be the one calling Aly.

"Yes, Poe is fine," Pete told her. Everyone in town knew their romantic relationship had ended some time ago, but those closest to them knew that they remained friends — and maybe more than that. "And don't blame Kinkel; I think he's doing enough of that himself. He just laid down in the middle of Highway 101 near his house."

"Oh my God! He tried to kill himself?"

"Well, not exactly. He did it in a crosswalk using orange road cones from a local construction project. But I'd definitely say it was a cry for help."

"Well then, what happened to Poe?" Aly asked, now starting to sound a bit more like a chastising ex, than just a worried friend. "He's a little stocky and eats too many cheesy sticks, but I figured he'd at least be in his 50s before he had that inevitable heart attack."

"That's for the doctors to figure out, so we'll see," Pete said, noncommittally. "But I did solve another mystery. Let's talk about your car seat: are there scorch marks on the bottom...?"

Hanging up the phone again — he'd never spent so much time at one rescue scene talking about another one — he had to admit he was still curious about the seat. He knew the what, but not the how and why. Knowing Ryan and his family as he did, he assumed he'd find it was relatively innocent. Stupid, to be sure, but not malicious — something that was definitely not the case at Mermaid in Oregon.

On scene less than an hour, the department's forensics team had found evidence of an accelerant in the debris, the exact nature of which was unclear. Indeed, it was something they'd never seen before. His guys were no CSI: Portland; they'd sent it to the state lab. But as to the crime of arson, they were certain of that. This wasn't even subtle; whoever had burned this up didn't care that someone else knew it. Looking around, he wondered if they might still be on scene.

It was well known that arsonists very often hung around to watch their handiwork. Looking up and down the street, Pete couldn't pick out anyone who seemed particularly suspicious: Two teenagers shooting video on their iPhones; a guy sitting in his vintage Volkswagen Bug staring out at the beach; a family of four, their small daughter clutching her mermaid doll, the dry suit clearly reading "Mermaid in Oregon."

God, Pete was going to miss the real thing — if he ever got the chance; his phone was ringing again with the same caller ID.

"Aly! Seriously, what do you have against me and my Mermaid fantasies? She's wearing a dry suit! I even checked with my wife, she's totally OK with it. Says it keeps her from having to go to the pool as much."

"I'm having lunch with your wife tomorrow; I'll let her know," Aly said, her frustration starting to show, too. "And far be it from me to interrupt your very active imagination in the middle of a blackened pile of timber, but this time I thought I'd tell you something you didn't know."

Pete was still not in the mood: "Let me guess, Bobby Nerker is on the way to the hospital; his insurance agent tried to kill him," Pete said. Even liking Aly as well as did, he was having a hard time imagining what could possibly be worth one more phone call.

"No," Aly said. "Bobby's fine, I guess; that kind of stupidity never really gets better."

Aly went on, now definitely more somber: "It's Margaret Tandy: She's on her way to the hospital. Every media outlet in Portland is going to be giving you a call. Thought you'd want to know."

"Well, shit... If she dies that's really going to screw up my plans."

"Pete! You don't mean that!"

"No," he said, his voice trailing off, "I don't," and he hung up the phone, now speaking to no one but himself.

"Except that I kind of do..."

Chapter 4
Margaret Tandy

It was good time to keel over and fall out of wheelchair.

Any earlier, and most of Surfland's fire and rescue crews still would have been at either Bendovren Coffee or Mermaid in Oregon. A department largely made up of volunteers, summer was always a busy time, but three emergency scenes at once just about had them at their limits. It was fortuitous, then, that the initial responders to all three scenes were concluding their duties when the call came in that Margaret Tandy was on the floor, possibly receiving CPR. That every last one of those responders went immediately to her house surprised no one.

Mrs. Margaret, as she was called, was the granddaughter of the first white family to explore the Surfland area. Although the family and the giant company they had founded had been located in Portland for more than a century-and-a-half, Surfland had been their summer home for as long as Surfland had been in existence.

Longer even: Surfland itself was only 44 years old, having been created from five smaller towns in 1968. Uniting so their residents could afford to build a sewer system, Mrs. Margaret and her family had been among the leading proponents for their small town of Whig City joining what was to become Surfland. Nearly a half-century later, the only bumper sticker on Mrs. Margaret's 1963 Jaguar E-Type remained:

"Surfland: Bonded in Crap Since 1968."

In the ensuing years they had done other things: Expanded the hospital, built parks, and funded what was believed to only section of a library dedicated completely to waterproof books, so residents could read them on the beach and not worry about them getting wet. The family even funded Surfland's first city hall, a building remaining in use today, though now as a microbrewery. A move Mrs. Margaret favored, she further endorsed it by knocking back the first amber when the brewery opened.

So when word came that her life might be in peril, it was not surprising that every rescuer in town went to her house to see what they could do. What they found, however, was beyond what anyone could have imagined, and although many people would recount the incident somewhat differently to Aly when she called to get notes for her story, the incident commander summed it up best: "Her dog was giving her CPR."

No one believed this, of course. Giant English Sheepdogs are not in the habit of giving a compression to ventilation ratio of 30:2, all the while making sure they don't break a centenarian's fragile ribs. Indeed, when Aly read the rescuers' statements back to each witness, every last one of them asked her to please change their answer to say it just seemed like that's what the dog was doing.

What they all did know, however, was that the dog seemed to be the only one doing anything. Among Mrs. Margaret's children, grandchildren and great-grandchildren, no one seemed to have any idea how to help her. If it had been any other family, some might have suggested they didn't want to. (Aly did, in fact, ask this, only to be ignored, insulted and told, "And you wonder why people think you're a homo-sapiens.")

Because this was not any other family, this was the Tandys. And although they had their flaws like any other family, everyone knew their lives, both personal and professional, revolved around Mrs. Margaret.

Indeed, having slid into profound dementia in the last several years, they had refused to put her in a care home or any other facility. That she was even able to attend this Friday's Tandy Family Tribute and re-dedication of Hope Falls Park was a testimonial to her family's care.

And so it was that after determining Mrs. Margaret had just passed out, and not had a heart attack requiring dog CPR or otherwise, Mrs. Margaret was put on a gurney for a trip to the hospital — just in case. Like a procession, the nearly two-dozen members of her family walked closely and quietly behind her as she was pushed towards the ambulance. Because all of them could not fit inside the ambulance, none of them did, choosing instead to follow in their cars. Not that Mrs. Margaret rode alone with the paramedics.

Her dog came with her.

For even if the dog had not given her CPR, it was understood this dog was special. Her constant companion for nearly 14 years, he was the biggest sheepdog anyone had ever seen. And whatever else her mind would or would not let her do, Mrs. Margaret never once let go of the scruff on the giant dog's neck. His name was Bekk, and no one said a word as he climbed into the ambulance, remarkably nimble for a giant dog of such advanced years.

Chapter 5
Pete Polanski

Even on a normal day, Surfland's St. Gangulphus Hospital didn't really look like a hospital. Sitting on the shore of Nelta Lake, the one-story structure was no bigger than a small suburban office building and from the outside even looked like one. Giving directions to visitors, locals often just told people to keep driving until, "You see the thing that looks like a bank on the left — and don't get confused by the drive-thru; that's the ER."

Today, however, it looked even less like a hospital; circus would have been more like it — and as Pete went through the ER doors into the back, he was running right into the center ring. Surrounding him was a snapshot of the day's activities. At one bed, Indy was holding a bag of ice on Ryan's jaw. At another, Aly was talking/lecturing to Poe; something about cheesy sticks. And in the corner, what appeared to be a psych-counsel with Kinkel, still clinging desperately to an orange road cone.

Dominating it all, however, was the Tandy family, each huddled around Mrs. Margaret on her gurney, still clinging fervently to her dog. Only one person, however was talking, Dr. Morton Bracewell. Relatively new, Pete only had the vaguest idea who he was — just as Dr. Bracewell had no idea who he was dealing with.

"Mr. Tandy, I don't care how much money you've donated to this hospital — my wife loved the Jacuzzi bathtub in the birth suite, by the way — that dog cannot be back here."

"First, call me Evan. Second, It's just a dog; he's quite clean I can assure you," Mr. Tandy said with no arrogance whatsoever. "We have him shampooed daily at the Aveda Spa."

"Mr. Evan, I mean, Mr. Evan Tandy, I mean, oh crap, Mr. Tandy, it's not that he's not — Aveda? Really? My wife loves that, too. Something about loofa sponges...

"But, sir, I already have a health inspector who hates me because I wouldn't label someone's vomit toxic waste. This would get the whole hospital in serious trouble."

Listening, Pete understood both of their views. The family wanted their mother to feel safe, the doctor wanted to make sure his job was. Certainly, it wasn't Pete's job to decide, but as the only one in the room with a badge, he did feel some responsibility to deal with what was happening.

Heck, Pete had a dog, loved him more than anything save his wife, and sometimes his wife would say that wasn't even true. (In Pete's defense, he'd never once actually told his wife she was the one who should sleep on the floor.) But even Pete understood dogs did not belong in the ER; if they did, Buffett wouldn't be asleep in his Jeep right now.

He did not look forward to what he had to do next.

"Mr. Tandy, I think—"

"Mr. Tandy," Poe said, now rising from his bed, Aly steadying him. "I think the dog is just fine, don't you agree, Pete?"

"I think you've been taking hints from her on interrupting people's thoughts," he said pointing to Aly. "Besides, you two ganging up on me violates the 'We Broke Up' code.'"

Poe appreciated Pete's attempts to lighten up what was clearly a very tense room. He returned the favor: "Fine, I'll lean on you; I'm still a little woozy from being close to dead," and by the time he crossed the room, it was all Poe could do to fall into Pete's arms.

All was not as it appeared, however, and as Pete held Poe up with his arms, Poe took the time to whisper to Pete. Eyes widening, Pete looked at the dog and back at Poe, mouthing only one thing: "Really?" A smile from Poe his only response, Pete gently moved Poe into a nearby chair and told the doctor, "The dog stays. He's a service dog... mental trauma kind of thing... very new."

Looking at Pete's badge, the doctor didn't argue any further, limiting his words to just self-focused muttering: "I knew I should have moved to Astoria. Craziest damn town I've ever seen..."

The dog now welcome, Mr. Tandy turned his attention to Poe: "Thank you. Whatever you said to this officer, it clearly made the difference."

"No problem. Dogs and I go way back," Poe said. "Ask my ex, she'll tell you I am one."

"Perhaps," Mr. Tandy said, clearly wondering if he should say anything else before turning his thoughts elsewhere. "I understand you've had quite the day yourself. Can I get you anything?"

"Me? No, I'm good. But you could tell Dr. Bracewell you're opening an Aveda Spa in his hospital; he seems to be having a hard day."

"Absolutely. Consider it done," and with that Evan Tandy walked off to find the doctor.

"I should have asked for a nicer car..." Poe mused.

"You already have a Jag convertible, what more do you want?" Pete asked with all seriousness.

Poe wasted no time responding: "Have you ever driven an Aston Martin? Pure British pleasure."

"'Pure British pleasure?' Uh-huh. Why do I have the feeling you're not the only freak in this room?" And with that, Pete was off to talk to Ryan.

From what he'd heard from the accident investigators, Ryan and Indy could have killed themselves. By all rights, Pete should be calling the cops, but that was the last thing Ryan's family needed. Instead, Pete administered Ryan a tongue-lashing of the highest order, one that included the words, "public safety," "menace" and for good measure, "amputation." By the time he was done, Ryan promised he'd never do anything like it again.

Next up for Pete was Indy, who was over at the counter to get her and Ryan's exit paperwork.

Not quite done with Ryan, however, Pete asked a question he hoped the kid didn't know the answer to: "Did you have any idea what those fireworks would do? I mean, you sent a car seat 50 feet in the air, across Highway 101, bouncing three times across the roof of the Surfland Siren, and into Billy Nerker's windshield. What were you thinking?"

"In my defense," Ryan said, trying to be funny, "the British make very small seats in their convertibles." Seeing it fail by the look on Pete's face, however, he quickly moved on. "Honestly, no. My sister picked them up someplace in Washington before her last trip home... we were saving them for July 4th next week."

Fully aware of all the reasons that was not going to happen, Pete tried to lighten up a bit on Ryan. "Well, the important thing is that no one got hurt. And I wouldn't worry about Billy; he told his insurance company it was an act of God."

"And they believed that?" Ryan asked?

"Hard to say, though I can't imagine God likes Billy any better than the rest of us."

"Thank God," Ryan said, chuckling slightly at his own joke.

"Did you think he was going to sue you?"

"No. I was afraid he'd tell my parents."

Giving Ryan a good-natured literal pat on the back, Pete promised Ryan he'd still be by for coffee in the morning. He knew Ryan's pardon would be short-lived. It was a small town; Ryan's parents would find out sooner or later. For now, however, Ryan seemed relieved as he caught up with Indy, who had called a cab to take them both home. Seeing them go, Pete resolved to talk to her later.

Also leaving was Mrs. Margaret, her dog, Bekk, still dutifully at her side. Pete had never seen such devotion in an— Well, never mind. Her family trailing behind as she and Bekk were helped into the ambulance, Pete considered the display impressive nonetheless.

"Really?" Pete asked Poe, this time actually saying it out loud.

His exit paperwork in hand as well, Poe had come up beside Pete at the ER's exit. "Really. Now leave it alone. Besides, you should have more important questions on your mind."

"Like why you keeled over and I thought you had died?"

"No. If I'd burst into flames, then I'd care what you think," Poe said. "I'll let the doctors solve that little riddle."

"Got any thoughts yourself?"

"Only that they took enough blood that I think I lost three pounds, they say I'm fine now, and that I can still help you out with your projects for Plink — assuming Mrs. Margaret lives that long. Thought about that?"

"All night," Pete said. "Worst case scenario: If she dies I'll just fake her, too."

"Are you also going to blow her up?" Poe asked with a smile. "That seems to go with it."

"Don't tell Plink you said that," Poe said, now starting to laugh a bit himself. "He just might."

Chapter 6
Indy Monroe

Standing at the ER doors waiting for their cab to arrive, Indy and Ryan had a chance to see the conclusion of what had been a very strange evening, even by Surfland standards.

In the waiting room outside the ER, the various members of the Tandy family were gathering their belongings; even the smallest of them seemed to have custom-made leather coats. Evan Tandy was still talking earnestly with Dr. Bracewell, who seemed rather earnest himself: "We'll make room for the spa by closing the pharmacy; everyone buys their drugs at Walmart these days, anyway..."

In the driveway, Kinkel's mom was strapping her son into the front seat of her car with his seat belt. Looking more like a mom buckling up an infant than a teenager, the psychologist who had been talking to Kinkel in back continued to do so out front, "Repeat after me: 'I am not an evil barista.' 'I am not an evil barista...'" Saying this at least a dozen times before sending the McGuires on their way, he suggested only that his mother let him sleep with the road cone Kinkel still gripped in his arms. That, and further counseling.

By comparison, Ryan was positively normal, with no apparent scars, physical or otherwise. Considering the exploding seat could have literally knocked his head off, a minor fracture of the jaw seemed a small price to pay. He wouldn't be chewing taffy or jerky anytime soon, but Indy knew him to be more of a mashed potatoes kind of guy anyway.

As Mrs. McGuire rolled out of the driveway, Indy saw the cab roll in, and soon both she and Ryan were on the way to their homes. "You sure you don't want to go get your car? I'll pay for the long way home."

"No," he said, uttering a sentence he would have thought impossible prior to tonight, "I think I've had enough of my car for the evening. I'll just walk to work in the morning; it's only a couple of miles."

"Good enough; I'll try to stop by tomorrow before my shift at Grind Me since I don't have to work for my pig boss until tomorrow afternoon."

"I am so sorry you have to work there; does he really expect you to call him 'Scrote'?"

"Yep," she said, trying to make Ryan feel better. "'Scrotum' would just be a little too formal for a coffee shop, don't you think?"

"I think you should kick him right in his name," Ryan said, still disgusted at the thought of her having to work there. "I see the way he looks at you; gives me the creeps."

"You should try working there," she said.

"I have a feeling I'm not exactly his type of employee; God, the man is a pig!"

"Not completely," Indy mumbled to herself, Ryan shooting her a quizzical look. "On the upside," she said, now back to reality, "I will admit I've never made so many tips in my life. Maybe I have a better rack than I thought," she said, laughing.

"You'll understand if the only rack I prefer to imagine you with is the one under my car, as you fix what are sure to be some serious burn holes in the floorboards."

"Good enough... " Indy said, her good humor covering the bitterness eating away at her. Even that thought, however, was cut short as the cab passed what had been the Mermaid in Oregon restaurant, now just a water tank and few still-smoldering embers. "Wow, and you thought you'd had a bad day."

"Jeez," Ryan said. "I wonder how many seats they blew up..."

Chapter 7

Ian Matthews

"All of them," said Ian Matthews to no one but himself as he sat in his car. "One down, all of them to go..."

Noting with satisfaction that the former crossbeams of Mermaid in Oregon were still smoldering next to the water tank, he remained slumped down in his seat. Worried that the fireman on duty might have seen him earlier, he made sure his head barely poked above the window-frame on his vintage Volkswagen Bug. It wasn't the most comfortable position in the world; quite painful, actually. But the joy of seeing the destruction of the restaurant was just too good to miss, right up until the glorious bitter end.

The frustrated owners, the unemployed workers — the crying mermaids were his favorite — the children clutching their toys: He relished seeing all of them absolutely miserable, as they deserved to be. Right up until the last firefighter left, mumbling something about his daughter's next birthday party, he watched it all — because he started it all.

One match, some special accelerant he'd picked up overseas, and a wooden building dried out despite more than 50 seasons in the rain, and it was done. One less piece of kitsch blighting the historic landscape of his beloved Surfland. The loss of the building bothered him somewhat;

it had only been Mermaid in Oregon for a decade or so. Before that it had been a fish market that he'd never actually gotten a chance to visit. But what it had become was intolerable, and he'd taken care of it.

There was much to do, however, in so many places, and as the last fire truck headed back to the station he sat back up in the seat. Waiting for a cab to pass, he pulled out onto the street and headed home.

Chapter 8
The Home of Martin and Sylvia Niemen

Surfland was a small town, but it wasn't full of idiots; people did lock their doors at night, no matter what the clichés might suggest.

But it was also a tourist town on the beach, and if there was one thing people loved it was listening to the roar of crashing waves at night. Forget a cheesy clock radio, or a child's sleep sheep — when did sheep start sounding like the ocean, anyway? — this was the real thing, and people wanted to hear it.

That's why even though the front door was locked at the house along Anchor Avenue, the sliding glass door was open. The bedroom separated from the outdoors only by a screen door with a lock long ago rusted open, the occupant not particularly worried about someone coming in via the third-story deck.

They should have.

Chapter 9
Buffett the Slumber Dog

WEDNESDAY

At the very western edge of the Pacific time zone, at precisely 45 degrees north latitude, the sun always rises early in the summer. But with the summer solstice just a few days past, it was rising about as early as it ever does: just before 6 a.m. Among the residents of Surfland that had been at the hospital Tuesday night, one definitely rose first: Buffett the Slumber Dog.

As always, he greeted the new day by going right back to sleep. Usually he switched positions, trying desperately to find space atop the covers that wasn't being violated by some bipedal mammal's legs. His favorite mornings were few: those when the bipedal mammal known as "wife" would go sleep on the floor.

Buffett was especially tired these days. His main bipedal mammal — a "Pete" — had been working on a very busy project that seemed to require them driving all over the place. Indeed, Buffett was far happier when the town was bursting into flames. Forced to stay in the Jeep and sleep so he wouldn't be in the way, Buffett was OK with being the lousiest fire dog ever. (Pete had even taken to carrying a stuffed Dalmatian in the front seat to compensate.) Not that Buffett lost any sleep over it — he rarely did — but he'd always been a bit of a disappointment...

No one knew quite where the puppy had come from; he'd simply followed the horseback ride back to the Seabiscuit Bed and Breakfast one day, and stayed. And while Katrina Snappell, the B&B's owner had no idea what kind of dog he was — maybe a husky mutt? — she had never seen such devotion in a dog. Everywhere she went on the beach, he followed.

Heading out for a private ride one day with her long-time significant other, Rip Rockford, she asked one of the staff to keep the dog inside. Making sure the dog was free to look out the window and down the beach, she left with instructions to release him in 20 minutes.

A mile and 22 minutes later, a dot appeared to the south of Katrina and Rip, a dot that quickly turned into the dog. Neither had ever in their lives seen a dog run so fast. Within seconds, Rip had given him a name: "Ladies and gentlemen, I present to you, 'Bullet the Wonder Dog!'"

In the ensuing months, Bullet continued to grow. Katrina began to suspect whatever might have been mixed in with the husky must have been quite big. When she saw him use his speed to leap 10 feet through the air and over the fences around the B&B, she even began to wonder if he might be part wolf. Concerned, she worried that if he ever became aggressive, he would have to go.

A week later, that was the least of her problems with Bullet.

It began with a normal horseback ride: a train of about a half-dozen horses, each one more docile than the tourist on its back. And — as always — Bullet followed, racing to catch up after his morning nap.

This time, however, instead of just running alongside, Bullet jumped into the air and landed perfectly across the back of the horse, right on top of the protruding pad behind the saddle. The horse took virtually no notice; one more fat kid on his back. Everyone else, however, thought it was hilarious. Even Katrina pulled out her camera to take a picture of the unique moment.

Three days later, Katrina and her guests had dozens more pictures of what was becoming an increasingly less and less unique moment. More, when Bullet got atop the horse, he simply fell asleep. Short of literally pushing him off — no easy feat with a dead-to-the-world 105-pound dog — nothing would move him from his roost.

By the end of the week, the situation had become intolerable. Bullet was now sleeping not just behind the saddle, but in it at times — a real problem when it was already occupied by a paying rider. And while some people still found it funny, the Facebook postings of a crying 7-year-old being pinned on top of a horse by a slumbering dog was no laughing matter.

Bullet had to go.

Here, Rip was indispensable. Whether it was because of all the people he knew, or just guilt at conceiving the worst name ever for a dog, Rip quickly found someone he thought could take the dog: "Pete! You're a fireman! You need Bullet the Wonder Dog!" A bit of an empty-nester with his grown son now out of the house, Pete agreed to take the dog home.

Within a week it became clear that Bullet was no wonder dog; he was barely a dog. He slept on everything in the house: leather couches, wicker chairs and stainless steel grills. Butcher block counters and ceramic stoves, thankfully none of them on. And finally, Pete's wife, every time she sat down on any of these things. A human being was no impediment to Bullet's desire for a quality resting surface. Soon, it was clear: someone had to go.

"Honey," Pete whined, "I can't take him to the pound. They might put him to sleep."

"How could you tell?" she retorted, before admitting that she didn't want to see him dead, either. She would just prefer he be dead-to-the-world somewhere else, so they reached a compromise: Pete would keep the dog out of the house any time he wasn't there. When he was, Pete would make sure he slept only on the bed. It was a California King; they'd all fit. Usually.

"You're lucky I've got a bad back," Pete's wife told him. "And one more thing: change his damn name; he's an insult to bullets, Wonder Bread and anything else you can think of..."

And so it was that Buffett the Slumber Dog came to spend most of his non-waking hours in the bipedal mammal's Jeep, sleeping in the back. Named for the noises that were constantly coming out of the speakers, Buffett didn't care what he was called as long as they didn't do it too often; he needed to sleep.

That's why the past few weeks had been such a pain. Everywhere he and Pete went, Pete was having to do things that screwed up his back seat. Something called "filming." And since the easiest place to put filming stuff — if such a thing was possible in a Jeep — was in the back seat, Buffett often found himself jammed in the front. Thankfully, Pete put away the stuffed Dalmatian at these times, but the seat was still tiny, ensuring Buffett was not a happy dog.

In this regard, Buffett felt he was fairly honest about his needs: all he wanted to do was sleep. He ate as little as possible so that not only could he spend more time sleeping, but with no calories to burn he wouldn't even get fat. Yes, he had chased the horses when he was a puppy, but puppies like challenges: It was fun trying to get a free ride down the beach and sleep at the same time. Was it his fault it took him until he was nearly full-grown to actually jump onto the saddle pad and get some rest?

Which brought him back to all this filming business. Not for the first time, Buffett wondered why he couldn't have been adopted by a real fireman, instead of a volunteer one who had to screw up Buffett's back seat. Indeed, before last night not one thing had really burst into flames in weeks, and short of the 12 hours' sleep he got every night on the bed, he was really quite exhausted. So, with this love of comfy sleep in mind, Buffett did something one morning he rarely did voluntarily: move.

It all started when he and Pete were somewhere up in the woods, near a lake or something, for what seemed like the 10th time that week. (Hard to say, really. In dog years, a week can be more than a month. And counting? Well, maybe awake dogs do it better, but that wasn't really Buffett's strong suit.)

Recognizing it was about to be another long day of Pete working with not-on-fire things that Buffett didn't care about, Buffett decided there just had to be a more comfortable place to sleep than the front seat of the Jeep. Actually choosing to get out of the Jeep for the first time in his life, Buffett jumped through the open window and went looking for a makeshift bed. There were the obvious places, of course: Moss-covered ground, piles of fern fronds, an old blanket.

But Buffett was no ordinary sleeping dog, and while he might have at one time enjoyed the challenge of being able to sleep on just about anything, his life of unmitigated comfort had spoiled him. His choice of bedding today reflected that: Moss was wet, old fern fronds were scratchy, and the blanket looked like it had been there for decades, even in people years. He was used to his comfy seat and bed, and he wanted something equally soft and clean now.

Finally his nose found something familiar; actually a bunch of somethings. Working to stick his nose and feet into a nearly invisible crack between two steel doors, he eventually succeeded. Not in breaking the doors or the lock, which was shinier than the doors, but it busting one of the doors off its rusted hinges. Moving the doors aside with his nose, he found a pile of pads. None of them were very big, but they smelled nice, like the couch back home. Finally happy, he dragged each of them out into the open, pushed them around with his nose into a kind of bed, and eventually settled down on them to sleep. Not the best spot in the world, but a lot better than the front seat of the Jeep.

How long Buffett stayed there he wasn't quite sure. But eventually he heard his bipedal mammal calling him and grudgingly rose from his pile to go back to the front seat of great uncomfortableness. Ambling back to the Jeep, however, he saw Pete had done a wonderful thing! He'd cleared out the back seat, working hard to jam the all the camera equipment into the front. It was the nicest thing anyone had ever done for Buffett. Resolving to do something nice for Pete, Buffett promised himself he would only take up two-thirds of the bed tonight.

Jumping into the back seat, however, Buffett was surprised to find himself caught on something as he laid down to sleep: One of the pads had snagged on his collar and was now in his way. This was not acceptable; now that the seat was his again, these pads were a poor substitute for a bed. Whining, he caught Pete's attention, who unhooked Buffett's collar from a tear his buckle had made in the pad.

"Amazing. Buffett: Only you could find a leather folder to sleep on in the middle of the woods," Pete said, and after looking at it for a few more seconds tossed it in on the floor. Neither of them paying it any more attention, Pete began the drive back to town, Buffett now appreciating Pete even more: *Hmm...* Buffett thought, *maybe I'll only take up half the bed tonight.*

In the weeks to come, Buffett and Pete returned to the park quite a few more times, more filming, scouting, whatever. And each time Buffett returned to his pile of pads, willing to make the sacrifice because he at least knew the ride home would be in his beloved back seat — until one day the pads were gone.

Buffett was sad that he needed to find a new makeshift bed. In some ways he'd even come to like his little spot hidden in the woods. He especially liked the fact that it smelled like the couch at home without someone always screaming at him to get off. But his depression lifted considerably when he realized that Pete was rarely alone when he visited the park these days and with those people came more cars, more open windows and more backseats. He even found one that smelled like the pads, although just like the couch at home it seemed to come with a lot of yelling.

Yelling... more yelling; the Pete's wife was at it again, just like that bipedal mammal at the park. His dreams now interrupted, Buffett began once again to distinguish them from reality, with the 5:56 a.m. rising sun now finishing the job that Wednesday morning. Working hard to ignore all of it, Buffett kicked his giant legs across the bed. Suddenly he realized: It was a special morning! The wife legs were gone — and so was the yelling! Assuming but not really caring that she was on the floor, he quickly fell back asleep until Pete finally rose and rousted him from bed.

Chapter 10
Poe

Rising just after the sun, Poe took stock of his life, as people are inclined to do after a seeming brush with death. He was in his mid-40s, packing a few more pounds than he should. His dark brown hair greying at the temples a bit, he was showing his age more these days — but not giving into it.

As he had been for most of his life, he was pretty relaxed. A writer, he'd spent his life cashing the checks of whoever would pay him. In his early years that meant he was a cog in the public relations machine of Chexon Oil, a job that sent him all over the world telling anyone who would listen how good Chexon Oil was for just about everybody. ("At Chexon Oil, we believe warming the globe is good for penguins; as you saw in that movie, they get very cold.") That he felt only one step up from being a tobacco company shill bothered him some, but not enough to quit the job and its multitude of international perks.

Eventually, however, whether it was the onset of a conscience or just middle age, he headed off to journalism school in Missouri. Motivated as much by a need to remove the taint from his byline as getting an education, he'd gotten both by the time he left. That, and a girlfriend, Aly Oliviera, with both of them graduating and heading for the Oregon coast for jobs. For Poe, both were over within a matter of months.

Nearly a decade later, however, he and Aly were still here. She running the local paper, and Poe freelance writing. And while Poe couldn't say writing stories about chowder festivals, the latest trends in tsunami survival, and crosswalk etiquette for the terminally slow were exactly stimulating, they did pay the bills. Later this morning he was meeting with the proprietor of Flipper's Music and Munchies, a former pianist who'd lost all but both middle fingers to a chainsaw and an ex-wife on a Absolut Bacon bender.

Not the best story to be sure; angry artists were not his favorite. On the other hand, at least it wasn't a dolphin-themed restaurant with naked mammals cavorting above his head, as he originally feared. It wouldn't be the easiest $675 he'd ever earned, but it was money, something he increasingly appreciated. Especially now that the economy had tanked for so many people in his adopted town of Surfland.

Indeed, it was that bad economy that had him throwing on one of his infamous ugly Aloha shirts at a time far too early for his tastes. As always, he grabbed the first one to the left; with 72 of them, decision-making took too much time. It might have matched his shorts, it might not, and since it was just a meeting with Pete, Dick and Plink, he really wasn't worried about it. He knew Pete and Dick wouldn't be bothered, and didn't particularly care if Plink was.

Heading for the garage of his small one-bedroom condo overlooking the ocean, Poe smiled in spite of the early hour. His little brush yesterday with whatever-it-was reminded him of what was truly important in life: friends, of which he had plenty; a pounding surf, which he took in every morning; and someone to love, his 2011 Jaguar XKR convertible.

The by-product of a lottery ticket he was even embarrassed to cash, she was British Racing Green, loaded, and faster than hell. That he rarely ever broke the speed limit on the streets of Surfland was beside the point. It was his, it was gorgeous, and if people thought it irresponsible that he should spend that kind of money on a car, they could kiss his flowered aloha ass. (He liked the shirts that hung down over his belt.)

Besides, if people wanted to question his sanity, there were plenty of other reasons: Why would he even have convertible in a town where it often rained 100 inches a year and rarely broke 70 degrees? Why couldn't he date anyone more than a year without pissing them off? And why would anyone go right back to the coffee shop where they could have died the day before?

Despite being the opening days of summer, it was raining as Poe drove north on Highway 101 towards Bendovren Coffee, the soundtrack from "Robin Hood: Prince of Thieves" cranked on the stereo. It was expected to clear later in the morning, but for now the early-morning sunshine had lost its battle with the clouds.

If the weather was conflicted, however, Poe was not. As long as Bendovren Coffee was open, he'd be their patron. Not exclusively; that was nearly impossible in a town of 10,000 with 18 coffee shops. But when he had a choice of where to start his day, have a meeting in the middle of it, or grab a drink to wrap it up, Bendovren was usually his first choice.

He'd interviewed the Nordins when they first moved to town from California. Refugees from the rat race, they'd been forced into the shop's name by Ryan's grandfather. Agreeing to bankroll their dream, it came with the condition that they indulge his rather bizarre sense of humor. Though Poe would never put it in his story, he rather liked the old proctologist's take on things.

In fact, Poe didn't put much of anything in his story; he'd profiled them as part of a bigger piece on area coffee shops. Even taking out the two coffee shops at the high school and one at the mortuary, no one business got more than a paragraph-and-a-half.

To Poe's horror, even in that limited space he managed to screw up their names, calling them "Norcross." To atone, he wrote a larger story on just them, choosing to focus on their discount drinks, an angle that brought them considerable business in the land of a $5 mocha. (The "Cheap Lei" with macadamia nut and coconut was especially popular.)

In the ensuing years, he'd become a friend as well as a patron. He'd gotten to know both of their kids, Eva and Ryan, through his volunteer work with the journalism class at Surfland's Harrison High School. Ryan and he had grown especially close because of their mutual love of cars and writing — and despite Poe's annoying tendency to still call him "Ryan Norcross."

It was that love of the family that kept him coming back now. He knew the bad press from what had happened yesterday would only make things harder for the entire family. Indeed, the timing couldn't have been worse; Eva had been hit by a bus while on a university trip to Vancouver, British Columbia. She'd be fine, eventually, but Ryan's parents were now spending most of their time north of the border, leaving the business in Ryan's hands until they returned.

Poe would be there when they did.

Parking in back, Poe could see the damage Ryan and Indy's little project had done to his car — and the efforts Ryan and already made to repair it. The floorboards nearly replaced and the seat ready to be remounted, Poe could hardly imagine what time of the morning Ryan had gotten there to accomplish it.

Walking into the shop, Poe saw that Ryan was working alone, yet still managing to keep up with his customers in the drive-thru and lobby. This was in part, sadly, because there weren't as many patrons as one might expect on a summer morning; Kinkel's vomit-inducing drinks were definitely taking their toll. But it was also because Ryan was the fastest barista Poe had ever seen. Indeed, just seeing Poe, Ryan went to work on Poe's usual, his hand raising one finger to show Poe how long it would be.

Walking into the back corner where he'd be meeting with the others, Poe momentarily shivered; not exactly the best memories in that space of late. But as he often did, he then looked at the historic photos on the wall, and that made him feel better. Copied old photos of the various towns and people that would someday come together to create Surfland, on less busy days he'd take them off the wall, sit down, and read the captions on the back.

Smiling at the thought he'd almost been history himself, he then turned his attention to what he always did, the stunning view from the floor-to-ceiling windows on the north side of the shop. Looking out over the GO River Wayside, the crashing surf, and the lighthouse in the background, it was one of Poe's favorite views in town.

Lost in his thoughts, he didn't even hear Ryan approach: "Hey, Poe, I made this one special — non-fatal."

Poe felt terrible: "Trust me, it'll take a lot more than a bad cup of Kinkel coffee to kill me," he said, trying to lighten the mood. "I ever tell you about the time I ate a UFO — 'Unidentified Food Object — when I was in Vietnam? I don't think it was cat—"

"Poe! Stop bugging that kid!" blared Plink's voice from across the shop. "I need my usual, we need to meet, and I'm not paying you to stand around. And where the hell are Pete and Dick?"

Sighing, Poe gave Ryan another pat on the back, both of them taking one last spectacular look down Highway 101 to the breaking waves below.

"Feel free to make him the fatal kind..."

Chapter 11
Pete Polanski

Despite Plink's insistence that Poe get down to business, the first ten minutes proceeded as their meetings usually did, with Plink and Dick yelling at each other. As President of the Surfland Tourism Advisory Board, Dick was actually Plink's boss, though it rarely seemed that way.

"Don't say it again, Dick!" Plink said, almost as if on autopilot. "We are not using 'The Beach is Back' for a marketing campaign!"

"Ih EL-unh JAH!"

"I don't care if it's Elton John! You don't see me telling people to eat crabs because it's the 'Circle of Life, do you?"

"WAH?"

"Why? It's in poor taste, it's juvenile, and you pay me to come up with these things, remember?"

Poe couldn't resist interjecting: "Actually, I kind of like it. Sort of sticks out from all the boring crap you marketing types usually come up with."

Plink got as angry as Poe suspected he would: "Well, if there's anyone who's an expert on poor taste, it's you: Madras shorts with a pink and orange Aloha shirt? Aren't there enough people throwing up? I swear to God, do you get dressed in the dark?"

Poe was really having fun now; when Plink got really angry his right eye would start to twitch in its socket. "Now that you mention it, yes —"

At this point, Pete cut him off, and whatever Poe wanted to say next he promised himself he'd remember for next time; Plink was so close to the twitch. Sadly — but maturely — Pete was trying to return some sanity to the conversation. "Gentlemen, I believe we came here to discuss the final preparations for Friday's event. Why don't we get back to that? Plink?"

"He started it..."

One of Plink's brighter ideas — and people were beginning to suspect those were a minority — was to make a media splash by stressing the town's history with one of Oregon's most famous families, The Tandys. To that end, he dug through the history books to see if there were something he could exploit beyond just the family's numerous good works; people all over western Oregon could claim those. Plink needed something special — and he found it.

In 1927, as the Roosevelt Highway — later Highway 101 — was being built through what would become Surfland, Rebekkah Tandy herself came to the city to dedicate Hope Falls Park. The wife of Josiah Tandy, she and her husband had come to the coast in 1847, the first white people other than fur trappers to do so.

Tragically, the formal dedication never happened, and history seemed to have made the park itself pay the price. The park had fallen into disuse and neglect, the lake never even given an official name. Indeed most of the town didn't even know it was there, hidden as it was on the east side of town in the forested foothills of the Coast Range. Its upkeep completely falling through the financial cracks when the towns merged to become Surfland, the only sign it even existed anymore was a locked gate on the road leading to the park.

Plink Blayton was going to bring it back to life. Better, he was going to have Mrs. Margaret Tandy there when he did it. To much media hoopla, she would finish what her grandmother could not; he'd even let her family name the lake. That she wouldn't even be able to speak bothered him little; she'd be there, and so would dozens of TV cameras and reporters.

There were doubters, of course — namely, everyone in Surfland. Most of Plink's ideas since his arrival in 2007 were downright nuts; his "Surfland Seagull Races" had produced far more poop in area parking lots than it had press coverage. And his ongoing attempt via Hollywood billboards to get Randy Newman to re-write the words to "I Love L.A." to include Surfland had resulted in thousands of wasted dollars and no phone calls from Randy. And his planned thing with the whale... well that was just nuts, YouTube generation be damned.

That's why most thought his park dedication idea would be a failure as well, mainly for two reasons: For one thing, Mrs. Margaret rarely came out in public anymore due to her fragile condition. Indeed, people had basically stopped asking for her to do anything out of respect for her family. For another, what few people could remember the park knew it was an overgrown mess of blackberry brambles and weeds, trees gone wild and a lake so banal no one even cared it didn't have a name.

When the Tandy family said they'd love to be part of "The Tandy Family Celebration and Re-dedication of Hope Falls Park," people were stunned — including Plink. This made solving his second problem all the more critical, and for that he called in Pete Polanski, volunteer firefighter and local video producer.

The first skill set made Pete ideal to help supervise clearing out the disaster that was the park; the man knew how to swing an axe. Better, he could dedicate his efforts to clearing the park in a way that made it ideal for news crews and other photographers. That Pete was friends with Poe was a semi-bonus; as Plink had no choice but to have Poe read all of his press releases, he could simply slip him into Pete's payment and call Poe a subcontractor.

That, and Pete might be the only thing that prevented Plink from killing Poe.

"...And I don't want you writing a damn thing about this, got it Poe?" Plink told him. "Wouldn't that be a conflict of interest or something?"

"Don't be ridiculous," Poe said. "You're implying I'm interested."

"Dammit, Poe! Do not screw this up! I'm still dealing with the mess you made last time."

"I'm not the one who lied to the Today Show. You should have known Ann Curry was from Oregon."

Once again, Pete could see his schedule getting blown out the door; he still had B-roll to film at the lighthouse and preparations to finish for blowing up a whale. "Gentlemen, I do not have time for this sh— This show," he said, realizing that everyone in the coffee shop was staring in their direction. "Can we please just focus on the final preparations at the park for Friday?"

Plink began: "First, Pete, when you come to the park on Friday don't bring that damn dog of yours; he keeps sleeping on the leather back seat in my car."

This was not the conversation Pete had in mind, and he was beginning to understand why Poe did the things he did. "Plink, that wouldn't happen if you didn't leave your rear window open."

"It wasn't open; he went right through it."

Pete did not have answer for that one — Poe did: "Not the dog's fault you bought a piece-of-crap Pontiac Aztek," Poe said, thrilled he'd finally gotten Plink's right eye moving. "Although you should probably thank him; he probably increased its Kelley Blue Book by 20 bucks."

In control again, Pete cut Plink off before he could say anything: "Plink: You'll be happy to know just about everything's ready for Friday's shoot, though I do have some bad news."

"What, your dog ran out of garbage to bring home from the park?"

Pete was going to kill Plink himself, as he probably should have a few weeks back.

Over the last few weeks, Buffett had dragged more than a few things out of the underbrush, mostly by accident. Some, Pete had just thrown in the trash, like the Oregon State University 1965 Rose Bowl blanket. Had it actually been there for 47 years? Possibly, that was before the towns merged and people genuinely cared about the park.

Other things, however, he thought Plink might want: A mug from long-gone Nelta Lake coffee, A "Pew '62! Go Harrison High Skunks!" pennant, a leather folder from "To St. Helens and Back," an old theme restaurant in Portland. None of them were gold, but they were interesting. Indeed, given Plink's attempts to cash in on the town's history, Pete figured he might want them, so he brought them along once to his regular meeting with Plink at Bendovren Coffee.

He figured wrong.

"I don't have enough to do without you bringing me this crap? An old mug? A faded pennant?" Plink began, his voice now rising to a full-blown yell as began to wave the folder around in the air: "And look at this folder! Pure gold! Money in the bank!" Starting to notice the stares, Plink lowered his volume, if not his ire. "Jesus, is this what I'm paying you for?"

And, just as he would again and again, Pete held his tongue as he tried to keep Plink from making any more of a scene. Indeed, the only difference between that day several weeks back and today was that the shop was a lot emptier. The unfortunate Nordin family aside, perhaps that was a good thing...

"No..." Pete said, remembering his drawn out response being the right one then — and hopefully now. "No, the bad news is that whatever might have been on and in that podium in 1927 is gone now. The dedication plaque, the locking steel doors that kept the elements out of the storage space underneath, everything but the stones themselves."

"Who the hell would steal that stuff?" Plink asked, now finally calming down.

"No idea; it was all metal. Maybe they were meth heads looking for something to melt down. Hard to say, and since it could have happened anytime between 1968 and now, I don't think we're ever going to find out."

"Can we make fake ones?" Plink asked. "No one has to know."

"Only if I'm allowed to blow them up..." Pete said, an unspoken thought remaining: "...and you're standing next to them."

Chapter 12
Plink Blayton

Plink Blayton had always believed what people didn't know wouldn't hurt them, especially when it came to tourism.

Did Walt Disney tell people that the top floor of all the buildings in Disneyland's Main Street were actually shorter than the other stories? No, he just let people enjoy the fact that the buildings looked taller. Do they tell people in Washington, D.C., that Thomas Jefferson and George Washington, the fathers of democracy in America, owned slaves? No, why screw up people's enjoyment of American history? (Actually, Plink had no idea if they told people or not; he'd never been to Washington, D.C. He just knew he sure as hell wouldn't tell anyone.)

So when it came to pushing Surfland as a tourist destination, it was his belief that the truth was a malleable thing. However he could use it to bring people to Surfland was OK with him, and he assumed the merchants who were raking in the bucks would agree with him.

This had gotten him in trouble a few times, no more so than when he'd been trying to explain to Ann Curry why the Oregon Coast was not a dangerous place. Having grown up in Ashland, Oregon, she was more than familiar with the hazards it presented for the unknowing visitor — one of whom just last week had fallen from a Surfland cliff onto the beach below. Thankfully at low tide, they'd just broken their legs instead of drowning.

Ann: "Don't you feel some responsibility to warn people that those very scenic cliffs they're standing on are also somewhat unstable?"

Plink: "Of course we do! And wherever we can place signs, we do! But, Ann, as you well know, we can't put signs everywhere!"

Ann: "Can you explain to me, then, why an anonymous Oregon State Parks employee sent us this video of you removing the sign one night after the park had closed several weeks ago?"

Plink: "Ahhhh... I, aaahhhh.... I wasn't removing it. I was simply replacing it with another sign."

Ann: "This video goes for another 10 minutes, Mr. Blayton. You never come back."

Plink: "Ahhhh... Urgh..."

Ann: "Mr. Blayton: Is there something wrong with your eye?"

That incident had almost cost him his job, especially after the video went viral. Assuring Dick that his replacement sign had fallen in the ocean, Dick convinced the Surfland Tourism Advisory Board of the same thing. Whether Dick actually believed him or not, Plink would never be sure. But knowing what Plink did about Dick, it didn't matter what Dick believed. As long as Plink kept his job, Dick didn't have worry about losing his.

Perhaps that's why Dick never asked Plink why he had done it — or whether or not he was likely to do something like it again. He was. The sign he'd removed was an eyesore; who wants to get home only to find their scenic coastal photos ruined with a stupid sign warning you could die? Never mind that if you're too stupid to understand gravity you shouldn't be near a cliff, anyway: Vacation memories should be happy ones, and signs saying you could die were definitely not in that category.

Plink did learn one thing from the "Curry Killing," as it had come to be known: The full power of the Internet. Not that he hadn't worked with it before then, but like many of his generation, it was something he used, not something he understood. Following some 154,396 blog postings demanding he be fired — he'd counted — he realized it was something he'd better understand — quickly.

And he did, which is what had brought him to his latest idea: Blowing up a whale. He wouldn't be the first to do it, of course. Indeed, probably the most famous moment in Oregon coastal history was an exploding whale — all of it caught on film more than four decades ago. Grainy and replete with those Technicolors that just screamed '70s, Plink had watched it several dozen times himself. The first time he saw it he laughed his ass off.

But what was good for his generation was not good for the Internet generation. They knew what they liked, how they liked it, and '70s Technicolor wasn't going to do it for them. But Plink knew what would, and if he had to blow up a whale to do it, so be it. He was simply bringing the truth into the future. It would go viral, he knew it.

Plink had been burned once by the Internet; never again. From now on, the Internet would save his bacon instead of cook it.

"Can we make fake ones?" Plink asked. "No one has to know."

"Seriously? Again?" Pete said, clearly exasperated. "Isn't the whale enough for one week?"

"I've been through this with you before; the truth is what I say it is, and I want this event to be perfect for the world to see."

"Well, on this one you're just going to have to stick with the real truth — God, now I sound like you," Pete said, sounding disgusted with himself. "No one even knows what the original plaque said; no one's ever even seen it."

"Perfect!" Plink said, almost giddy. "We can make it say whatever we want!"

Actually looking to Poe to back him up, Pete saw his friend now on the other side of the coffee shop talking quietly to Dick. Whether Dick was there because he actually needed to talk to Poe, or just didn't want to know what Plink was doing in the name of Surfland, Pete didn't know. In any case, Pete needed to get out of here and get to work — and decided it didn't matter, anyway.

"Fine, Plink, if you can get someone to make you a plaque in just over 48 hours, I'll film whatever you want. Good luck with that."

"You know, you're right," Plink said, for once in his face looking thoughtful. "I'll just write something, put it in front of Mrs. Margaret, and tell everyone I found a copy of the text in the archives and make a plaque later. She was the only one there then, and she's senile now. No problem."

All Pete could mutter was, "You are amazing."

"Yes, I am, aren't I? Now there's something else I need you to help me with..."

Chapter 13
Poe

If it was true — as Plink believed — that Surfland should be a place where the dimwitted and clueless should be free to fall and hurt themselves in pursuit of a wonderful vacation, it was equally true there were places they could even pay for such opportunities.

Fronting the ocean along Surfland's seven miles of beachfront was more than one hotel lined with balconies. On most days these balconies were used for their intended purpose: sitting back with a drink, watching a sunset and even the occasional romantic rendezvous between people that never seemed to remember there were more than just seagulls watching. (The Jacuzzi suites were a particularly mixed blessing; while they kept the most graphic views underwater, there were still a whole lot of naked people running around before they got into the water.)

Every once in awhile, however — alcohol was usually involved — someone would decide to jump off their balcony and see if they could make it into the pool/surf/hotty's pants below. Aside from being terrifying to the people in the pool/surf/pants, it was also dangerous as hell, as drunk people have terrible aim. Nowhere was this problem greater than the The Inn at Roca de la Muerte Dolorosa.

Built alongside and bolted to a basalt cliff, it towered 10 stories above the beach. Known for some of the highest scenic views in

Surfland, it was also a favorite spot for drunk people looking to jump up to 100 feet into a pool. A problem since the hotel was built — the architects not having thought like drunken frat boys — it was a miracle that no one was hurt, killed or sued as the years went by.

So it was in the spring of 2006 when a member of the OSU chapter of Chi Psi spotted a hot girl in the pool below, got naked, and jumped eight stories in an attempt to get closer to her. If he'd gotten any closer it would have killed her. As it was, he knocked one of her eyes out of its socket when his "male organ," as the police report put it, thwacked her right in the head.

Like the dozens of previous Spring Break incidents, everyone expected the furor to pass as it always had; veteran cops even had a name for it "Assault by falling M.O." Except this time the girl in question was the daughter of the owner of The Inn at Roca de la Muerte Dolorosa, and he was definitely not amused.

To that end he had cameras installed, enough that any balcony could be seen at any time by the hotel's security staff. The moment anyone even appeared drunk on a balcony, loudspeakers would erupt, warning the individual to go back inside. This usually worked — and when it didn't, guests suddenly found some very large men knocking at their door. The cameras were a success, and soon the security staff began finding other uses for them.

Pointing some out towards the water, they could see when a giant beach log might be ready to come in on the tide and take out the first floor conference room. During storms, they were particularly useful, and more than once had spared hotel guests and workers from tragedy. (No, nothing stopped the logs from taking out the first floor windows, but at least the buffet had been moved to the second floor.)

Other cameras they pointed down the beach to see who might be approaching and leaving the hotel. This was necessary when it was discovered someone was slipping into the pool and filling the filters with dead salmon. Somehow aware of the camera angles and security guards' schedules, they managed to elude capture until a new camera pointed down the beach caught them going back to their car. A part-time musician whose car was immediately recognized — there was no room for him to play Barry Manilow tunes when the buffet moved upstairs — the new cameras had proved themselves an immediate success.

Not that everything the cameras focused on was related to the hotel, which presented Plink with his latest public relations nightmare.

"Did you see this on YouTube?" Plink could be heard yelling at Pete. "It's called *Surfland Men Have Crabs!*"

Even across the room, Poe laughed so hard he almost spit coffee on Dick Yelpers.

Having earlier gotten him and Dick away from Pete and Plink, Poe was once again listening to Dick's pitch for "The Beach is Back — or, in Yelper-speak, "Tah BEE ih BAH" — when Poe heard Plink's latest outburst. What returned him quickly to the table, however, was what Plink said next: "He's naked, for God's sake. And he has crabs!"

"A couple of two-pounders by the looks of 'em," Poe said, somehow picking the perfect time to come back to the conversation. Actually sounding for once like he wasn't trying to piss Plink off, Poe couldn't take his eyes off Plink's iPad where the video was playing. "Where'd you get this?"

"The Internet, you idiot," Plink said. "Don't you watch YouTube?"

In truth Poe didn't, not much anyway. Not anything against it; he just had other things to do. On this matter, however, it was clear Poe knew more than Plink — not that he was going to let Plink know that.

"You have no idea who shot this or where it came from?"

"No! All I know is it was shot on an infrared camera, sometime at night. That, and it's got a naked man running around with crabs; thank God the resolution isn't very good."

All true Poe thought — and he knew who it was nonetheless.

What he didn't know was when the Inn had gotten the upgraded infrared cameras. His friend Rip had helped install the originals; heck, Poe had even used them to catch a puppy poacher a while back. That's how he even recognized the low-resolution sight lines in the video. These new infrared and telephoto capabilities were unknown to him, however, and surely to his friend in the video.

"Honestly, Plink, I don't know what the big deal is," Poe said, now deciding it made sense again to annoy Plink. "It's a naked guy on the beach; it's not like it's the worst thing this town's ever had on YouTube. You saw to that."

"Poe, dammit! Don't tell me you're not the guy who called the Today Show; 'anonymous employee at Oregon State Parks,' my ass," he said, almost spitting. "Do you know there are 154,396 different links to my name on Google that call me some nasty name?"

"Actually, I just checked: it's up to 154,428," Poe said with absolute certainty. "A media ethics class at the University of Missouri just weighed in."

"Missouri? Why the hell would they care about it all the way out there?"

"I sent it to them; seemed a good case study on what never to do."

Watching Plink's right eye start to twitch again, Poe hoped the man was distracted and angry enough to forget about the naked man on the beach.

No such luck.

"Pete," Plink said, trying to ignore Poe, "I really want you to find this guy. Just add your hours onto your filming bill. No one will know the difference."

"Me?" Pete asked incredulously. "Get Poe; you're paying him, too, and he actually used to investigate things when he worked at the paper. I'm sure he can find this guy."

"First of all, you have a badge, that's why," Plink said, as if that explained it all. "And second, I was forced to hire Poe to proofread things. I may have to let Poe make sure I use the media properly, but I'll be damned if I'm going to pay someone extra who keeps trying to ruin my life in it."

"You have no proof I called the Today Show," Poe said, knowing full and well he had. "And remember, I'm not the one who took down the sign, jackass. Although that bright neon orange one you had to put up in front of all the Portland media looks reeeaaaaal nice."

Refusing for once to take the bait — God he hated that sign — Plink continued his verbal assault on Poe and the media: "And the article in the New York Times where you called Oregon 'A Great Place to Die'? Do you know how many calls I took over that?"

"That's hardly my fault," Poe said. "And isn't that your job?"

"Not your fault? You wrote it! And no, it is not my job to tell people why vacationing here WON'T kill them!"

"You're right; that's what we have signs for. Oh, wait..."

Pete was growing more exasperated by the minute as his morning continued to evaporate. "YOU!" he said, pointing to Poe, "Shut up. And you," he said now returning his attention to Plink: "I do have a badge, but what I don't have is time. Forget it. You want someone to investigate? Call Rip Rockford, that's what he does."

Pete now pointing Plink towards the door, Plink packed up his things, indifferent as always to the scene he'd created. Throwing the door open, he turned back to look at Pete: "You just get your job done, and I'll do mine!" And with that, he found Rip's number on the Internet and pressed "send" as he stomped out into the rain.

Watching him go, Pete was exhausted — and even with Poe, a bit. "Poe, why do you do that? He's only a problem if you take him seriously — and all you do is make him take himself more seriously."

"That's why I do it; he's a serious prick."

"Maybe, but he's also paying our bills right now, so can you just cool it a bit? Poe? Are you even listening to me? Who are you texting?"

"The same person Plink's calling; even a prick can be a serious problem."

Chapter 14
Poe & Oregon

Although no one place can ever claim to have exclusive run on tragedy and bad news — Detroit since 1980 notwithstanding — just about every piece of news coming out of Oregon in December 2006 seemed to be bad. And no matter how bad the headline was, another one seemed to come right after it that was even worse.

Two major stories dominated the news for weeks. First was the disappearance of a San Francisco family of four, who had vanished somewhere in the Coast Range while on Thanksgiving vacation. Ten days later, the mother and two children were found in their snowbound car, while the father was found the next day frozen to death, having died looking for help.

As that story wrapped up, three climbers disappeared on Mt. Hood. Caught by a blizzard, one had time to call his wife before he froze to death in a snow cave. The other two were never found, despite one of the largest search and rescue operations in Oregon history.

In the middle of this there were smaller stories of tragedy. In the Mt. St. Helens National Monument, an avalanche of snow and rock swept down below the Coldwater Ridge Visitors Center and carried two men to their deaths. True, it happened in Washington, but both victims were Portland residents, one from a prominent family well-known in restaurant circles. Their bodies, too, were never found, presumed to have been entombed at the bottom of the lake by the fallen rock. Captured on grainy video by a cross-country-skiing videographer on the opposite ridge, it probably would have made national news itself had the tragedy on Mt. Hood not occurred.

And in Surfland, a giant catamaran in transit from South Africa to Seattle washed up overturned on the beach after a storm. The only sign of the crew of three was a tether strap lashed to the propeller, tied there after the boat capsized by someone desperately trying and failing to stay with the boat.

Indeed, when Christmas finally arrived in Surfland and the rest of Oregon, it was with a sort of mental exhaustion as well as merriment. Poe as much as anyone felt this; much of the Surfland Siren's staff out on vacation, he'd covered the wrecked catamaran for Aly. Still haunted by thoughts of that last sailor fighting for his life as he tied off the strap, Poe went to his parents' home in Colorado for New Years.

There, Poe found virtually no one understood how all those crazy things could possibly happen in one place, at one time. Trying to explain it proved fruitless, and when he got a call from Aly in New Jersey noting the same thing, a piece of writing began to compose itself in his head. When it was done Poe read it back to himself, as he always did, hoping his fingers had done justice to what his mind hoped to write:

People don't know a great deal about Oregon.

Generally speaking, they know the basics: it rains a lot, we have big trees, crab comes from somewhere around here — and it rains a lot. Beyond that, however, they seem pretty clueless. True story: A couple of years ago I had someone in Philadelphia ask me, "Ore-GONE, is that one of those ocean states?"

Yes, it's where the crabs come from.

But having recently returned from the land outside Oregon, I've decided a little geographic confusion isn't all that bad. It's certainly better than what the nation's been hearing about Oregon these days: "Father dies trying to save family," and "Climbers disappear on Mt. Hood." These were the national headlines for three straight weeks, and on the heels of that more than a few people out there seem to be wondering if Oregon isn't a great place to die.

It's not that people don't die everywhere else. There are so many people murdered in New York City every year that they don't even make the opening of the evening news. A traffic fatality in Los Angeles might not even make the news.

But there is something epic about life and death here in Oregon that makes it different. At first glance it would seem to be the nature of where we live. Snowed in on a mountain road, lost in a blizzard, and locally, drowned at sea: nature itself killed these people. Yes, they made choices that put them in harms' way, but it was ultimately nature that made those choices fatal.

I think that's too simple. I spent three decades living in Colorado where our mountains are higher, our winters longer, our temperatures colder. I do not ever remember a family getting stranded on a mountain road, yet it's happened twice since I moved here. I do not ever remember climbing parties just disappearing on the side of mountains never – as yet – to be found.

Certainly, some of this is the media. (Yes, us.) It's the slow season in the news world; the elections are over, congress has gone home and there's nothing better to fill the 24-hour news cycle quite like a story of a family/ father/climber (choose one or all) in peril. Not to be crass, but a mother breastfeeding her children to keep them alive and a last cell phone call from 11,000 feet in the sky is the stuff television is made for.

Indeed, it's the stuff that drama is made for and always has been. Be it Jonah vs. the Whale, or Prospero battling "The Tempest," the constant struggle of man against nature is as timeless a story as has ever been told. A father's death in the snow just a mile from his family seems a Shakespearean tragedy for our times.

But even that misses the mark. "Romeo and Juliet" is "West Side Story," not the west. Who has time for Sharks and Jets in Oregon?

We're too busy with plain old sharks. This is not to romanticize death in Oregon or any other place, but these types of things don't happen in Manhattan.

But neither does standing on a deserted beach and watching whales off the shore. Neither does the opportunity to hike into the woods and stand in a spot where no other human has been for possibly decades, centuries ... ever? That's Oregon, especially my little coastal slice of it: Life on the edge — literally.

And having spent our lives with the daily intoxication of life on the edge, we can't imagine living any other place. There is a vitality and randomness to life here in Oregon you can't find anywhere else. And while every moment may not be an adventure, there is always the chance that the next moment will be — because so often it has been.

Yes, life in Oregon is volatile and violent, beautiful and bestial. It is as often tragic as it is triumphant. But it is a life like no other.

And it is not only why we live here, it is why we couldn't live anywhere else.

Content that it was good as it was going to be, but still not entirely happy (he never was with his writing) Poe emailed it off to a friend of his at The New York Times, hoping they'd want it, but very much assuming they would not.

So Poe was as surprised as anyone when Plink Blayton called him one January morning in 2007. Plink had only been in his job as the Executive Director of Surfland Tourism a few weeks, and Poe had never even met him. Seeing Plink's name on the caller ID, Poe had no idea why he'd be calling at 8:02 in the morning, but he didn't worry too much about it. Poe got along with just about everyone. He assumed his relationship with Plink would be the same.

"You A-hole! What the hell were you thinking running this in The New York Times?"

"Huh?"

"Did you know 8 a.m. in New York is 5 a.m. here? That's when I started getting calls from members of the advisory board, MSNBC and La Leche League International! What the hell were you thinking?"

Here, Poe was starting to ask himself the same thing about the clearly insane person on the other end of the phone. Before answering, however, he made himself two promises:

1) He'd start checking his voice mail more often. Clearly ignoring that message with the New York City area code had been a bad idea.

2) He was never going to have to worry about being friends with Plink Blayton.

"I told what I call the truth, as least as I see it, and that's my right under the First Amendment. I'm surprised as early as you got up you didn't have time to review it."

This did not make Plink feel better. "The truth?! The truth is what *I* say it is!"

Just as Poe had intended.

And so began a feud that more than five years later was just as intense as ever. Poe refusing to see his Surfland as any more or less than the imperfect little town he loved. And Plink thoroughly committed to spinning a perfect version of Surfland for all the world to see and buy.

It wasn't that Poe couldn't sympathize with Plink; Surfland wasn't the easiest place to market in the best of times. Amidst the worst economy in generations, Plink's job was considered by many to be impossible. Maybe that's why Plink had lasted so long despite his litany of bad ideas: No one else wanted the job.

The truth about Surfland — as anyone but Plink would admit — was, well, that it was kind of unattractive. In contrast to the historical ambiance of Astoria, the fun of downtown Seaside, the funky weirdness that is Yachats, or the vintage charm of the riverfront in Old Town in Florence, Surfland seemed more like a sprawl of motels, interrupted by occasional bursts of quaint urban redevelopment and ugly rock and gravel yards. Anyone looking for the idealized romance of a Pacific Northwest beach town would certainly go somewhere else.

But whereas Poe loved these things about Surfland, Plink despised them. Would Poe market the gravel yard? No, but he wouldn't pretend it wasn't there. (Plink's plan: Erect giant billboards on the side of Highway 101 the length of the rock yard to block people's view of the business. Thankfully, other than the area casino's marketing department, everyone thought it was a terrible idea, including the Oregon Department of Transportation.)

And whereas Poe was proud of the fact that Surfland had more hotel rooms and beach rentals than any Pacific coast city between San Francisco and Seattle, Plink despised it. Saying it made Surfland sound cheap and itinerant, Plink refused to put those facts in any marketing materials or tell the truth when asked about it. Poe, on the other hand, thought this was great: More rooms, more tourists, more happy memories. What could be bad about that?

It was all a matter of perspective to Poe; people would see what they wanted to see, might as well let them see the truth. And if helping them see that truth — as when he'd forwarded a certain Oregon State Parks employee's video on to a friend at the Today Show — well, so be it. The truth sometimes hurt, and the fact that Plink was often collateral damage, well, that was just plain fun.

Perhaps this was because the man, despite stunning incompetence and outright failures both public and private, seemed to be made of Teflon. Who else could survive offending lesbians, gays and half the ethnic groups in the Middle East — all at the same time — and keep his job? To the original surprise and now just resigned acceptance of everyone in town, no matter the screw up, Dick Yelpers and the rest of the tourism advisory board seemed to forgive him.

Poe had known all of this for years, of course. It was a small town and as well-connected as Poe was, he'd have to have been as out of it as Mrs. Margaret was to not have some idea how people felt. But knowing his own bias towards Plink — not too many people called Poe "A-hole" before he was even awake — he elected to keep his distance from the whole mess.

The time he had spent with Plink in the last few days had changed all of that, however. And while Poe might have felt inclined to do something in any case, his journalism senses were telling him something wasn't right with the guy. Plink's interest in the naked man on the video sealed the deal. Watching Plink back his Aztek out of Bendovren Coffee's parking lot, he hoped to God Rip got his text before he acted on Plink's phone call.

Or that Plink's car would just spontaneously explode; God that thing was ugly.

Chapter 15
Pete

Waiting until Plink was long gone to head back to their cars had one other advantage for Poe and Pete: It had stopped raining. For both it meant convertible tops down, stereo up; Poe with the push of a button, Pete with a few undone snaps and some elbow grease from both him and Poe.

Pete started the conversation: "Hey, you sure you feel up to all this running around today?" Pete asked, clearly concerned for his friend. "It's not every day you almost die."

"Nor was it yesterday; just because your heart sort of stops for a second doesn't mean you almost died," Poe said, trying to brush it off, not entirely convinced himself.

"Uh, huh. Doctors give you any idea why it just 'sort-of stopped'?"

"No. They took some blood, ran some tests, told me they'd get back to me in the next couple of days. Said don't do anything stupid — and I'm going to ignore that, because that would mean I couldn't spend any time with you."

"Does Aly know you're up and around?" Pete asked, now teasing a bit more.

"No. And since she dumped me, I can do whatever I want," Poe said.

"That must be why she was with you at the hospital last night..."

"Look, if you're asking me to explain our relationship, I can't," Poe said, as he and Pete secured the last of the straps tying the Jeep's top down. "But if anyone has to explain a relationship its you," Poe said, now looking down into the back seat. "Has this damn dog even moved a millimeter since you parked here?"

"I hope not," Pete responded nonchalantly. "I can't afford an alarm."

"How you stay married is beyond me," Poe said, still looking at the dog. "You make your wife sleep on the floor, and I'm the one who's single."

"It's good for her back, I swear," Pete said, as he used the spare moments to tidy up his Jeep. "Besides, you should be nice to Buffett; when we go to the lighthouse, he's going to have to sleep in the front seat."

"I'm devastated, truly," Poe said, clearly not, as he saw Pete make his way towards the garbage can with a mixture of fast-food wrappers, receipts and a gray folder. "Hey! What's that folder in your hand?"

"Oh, just an old piece of junk Buffett dragged in when I was out scouting and cleaning at the park."

"That's amazing!"

I thought so, too! But Plink hated it. He screamed at me, saying that finding a bunch of old kitschy crap wasn't what he was paying me for..."

"No, I meant it was amazing that Buffett actually did something, for once."

"Hilarious," Pete said. "Someday you and this dog are going to be really close, you'll see."

"Only if Super Glue is involved," Poe shot right back. "But I also did mean the folder. Isn't that from 'To St. Helens and Back'?"

"Yeah, so what?"

"Well, that was that big theme restaurant up in Portland, with a few others scattered up and down I-5. And in, like, six months everyone important affiliated with the chain died in some God-awful accident," Poe said, clearly pulling something out of the database that was his writer's brain. "In fact, the son and the chain's CFO were out scattering his parents' ashes on the mountainside when they were swept away by an avalanche. The whole chain was out of business within months."

"Wonderful. Now, will you please tell me why you care about this and why I should?"

"I wrote about it once, in that New York Times article that totally pissed off Plink," Poe said. "You tend to remember the best parts of your life. And that's why you should care, too: Think how mad that folder made Plink: Isn't that worth something?"

"Since — again — he's writing my check, no."

"Well, thankfully you and Plink are both wrong here; it'll be worth a lot at this Friday's charity auction here at the shop."

"Who is going to pay money for an old folder from an out-of-business Oregon restaurant chain?"

"The same guy who pats his friend on the back at the hospital, says, 'Well, seems you're going to be OK. Gotta go!' and then runs off to the charred ruins of a restaurant to see if he can salvage anything."

"That's where Rip was?" Pete asked, somewhat incredulous. "At Mermaid in Oregon?"

"Yep. He wanted to see if any of the brass fixtures had survived the fire. If it's Oregon and kitsch — even a crappy folder that no one wants — Rip's gotta have it."

Chapter 16
Rip Rockford

"Oh my, this is wonderful," Rip said as he looked over the folder, not even noticing the tiny tear Buffett's collar buckle had made in the fabric. "Real leather, actual ash embossed in the restaurant's name, 'To St. Helens and Back' stationary still inside... Look! The papers even have signatures on them! Ooohhh..."

"Should I leave you two alone?" Poe asked.

"Where did you find it? How much do you want for it?"

"Where doesn't matter; let's say it took dogged determination to find it," Poe said, ignoring the questioning look on Rip's face. "How much? You can tell me that on Friday when we auction it off during the fundraiser for Indy's mom."

"What if someone else gets it?" Rip asked.

"They won't," Poe said. "We're not telling people about it because nobody else would care."

"Then why not just give it to me?"

"Three reasons: One: you want it badly. Two: You're loaded, and Indy's mom needs the money. And three: You left me at the hospital to go look at melted mermaid parts."

"Still mad about that, are you?"

Rip and Poe had been friends since Poe moved to Surfland, and like Poe, Rip had come to the coast looking for a new start. An avid fan of '70s detective shows — you spend a lot of time cloistered in front of your TV when your last name's Snodgrass — he'd decided at the age of 40 to become a private investigator. Cashing in his Microsoft stock options and his last name, he left Seattle, moved to Surfland where his family had vacationed in his childhood, and became "Rip Rockford, P.I."

Wearing Aloha shirts like Magnum (and Poe), driving a red 1976 Ford Torino like Starsky, and keeping his prematurely greying hair cut like Mannix, Rip appeared to be a stereotypical beach bum. But behind his usually unshaven face was a quick mind. As the booming world of the Internet brought all the information of the world literally to his fingertips, Rip built a nice side business doing background checks and digging up information for anyone that Rip felt inclined to help.

Being loaded from his Microsoft days, Rip didn't have to do anything he didn't want to for anyone he didn't want to. So he spent his days helping the people he liked, riding horses on the beach with his significant other, Katrina Snappell, and spending his money on people and things that amused or interested him. Talking to Poe and Pete in Bendovren Coffee's parking lot, Rip's conversation was about to involve all of those things.

"Still have the dog, I see," Rip said. Looking in Pete's back seat, Rip was clearly trying to change the subject; he really did feel badly about leaving Poe at the hospital. "Did you ever determine if he has a pulse?"

"You're just mad because he flattened a saddle and Katrina wouldn't sleep with you for a week," Pete shot back.

"No, I was mad because he did it when there was a 62-year-old spinster from Ft. Wayne in the saddle," Rip said. "Did you know I had to track down every boy she dated in high school just so she wouldn't sue Katrina?"

"Did she find love?"

"I doubt it; I can't imagine anyone finding anything good in Ft. Wayne…" Rip said, letting the conversation trail off. "OK, Poe: What's so damned important that you had to see me now? I can't imagine it was just to show me a folder you know full well you're just going to gouge me for on Friday."

"I needed to see you before you did anything for Plink," Poe said.

"Why would I do anything for Plink? He's an ass," Rip said. "Did I ever tell you about the time he got pissed at Katrina because she wouldn't spray-paint one of her horses so he could film it and claim 'Black Beauty' happened here?"

"Good point," Poe said. "But if you don't do it, he'll just get someone else to. Can you just take his money, say you're doing it, and then tell him you didn't find anything?"

"Isn't that kind of theft?" Rip asked, not entirely sure of this plan.

"Not if you give it all to Indy's mom."

"That's some serious rationalization," Rip said. "But OK. What's he asking me to do anyway?"

"I'll let him tell you when he finds you," Poe said. "And promise him you'll find an answer. Just make sure it's one he'll buy, if you don't mind."

"No problem," Rip said. "Anything else?"

Before Poe could answer, Pete's horn let Poe know his friend and Buffett were leaving to go back to Pete's house to load up the photo equipment. Each tossing each other a small wave, neither said a word; they'd see each other in a few hours at the lighthouse, anyway. And for the conversation Poe needed to have next, it was better that he and Rip be alone, anyway.

"Let's take a walk," Poe said, now pushing the button so his automatic top would go back up. "There's something else I need."

Chapter 17
Poe

Jackson Poe was not in the habit of digging into people's pasts; he'd come to Surfland in a sole desire to get away from his. Lots of people had, and while they might not all change their names like Rip had or come for business reasons like Dick Yelpers, Poe figured as long as their pasts were behind them, what they chose to be in Surfland was their business.

Maybe that's why Poe was OK with asking Rip to dig into Plink's past; Poe couldn't help but feel that Plink's nonsense in Surfland had a long history somewhere else. Worse, Poe had a growing feeling that Plink's mechanizations of the truth would have nothing but a bad end for Surfland. The Surfland Seagull Races going horribly awry was one thing; cars can be repainted, shattered windows replaced, hair transplants replanted. But what gnawed at Poe was something else.

That, and the guy was just a dick.

That Poe actually worked with Plink still caused him no end of amazement; every word Plink wrote had to go through Poe's editing pen first. After the mayor's horrifying debacle on Lebanon's St. Maroun Day, she'd wanted Plink fired immediately. But once again Dick managed to convince her to let him stay, and once again she capitulated — but this time with a caveat: Every single thing he wrote for public consumption had to be edited by an outside source.

Their first thought was Aly at the newspaper. She said no immediately, citing journalistic ethics. That, and she hated Plink as much as everyone else. (Just because Plink screamed in her face that a trained crab doing the Electric Slide was big news didn't make it so.)

Next up was Poe, probably Surfland's most famous writer. Neither Poe nor Plink initially warmed to the idea, although Poe was more easily convinced once he saw what he was being paid per word. Plink, even to this day, still had not really accepted it, much to Poe's delight. Indeed, among Poe's favorite days were those when the mayor reminded Plink how much better things were going "with the writer from The New York Times." On those days, Poe thought Plink's eye might come right out of its socket.

The last time that had happened was several weeks ago, Poe now recalled. But after months of watching Plink abuse his friends and his town with one crazy idea after another, Poe had had enough, and for what he had in mind next he needed Rip. Taking advantage of the blue sky now filling the horizon, Poe and Rip were walking down the hill from the coffee shop to the GO River Wayside as Poe tried to explain himself.

"I'm just convinced he's bad news," Poe said. "And the fact that everyone seems to know it but Dick... What is that all about?"

"Maybe Plink has something on Dick," Rip offered.

"That would explain it, I guess," Poe said. "But what could that be? The guy's one of the most loved McOwners in the universe, and it's not like he said something offensive. Hell, it's not like he's said much of anything; he's had a speech impediment to overcome for 35 years."

"I still won't eat a frozen pizza..." Rip said, shuddering in sympathy before coming back to the conversation at hand. "OK, I'll look into Mr.

Blayton. Shouldn't be too hard; everyone knows his last job was helping rebuild the Gulf after Katrina. I'll start—

"Hold on!" said Rip, as he stopped so suddenly that Poe almost bumped into him.

Rip hardly noticed. Rummaging through his jacket, shirt and pants, he was looking for something. Stopping as he found what he was looking for, Poe watched as Rip pulled a hundred-dollar bill out of his Aloha shirt pocket and trotted over to the corner where the GO River Wayside parking lot met Highway 101. Stopping to speak to the homeless man standing there, Rip passed the hundred to the man before walking back to a stunned Poe.

"I don't know what surprises me more: That you carry hundred-dollar bills around wadded up in your pocket, or that you just gave it that smelly homeless guy," Poe said. "Forget working for food; how about a shower?"

"You ever talked to him? He's not smelly at all; just looks that way," Rip said.

"I should think not; you pay him enough to rent a room for well more than an hour," Poe said, still incredulous. "Hell, he probably stays two hours and takes a bath."

"Sometimes you are not a nice person, you know that?"

"Nice, shmice," Poe said. "I see that guy walk by here almost every morning. You know they just go back to a car and go home with their other corner-parking buddies, don't you? "

"No idea," Rip said. "What I do know, however, is that last week when an old man collapsed in the parking lot and stopped breathing, that guy rushed over, administered CPR and kept at it until the ambulance came."

"Did he make it?"

"I hope not; the guy was telling his wife he was dying of cancer and having to go out of state for cancer treatments, when the whole time he was out here sleeping with a 19-year-old bimbette," Rip said. "His wife had hired me to spy on him. What I do know, however, is that the homeless guy over there did everything he could to save that guy's life, and that seemed worth $100 to me."

Slightly embarrassed, Poe patted his friend on the back. "That's very decent of you. And if it means anything to you, I think you should give yourself $100 for saving my life yesterday."

"I thought you weren't dying..." Rip said, wondering where this was going.

"I wasn't. But I want to make sure you have that kind of money in your pocket this Friday when it comes time for the auction," Poe said, now starting to leave Rip behind as he began the walk back up the hill to his car. "I have a feeling it's going to take at least that much for a certain folder."

Chapter 18
Kitsch & Rip

Like many of the people in Surfland, the origins of the word "kitsch" are somewhat ambiguous, with numerous possible origins and histories. The English have staked their claim, saying it derives from the word "sketch." Further south, some French claim — while others refuse to — its beginnings as a perversion of the word "chic." Even the Russians have weighed in, saying it's from the word "keetcheetsya," which basically meant to be full of one's self for no reason whatsoever. (Which, ironically enough, to many seems very French.)

The most credible etymologies, however, have "kitsch" coming from a German word, and given people's tendency to speak the word with disdain and no little bit of spit, this makes some sense. Thought to derive from the word, "kitschen," meaning to collect trash from the streets, it certainly fit the kind of thing Buffett had dragged back to Pete's Jeep.

Another German theory of its origins begins with a verb: "verkitschen," meaning "to render worthless," something Plink would certainly agree with. Indeed, given the anger with which he dismissed Pete's finds from the park, the German language almost seems to be mandatory — to say nothing of the spittle that often accompanies such tirades.

Whatever the word's origins, though, it seems to have gained popularity in 1920's Germany as a revolt against those works perceived to be a tacky imitation of real art. Why anyone in post-World War I Germany would care about such things in the midst of a depression that was bankrupting the country is hard to say. Maybe they were angry that kitsch was the only art they could afford.

Today, that view continues to hold sway with many. Seen as the ultimate condemnation of cheap and mass-produced objects, it's hard not to argue with the idea when every Planet Hollywood in America seems to have a naked Sylvester Stallone hanging somewhere above the dining room floor.

Sometimes, however, the very thing that makes kitsch horrifying in its time makes it exactly what people want long after that time has passed. What is easily dismissed as excessively sentimental and conventional at the time of its creation becomes delightfully so when all the other conventions of life have changed. Elvis 45s for record players long discarded, He-Man action figures too big to fit into today's high-tech toys, Atari consoles with their block-head basketball players that just make X-Box kids laugh: All of them a symbol of a time gone by. A reminder to someone of what they remember as a better time, a simpler time — a time when people threw all that stuff out because they just figured it was worthless crap.

Like many men of his generation, Rip Rockford had made it one of his missions in life to find this crap. This — as the Germans would have called it — worthless stuff from the streets, which turned out not to be so worthless after all. Because no matter how much stuff is produced, if most of it ends up in landfills and/or smashed to pieces by use, what remains becomes valuable, just waiting for the right sentimentalist to come looking for it.

Rip didn't buy everything, of course. He had never paid $750 for an action figure, and he certainly had never paid $11,400 for an Elvis record, as others had done. (He did recently arrange to buy an Atari

2600; the obscene price still under negotiation, as it was still the only video game he'd ever managed to understand.) Rather, Rip focused his energies on kitsch from his childhood family vacations. If it had something to do with those trips to Surfland, he wanted it.

The first ten original Oregon mile markers from what was then called the Roosevelt Highway: $872. Three stone arches from the original bridge that crossed the Weolitz River north of Surfland: $78. The original 1960s sign from Surfland City Hall, made completely with flotsam and jetsam found on the beach: $265. A plush crab, complete with wooden mallet dated 1974, from Bo's Crab and Anvil: $135. (A limited edition, only 22 survived the Great Coastal Flea Invasion at Bo's warehouse.)

All of these were markers of Rip's childhood: The trip down Highway 101 from Astoria, his excitement at crossing over the bridge into Surfland, getting a fishing license at city hall, pounding a crab shell at Bo's until there was nothing left but powdered meat and shell. Tangible reminders of his long-gone youth, Rip was willing to pay a lot to get them — and since he had the means to do so, why not?

As Rip caught up with Poe walking up the hill back to Bendovren Coffee, it didn't really bother him that his friend intended to get every dime possible out of him for the folder. All the money went to a good cause, and it wasn't like he was going to find another one, anyway. Indeed, when he thought about it, this was the only piece of memorabilia from To St. Helens and Back he'd ever seen, and with that knowledge he ran to catch up with Poe.

"Please tell me you're not just going to throw that in the back seat of your car," Rip almost pleaded. "I remember what happened to Aly's dog."

"First of all, that was the dog's fault; it shouldn't have tried to get onto the trunk while the car moving. And second: Stop whining; I'm going to give it to Ryan for safe-keeping until Friday," Poe said. "What is it with you and this thing, anyway? It's. A. Folder."

"Didn't you ever go to To St. Helens and Back when you were a kid? It was awesome!" Rip said with genuine enthusiasm.

"No, and neither did you," Poe said. "Weren't you already a teenager after Mt. St. Helens blew up and they opened that place? Hardly a kid."

"I suppose," Rip said, now sounding a bit melancholy. "But when I got older and busier, that was still the one thing my family and I did together. Kind of stupid, and it was more for my younger brothers and sisters, but they loved the whole fake-volcano-thing erupting on the hour — and I gotta admit the girl that dove into the volcano for the ritual sacrifice was pretty cute."

"A ritual sacrifice? In Oregon? Isn't that more of a Polynesian kind of tacky?" Poe asked, not having even moved to Oregon until after the chain of restaurants had closed.

"Well, yeah; you didn't go to St. Helens and Back for a precise view of Pacific Northwest history," Rip said. "You went to feel the grainy ash laid into every leather menu cover, the booming bass as the volcano 'erupted,' and the 'Colossal Caldera' dessert; it actually spewed chocolate after they put it on your table."

"Sounds delightfully horrible. No wonder you can keep your cheesy sticks down in the presence of naked Stallones," Poe said, shaking his head as he started to lower the top on his Jag one more time. "You've been stomaching God-awful kitsch all your life."

"Whatever. You spend your money on your stupid passions," he said nodding his head toward Poe's car, "and I'll spend mine on mine. Now take my leather menu cover inside before you forget and let it blow out of your damned car."

Chapter 19
The Tandy Family & Surfland

Hanging up the phone, Evan Tandy turned to talk to his mother: "That was Plink. What a nice man. He just wanted to make sure you were feeling all right and to let me know he'd have plenty of chopsticks at the rededication on Friday. He's even bringing glue so the kids can make log cabins out of them. He seemed surprised when I told him we'd taken care of the plaque, but I insisted it wasn't a problem."

Evan said this as he looked out the windows of the Tandys' beachfront mansion overlooking the GO River Wayside. Hoping they'd actually find some time on this trip to spend on the beach, he turned to talk to his mother: "Wouldn't that be nice, Mom? Some time in the sun?"

As had been the case the past several years his words were met with silence. It had been more than five years since Mrs. Margaret had spoken a word, and even before that her speech had been slowing. Not diagnosed as Alzheimer's, it was dementia nonetheless. Not uncommon in a woman a couple of years over a century, it was known to run in the family and apparently untreatable, despite the money and power of the Tandys.

Looking achingly at his mother's nearly 6-foot frame sitting absolutely upright her wheelchair, he was reminded that the family had debated briefly about putting her in a home, but quickly discarded the idea. Physically, she was as fit as anyone could be; she still was able to help with her physical needs, just not her mental ones. Her blue eyes still radiated color, if not intelligence. Her hands still grasped a handshake reflexively, if not the meaning behind it.

No, a home just didn't seem right, so Mrs. Margaret accompanied the family everywhere they could take her. The leader of the family through four generations, she would draw her last breath, whenever that was, in the presence of her family.

Gazing into her blank visage, Evan couldn't help but weep for all the stories she would never tell again...

Rebekkah Talmedge was 15 when she boarded the *Magna Vomere* for her trip to her new home in the Oregon Territory. Accompanied by her friend from church, Adeline Rogers, also 15, it was June 1836, and both were about to embark on the greatest adventure of their lives.

Setting sail from Boston, they were on their way to Fort Vancouver in the Oregon Territory to re-unite with their future husbands, missionaries from the Methodist church. The families of their husbands-to-be sparing no expense in getting them safely west, they were embarking on the most modern vessel of its time. A packet ship, the 230-ton *Vomere* was designed for speed to keep its cargo of both passengers and mail on schedule.

The ship arrived first in Honolulu after its trip around Cape Horn, as did most of the ships of the time. The major port of trans-Pacific trade, the ship stayed in harbor for several days while mail was unloaded and loaded and supplies replenished. Taking advantage of the time in port, Rebekkah and Adeline wandered about the exotic island. Their first experience with palm trees, coconuts and other exotic things from the tropics, both of them would reminisce about those special days for the rest of their lives.

Sailing from Honolulu, they crossed the Columbia River Bar on March 20, 1837, arriving in Ft. Vancouver not long after. Less than a week later, both women were married to the men that they had said farewell to so long ago, the men having sailed early, in the spring of

1834. But if the wait to get married was short, the honeymoon was not.

Riding on horseback, they took two days to reach the summit of the Coast Range and the headwaters of the Weolitz River on the west side of the mountains. Picking their way along the river's banks headed west towards the ocean, they were navigating a route only Native Americans and fur trappers had ever taken.

It was a harsh route; clusters of trees each as big around as a small house often forced them off their chosen path. Dense stands of ferns and other plants on the ground often blocked the horses, forcing their riders to pick their way through the foliage by hand. Tributaries that on the map were only streams were often raging rivers, requiring more deviations from their planned route as they looked for a safe place to cross.

But cross they did, and with a zeal undamped by the obstacles, Rebekkah and her husband forged ahead on the fourth day, reaching the Pacific on March 28, 1837. In an area that would become known worldwide for tourism, Josiah and Rebekkah Tandy had become the first tourists on the central Oregon coast.

Catching up a few hours later, Abraham and Adeline Grey joined them, and the four couples spent the next week exploring all the places that would become Surfland. They camped at the falls and lake where a park would be named in their honor. They swam where the river meets the ocean at what would become the GO River Wayside. And in the place where the lighthouse now stood on Ageya Head, the two young couples held hands, and thanked God for what the Lord had allowed them to see that week.

Pulling out a small bottle of wine they had managed to carry all the way from Ft. Vancouver for this moment, all of them toasted the virgin spaces they'd been allowed to cross. Sitting in a circle, all of them could see the ocean to the west, save for one: Josiah, looking east at the trees.

By the age of 16 Maggie Tandy had heard this story about her grandparents more times than she could count, especially the last part.

For as everyone in Oregon knew, Josiah's vision of the lands to the east instead of the vista to the west would change state history.

For upon returning to the Willamette Valley, Josiah did not stay a missionary long, believing instead he might better assist the Lord by spreading Christianity through financial means. Dedicating his life to financially backing the Greys as they worked with settlers and Native Americans, Josiah saw the future as most men could not. Getting in early in the logging and shipping industries and later railroads, Josiah built an empire that not only allowed Methodism to grow, but Oregon itself. When he died at age 90 in 1900, his wife, Rebekkah, kept the company stable in preparation for the next generation of Tandys. Maggie was the first.

All her life, Maggie had read the textbooks that held her family's story, as well as other kinds of books, like business, math and science. A young woman well ahead of her time in terms of independence and intelligence, she knew the Tandy Family legacy and empire was hers to preserve — and she took that responsibility seriously. Learning everything she could from books and teachers, she was ready for college at age 16. When no local university would accept her on account of her age and gender, her Grandma Bekk, as Maggie called her, called up a Portland college and asked how big of a donation they would need to start a new business school that accepted women.

That was the summer of 1927, and before Maggie went off to school, Grandma Bekk had her come out to their beach house in Whig City the night before the dedication of the Hope Falls Park. They had always had a special bond, and the family having just returned from a trip to Hawaii, Maggie was worried about her.

What was supposed to be a triumphant return of Rebekkah Tandy to the geographic beginning of her life-long adventure on the Pacific had seemed to Maggie anything but. Indeed, as the rest of the family played and romped, her grandmother said little, often just gazing off to the east. More than once, she heard her father and mother wonder if it wasn't dementia. On the voyage home, Maggie stopped by her Grandma

Bekk's stateroom frequently to see if she was OK. All she would say is that they'd talk about it when they got back to Oregon.

That time finally came as Maggie and Rebekkah sat on the deck of the Tandys' beach house perched atop a cliff overlooking the GO River Wayside. It was not a big house, but it was the only one within a hundred yards in any direction as the Tandy family owned the neighboring four lots. Indeed, with the entire family in town, everyone else had decided to take their families to other beach houses and hotels in the area. Sitting on the deck alone with Maggie, Grandma Bekk told her granddaughter all the stories she'd never heard, the truth behind the legends. Talking long into the night, both of them slept in far longer than they should have the following morning.

The dedication of Hope Falls Park and the adjoining lake was a big deal to not just the family, but also to all the local coastal residents and indeed the entire state of Oregon. The central Oregon coast section of the Roosevelt Military Highway nearing completion, this park would tell the entire nation that the area was open for business.

Rebekkah Tandy had overseen the dedication ceremonies herself: The naming of the lake and falls, the construction of the podium on which the plaque would be placed. Even the plaque itself was commissioned by Rebekkah. A final tribute to her husband and the world they had built, it was lying in the garage wrapped in paper. Indeed, when workers from the town offered to come get it, Rebekkah declined, promising she'd make sure the plaque got there the next morning.

It never made it.

Rising at 8 a.m. on the day of the dedication, Maggie couldn't believe she and Grandma Bekk had overslept; both of them were chronic early risers. Running down the hall to her grandmother's bedroom, she stuck her head in the door expecting to see her grandmother also moving frantically. But she did not, nor would she ever again. Suffering a heart attack in the night, Grandma Bekk was barely breathing.

Running to the phone, Maggie first called the fire department, then her father. Within minutes, both were there, but there was nothing that could be done. Gathered around the bed, Maggie stood nearest to her grandmother. Mustering strength for what would be her final words, Rebekkah Talmedge Tandy, age 106, looked at her gathered family and said simply, "She is me," pointing her finger at her youngest grandchild. And then, with her last breath, said something that only Maggie would fully understand: "Remember."

Margaret Tandy entered business school that fall remembering everything her Grandma Bekk had told her both on that final night, and every day earlier. Working through school in just three years, she eschewed anything that distracted her from her goal. Late-night partying, boys who wanted to spend those nights with her, she declined them all, more than once hearing from the rejected that perhaps she was "one of those" that didn't like men at all. She did, but not as much as completing what her grandmother had started.

By the time she was 22 she was actually running the company, not even choosing to marry or have children until she was in her early 30s. Only when the company was on solid footing during The Great Depression and soaring during the massive government spending of World War II did she finally take the time to raise a family. Evan was the first, and like her grandmother before her, she had him and all of her children be a part of everything she could. From financials to philanthropy, she wanted the kids to understand everything that went into the Tandy Family Empire.

In many ways they were easy lessons; Margaret made her business decisions from the things she learned looking at her own family. For as she looked to add to the family's traditional portfolio of timber, shipping and railroad interests, she let their interest as Oregonians guide her thoughts. Thinking them at least common in their likes and dislikes, she watched their needs and desires carefully, in the hopes that the Tandy Family would continue to be a part of Oregon's future.

In the 1950s they became involved in transportation again, this time in construction. Using their contacts from the war to land one government contract after another, they were key in building the western portions of the interstate highway system, and just about every other modern highway in Oregon. Margaret made this decision after reflecting on the hours her family had spent in the car going to Surfland. Everyone, she reckoned, would be doing the same once they had their own car, and she was right.

In the 1960s she watched Evan's fascination with the burgeoning space program. This inspired her to purchase a number of small high-tech companies and become part of the massive spending associated with NASA. In the 1970s, as she watched Evan's growing waistline, and the vanity with which he viewed it, she decided to invest in sporting goods companies that were suddenly springing up all over the Willamette Valley. In the 1980s and '90s she saw her grandkids' fascination with the very first personal computers, and how frustrated people of Evan's generation got with them: "Argh! What the hell is a DOS?" This inspired her to invest in a number of micro-computing companies up and down the West Coast. That Oregon became known as the Silicon Forest was in large part because of the Tandys.

Not all of Margaret's decisions were successful ones, of course. Having gotten a sneak-peak at the Ford Edsel in 1957, Evan thought it was the greatest car ever, leading Margaret to invest in Ford. In the early 1980s, along with buying Apple and Microsoft, she put millions into Commodore as that was the computer her grandkids liked the most. She invested in the Sharper Image — twice — her judgment clouded by the staggering amounts her family spent there on a variety of brushed-steel disposable doo-dads made in Asia. (She actually kept one of the company's ionic air "cleaners" in her office with a sign and a mirror atop it reading, "Moronic Breeze.") She'd taken one of the biggest write-downs in the history of the company in the early 1990s when they had to unload all the small companies they'd bought that were involved in oat bran. Elevated cholesterol, it turned out, was better fought with high-tech drugs and exercise than muffins and potato chips.

The family's latest failed venture was motivated by her children, as well. But when she looked in the mirror she had to admit that on this one the moronic breeze came entirely from her.

"To St. Helens and Back": She loved the name, and while that was no excuse for an investment strategy, the truth was the money she'd put in was but a drop in the Tandy Family bucket. In retrospect, however, she'd made more mistakes on that investment that any other in her decades running the family business, and that bothered her more than anything.

For one thing, she actually ignored her family when they told her they thought it was a poor excuse for a theme restaurant. "Gramma Margaret," her 7-year-old grandchild told her one day as they finished a Colossal Caldera, "everyone knows there aren't any Tiki Gods in Oregon volcanoes."

She'd ignored them, however, as she'd known the family that owned the restaurant chain for generations. Indeed, the Niemens were not only friends from Portland, but Surfland as well, where they had once owned Niemen Seafoods and still owned a beach home. She and Matti Niemen even had a bit of a fling in the summer of '26. Promising to call her when they got back to Portland in the fall, he never did, and by 1927 he was just one more memory, if a bitter one.

Perhaps if she'd remembered that, instead of all the good times with the Niemens, she wouldn't have kept pumping the hundreds of thousands of dollars she did into the restaurant.

Originally the creation of Matti's son and wife, geology and mass communications professors at Oregon State University, the Mt. St.

Helens-themed restaurants were ripe to take advantage of American's interest in the mainland U.S.'s only truly active volcano. They'd begun when, following their father's death in 1984, they sold the family business and parlayed that money, some Tandy Family venture capital, and their knowledge of Mt. St. Helens into a whole new kind of empire. Going from just one location in 1985 to around a dozen 20 years later, the chain seemed to be doing well despite its kitsch.

The beginning of the end came in 2005 when The Niemens' car soared off a cliff on the way back from Mt. St. Helens. A family weekend gone tragically wrong, their car tumbled so many times down the face of the volcano that the only thing recognizable from the wreckage was an engine block, a toupee, and a stiletto shoe with Mrs. Niemen's foot still inside it.

The middle of the end was the avalanche at Coldwater Lake that killed their son, Isaac Andrew Niemen. An odd sort, he was stereotypically ill-suited to the world of business in his Birkenstocks and flannel shirts. But if he was weird, he was also typically Oregon, and though he was grieving the loss of his parents, Mrs. Margaret continued to back him as he looked to grow the business. When he was killed with the chain's CFO in December of 2006 while scattering his parents' ashes near the same volcano, the tragedy was just compounded.

The end of the end was discovering that the now deceased CFO had been bleeding the company dry in the years leading up to Ian's parents' death. A long-time family friend of the Niemens, everyone had trusted him. Only a misplaced spreadsheet on his computer discovered after his death had given him away. A trove of information for all of its incriminating data, it was still missing the one thing Mrs. Margaret cared about: the location of the bank where it had all gone. She and other investors' money likely stashed away in some secret Swiss account somewhere, she hoped the CFO would someday find himself answering to one of his restaurant's flaming Tiki Gods on his way to the next life.

She almost found it funny: Both ends of her business life bracketed by bitterness with the Niemens.

This failure to see what was coming — and that personal feelings and sentimentality had kept her blind — was one of the main reasons she'd decided to start stepping down from the day-to-day operations of the company. As always, it wasn't about the money.

An investment in the low seven-figures was really nothing compared to the overwhelming success Margaret had found during her two-thirds of a century running the company. The Tandy name was on hundreds of civic and educational projects all over Oregon and the Pacific Northwest — and on hundreds more where they had given anonymously. By the early 21st century, the Tandy Family weren't multi-multi-billionaires like the Waltons in Arkansas, but they were close enough.

Still, her willingness to let her personal feelings trump the principles by which she'd always run the family business were a reminder that she wasn't getting any younger. Well over 90, Mrs. Margaret, as she had come to be known in social and philanthropic circles, was still as physically fit as a woman 20 years younger, but she was mentally ready to let someone else in the Tandy Family take responsibility. Sentimentality and kindness, no matter how well intentioned, couldn't take the place of common sense.

There was just one problem, however: the same one that had vexed her for the last 30 years. Who would be next to run the Tandy Family businesses? None of her children or grandchildren seemed ready for the job, in her opinion. Indeed, none of them seemed to really want it, even though the day was coming when she would no longer be able to do it herself. A huge problem but one simply stated: She had no idea who she could point to and tell the family: "She is me."

And now she never would, thought Evan as he looked again at his mother. He was sitting now, having pulled a book from their library's shelves. His mother wearing the same blank stare she'd maintained for a half-decade, he once again read to her from her biography in the hopes it would jog some sort of memory. Flipping to the chapter where it discussed the family's history and role in Whig City and then Surfland, he was reminiscing about better times when his daughter called to him from the next room.

"Dad! Doctor Bracewell's wife is on the phone. She wants to talk about the Aveda Spa!"

"OK," Evan said, happy to be helping out the hospital. "Just bring the phone in here — and remind me: What makes an Aveda Spa different from any other spa? "

"It's a loofa thing, I think..." she said, not entirely sure herself. "Oh, wait! Grandmother's minister is here; he heard about her trip to the hospital."

"OK, send him in here, instead," Evan said, knowing the minister needed privacy when he prayed with his mother. It seemed pointless to him, but it was one of the last things his mother had insisted on when she was still communicating with the family. "I'll come out there and get the phone."

"Sounds goo— Dad! The dog's back!"

"Bring him in here, too," he said, looking at his mother one last time. "I think he's costing me more than the spa."

Chapter 20
Indy Monroe

Walking down the hill to the coffee shop from her family's small house, Indy Monroe felt like the day itself: Still wet from a morning shower, but definitely fresher. The filth of her second job only figurative, it still felt good to get clean. Her backpack slung over one shoulder and her cell phone balanced on the other, she was wrapping up a phone call with her dad in California.

"When I left she was sleeping so soundly even that crazy-ass 'Red Alert' doorbell you had me install didn't wake her up... Yes, I know she likes it... Uh-huh, I finally got the last package... Only time I've ever seen a FedEx guy carry a body-sized box with one hand... Yes, except for those weird French people at Cirque Du Soleil... Dad, I gotta go..."

Stopping at the intersection, Indy hated to cut the call short with her dad. She hadn't told him about last night's misadventure with Ryan yet, and she knew he'd appreciate the story more than anyone. But Surfland's chronic lack of crosswalks with which to cross Highway 101 would have her dodging traffic shortly, and one trip to the hospital per 24 hours was enough. The city filled with tourist drivers paying more attention to beautiful views and their own cellphones than the road, she knew she'd have to be the one to focus if she was going to get across the highway alive.

"Yep, I love you, too," she said, her voice heavy. "I hope I get to see you one of these days..." Cutting off the call, Indy turned her attention back to the highway and waited for the right time to cross. Seeing an opening, she darted across the four lanes of highway and got to the sidewalk on the other side. Relieved once again not to be killed by a distracted driver, she found herself distracted now. Gazing down the hill, she could see Bendovren Coffee's giant picture windows, Ryan working, and a whole host of memories — each of them growing more distant each day.

God her life sucked.

That Indy was born in Hollywood didn't really explain her name; lots of people in California had odd ones. That she was conceived while her father was doing makeup on "Indiana Jones and the Last Crusade" did. In deference to her mother her legal name was India Marion Monroe, but her father had never called her anything but Indy.

Growing up in Hollywood was fun, especially when her father got her onto the sets of all kinds of movies. A makeup artist on some of the biggest sci-fi movie franchises in Hollywood history, he'd worked *Star Trek*, *Star Wars*, *Aliens* and so many smaller films she'd lost count. Hanging out with him, she kept quiet and watched and learned. Not that she wanted to be a makeup artist when she grew up, but it was quite cool watching her dad turn someone known as Hollywood's biggest bitch into a literal one. (*The Boy Who Cried Werewolf II: First Litter.*)

But it was on the set of *The Abyss* that she first heard her dad say the words that would change her life: "CGI? What the hell is that?" Industry shorthand for computer-generated imagery, her father was learning about its early uses from the film's director, James Cameron, who would later go on to use it in *Terminator 2*, and *Titanic*, winning Academy Awards for both.

At first, her father didn't think much of it; indeed he'd been part of the makeup team that had won an Academy Award on Titanic, as well.

But as the technology evolved, her father saw that it could be used to modify more than sets and robots, it could be used to modify people, too. Within a decade, he was virtually unemployed, his skills with a makeup case now replaced by a kid with a computer.

His career dying, he moved to a tiny studio apartment on a direct bus line that ran near the studios, basically living a pauper's existence. Meanwhile, Indy and her mother were sent back to Surfland, where the maternal side of Indy's family still lived. Far less expensive than Hollywood, what little her father was making would pay the bills there, as Indy, her mom and grandmother all lived in a small two-bedroom house in the middle of town. Indy slept on the couch in the living room.

Much of this would not have been necessary had it not been for her mother's illness. Tired almost all the time, different doctors had diagnosed it as chronic fatigue syndrome, fibromyalgia, and a whole host of other Latin words that Indy could never remember. Her mother always tired and in pain, she saw the doctor when she could, but everything seemed to be a temporary fix at best. To Indy's relief her mother didn't seem to be getting any worse, but she wasn't getting any better, either, keeping the entire family in kind of a holding pattern.

That pattern meant Indy and her father, who had always been close, virtually never saw each other as her father moving to Surfland was never an option. Even nearly unemployed, her dad's union health insurance paid her mother's bills. Afraid to jeopardize that by refusing to take even a last-minute a job, her father stayed close to the phone in California, and continued to work his contacts from when days were better. But aside from some God-awful SyFy movies like *Sharktopus*, *Mega Death Worm* and *Mansquito*, he had virtually no jobs. His latest paycheck, from *Farmageddon*, was almost gone, Indy knew.

He'd never admit this to her directly, of course. When he called, everything was always fine, and certain to get better. Discussing a job that earlier in his career would have mortified him, he told Indy how proud he was to turn a host of sexy no-names into farm animals. To hear him tell it, her dad thought turning a former Playboy centerfold into a cow was among the best work he'd ever done.

It was that lesson, to do what it takes to get the job done, that had driven Indy to make the decision that pained her every time she looked at Ryan through the bay windows at Bendovren Coffee. Putting her mom's needs first, she'd left her long-time job with the Nordins when she'd been offered a job at Grind Me Hard Coffee. The tips there were easily triple, Oregon's vacationing letches willing to pay up to watch her shake her ass and chest as she made them their half-caf, 1-percent, whatever-the-hell-they-wanted mochas.

The Nordins had understood, of course. Their daughter's medical needs consuming their time and money, they certainly knew where she was coming from. But having walked away from people that had worked around Indy's every need for nearly four years — her mom, her softball schedule, her other jobs — she felt terrible about it all the time. It wasn't so much that she had made the wrong choices, as it was the feeling that she'd never really had any.

Finally nearing the door to Bendovren Coffee, Indy's mood lightened somewhat as she saw the shop was nearly empty, leaving Ryan free to work on his car, now parked in front of the shop. Putting on her green sunglasses to block out the sun that was now filling the sky, she hoped they would also keep Ryan from seeing she'd been crying. Trying to lighten her own mood, she called out to Ryan: "Mr. Bond, you've got company!"

Chapter 21
Ryan

"No problem, this is a company car!"

Returning the line from *Octopussy* almost instantly, Ryan didn't even have to look up to know it was Indy approaching. Both of them movie freaks, quoting movies was a little game they'd played for years, though with Indy's background in Hollywood he lost most of the time. Only since they'd both enmeshed themselves in the Bond universe had he stood a chance.

Bolting down a piece of sheet metal — the old floorboard having been incinerated — Ryan kept up the conversation without ever looking up. "I assume your headache from our little adventure last night isn't anything close to mine."

"Concussions can do that to you," she said, surprised she didn't have one herself.

"Concussion, hell," Ryan said, now sitting up to look at her. "I'm talking about Pete damn-near ripping my head off again this morning for playing with fireworks."

"I take it you didn't tell him about the pile still in your garage...?"

"Uh, no," Ryan said sheepishly. "Let's just say when I get some time off I'm going to take a little stroll down to the river... assuming I ever get any time off."

As Ryan expected, Kinkel had not come back to the coffee shop. The scorn from making bad coffee and the trauma involved in thinking he'd almost killed Poe had been too much for him. Last Ryan heard, Kinkel was trying to get a job as a towel boy at a pool. Or maybe a boy as a pool towel; at least just lying there he couldn't hurt anyone. Whatever it was, he hoped Kinkel would be better at it — and keep his shirt on. That impression of Lewis & Clark with a nipple where their heads should be just looked weird.

Not that Kinkel's services were needed. Despite a small rush this morning and the ongoing business Poe and Plink's specialized coffee addictions brought him, business had virtually dried up in the last month. Timed almost perfectly to his parents leaving town to tend to his sister in Canada, it seemed like a giant conspiracy was afoot to make his life miserable. As always, it was Indy who tried to cheer him up.

"Maybe the fundraiser Friday will bring in a lot of people," she said. "And you can keep the money from the coffee; my Mom's going to make enough in donations from the auction."

"No, and that's that," Ryan said, knowing there were a lot of bills related to health care that health insurance didn't cover. "And before you say another word, I'm going to change the subject and tell you Poe dropped off something else for the auction this morning, and that your tip jar has another $36 in it."

The entire time Indy had worked at Bendovren Coffee, it had been public knowledge that all of Indy's tips went to help her mom. When she left, Ryan and his family just left it out knowing people would still like to help. Keeping it nearby just to be sure it didn't somehow walk off when he wasn't in the shop, Ryan pulled it out to show her.

Smiling, a perplexed look suddenly crossed Indy's face. Digging her hand into her pocket, she pulled it back out with a wadded up bill stuck between two of her fingers. As she tossed it in the jar, Ryan didn't immediately recognize the face on the bill, so he assumed it was a big one. "Was that Benjamin Frank—"

Before he could finish, however, the noise of sirens began to fill the air — lots of them. Instead of coming at them quickly, however, it was a long time before they were within sight of the shop. "Well, that's not good," Ryan said half-jokingly. "You only drive the ambulance slow when they're already dead."

"You're not far off," Indy said, now pointing at the motorcade rolling by the shop. "It's the Tandys, and if Mrs. Margaret is actually alive in that back window, she's so close to being a vegetable she might as well be dead." Silence fell on both of them as they looked at the sad truth of Indy's statement. Sitting upright in the back window of a black Cadillac Escalade SUV, Mrs. Margaret looked like the only thing holding up her pale form was the seat-belt. Both of them had read her biography in school, and while she may have lived a life of adventure once, that was clearly over now.

The motorcade now rolling out of sight, someone whose life was still an adventure was immediately following them. Splitting off at Bendovren's parking lot, Paxton Dell rolled in driving his 2011 Bullet Edition Ford Mustang. A current friend and former student at Harrison High School with Ryan, Paxton now spent his time with The World is United in Song. Made up of some of the best young-adult singers in the world, the group traveled the world while its members both entertained people and got an education with the show's traveling school.

"Paxton! You made it! Give me your keys!" Ryan yelled happily.

"Only when I'm not here," Paxton said through the open window, fully intending to let Ryan continue keeping the engine warm when he returned to his travels next week. "And maybe when you're not... Jesus, what did you do to your car?"

Even with the floorboards fixed, the scorch marks on the perimeter of the door frame let anyone and everyone know something had gone very wrong with the car. But excited to see his friend, and eager to show both Paxton and Indy what else he'd been working on all morning, he ignored the question.

"You gotta see this," he said, his hands pointing Paxton towards the passenger seat of the Sunbeam. But even as Paxton moved cautiously towards the car, Indy seemed to be speaking for him: "Oh God," she said. "Tell me you didn't put the ejector seat back in."

"No!" Ryan said. "Well, yes, but only the mechanism, just to hold the seat up. No explosives, I promise."

Now understanding what the scorch marks were from, Paxton started to get out of the car. "Ryan, do I need to get the extra key to the Mustang back from you?"

"No! I swear! This is completely different," he pleaded as he pushed Paxton back into the passenger seat. Handing Paxton a piece of sheet metal left over from the floorboard repair, Ryan told him simply: "Hold this in front of your chest."

Running around to the driver's side, Ryan began to explain his latest creation to Indy and Paxton. "OK, the ejector seat was a bad idea. Good for Bond, bad for me," he said, now getting really revved up. "But any good spy still needs a way to protect himself from those who carjack him."

"My God, you are going to blow up the car," Indy said, only mostly kidding.

"Ha ha." Ryan said, pausing only for a moment. "No, what I've done is make it so whoever might be in that seat is incapacitated instead of ejected."

Paxton's eyes beginning to grow wide with alarm, Ryan hurried to slide into the driver's seat to make his friend feel better: "Dude! That's what the metal is for: So when the racquetball ejects from under the dashboard it just bounces off!"

And before anyone could say anything, Ryan pressed the hidden button that sprung open the lid between the seats. Flicking the second button to the right — the first was still wired for the ejector seat — all three of them were greeted by the sound of building gas pressure under the dashboard. Smiling ear to ear, Ryan thrust his hands into the air triumphantly as the ball shot from the tube under the glove compartment.

And drilled Paxton right in the gonads.

Chapter 22
Indy

Walking the half-mile between her old job and her new one, Indy could still hear Paxton's screams and Ryan's horror: "Augh!"/"It wasn't supposed to be aimed that low!" "AUGH!"/"I must have moved it when I tightened the nuts!" "AUGH!"/"It's not my faul—"

Chuckling as she remembered Paxton actually choking Ryan as he tried to finish the sentence, Indy reflected that it might not have been the best time for Ryan to mention "nuts." Now actually laughing out loud, she wondered if The World is United in Song needed another soprano.

Her mood, however, quickly soured as she approached Grind Me Hard Coffee. A tiny shop in an old A&W Restaurant location, it was wedged in between two buildings built much later and much taller. A perpetual shadow always covering the shop, the lighting inside was as dark as her disposition as she headed inside to change into her work clothes.

Indy found the bathroom at Grind Me Hard Coffee as appalling as the rest of the place. Jammed into a tiny janitor's closet after her boss had converted the original bathroom space into his office, Indy laid a layer of paper towels down on floor in the event anything should actually fall to the ground.

Getting dressed at home certainly would have been easier. Even if she wasn't proportioned more like Serena Williams than Esther Williams, the fit inside the bathroom was a tight one. Peeling off her jeans and long-sleeve T-shirt, she had to contort her body around the utility sink and toilet jammed in the corner.

Indy refused to get dressed at home, however, for the same reason she refused to wear her uniform anywhere outside the shop: She hated it. A skimpy black bikini top, cut-off cargo shorts, and a utility belt holding an espresso scoop: That was her uniform. The standard attire at each of Grind Me Hard Coffee's 14 outlets throughout Oregon, the only thing that set Indy apart from all the other girls was her shoes. Most girls had to wear stilettos, while Indy got to wear something closer to an open-toed sneaker. Even that, however, came with a price.

"Indy! Get that rocket-arm out here!" her boss screamed from outside the bathroom. "The guy six cars back needs a muffin!"

Knowing it was no use to pretend she couldn't hear him through the paper-thin door he'd installed, Indy sighed, and got ready to clock in. Checking one last time to make sure her blond hair wasn't going to fall over eyes during her shift, she picked the towels up off the floor, collected her things, and headed out to face the day.

"Oh my sweet thang,
She lays in the hay and sighs.
Come to me and let's combine,
And pull the wool over my thighs..."

As always, her boss's favorite band — Sheep Pimpage — was playing on the stereo in the lobby. A freakish combo of Screamo and Country — *Deliverance*-style — she assumed they'd only made one CD, as that was all her boss ever seemed to play. She used to complain about it, but after the eighth time she realized the only person she was pissing off was herself, so she changed tactics.

"Hey, boy," she said to her boss as she walked behind the counter. "You got a real pretty mouth ain't ya?"

"Do I now? I knew you'd come around. Finally gonna let me see what's..." Here, however, he paused, now understanding that once again he'd been the butt of a joke that only she understood. "That's another one of those movie lines, isn't it? I wish you could just talk like a real person to me. I hate those movie lines."

"Just like I hate it when you tell me my bikini top won't shrink in the wash, yet every time it does," she said, eyeing the distance to the sixth car in line. "Quite frankly, Scrote, you don't pay me enough to care what you hate."

"What are you trying to tell me?"

"Anywhere else it would be, 'Kiss my ass; I love movies.' But since I know you'd probably try to do it, let's just try to get through the day without you getting your hopes up, OK?" she said. Her voice heavy with weary resignation as she grabbed a blueberry muffin from the pastry case, brushed him aside and spoke at the same time. "Now shut up and get away from the window."

Sticking her entire upper body out through the drive-thru window, Indy fast-pitched the muffin straight into the open window of the sixth car in line. The customer would pay for it — and tip handsomely — when he got to the window. That Scrote leered at her the entire time she did it bothered her not at all; he rarely did anything else, anyway. It was good money — and it gave her an excuse not to wear those damned stilettos like everyone else had to.

Easing her upper body back through the window, Indy once again shook her head at how low she'd stoop to keep her and her mom's bills paid. One day she was tossing a forgotten scone to Ryan across Bendovren's lobby, the seeming next she was delivering pastry items via her softball skills on a regular basis. She had no doubt that Scrote was the slowest barista in the world, but ever since he'd discovered how quickly and accurately she could throw overhand, he almost seemed to have gotten slower. Just as he had been before her toss, he was jabbering with the guy immediately outside the drive-thru.

"Scrote, you've been talking to that guy since before I got here! Get moving!" To this she received no response, other than a brush off and a mumble. Something about a "sweet ass," she thought. Pushing Scrote's latest disgusting comment from her head, Indy went to the espresso machine and began churning out drinks. Everyone in line was one of their perverted regulars, and when Scrote finally shut up, she'd have their drinks ready for them.

Most of their regulars were disgusting pervs, locals and tourists alike. A few were her friends, who came by to help her, holding their noses both figuratively and literally as they waited in line at the drive-thru that ran next to the dumpsters. And then there were the non-regulars: people who had no idea what kind of place they were pulling into. "Coffee" was the last word on the sign and that was the one they acted on as they pulled well off the highway.

From this Indy took some solace; as hidden as the building was, she wasn't on display to every passing motorist on Highway 101. Unfortunately, this did nothing to mitigate the hundreds of pairs of leering eyes that came into the lobby every day. Learning to simply look through people even as they looked right at her (from the neck down) had become a survival skill.

Lining up the completed drinks for whenever Scrote got done — it was amazing how long perverts with a caffeine addiction would wait for her to lean over and give them change — she headed into the lobby to do a bit of cleanup. Leaving the noise of the espresso machine and Scrote behind, she was reminded again of just what was playing on the CD player.

"Silently ewe come and creep,
Please don't tell me lies.
Truly you're my love sheep,
So pull the wool over my thighs."

Trying as best she could to block out the song while simultaneously straightening up a pile of magazines with names like *Muddin'*, *Shootin'*, and *Goat Fantasy* she was stunned when an unknown male voice said a word she had never heard in the lobby in all her time at Grind Me Hard Coffee: "Thanks."

Momentarily perplexed by the man with an iPad and laptop computer, she decided he was either mentally challenged or lost. Either way, she was certain he didn't want to be here. "You know, there's much better coffee just south on 101 at Bendo—"

"Indy! Get over here!" Scrote screamed. "I'm almost done, and the guy wants another one of your muffins, heh, heh..."

Not wanting to delay and give Scrote any chance to poach her tips, Indy headed back behind the counter wondering what a seemingly decent guy could doing in a place like this. Grabbing another muffin, Indy once again leaned out the window and delivered it right where it was supposed to go, just like last time, right down to the same six cars now seemingly parked in the drive-thru.

"Jesus, Scrote! I'm not here for my health!" Indy yelled at him. "You're not even talking to a hot woman in a convertible; it's a guy in a Volkswagen. What, are you not feeling well? Are you switching teams?"

Once again taking Indy's exasperation as a possible opening, Scrote actually seemed to talk to her as a person for once. "Now that you mention it, I'm not feeling well. My nose itches, and I think my skin's starting to get a little flush...," he said, now turning his backside to her.

"You are NOT going to show me your ass," Indy said. "There's no tips on Earth worth that. So unless you want your number one revenue stream to walk out the door, I suggest you turn back around, say goodbye to your buddy in the drive-thru, and get us both making money again."

Thankfully, Scrote did all three, and within 10 minutes the line at the drive-thru was cleared. No one waiting in line any longer, all was quiet, with Scrote now once again checking his visage in his mirror. The lobby was also empty, the man with the laptop gone. Pondering once again why such a seemingly decent — OK, geeky — guy would be in a place like this, Indy allowed herself a smile.

"Come on honey, have no fears.
I can soften your cries.
I'll hold you close with my love shears,
As you pull the wool over my thighs..."

Never mind.

Chapter 23
Scrote

Walking back into his office, Scrote couldn't help but smile at himself in the full-length mirror he had hanging on his door. Things were good, because while Scrote didn't remember everything Indy said to him, he'd heard her say "ass" — and that was enough. Heard like a melody, he took it as a good sign: She was warming up to him. Any day now he'd be watching her peel off everything from her green sunglasses on down. Better, as he told his partner, she'd be doing it all in Grind Me Hard Coffee's new location. Chuckling at his own joke, he mused, "Man, what I could do with that sweet glass..."

Scrote didn't usually meet with Ian through the drive-thru window; their meeting spot at the wide-open parking lot at the GO River Wayside had far fewer neighboring ears. But Ian had bailed on their meeting last night and Scrote really wanted to talk to him. That a half-dozen cars were waiting in the drive-thru bothered him little; more chances for all of them to see Indy all stretched out in that softball-thing she did. Opportunities for everyone, it seemed.

After several months of uncertainty — and downright fear — things were getting better at Grind Me Hard Coffee. Although sales in The Valley were still down, out here they were at record highs. All Indy, he had to admit, so he was excited at what she'd be able accomplish at the new location. Hell, she'd been the inspiration for the plan from the very first minute.

Not that she knew that.

Kirby Ionescro was the seventh son of 13 children born to two Romanian immigrants in Fresno, California. Basically raised by his older siblings who found his younger sister much more fun and adorable, Kirby spent much of his youth getting into one mess after another — and never learning from it. Surviving with limited resources and attention from his family, Kirby had decided that his failures were never his fault. That he would have succeeded if he'd just had more... something. Everything would have been OK, if only... somehow. People would have done what he asked, if it weren't for... someone.

Women in particular were a source of frustration for him. This was likely a result, again, of his younger sister, who was everything Kirby was not: decent, fun, and cute to boot. He became twisted by seeing her use her pixie personality and cuteness to never fail at anything (never mind all that studying and working and stuff). It was then that he realized the path to success lay in making sure he attached himself to the right women... whoever they were, so they could get him whatever it was... so they could learn to know the real him... so he could never fail.

Kirby's first foray into the world of women for fun, romance and profit ended poorly. Joining the cheerleading squad his senior year in high school as a yell leader, coaches found his stocky physique perfect for making the base of a pyramid. The go-to guy on the squad — the more wiry guys had a tendency to collapse and drop the girls on their heads — he tried to parlay his relationship with the school's cutest girls into cash by offering to pimp them out for a fraternity party at the nearby college. He had a particular sweet spot for Sally Tittledge, the team captain.

By Scrote's recollection, the plan would have worked had Sally's brother not been in that fraternity. Horrified to find his sister the cheerleader eighth in Kirby's "Pom-a-louge of Women," he went to his father. (Just after selecting the first seven for a manage-a-sept.) This sent Sally's father into a rage untempered by laws regarding felony murder of juveniles.

Deciding a high school degree — and romancing Sally Tittledge — was something he could complete later, Kirby packed his bags in a hurry, stopping only to tell his younger sister that she'd never know how good she looked on page 12. Taking what little he had in savings, he headed for the local truck stop and headed out with the first person that would give him a ride.

The driver turned out to be a roadie for the band "Sheep Pimpage," a small screamo/country hybrid out of Modesto. Heading for their next concert date in Grants Pass, Oregon, Kirby offered to work for her for free, as long as she'd give him a place to sleep and feed him on occasion. He did this for six months, discovering along the way a great deal about farm animals, angry Goth kids and show life.

He also discovered he was good with numbers, having to use them during load-in and load-outs in the various venues. Nothing spectacular, but where most people needed a calculator to do measurement calculations and multiplying load tolerances, Kirby could do them in his head. In Vancouver he'd actually been right where the show electrician had been wrong, something that had became horrifyingly obvious when the show's accountant was electrocuted in a homemade hot tub made out of barnyard troughs and feed barrels.

The show now in need of an accountant (and an electrician, who was in the hot tub showing the accountant how pigs procreate even when immersed) the show manager put Kirby in charge of the books. Just one year after leaving home, Kirby Ionescro was now the financial manager of a thriving music group. He even finished his high school diploma online. Now more educated than most of the people he worked with, his degree and abilities gained him the respect of those both on stage and back — and a nickname. "Scrote," they called him. And while

Kirby did decline their offer to tattoo his new name on its namesake, he did appreciate the manly tenor of the name. He just knew women would love it.

Over the years it had surprised him how many women had not loved it — or him.

In Seattle, he was meeting with the manager of KeyArena to finalize the performance contract and possibly land himself a job at the arena when he decided to ask her out. He never even got the chance, however, choosing instead to take her rather pointed decision to pour her superheated Starbucks espresso on his groin as a "No." That, and she had taken time to write "S C R O T E" in the white boxes down the side of the cup — and then crossed out each one.

In Portland he was working as a junior accountant at To St. Helens and Back, when he casually mentioned to the woman playing the sacrificial virgin that if she was tired of flaming co-workers, there was "Nothin' hotter than a Scrote." Angry that she'd been outed — Kirby had no idea she was a lesbian — she not only slapped him, but pinned his corporate name tag to his groin. This did not impress the head of accounting, who while knowing his daughter jumped half-naked into a volcano every night, did not know she was a lesbian.

Like most his jobs of late, he went immediately to human resources; he knew where to submit his exit paperwork. Pondering once again the sheer mystery that were women, he intended to hit the road soon — a road that would eventually lead to Surfland.

Some things never changed, of course.

In Surfland he knew Indy hated his name. Inviting him once to a "Pig-In-The-Poke 'Em and Scrotum Festival," she'd given him an address and said she'd meet him there. Only, when he went down to his car to leave, he found someone had filled his car with pork rinds. He'd known she'd done it, of course, but he liked her — a lot. More, staying with her was the key to his professional and personal plans, so he'd put up with it — and damn near everything else, in the weeks since.

He had to admit, though, even his partner, Ian Matthews, didn't seem to like his nickname very much at the moment, even though they'd been working together nearly a decade now. To that end, Scrote had been harassing Ian in the drive-thru about his choice of names, when his partner snapped at him: "You pick your name, I'll pick mine."

Momentarily, Scrote wondered if Ian might dump him like Sally Tittledge had all those years ago. Scrote's photo still up on the walls in the Fresno post office, police department, high school, Chuck E. Cheese and mortuary — the girl on page 23 of the Pom-a-louge of Women had actually been a corpse — he was not eager to return home, now or ever.

Ian's ire soon passed, however — "No damage done," he said. — and soon they were back to talking about the future of Grind Me Hard Coffee.

A business idea born of men's mutual love of hot coffee drinks and even hotter women, Scrote had opened more than a dozen outlets in the Willamette Valley in the past five years. The recession that followed the Wall Street collapse in 2008 had nearly wiped out the company, as it had many people. But buoyed by his silent partner, Ian, Scrote had put together a new business plan.

It was pretty much the same as it had always been: Combine obscenely high prices for coffee with an even higher surcharge for being served by a woman whose breasts could be used as a topographic map for Mts. Rainier and Adams.

But whereas before suburbanites appetites had been curbed by financial realities — and wives riding shotgun — his new plan relied on neither of those. Now it relied on Indy, the perfect location, and the perfect town to wrap it all up in. And even Ian, who usually seemed a cold fish about such things, had to admit things seemed to be going just about perfect.

Truth was, Scrote would also be happy to no longer have to draw on his partner's seemingly bottomless resources. He'd seen what happened to people Ian got tired of. Brushing that thought aside, however, Scrote got positively giddy as he recalled again the sweet way Indy had said, "ass." Looking over his shoulder one more time, he knew she'd eventually see things his way. And where every other woman he'd ever tried to work with and build a relationship with had rejected him somehow, for someone, for something, he knew Indy would not. She didn't have a choice. Turning one last time to Ian — Indy had mentioned "switching teams" and that was never a good thing — he patted the Volkswagen on the roof and sent his friend on his way.

"Believe me, the days of you being the only bottomless thing in Surfland are over — forever," Scrote said to the Bug as it rolled out of sight. Now laughing only to himself, Scrote turned his imagination to seeing Indy's uniform bottomless. Maybe if she switched her top to white, she could wear it at their wedding; that would be perfect.

Now, if he could just get his ass to stop itching.

Chapter 24
Ian Matthews

Pulling out of the drive-thru at Grind Me Hard Coffee, Ian was worried that Scrote was on the verge of another personal letdown with a woman and a plan. Not that he really cared about Scrote, but he did want the plan to go through. The building Scrote craved was important to Ian personally.

To say this attitude would have surprised the people who knew Ian would not be true; no one knew him. No one ever had, actually, save for one man, and he was dead. Lacking connections with anyone, even Scrote, Ian had become a solitary zealot, crusading against the fake and faux. And like most zealots he saw himself a man of genuine substance — with zero ability to tolerate those who weren't.

Nowhere was this more evident that in his contempt for the things that had sprung up in his longtime home of Surfland in the last 20 years. Most recently it had driven him to torch Mermaid in Oregon; the place was a crime against decency.

At first glance, it might seem that Grind Me Hard Coffee was more of the same: artifice in the name of greed. But what Ian appreciated about Scrote's idea was its sincerity: It was about boobs, sex appeal and over-priced coffee. No pretense there whatsoever. Was it trashy and splashy? Certainly, but Scrote was honest about it. And even if it wasn't Ian's thing, it served his purposes to a tee.

Heading back to his cottage just south of the city limits, he shifted from second to third gear in his Bug as he accelerated down Highway 101. Operating as perfectly as the day his grandfather had bought it new in 1964, Ian looked out the window to see numerous cars far more expensive than his. That he had the wealth to buy all of them while he drove a spartan Volkswagen bothered him not at all. He loved it, his grandfather had loved it — and his parents had loathed it.

Perfect.

Go-go society types, his parents had spent Ian's youth constantly dragging him off to events in Portland and Seattle where he needed to press flesh, schmooze people and engage in all kinds of insincere crap that he cared nothing about. Every person he met was to him reinforcement of his parents' money-driven values, so he hated them, too — and himself, just a bit.

For while Ian loathed his parents' money, after a decade or so of rejecting them and it, he'd finally allowed himself to start indulging in it. Sending himself off for multiple degrees in the sciences at Oregon State University, he'd used their bank accounts to fund his education and his travels all over the planet. That he was a hypocrite bothered him some, but he rationalized it by telling himself that the things he was learning about the people and cultures of the world were worth it. Indeed, how many people had a Cambodian orphanage named after them?

These were the things he told his parents about, not that they cared. Still engaged in fantasy, his parents continued in the belief that someday their only child would take over the family business, one that was beginning to bore them. Meanwhile Ian, convinced more than ever that they were two worthless people that the planet would be better off without, wondered how much longer he'd have to put up with them — and how he might speed up that process.

Especially awkward for all of them was when he would return from overseas and show up unannounced to their events. Required to be there if he wanted the money to keep flowing, he'd arrive in his Volkswagen Bug with a scraggly beard, unkempt hair and a suit straight off the Goodwill rack. All of them miserable with his presence, Ian took some pleasure in knowing he'd made it worse by taping a day-old anchovy in one of his armpits.

But that was nearly a decade ago, and knowing that such conversations were now not only years in the past but impossible in the future, Ian smiled as he pulled into his driveway. His home was a simple place on the bay; just a couple of bedrooms with a small deck that allowed him to see over the dunes to the ocean beyond. Like his car, he had better alternatives.

His family had owned a house on Anchor Avenue for generations. But just as he had loathed his parents, he'd always hated the monstrosity of a house they'd built as a testament to their wealth and greed. Who the hell needed 4,500 square feet, three floors and two kitchens? He was happy to let Scrote stay there.

On this trip home, however, he didn't even enter his small cottage, aside from pulling into the garage. Searching through the meticulously sorted shelves that he and his grandfather had built together, he quickly found what he was looking for. Taking advantage of its wheels, he dragged it across the floor and then lifted it into the trunk on the front of his car.

Watching the car sag a bit on its front axle from the weight, Ian pondered no more than a moment the type of crime he was about to commit. It wouldn't be his first, although if it had been it wouldn't have bothered him. Arson, murder, it was all in a creative day's work at this point.

But it would be his most public, and there was a risk of getting caught. The last time he'd killed someone in public, he'd been at the top of a mountain when they died. This time he'd be right there, and though the location was secluded from the public, it was a state park. But far from dissuading him, it gave him an extra thrill. His grandfather would be proud of him; this is how he would have done it.

Satisfied with his solution, he slammed the trunk shut and got behind the wheel for his trip back up Highway 101. A journey of only a few miles, the tourist traffic could make it a 45 minute-journey and he didn't want to be late. His timing at the lighthouse would be critical.

Chapter 25
Ryan Alexander Reynolds

"Goat you know me, baby-bee?"
Goat you know you're the reason I live?
So let's bed down in the hay, girl,
And pop out a herd of kids."

Returning to the confines of Grind Me Hard Coffee, Xander was reminded how God-awful the music they played inside was. Having forgotten an external hard drive in his van, he'd left the shop for a moment and found the respite from the music glorious. He returned, however, for the same reason he always did: Indy Monroe.

He'd had a crush on her ever since he first talked to her — and last talked to her, as it turned out — in the library at Harrison High School four years ago. Walking through the door, he was actively looking for her when their eyes suddenly locked as she stepped from the bathroom. Awkwardly, he looked away and headed for his table. The last thing he needed was for her to think he was a stalker or something creepy like that.

As he took his seat, however, he could see she was making her way towards his table. Oh, crap. What was he going to say? He needed to be cool and self-assured, but not arrogant or clichéd. *Oh, crap, here she comes. Oh, crap, she's opening her mouth to speak... Be cool...*

"Hi, I'm Indy," she said. "I thought you'd gone, just like every other decent person."

Her voice like an angel, Xander she knew she wasn't insulting him, just being friendly and funny. *Be cool... Be cool...*

"Where did you go?"

"I went to hell and back, Indy. I went to hell and back."

So not cool.

Following graduation from Harrison High School four years earlier, Ryan Alexander Reynolds, as it said on his diploma, had taken his love of computers and went to work for his uncle at a globe-spanning NGO in Portland. What he lacked in an actual degree he made up for with his work ethic and his ability to make computers work and interface with just about anything. Coupled with a voracious desire to learn about everything — when he was hired, his Kindle had open books on photography, poetry, plasma physics, chemistry, remote control interfaces, gardening, and lasers — he was a man of unique talents.

Ryan was a geek.

Soon, his skills were taking him all over the globe setting up computer systems for his employer in locations both exotic and otherwise. Not by choice, he found his horizons broadened to subjects like explosives, weapons and how computers might be used to predict and mitigate the damage of both. By the age of 22, he'd spent more time in former war zones and current hot-spots than anyone outside the military — and seen the horrors that often came with that.

That's why he'd returned to Surfland: he needed a break. On long-term leave from his job, he'd gone after a temporary employment opportunity with Surfland Tourism. Seeking someone with experience in both computers and low-yield explosives, the opportunity seemed heaven-sent. When he realized that the angel that occupied his mind every waking moment of high school still lived in town, he knew a benevolent God was somewhere at his back.

Until he spoke — and totally screwed it up: "I went to hell and back, Indy. I went to hell and back."

"Yeah, that's how I feel about this place, too," she said, now laughing again. "What's your name?"

God, apparently, was giving him another opportunity.

"My friends call me 'Xander.'"

""What do your enemies call you?"

"'Geek,' if I remember Harrison High School correctly."

"Oh, my God! I remember you! You're the geek!"

And there went God right out the door. Slowly starting to pull his stuff together, Xander had never felt quite this low. Four years and two war zones later, 20 pounds of muscle added, one pair of thick-rimmed glasses subtracted, and he was still the geek. Forget the temp job; picking through the remains of an Iraqi IED was seeming better and bet—

"I loved you in high school!" Indy nearly screamed. "You were in the library, and you rescued my history paper after I accidentally deleted it! Whatever happened to you after that? It's like you fell off the face of the Earth."

With that invitation — Thank you, God — he began to tell her.

"Seriously," Indy said. "You came back here to blow up the whale? I wondered what the hell that was all about."

"You know about the whale?"

"Where do you think Plink got the whale?"

Before she could even start that story, however, a voice bellowed from the drive-thru: "Indy, get that cute ass over here," Scrote bellowed. "One of those old Chevy van's got a broken porthole window and I need you to pitch some compost through it!"

"Like a '70s van needs more decay in it..." Like always, Indy was speaking aloud to herself, ironically as a way to keep sane at this horror of a job. That her new friend appreciated it made it all the better.

"Look at the bright side," he said. "If you miss, all you'll hit is a Day-Glo painting of a beach."

Laughing, Indy nodded her head in agreement. "We'll have to continue our talk of exploding whales later."

"I'd like that," he said, barely containing the enthusiasm in his voice.

"Me, too... Say, why 'Xander'?"

"When I got back to the United States, I found out the other Ryan Reynolds was the 'Sexiest Man Alive.' Just seemed like a lot to live up to. And I hated *Green Lantern*."

"No kidding," she said, now heading back to the drive-thru. "Not a single good line in that movie."

Laughing, Xander had to admit he had no idea what she was talking about — and he didn't care one little bit.

Chapter 26
Poe

The sun now having burned off the last of the morning clouds, the south end of Surfland was getting a full-blast dose of the orchestral theme from the newest Star Trek film. Rationalizing people didn't need to sleep past 1 p.m. anyway, Poe kept the volume up as he headed for the home of his strangest and certainly most reclusive friend.

Called Fuzznut, he was a mascot by trade, a nudist by choice and gourmet chef by passion. Never, obviously, practicing the first two at the same time, the same could not be said of the last two. Aged somewhere in his 50s, it was a miracle Fuzznut had never burned anything important, despite his love of frying bacon.

What traditional conventions of cooking Fuzznut ignored, however, he did try to apply to his friendships, however. In recent years he'd taken to wearing an apron when Poe came over out of respect for Poe's sensibilities. (That, and an awareness that eventually the declining mobility of age and sautéed crabs exploding in butter might pose a serious problem.)

Counting on that, Poe knocked on the door — and was surprised not to get an answer. It wasn't like Fuzznut to miss a scheduled meeting, and today of all days was not a good time to start. Certainly, Poe could get the eagle costume from Fuzznut later; it was still nearly two days until Paxton was supposed to wear it at the Friday fundraiser.

This morning's meeting at Bendovren Coffee, however, had suddenly given the appointment new urgency — and Fuzznut's eccentricities an added sense of danger.

Fuzznut's number one eccentricity — outside the house, anyway — was that he never went out in public without a mascot costume on. Probably the most famous furry face in Surfland, no one had ever actually seen his real one, or even knew his real name. Walking or biking to most of his jobs on nice days and changing in a van he owned when it rained, Fuzznut was furry and then forgotten.

Except one time a day.

That time came before dawn, when a naked Fuzznut would walk out his back door onto the beach and dive for crabs from the rocks in the surf. The freshest seafood he could get, it kept him in amazing shape. The water a crisp 44 degrees year-round, his daily expeditions in the hour before sunrise had always been private — until now.

Now there was a video of a very grainy Fuzznut, shot by someone at The Inn at Roca de la Muerte Dolorosa and put on YouTube. Only Poe knew those details, of course, and he had no doubt he and Rip would be able head Plink's manhunt off. Still, however, he wanted Fuzznut to know he might want to lay low for a while, at least until Plink's obsession — and the Inn's cameras — focused on something else.

Obviously, that would have to wait, however. Heading back to his car, Poe recalled that Fuzznut had said how crazy his current job was, including the need to be on the job virtually all day long. Assuming that's what was up at the moment, Poe just hoped his schedule would keep him out of the ocean, as well.

Poe's next stop was a quick run through Bendovren's drive-thru — thank God Ryan was back at the espresso machine — for one of his signature cups of coffee. His own custom blend, the Nordins roasted Poe's beans separate from all the others. A service they provided for their most loyal customers — even ones annoying as Plink — it wasn't cheap, but it was worth it.

Letting the familiar smell of caramel tickle his nose — it was his second today — Poe smiled at what seemed like a perfect world. Raising the java to his lips, however, Poe was surprised to find his drink was now dragging his mood in the opposite direction.

Seeing Ryan's drawn face was a stark reminder that Bendovren Coffee was on the verge of closing, despite the young man's exhaustive efforts. As Poe eased his Jag out of the drive-thru something was nagging at him; something that didn't seem quite right. Not that Bendovren would be the first coffee shop the recession had laid low, but it would be the first owned by his friends. Maybe that was it.

Turning the volume back up on his stereo, Poe hoped his music would boldly take him where it had before as he and his Jag cruised past the GO River Wayside. It worked, and among those forced into ambient listening were some who liked it and some who didn't — not that Poe worried too much about the latter. People who couldn't appreciate a booming crescendo: Well, there was just something wrong with them.

Curious to see if Rip's favorite street person might be giving CPR again — people told Poe all the time the throbbing bass could induce a coronary — he was surprised to see the bum had left his corner. Working for food, perhaps — but probably not.

His mood once again light, Poe soaked up the summer sun. True, it was only 62 degrees, but on a sunny day in Surfland it felt more like 80. Sun-induced goose bumps but without the threat of melanomas: that's the way he liked to think of it. It was the perfect preventative to what he had to do next: Spend more time with Plink.

Officially Pete's assistant on Plink's list of expenses, he was actually serving in that capacity today. Pete was shooting background footage on his newly acquired HD cameras, and he wanted to return to the lighthouse one last time before putting together the final cut of Plink's "Water-ful" promotional video. Having worked with Pete numerous times over the years, Poe was the perfect person to help him get everything set up and ready to go. It certainly wasn't the worst job he'd been paid for in his time in Surfland; freelance writers took what they could get.

But not today. Further lifting Poe's mood was how well the restaurant story for Sunwest Magazine had gone. Certainly, when he'd left Bendovren Coffee for the first time that morning for Flipper's Music and Munchies, he knew he wasn't headed off to talk to dolphins. But what awaited him didn't thrill him much either: Phil "Hacksaw" Luber, whom he assumed to be one angry dude. Poe knew he'd be that way, too, if his ex chopped off all but two of his fingers.

What Poe found, however, was a man who had embraced his lot in life and put it to work for him. Opening a piano bar, Phil could play damn near anything on two fingers, including 57 versions of Chopsticks. He could also play wine glasses like a cello, making each one of the 36 sing like Liberace. Bitter not in the least, Hacksaw saw the incident as a blessing, although Poe did notice Hacksaw's middle fingers got especially taut when he played country western songs about ex-wives.

Suddenly, Poe's music cut out as the Bluetooth on his iPhone kicked in. A handy feature in a state where hands-free cell phones were the law in cars, he reacted to it as he always did when his music was on: "Dammit!" And, as he always did when his music was on, he went to cut off the call. This time, however, he stopped when he saw who was calling: the ER doctor at St. Gangulphus Hospital. Answering the phone, Poe went straight to the point:

"Dr. Bracewell, I presume? Tell me what I already know: I'm fine and that Kinkel McGuire is the worst barista in the universe."

Taking a moment to catch up to Poe, Dr. Bracewell didn't seem entirely sure what to say: "Well, having no idea who Kinkel McGuire is, I can't really speak to his barista skills. But if he's the one that made your drink you might want to put a little bit more in his tip jar."

"Why's that?"

"Maybe then he wouldn't try to poison you again."

Chapter 27
Dick Yelpers

Dickie Yelpers was exactly 12 years old when he met Elton John. And while it would be terribly overwrought to say the visit changed his life, the incident that created the meeting definitely had. Combined as the two events were, it was not surprising that Dick spent considerable time trying to figure out how to show the musician he appreciated his kindness.

Raised in Lake County, California, Dick's parents were groundskeepers at one of the largest family-owned wineries in the state. Like all employees, they were considered extended family, and when special occasions were held, everyone was invited. If it seemed strange to outsiders that a 12-year-old would have his slumber party in a vineyard, it didn't to anyone in the family (although they did keep the door to the cellars locked).

So it was that Dickie and seven of his friends were about to dive into gallons of Coke and enough freshly baked Tojino's frozen pizzas to kill a horse, when one of his buddies scooped a handful of dirt out of the ground and dared Dickie to eat a worm. There were numerous reasons to say no — and being 12 Dickie ignored all of them. Shoving the mass of worm and dry earth into his mouth, the soil combined with his saliva to coat the inside of his mouth — but the worm went down.

Thrilled with his victory, Dickie shoved a giant wad of hot pizza into his mouth.

The resulting tragedy would change Dickie Yelper's entire existence.

It's well-known that magnesium basically explodes when it comes in contact with water. A staple of high school chemistry classes, its highly visual reaction is a favorite among students, especially when placed on the edge of a toilet seat. Dickie and his friends, however, had not entered high school yet, not that Lake County schools would have covered soil consumption.

Ignorance never a barrier to the laws of chemistry, Dickie was horrified as latent moisture from the frozen pizza, combining with the abnormally high magnesium content of the soils in the vineyard, basically set his palate afire.

Rushed to the hospital, oral surgeons managed to save his tongue and vocal cords, but his palate was destroyed. Drifting in an out of consciousness on his birthday, in Dickie's moments of lucidity he lamented that he would never talk again, never kiss a girl the way God intended, never live life the way he had planned. He wanted to die, and as a bacterial infection spread from his mouth to his brain stem, it seemed he might.

And then Elton John came to visit.

It happened as Dickie came back to consciousness from one of the morphine shots they were giving him for the pain. Clad in feathers, sequins and giant sunglasses, he placed his hands on Dickie's still bandaged and swollen face and simply said, "Don't go breakin' my heart," and begged Dickie to live.

Almost instantly Dickie began to rally, and by the following morning even the infection seemed to be disappearing. Dickie still had a long way to go, but it seemed he was going to live. Which is why his parents never told him that who he thought was Elton John was in fact his very strange Uncle Desmond, who later would undergo his own surgery and become his Aunt Desdemona.

As the years went on, Dickie never forgot the will Elton John had given him to live. Largely because his parents never told him the truth. But also because Dickie was a genuinely decent person, one who tried to remember the people who had helped him through the difficulties his post-pizza life had presented.

First among those in his corner was the family that employed his parents and owned the vineyard. Motivated by a genuine desire to stop palate burns by overheated frozen pizzas, they hired the very best lawyers money could buy and sued Tojino's Pizza Co., Inc. That it was their son who had actually dared Dickie to eat the dirt and worms, well, that was just a coincidence they said. In any case, by the time he was 15, Dickie was a multi-millionaire, the money just waiting in a trust.

Money not an issue, life was still hard for Dickie, as was just about every form of oral activity. As he had lamented in bed on his 12th birthday, speech was nearly impossible, despite the best speech therapists money could buy. Not that his speech didn't improve; it did. But that was small consolation as he embarked for college: He didn't want to kiss his speech therapist.

A business student at San Francisco State, his social isolation got worse. Finding a woman who could accept never being kissed in a normal way was compounded by the fact that finding guy friends was equally impossible. He tried rushing a fraternity his freshman year in the belief that most of the people there sounded drunk half the time, anyway. Indeed, when they found out how rich he was, they were happy to take him. He quit within a week, however, when he discovered new pledges were required to cook frozen pizzas for the upperclassmen twice a week.

Dickie spent most of his time alone, even choosing to eat away from the dorm, the social groups surrounding him a reminder of what he didn't have. He especially liked McDonald's; the thick shakes made his mouth feel better. One night, however, he met someone who finally understood him: a mime.

Now, Dickie hated mimes as much as the next guy, assuming that the next guy isn't a French theatre major. But this mime was different:

her father was the owner of the McDonald's on Winston Street where Dickie ate most of his meals. She'd been watching him, and while she didn't understand him any better than any other woman, her training as a mime meant she didn't need to. She was used to communicating without words — and she liked Dickie.

Within a year they were married, and three years after that he graduated near the top of his class. With her father's backing, Dickie — now Dick — was offered a franchise in Surfland, Oregon. Neither of them had ever heard of the place; it seemed like to end of the Earth — literally.

But it was also a start, and soon they found themselves content with one another and their franchise, popular among tourists and locals alike. And it probably would have stayed that way, had not a grandma spilled coffee on her crotch in the winter of '92. A case that became famous around the world for lawsuit abuse, insanely hot coffee and more discussions of a grandma's private parts than any human wanted to know, Dick argued within the company that they should just settle it. Didn't matter if they were right and she was wrong, he knew from personal experience how costly a combination of lawyers and burned body parts could be.

"Shuh's guh-nuh skru uh."

And screw McDonald's she did. Final settlement amounts were private, of course. But after the lawyers, the bad press and the check they wrote out to grandma, the costs was in the millions. Within the company, it was largely agreed that Dick Yelpers had known what he was talking about. When a string of McDonalds up and down the Oregon coast became available in the late '90s, Dickie was given the first chance to buy them, and he did. A bit more than a decade later, Dickie was one of the most successful restaurateurs in Oregon.

And it was all about to come crashing down.

He should never have put his name in for President.

The secretary of the Surfland Tourism Advisory Board, Dick had been surprised when Plink Blayton suggested he run for president. Both were unpaid positions, but the presidency had a higher profile, more of a chance to make an impact. Having been largely responsible for bringing Plink to Surfland, Dick believed him when Plink said Dick's stature as a businessman more than outweighed his speech impediment.

At first, it had been a mutually beneficial relationship; they seemed to work well together. Certainly, Plink had some crazy ideas, and early on Dick had shot some of them down. (Just because the city had horses and sand didn't mean restaging "Ben Hur" was a good idea.) Others he figured he should let Plink try. (In retrospect, when it came to the Surfland Seagull Races shooting them down might have been a better idea.)

But even before the incident with the Girl Scouts, Plink had become increasingly arrogant. Despite being Plink's boss, he had never seriously considered Dick's marketing message: "The Beach is Back." True, "Tah BEE ih BAH," as explained by Dick didn't exactly engender goose bumps. But more than just Dick's salute to Elton — not that Plink knew that — Dick genuinely thought it had merit. A way of celebrating all the reasons people come — and come back — to the beach. Plink never listened to a word of it.

And he'd never have to.

Looking back on it now, it seemed inconceivable that Plink had planned out all the events of the last few years. The election, certainly; it was a foregone conclusion that Dick would win, as everyone else dropped out once he announced he was running. But everything else? The incident at the GO River Wayside? The television crew? The tape? There was no way he could have planned that. Or was there?

Whatever the case, Plink's ideas and attitude were becoming increasingly dangerous. Perhaps not physically, but certainly to the reputation of Surfland. Someone had to stop him, and while Dick knew one man who might, he really didn't have much hope. Plink had Dick by the balls — and they both knew it.

Chapter 28
Ian

Like many of Oregon's coastal beacons, Surfland's Ageya Head Lighthouse sat atop a rocky promontory. Formed millions of years ago when a lava flow froze in place upon meeting the frigid waters of the Pacific, it was basically a big two-tiered plateau with a rocky knob on the end. The top of it long ago covered by topsoil and grass, it had been a favored gathering spot for the Ageya Tribal nation for generations, Josiah and Rebekkah Tandy in the 19th century, a rock quarry at the beginning of the 20th, and thousands of tourists ever since.

It was the rocky knob on the end, however, that interested Ian Matthews today. Driving up the all-but forgotten forest road on the north side of Ageya Head, every dimension of the historic site came easily to mind. He hadn't been there in years, of course, but as he parked his car about a quarter-mile east of the lighthouse, he didn't need to see it to recall exactly what it looked like. It had two tiers, the lower and flatter one being the site of the lighthouse about 75 feet above the ocean. The upper tier was about 100 feet above that, at the top of a 45 degree slope, it's jumbled piles of quarried basalt slowly turning to soil and grass as one went east.

Not even bothering to lock his car, Ian went to the Bug's trunk and took out the jack he'd taken from his garage. There would be no rolling it where he was going, so he strapped it instead to a backpack frame. Not exactly comfortable, he had to admit, but that wasn't what was critical on this hike. Speed was the only thing that mattered.

Starting his walk up the trail, Ian reflected how similar this was to the last time he'd strapped on a backpack this heavy: Going unnoticed was critical, his surroundings were stunningly beautiful — and he was going to kill someone.

Ian had grown up killing things on the Oregon coast.

His grandfather, known simply as "The Captain," had been a commercial fisherman since the 1920s out of the Port of Lenobar in what was then the town of Harrison. Starting with a few boats in the years before the Great Depression, The Captain and his father rode out the lean years by working on some of FDR's WPA projects by day, and keeping the business alive at night.

Often, this required creative solutions, like the day the bank repossessed their flatbed pickup. One 38 Ford sedan and one chainsaw later, problem solved. (One tarp was needed for the rainiest days.) Not the most elegant solution, but The Captain was known as a man of his word, which meant personally driving their boats' catch from the coast to their downtown Portland neighborhood each night, no matter what the obstacle.

Their sales were tiny; the demand just wasn't there. But it did pay the mortgage on their homes in Portland and the coast, although they often wondered if it was worth it. Making virtually no money throughout the 1930s despite constant work, they spent very little time in their Portland home or the cottage south of Harrison. (That their coastal living room was also used as a boarding house for fishermen who rarely showered made the absence somewhat less frustrating.)

As the dark days of The Great Depression lifted, however, so did the fortunes of Ian's family. Having established their business in the worst of times, they were primed to grow when the good times returned. In the 1940s they made millions selling to the government via wartime contracts. In the 1950s and '60s, as the middle class boomed and spent more of their leisure time — and money — on coastal tourism, they grew even wealthier as seafood restaurants opened up and down the coast. In the city, they were the largest supplier of fresh fish, by far. By the 1970s and '80s, when Ian was regularly spending every summer day with The Captain, the family was incredibly wealthy. And while they might not have been as well-known as the Tandys in Surfland and Portland, their presence was every bit as prevalent: Half the fishing vessels in the Port of Lenobar belonged to Ian's family, as did 40 percent of the fish sold in Portland.

Enjoying the fruits of the family's labor, Ian's father was different from The Captain in every way possible. A science professor at Oregon State University, he enjoyed living well above the means his academic job would have solely provided him. Married to a similarly frustrated academic, both of them were more than happy to spend the family money on fancier cars, sharper clothes and bigger homes. Both in The Valley and Surfland, they had their original homes scraped from their lots and replaced by mansions. Eventually, both of them came to see teaching as a distraction to what they really liked to do: Being rich and flaunting it.

Summer was a particularly busy time for them. In a state where it often rains continuously from October to June, they made sure they were out — literally — most every summer night. Leaving very little time for parenting young Ian, they pawned him off on The Captain, who continued to live in the cottage he and his father had built just south of Harrison in 1921.

It was from The Captain that Ian learned to kill things — and why respect for them was just as important. Certainly, his family had made their living off the bounty of the ocean. But whereas many commercial fishermen had over-fished their parts of the sea, The Captain never had. Having virtual control of the seas off the central Oregon coast, he'd made sure to protect the area from those that would destroy it just for short-term profit.

Here, too, The Captain insisted his young grandson learn creativity; one could not simply go about attacking other fishing boats. Instead, it was a matter of doing things creatively, quietly, and with a certain degree of style. That, and it was a lot easier if everyone just assumed things were accidents. The brash might put sand in a poacher's fuel tank, while The Captain would jam it with oyster shells. (Drunken fishermen were always dropping those things.) People without imagination cut nets, The Captain preferred to coat them with peanut butter, ensuring they became a seagull buffet.

It wasn't just what you did; it was how you did it.

This was how Ian spent his teen and early adult years: Spending the academic year with his parents who treated him like an accessory, and his summers with The Captain, who made sure Ian came to appreciate the things that truly mattered. Society vs. sustainability, profits vs. protection, faux vs. fauna. Even his summers became the opportunity to learn what his parents and school should have been teaching him. He learned biology on the seas and in the woods. He excelled in math and English as The Captain taught him the family business. He even learned history, as his grandfather showed him various things he'd built during the Great Depression, including the home of what was now Bendovren Coffee.

As Ian approached adulthood, he and The Captain spent less time on boats, and more time just sitting. Destined to take over the company one day, The Captain wanted Ian to understand what was special about Surfland — and more than ever what it took to protect it. They were quite the team in those days, especially since Ian looked exactly like his grandfather: Fair of skin like most Nordic peoples, not tall, but not short, either, and lean, as most fishermen tend to be. Indeed, more than one photo of the pair sat in the archives at the local history museum, icons of Surfland's nautical history. In one photo, taken on the porch on

The Captain's cottage, one would have thought they were two identical halves of a Norman Rockwell painting, save that one half had been painted 50 years later.

Assuming, of course, that Norman Rockwell was painting crazy people.

For as The Captain aged he was also slowly slipping into... something. Not dementia exactly, as he could still remember key events in his life. And indeed the beginnings of his stories were unfailingly true — which was a problem, since the end seldom was.

Wild stories replacing memories, they nevertheless seemed to all listeners like things that could have happened, so exacting was his detail. It helped, too, that his stories were never fanciful; he didn't invent space aliens that probed him, (although he did once intimate that Rita Hayworth had). And if he occasionally started a story with, "See that guy over there? I killed him once," that was usually forgiven, especially since Ian was the only one really listening, anyway.

But listen he did, and as Ian began forming the moral compass that would guide him in life, it was being warped by someone whose compass was pointing straight towards batty. A tale that truthfully involved putting oyster shells in the engine of a poacher's boat, now ended with The Captain blowing it up. A lesson in how to ruin someone's nets ended with how to put a body in them. And while most people would dismiss the claim that The Captain had induced dysentery simultaneously on three different cruise ships docked in Lenobar Harbor, Ian believed it all. (CNN being a major help in this regard.)

Certainly, Ian noticed that these stories all seemed to vary from the ones he'd been told as a child. He chalked that up, however, to The Captain censoring the grimmest parts to spare his childhood. He was an adult now, and obviously, hiding the ugly truth wasn't necessary. That's why Ian felt he was more than ready — in so many ways — to take over the company when The Captain died in 1984. And why he was so betrayed when his parents turned around and sold it soon after to a giant corporation out of Seattle. Their lives and businesses were in The Valley; they had no time for the rainy coast and other dreary things, like fish.

Enraged, Ian retreated to The Captain's cottage, which his family let him keep. Spending nearly a decade living there, he kept to himself, occupying himself with two things. The first was watching the sea: the creatures in it, the birds soaring above it, just as he and The Captain had always done.

The second was killing his parents.

For years, he pondered The Captain's stories and wondered if there wasn't some way to use them on his parents and turn back the clock. Once again observing nature, he drove all over Surfland, looking at the rocks, the cliffs, the trees, the ocean, the bay, even the weeds on Highway 101— one giant patch hid a transformer box — trying to figure out a way to kill his parents and get away with it. Indeed, before Ian knew it, a decade went by as he tried to figure out how burning/crushing/ shooting them and their sparkly new homes/SUVs/faces might return him to the deck of The Captain's fishing boats.

But not one of the Captain's stories had told him how to get back the company, only how to preserve it. And while Ian certainly could calculate what to do with his parents once they were dead — he still knew where to find a drift net — he had no idea how that would help him. Just having their money wouldn't change anything; the company was gone.

And so was Ian, as far as Surfland was concerned. Once one of the most familiar faces in town, the only evidence he even remained in Surfland were his weekly trips into town in The Captain's Volkswagen Bug to buy groceries. Even here, however, long-time residents failed to identify him as The Captain's grandson, so disheveled had his appearance become. Rarely cutting any of his hair or even showering, he was the kind of person many people learned to keep their distance from. At the IGA he was often mistaken for the fish section.

That Ian repelled people bothered him not at all; they repelled him. When he'd needed them to protest the sale of a locally owned, environmentally friendly company to a big corporate conglomerate, they said nothing. Eating their seafood on the waterfront every night, what did they care where their food came from? Just as long as it was cheap. Most days he felt like killing them all, as he was sure that's what The Captain would have felt like doing.

Even in his fugue of hate, however, Ian realized that could not be done. He did, however, on the anniversary of his grandfather's death, randomly pick out one Surfland restaurant with fake food in the window for the purposes of vandalizing it. It wasn't much, but it did make him feel better, especially since The Captain had once done it to every restaurant in San Francisco — in one day.

After a decade of being a virtual hermit, however, Ian came to realize that the solution to his problems lay not in hiding from the world, but in engaging it and learning from it. That's when he went off to OSU and got his degrees, and began traveling the world. From Cambodia to Cameroon, Albania to Zimbabwe, Ian discovered a happiness he had not known in years.

And the way to finally kill his parents.

The plan began in late 2005, when Ian came home from three years overseas in Southeast Asia. Declining to ride in a limousine longer than a fire truck, Ian instead arranged to have The Captain's Volkswagen Bug left for him at the airport. Having not cleaned himself at all on the plane — or the prior two weeks — he went directly to a party hosted by his parents at their favorite restaurant. The 20th anniversary of their decision to sell The Captain's company and start their own, Ian was on edge the minute he walked through the doors of Captain Chang's Chinese Restaurant, which his parents had rented.

His horror was complete, however, when he saw the crab at the buffet and his mother's chest. Both were fake — and any reticence Ian might have had about killing his parents disappeared. It wasn't enough that they had rid themselves of The Captain's company, they were now ridding themselves of any responsibility at all to their heritage. They were actually making the world worse for other men and women of the sea. Something had to be done — and Ian would do it.

And he did; within a year both his parents were dead. The victims of a tragic "accident," hundreds of Portland's hoi-polloi came to pay their respects, including Ian, who sat in the front row holding his parents' ashes. Strangely non-emotional, most of the guests assumed it was because in addition to saying goodbye to his parents, the original site of his parents' funeral had burned to the ground just last night. Arson, it had destroyed not only Captain Chang's Chinese Restaurant, but also the thousands of personal items Ian had brought from his parent's home for the service. The fire vaporizing the place into nonexistence, the only evidence it had ever been there at all was a pile of melted fake food on the sidewalk out front.

Smiling as he worked his way towards the rock quarry, Ian delighted in the symmetry of the moment. Nearly a decade ago he'd killed his parents and burned down a restaurant, and now in a period of couple of days, he was going to do the same thing again.

And just as it had been then, it would be easy.

Torching Captain Chang's had actually been an afterthought. He'd originally gone there just to prepare his parents' mementos for a public auction — and steal the fake food out of the window. But as he stared at the sign on the door, he became enraged again at how his parents had so easily dismissed The Captain from their lives, only to replace him with this fake one. The place had to go — and it did. Ian had learned a lot overseas about just how the rest of the world dealt with inconvenient problems.

But standing there in the cold October rain, a smoldering pile of fake Kung Pao Chicken and Mumu platters at his feet, Ian realized something: As long as he was surrounded by the bitter artifices of his

parents' life, he'd never find peace himself. Certainly, killing his parents
didn't bother him. But there were just so many other things he wanted
to do, and as long as he was chained to his parents' legacy, those things
were impossible. It had to go away — and so did Ian.

And he would have still been away, had the events of the last few
months not transpired at Hope Falls Park the way they had. Returning
to Surfland, he was at first worried someone would recognize him.
Within days, however, he realized that as long as he kept his trips in and
out of the house low-key, no one would connect the clean-cut man in
the Volkswagen with the Grizzly Adams-like hermit that had roamed
the streets of Surfland nearly 20 years ago.

Feeling free to roam a bit, he found himself driving up and down
streets he had not explored since his youth — and being horrified
by what he saw. So many of the places that had been part of his past
were now gone: The little family-owned restaurant where he'd played
backgammon with The Captain was now replaced by a vegan bistro/
porn shop. The giant grassy field at the north end of town where they'd
run the annual All-Star Joan of Arc Memorial Horse Race and Bonfire
— he'd met Florence Henderson there once — was now a casino. The
old Whig City Oyster and Clam Market was now a cheap and kitschy
restaurant. This one bothered him most of all, partially because he'd
never actually gotten to go there; The Captain insisting all the shellfish
had beards, whatever that meant.

More, however, he considered "Mermaid in Oregon," an abomination.
First of all, there were no such things as mermaids, although he could
have handled that. After all, Ian had nothing if not respect for the
environment. If they'd actually used the draw of the mermaids to inform
people about life under the sea and how to preserve it, that would have
meant something to him. Instead, the place was a nightmare of brightly
colored people in tacky dry suits looking to sell anything and everything
cheap and plastic to passing tourists. Rather than being arrested for
burning it down, he should have been given a medal.

Lost in his thoughts, Ian was surprised to find himself already edging out of the forest onto the grassy summit of Ageya Head. Slowing to make sure no one was looking in his direction, Ian stopped when he realized there was a large party of people off in the distance. Lying low, he paused, wondering what he should do before he realized they weren't actually moving. All huddled around someone or something, none of them were even looking his way.

Feeling safe to once again move across the grass towards the rocky slope above the lighthouse, Ian's instincts were vindicated as he found his only company at the old rock quarry to be a Giant English Sheepdog sleeping in the grass.

Relieved to finally get the weight of the jack off his back, Ian stopped for a moment to watch a bald eagle soar above his head and smiled once again to no one in particular. Not only was he about to solve a major problem, but he was going to use this unnatural abomination of a rock quarry to do it. Quickly locating the fulcrum point of rock he'd known for 20 years he had planned to use for this purpose, Ian shoved the jack underneath and began to pump the handle.

Chapter 29

Poe

"Kinkel? Poison me?" Suddenly aware that his voice had actually gone up an octave, Poe had to stop himself from actually laughing at Dr. Bracewell over the phone. "Himself, maybe. But someone else? No way."

Sounding incredulous himself, Dr. Bracewell continued on: "Perhaps you're right," he said, still remembering the day Kinkel came into the ER with the penny-stamper still attached to his nipple. "But if not Kinkel, then someone else. There was definitely a foreign substance in your system."

"'Foreign substance'? Doc, Germans wearing Speedos on the beach are a foreign substance. What the hell does that mean?"

Left briefly speechless by the image that had now burned itself into his mind, Bracewell took a moment before telling Poe he had been poisoned by something natural, but completely unknown to him. Having already FedExed the sample onto the Centers for Disease Control in Atlanta, Bracewell hoped to have an answer within 24 hours. He did know one thing, however:

"If you'd drunk even another sip of that coffee, you'd be dead, Mr. Poe," Dr. Bracewell said. "If Kinkel really wasn't the one that poisoned you, then his coffee being too terrible to drink saved your life."

Bothered more than he'd like to admit by his close call — and the name "Mr. Poe" — Poe tried to make a joke of it. "And here I thought my rugged physique and physical prowess saved my life."

"If you mean eating too many pizzas and cheesy sticks, you're probably right," Dr. Bracewell said. "A man of, let us say, smaller dimensions probably would not have survived."

"I knew it!"

"At least until you keel over from a heart attack."

"You're a lotta fun, Doc," Poe said, now a bit more somber. "Call me the minute you hear anything from Atlanta."

Punching the button to disconnect the Bluetooth connection, Poe suddenly no longer found himself in the mood for *Star Trek* music. Shuffling through his list of songs, Poe needed to find just the right theme song. One of Poe's many quirks, every single song on the Jag's audio hard drive was a soundtrack from a TV show or movie. He had one for every occasion, though this was a tough one. What is the right music for, "Who wants to kill you?"

As Poe headed towards the gates at Ageya Head State Park, the security guard simply waved him through. On Plink's list of approved vehicles, the booming theme from *Sherlock Holmes: A Game of Shadows* was audible long before Poe was actually visible, ensuring the gate was up long before he got there.

Normally, on a summer day, there would be traffic, but not today. Plink had closed the park to the public just to ensure Pete got perfect shots uninterrupted by ugly people and ugly cars. (In Plink's view, everyone.) At first, Oregon State Parks had protested, but when Plink also explained that Margaret Tandy and her family were having a picnic on the grassy summit and wanted privacy, the request was immediately granted. Glancing at the gathered family as he drove by them on the southern road paralleling the grassy summit, Poe idly wondered if this was what had kept Fuzznut from their appointment.

Turning his attention back to the view, Poe was reminded again of what a beautiful place Surfland was. The town spreading down the beach to the south, the mighty Pacific to the west and north, Poe noticed Pete had a camera set up on the side of the road, presumably taking in the whole thing. Continuing down the road past the jumble of boulders that remained from the area's days as a basalt quarry, the grass dropped out of sight as the lighthouse and parking lot came into view. Poe could see Pete's jeep parked at the base of the rocky pile, while next to him was another HD camera. Along with Plink, clearly micromanaging Pete. Although from this distance Poe had no idea what was actually being said, he was sure it was annoying.

Seeing Plink, Poe couldn't help but wonder again if Plink might have tried to kill him. He certainly hated Poe enough. Just as quickly, however, Poe dismissed the idea; dead local writers create a lot of bad press. Who then? Certainly, Poe had made a few enemies over the years. But the only one he could think of who would actually want him dead was dead himself. Poe had seen the guy go flying out his front windshield at more than 100 mph; he knew it wasn't him.

Before he could ponder the problem any longer, his tunes were once again interrupted by the Bluetooth. This time, however, Poe cut off the ringing, promising himself to get back to Dick later. Even if he hadn't been in a hurry, the roar of the crashing surf below made it nearly impossible to hear anything, anyway. Continuing behind the lighthouse to the outer parking lot, Poe made sure the building blocked his car from Pete's cameras, as had Plink when he parked his Aztek.

Leaving the top down on the Jag, Poe walked back across the parking lot, his first sight being Buffett working his way up the pile of boulders towards the grassy summit. Likely sent there to make sure he didn't screw up the shot, Poe envied him; at least he was away from Plink. Not so fortunate was Pete.

"Pete, I'm going to say it again," Plink intoned as if Pete had never filmed anything. "I want the lighthouse in the center of the shot."

Pete, patient as always, tried to talk to Plink, the loud surf making it more like shouting. "You don't want it in the center; you want it to the left or right! It's called the rule of thirds: Put the subject of interest in the left or right—"

"Rule of thirds? What the hell is that? The lighthouse is the most important thing, put it in the middle!"

Poe couldn't resist: "Plink, he's right; it's called the rule of thirds: Never listen to photographic instructions from people that only use one-third of their brains."

Plink was not amused. "Where the hell have you been? You need to man the other camera. And did you make sure to park your car out of sight?"

"Right next to yours, which I noticed you parked in a handicapped spot," Poe said as he started to gather the third camera from the back of Pete's Jeep. "How lazy are you?"

"Oh, for God's sake, there's not even any handicapped people here!"

Resisting the urge to say, "Look in the mirror," Poe turned his attention to Pete, once again raising his voice to be heard over the crashing waves below. "You're sure the Tandys are keeping to the east side of Ageya Head? And the camera's already filming alongside the road?"

"Yes and yes; I'll just edit out the stuff I don't want, like you and that Gawd-awful crap you play on your stereo. Four thousand dollars worth of upgraded audio, and you can't play a single song with words?"

"I'll let Jimmy Buffett know you care," Poe said as he continued to gather the camera equipment.

"Will you two shut up?" Plink yelled. "Some of us actually work for a living."

Staring at Plink for just a moment, Poe once again said nothing; he wanted to get out of here, too. Noticing that Plink's right eye was starting to twitch, Poe found himself almost wishing Plink had tried to kill him. Strangling him would have been so much easier to explain if it was simply self-defense.

Chapter 30

Ian

Jacking the giant boulder into position was a simple matter for Ian; he'd been studying this particular rock for years. His parents often hosted catered parties at the lighthouse, and more than once he'd dreamt of this very rock crashing down the hill, setting off an avalanche that would kill everyone below. Everyone would just assume that nature had taken its course, albeit at a very tragic time.

Certainly, it would have been easier if the poisoned coffee had worked; that plan had seemed perfect. He'd been lacing the beans for weeks, trying to get just the right amount to induce a heart attack. Each time, he used too little. Not surprising, considering how rare the poison was. So this last time he'd used a lot, and while it had produced all manner of chaos, it obviously had not accomplished the goal, or he wouldn't be here.

Curiously, in some ways that made him happy. The Captain would have liked the audacity of this plan so much better. Yes, running all the way back to the car with the jack wasn't going to be easy, but he had a feeling that amidst the chaos and death down below, no one would be searching the grassy summit for a while. The man who knew Ian's secret would be dead, and Ian could go back to his carefully crafted life overseas.

Looking once again around the grassy summit, everyone was still in the same place: The gathered family to the east and the sheepdog just a few dozen feet away to the south. Down below, everyone was exactly where he'd hoped they'd be: Gathered at the base of the cliff. Certainly, that part had been a guess, but from the Xeroxed schedule Scrote had stolen out of the Jeep, Ian assumed that to "HD film lighthouse," they'd want the ocean in the background, and he was right.

Now was the time to send the boulder crashing below. He could see that they were starting to gather cameras and other gear from the back of the Jeep and would likely soon be breaking up. Focused on nothing but the rock and the group gathering below for the past hour, he knew at that very moment that all the pieces had fallen into place.

Even better, one had not: The cameraman's dog, some kind of husky mix, was coming up onto the grassy summit. Originally this had worried him; he didn't want anyone having a reason to look up the slope. But when it became apparent no one was watching the dog, he was happy that the dog would not meet the fate of his owners.

Natural selection, indeed.

Chapter 31
Buffett

Buffett was not having a good day.

First, he was forced to sleep in the front seat of the Jeep because the back seat was filled with camera gear. Then, when he managed to find a comfy spot to sleep in the shade of the lighthouse on a small patch of grass, the very loud and annoying bipedal mammal made him go really far away. Wandering up the rocks, Buffett decided this was the hardest he's ever had to work to find a place to sleep.

Upon arriving at the top, Buffett was very excited to see another dog lying in the grass, which meant it must be comfortable. Walking slowly towards the other dog, Buffett was surprised he could not smell the other dog. All he smelled up here were bipedal mammals. There were lots of them to the east, and there was one standing in the rocks moving a big stick up and down.

And there was one in front of him, where the dog was sleeping in the grass. This made no sense to him. Dogs did not smell like people, though certainly the opposite was true. His bipedal mammal, Pete, often smelled like a dog when they both woke up in the morning. But a dog that smelled like people? That just made no sense at all.

Just as it didn't when the dog jumped up on two feet and screamed.

Chapter 32

Fuzznut

Bekk the Dog was definitely out of character. Bekk did not normally stand on two feet. Bekk did not normally verbalize anything unless told to. Bekk did not normally scream, "POE!" But then what was normal for Bekk anyway? He'd been dead for a half-decade anyway.

Bekk VI, a Giant English Sheepdog, had been Mrs. Margaret's companion since he was a puppy, in 1998. One of a series of loyal dogs of a variety of breeds that had kept her company throughout the decades, he was named in honor Margaret's Grandmother Rebekkah. He went with her everywhere, to everything. And while it might have been that some places were inclined not to allow dogs, exceptions were made when the dog's owner had naming rights on the building or business.

When Bekk died young in 2005, the family was stunned. The theory was his heart had just given out, and the recriminations began as to just who was at fault. The great-grandkids for riding the dog, the grandkids for chasing him at the beach, the kids for allowing him to eat caviar at civic functions. Most likely it was none of these; at well over 100 pounds, his heart was probably never meant to accommodate his atypical size.

What was agreed on, however, was that in her fragile state, Mrs. Margaret could not possibly handle the stress. Already slipping away from reality, they feared the death of her beloved companion would send her completely over the edge. A search was made, of course, for another truly Giant English Sheep Dog. But Bekk VI's unique size and coloring made him impossible to match, no matter where they looked.

So, they had a new one made.

It was what costumers call a "quad suit," a costume in which the performer runs around on all fours. Their arms extended by crutches with shock absorbers built into the extensions, the person inside basically runs around on the arms and legs. Used by street performers and in stage-shows, quad-suit performers have an uncanny knack for looking like the real thing, albeit for short periods of time.

What the Tandys needed, obviously, was quite beyond that, but nothing that their money couldn't buy. Commissioning a suit from the same costumers that made suits for Disney and hiring the understudy from the latest King Kong film, the Tandys managed to bring Bekk back to life. Certainly, he was a bit bigger than the original, but in Mrs. Margaret's diminished state, they were sure she would never know the difference. Sitting in a wheelchair, she was getting relatively shorter, anyway.

The arrangement had worked just fine until this summer, until just about a week earlier when Bekk was appearing with Evan at a charity function for the Portland ASPCA. Appearing on KPRO's "Good Day Portland," Bekk and Evan were standing amidst several other dogs when one of the larger Great Danes and a Bernese Mountain Dog took a shine to Bekk on live morning television. In full view of the cameras, Bekk was mounted as surely as a marlin on a wall, while Evan kept talking to the camera, too horrified to do anything. By the time it was over, Evan vowed never to do live television again, Bekk was flat on the ground under a Dane feeling greater than ever, and — thanks to repeated replays on local television and websites — donations to the ASPCA had jumped 83 percent.

What wasn't jumping anymore was Bekk, or rather the man inside him, who had four cracked vertebrae. With the Tandy Family Tribute and re-dedication of Hope Falls Park just days away, a replacement was needed, and quick.

It also turned out to be close, when Evan's daughter recalled seeing "U. Otter B.," at the Surfland Aquarium of the Pacific during her birthday party. The entire family agreeing he was the best mascot they had ever seen — he could make balloon animals in costume — the family lawyer was dispatched to see if they could hire him for a solid week, no matter what the cost.

Five days later, Fuzznut had to admit it was the hardest job he'd ever had, and in a 40-year career of performing as every costumed character known to man, that said a lot. The costume weighed close to 50 pounds, 14 of it in the head, and another 15 in each of the metal front legs and shock absorbers. His neck hurt all the time. He had knots so big in his shoulder that he didn't know if he should call a massage therapist or a boy scout. And last week, when he'd forgotten to put on the spiked front feet, his left arm slipped so forcefully in the wet grass that he ruptured a bicep. (Constantly having to switch between indoor and outdoor feet, he didn't know what was worse: tearing a muscle, or the sickening sound of his one-inch spikes sinking through the hardwood flooring.)

To top it all off? He was absolutely sure he was developing instant scoliosis. If he could see himself in profile, he was pretty sure he was developing a sag worthy of a horse in a Tex Avery cartoon. (Stupid great-grandkids.)

But if it was the most painful job Fuzznut had ever had, it was also the most lucrative. Pulling down $5,000 a dollars a day, he was even allowed to keep the costume when he was done, on the theory that after two sweaty guys in one week, no one was going to wear the thing again, anyway.

The job had other perks as well, namely that since everyone thought he was a dog, they did all kinds of things around him they would never do otherwise. The costume that realistic looking, he'd heard more discussions that no human was ever meant to hear than any mascot in history. Better, spending time with the Tandys, he got to hear conversations about just about everyone in town.

From his time lying down in the mayor's office, he knew she had the numbers of at least 17 Aussie firefighters on speed dial — and that she was running out of minutes. From his time around Mrs. Margaret's minister he knew that many men over 50 still had a mom-crush on Florence Henderson. And from his time around Plink on the back deck of the family house, he knew the man was a jerk; after-all, who self-censors when the only ones around are a dog and an old woman seemingly one step from the grave?

What was even more remarkable to Fuzznut was that the Tandys, too, seemed to forget he was just a guy in a mascot costume. Not that they said anything really juicy; they were too nice and boring for that. But when he heard Evan explaining why he'd built a science fiction museum in Portland — without any idea what that actually was — Fuzznut knew the family had pretty much forgotten he was there.

Two days after that, Evan was still talking about it with his sister as the family stood around on the grassy summit of Ageya Head.

"It came from a group called Star Trek In the Park, they do performances to *Star Trek* dialogue, or something like that," Evan explained. "So I accepted their grant request."

"Evan," his sister said, "they asked for money to buy new outdoor stage lighting and you bought them a downtown theatre and the empty office building next to it."

"I didn't want them to be in the rain..."

Fuzznut was stunned: Nice guys definitely did not finish last, at least not this family. Of course, as an enormous benefactor of that largesse, he definitely wasn't going to look it in the mouth. Or the crotch, as his bent-over height would allow these days. Nevertheless, he needed a break, and so he wandered west through the grass, hoping to find a place far enough away from the family that no great-grandkid would want to ride him.

He found his spot about 40 feet away from the rocky point that made up the west end of the summit. Virtually falling over, he took a giant draw from his Camelback and was asleep almost as soon as he hit the ground. How long he slept he really didn't know. Gradually though, he came to his senses, awakened by someone moving around in the rocks to his west. Whoever it was was doing something with a lot of repetitive motions, but just what he couldn't be sure, his view limited by the costume.

Just as he was pondering that, he heard a stereo playing something incredibly loud; Hans Zimmer, if Fuzznut's experience with his friend had taught him anything. And it had: within moments, Fuzznut could see Poe's Jag rolling along the road aside the grass. As low as Fuzznut was, he doubted Poe could see him — which would make it even more fun to harass Poe later.

Catching his attention next was a dog — a big one, coming up over the rise, likely from the parking lot below. The dog looked familiar, but he couldn't be sure. After hearing Evan's story about the events that led to Fuzznut's hiring, the lifelong mascot had no interest in being the next one to be crushed by an over-stimulated, under-sexed pooch. To his relief, however, he finally recognized the dog as Buffett; everyone in town knew him.

Content that he wasn't about to be molested, Fuzznut returned his attention to the man in the rocks, whose actions were now very clear. He was tipping the biggest rock on the slope towards the edge. How this was possible, Fuzznut had no idea, but he didn't have to. He just knew what he could see — and who was standing down below. Forgetting his character and every other thing about mascoting he'd learned in his career, he jumped up and screamed as loud as he could: "POE!"

Chapter 33
Poe

Gathering the last of his camera gear, Poe could have sworn the wind had called his name. Absent-mindedly looking quickly to either side, he saw no sign that Plink or Pete had said anything to him. Reflexively, he even glanced up, knowing full well the park was empty. Except that it wasn't.

What caught his eye, however, was the biggest boulder he had ever seen starting to tip towards him. Briefly cocking his head, as if changing position would change what he knew he was seeing, he took only the time he needed to inhale to choose his next action: "RUN!"

Dropping his camera gear first, Poe simultaneously tugged on both Plink and Pete, forcing them to drop their gear. Spinning them forcibly around and pulling them, he yelled again, "RUN!"

Sprinting west away from the Jeep, Poe was first, followed immediately by Pete. Plink, taking a half-second to judge if Poe was kidding — and reckoning by Poe's speed he definitely was not — was immediately after them.

Looking over his shoulder to make sure Pete and Plink were right behind him, Poe could see the boulder now tumbling down the face of the slope. Each bounce setting another boulder in motion, soon it seemed every rock on Ageya Head was cascading down the slope.

Despite what seemed like an eternity, however, the whole thing was over in 30 seconds. The three men largely unscathed save for some tears in their shirts where flying smaller rocks had pierced their backs, it was clear Poe's early warning had saved their lives.

The same could not be said, however, for Pete's Jeep and camera equipment, crushed into a mangled mess of steel and rubber. The three of them stood in stunned silence as the surf continued to roar and the dust settled. Turning to Poe, Pete seemed oblivious to what had just happened to his Jeep.

"How the hell did you know to run?"

"I could have sworn I heard someone call my name," Poe said, still staring at the top of the slope.

"How you could hear anything? I could barely hear you over the surf half the time when we were talking right next to each other."

"No idea, but I know who it wasn't," Poe said, finally starting to collect himself.

"Who?"

"The guy who pushed the rock down on us; I saw him at the top of the slope."

"Push? That rock?" Pete asked incredulously, now staring at the massive boulder that sat atop his Jeep. "Are you sure one of those flying pieces of debris didn't hit more than your shirt?"

"I just know what I saw and what I heard," Poe said, sounding more than a little pissed. "One tried to end my life while the other tried to save it."

"Seriously? You think someone tried to kill you?" Pete asked, now finally starting to walk towards the ruins of his Jeep. "Who would want to do that?"

Now shooting a glance at Plink, who had yet to move or even seemingly breathe, Poe was even more sure of what he'd concluded before: "I have absolutely no idea, and it's beginning to be a serious problem."

Plink must have stood on the same spot for a full 15 minutes before he began to move. When he did, it was not the arrival of emergency vehicles or sirens blaring that roused him from his catatonia. It was Pete.

"Here, Plink, the phone's for you. It's my insurance agent. I told him the city owes me a new Jeep and a whole lot of cameras."

"What?"

"City business, your insurance."

"You have GOT to be kidding, I'm not paying for this. That was an act of God."

"Too bad my insurance agent is an atheist; he wants to talk to you..."

Poe heard all of this as the pounding surf had once again randomly dropped in volume, and by now Plink could be heard screaming into the phone all over the parking lot. Walking away from him, Pete could be seen smiling, albeit meekly. Approaching Poe, he was clearly trying to make the best of a bad situation.

"Well, it would appear there was a miracle today," Pete said, once again staring up the slope.

"No one was killed?" Poe asked.

"That, and my wife was actually happy to hear Buffett isn't dead."

Chuckling, Poe started glancing around. "Where is that dog, anyway?"

"Sleeping in the back of a patrol car, I think."

"How appropriate," Poe mused. "Maybe they can take his statement and he can confirm that there was someone up there pushing that rock."

"You still think that's what you saw?"

"I'm sure of it, though at my age it's not like I have a photographic memory," Poe said.

"No, you don't — but I do," Pete said, a gleam forming in his eye.

"You? You flirted with a drag queen last year during the July 4th Parade."

"I told you," Pete said, amazed that Poe would remember that now. "I thought she was an East German exchange student I met in high school."

"My point exactly; your memory sucks," Poe said.

"Perhaps. But cameras don't, and here comes one now."

Following Pete's finger pointing up the hill, Poe could see a Surfland Police Department patrol car coming towards them. Slowing as it approached, the officer driving stopped the car and handed Pete the camera that Poe had passed as he entered earlier. Pete, seemingly distracted as he took the camera, stared into the backseat of the car, stopping only when the car started back up the hill.

"What are you looking for?" Poe said, now anxious to get a look at what the camera contained. "I assume this is the camera you left running."

"Uh, nothing," Pete said, taking one last look around the parking lot before he returned his attention to the camera.

Popping open the screen on the side of the camera, Pete rewound it to the beginning of the tape and then began to watch. Even on the small screen, the HD quality was amazing, and soon he and Poe saw a tiny man emerge from behind the hill carrying something on his back. Within minutes, it became clear how one man could unleash a torrent of boulders.

"He carried a jack with him!" Poe said to no one in particular. "My God, someone really does want me dead."

Up until now, Poe had pondered the question as more of a mental exercise. It was inconceivable to him that anyone should want him genuinely dead, so even as he thought about it, he never really believed it. Now he did, and he repeated himself: "Really. Somebody wants me dead."

Still looking at the video playback, Pete wanted to see if the actual moment the boulder came down would tell him anything. That didn't keep him from multi-tasking: "You don't seem as surprised by that as you should be. Is there something that I should know?"

"There is, but I'll need to tell you later," Poe said now looking back up the hill. "That cop is headed back our way."

As the car rolled to a stop, Poe saw Pete once again look in the backseat. This time, however, something registered on his face, causing Pete to pull the door open. Poe could now see the aforementioned jack, looking oddly old and brand-new all at the same time. Careful not to touch it lest he disturb any evidence that might me on it, Poe could see clearly on an attached brass tag where it had come from: "Harrison Hardware."

Handing Poe and Pete both a pair of rubber gloves, the officer asked them if they could carry the jack over to the evidence van. Happy to be able help, Poe had just one question: "Where's the evidence van?"

"Over there," Pete said, "The pink one, with cats."

"That's the evidence van?"

"They just got it; seized it in a drug raid."

"From who? Six-year-olds?"

"No, just a couple of 'Hello Kitty' fans with a penchant for making meth."

"Are they going to keep it that color?"

"I think so; the budget's low, and it makes a great presentation venue for the police department's DARE programs."

"I'm sure it's a big hit with sixth grade boys..." Poe said, grudgingly admitting it wasn't a half-bad idea as he lifted the jack. Carrying the weapon of rock destruction to the van, it was definitely heavy, but nothing that one man couldn't carry on his back, as he'd seen the man on tape do. What was more mystifying was the brass tag attached to it: No one used those anymore, and certainly not Harrison Hardware; that had closed long before Poe had even moved to Surfland.

One more mystery now rolling around in his head, Pete and Poe reached the evidence van and set the jack inside. Looking around inside, Poe had to admit the van was pretty nice, assuming one got their tastes from pre-teen girl pimps. Lined with plush pink couches and deep pile carpeting, there was even a pink-framed HD TV hanging on one wall of the van — which gave Poe an idea.

"Pete: Can you hook your camera up to this TV? Maybe we could get a better look at our jack of all trades."

Groaning at the pun — and the realization he should have thought of hooking up to the TV himself — Pete started fiddling with the back of the flat screen and within minutes had the camera hooked up. Rewinding the footage, they now had a much larger look at Poe's attacker. Using the camera's in-camera freeze-frame and zoom tools, he was bigger now. Unfortunately, he was more pixelated as well. Looking about as generic as a person could look, Pete stared at the image for several minutes before finally admitting he still had no idea who the guy was.

For Poe, however, there was something oddly familiar about him. Wracking his brain, he tried to place the familiar face, but nothing came to him. Worse, the more he thought about it, the more elusive the answer became. It was like he'd seen him just yesterday, and yet never met him. This man wanted to kill him, and even though Poe now had a picture of the guy, Poe was even more confused. After about five minutes, Poe gave up and told Pete just to let the tape run.

Just as they'd seen on the small screen, the man came from behind the crest of the summit, placed his jack, and began pumping the handle. Like he had been planning the moment all his life, he had no hesitation whatsoever. Soon, Buffett came into the picture, and recognizing that they were about to see the beginning of the rockfall, both of them leaned into the screen — when suddenly a dog sprung straight up from the grass and screamed.

Startled, both Poe and Pete jumped back. "What the hell was that?" Pete asked, but Poe already knew.

"That's the voice on the wind that saved our lives."

"A screaming dog? Now I am convinced you got hit in the head," Pete said.

"Remember what I told you at the hospital last night," Poe said, starting to laugh. "That's no ordinary dog, that's Margaret Tandy's dog..."

"Holy shit..." Pete said. "You're right..."

Turning back to the patrol car, Pete yelled at the officer to inquire if the Tandys were still on the summit. As he feared, however, they had gone home with the first sirens, and surely taken their "dog" with them. Not that Pete saw that as a tremendous problem; he had a feeling Poe knew just where to find him. Perhaps he'd even seen where the attacker had gone, though Pete had a feeling he'd slipped into the woods as easy as he'd slipped out of them.

Unplugging the camera, Poe was anxious to get everything unplugged before any of the police officers saw what was on the video. The screaming dog would be hard to explain, to say the least. Indeed, Pete and Poe both agreed that whatever information might come from the "dog" it would be best handled by Poe alone.

Hanging the camera by its strap over his shoulder, Poe and Pete began to walk back to the Jag as afternoon shadows begin to fall long from the east side of the lighthouse. Intending to mentally and physically regroup at the coffee shop, they went to tell Plink where they were going. Neither was particularly looking forward to meeting with him, but after the day's events, it seemed necessary. As when they had left him, Plink was screaming into the phone.

"No Dick, this does not mean we're getting a new tourism slogan!" Plink yelled, with a volume now having nothing to do with the surf. "How should I know?" he screamed louder, his right eye now twitching virtually every half-second. "If Poe's as good at pissing other people off as he is me, then I'd imagine there are hundreds of people who want him dead!"

Simply looking at his friend, Poe said quietly to Pete: "We'll text him."

Resuming their walk to the car, Pete stopped several times to look back across the parking lot. Poe tried to be sympathetic: "Look, if you need to go back to your Jeep and get some stuff, I'm in no hurry."

"No..." Pete said. "There's nothing left I can't get later off the wrecker truck..." And once again walking forward, he now seemed to speed up, easily beating Poe back to his own car. Poe soon saw why, as a pair of furry ears poked up above the top of the door.

　　"Oh, hell no!"

Chapter 34
Dick

As President of the Surfland Tourism Advisory Board, it was Dick Yelper's job to visit each of the town's businesses. Nevertheless, he had never even set foot in Grind Me Hard Coffee, and one look at the barista in her official uniform reminded him why. Never adept around women because of his speech impediment, the incident at the GO River Wayside had made him absolutely terrified of them, as Plink never failed to remind him.

Still, just coming into a business and ordering nothing was rude, so he did his best to order a plain latte. Or, as he told Indy, "Uh play lah-EH, Plee." Her reply, "One plain latte, coming right up," was music to his ears, and he took a seat, remarkably less terrified than he had been.

Actually, Dick wasn't even sure why they were all meeting here; Bendovren was their usual spot. But he'd gotten a text from Plink saying the location had been changed, and after everything that had happened today at the Lighthouse, he wasn't about to miss this meeting. Waiting for his latte, he found himself humming along to the music:

> "Mule be in my heart,
> So just stop your jerkin'.
> Hooked to a wagon of love,
> Mule be my only beast of burden."

Just starting to notice how terrible the lyrics were — and praying the coffee was better — Dick was actually relieved to see Plink and his project assistant, Xander, come through the door. Both of them sitting down at the table with him, Dick could see Xander's attention was largely on the girl behind the counter. What surprised him, however, was that as she brought Dick's latte to the table, she seemed to be equally interested in Xander. Not exactly a master of vocal expression, Dick had made himself an expert in other forms of communication, and he had no doubt what these two were saying to each other.

Not that Xander's boss noticed: "Thank you miss, you can go now," Plink said to her. "We have work to do."

"I'll bet you do, Plink," the young lady shot right back, before heading back to the drive-thru window. Clearly, she knew him, even if Plink was pretending not to know her. Was there anyone Plink didn't make angry?

"OK, before we begin," he said, pointing at Dick, "if you even mention 'Tah BEE ih BAH,' or any similar nonsense, I'll punch you — or worse. I've had a crap day, and I don't have time for any of your nonsense."

"How about my nonsense?" Once again, Poe had timed it perfectly as he and Pete walked through the door.

"I swear to God, you should come with a bell," Plink said in frustration.

"Now, is that anyway to talk to someone who just saved your life?"

Chapter 35
Poe

Remarkable, thought Poe. In an afternoon where he was almost killed by a homicidal rock fall by an unknown assailant for reasons he couldn't even begin to fathom, things had actually managed to get worse.

First of all, his mouth was full of dog hair.

After finding Buffett in the backseat of his Jag, Poe had suddenly realized what Pete had been looking for all those times back in the parking lot. Worse, he was absolutely sure Pete knew the whole time where Buffett was. Upon discovering both guilty parties, Poe had told them they needed to catch a ride with someone else; the Kittymobile seemed to have comfortable enough seats. But after 10 minutes of begging from Pete, Poe agreed to drive Buffett back to Pete's house. Apparently Buffett had already been thrown out of the patrol car for sudden flatulence — Pete called it stress-induced — and everyone but Poe thought it best Buffett be taken home in a convertible.

Surprisingly, upon arrival at Pete's house, his wife had no problem watching Buffett herself. His brush with death fresh in her mind — Pete had embellished a bit — she was looking forward to some quality time with him.

Poe's next disappointment was that Bendovren Coffee was closed early. Where was he going to get his special blend of beans? Certainly it wasn't the first time he'd had to go without, but after the day he'd had, it just added to the misery of at all. On the other hand, he hoped it that meant Ryan had gone home early for some much needed sleep. That, and it would delay for at least a little bit the inevitable conversation Poe needed to have with Ryan about just how poison got into his coffee.

Texting Plink that the meeting needed to be moved, Pete and Poe agreed that Grind Me Hard Coffee would be the next best place. For one thing, it was one of the only other places open into the late afternoon. More, though, it would give both of them a chance to see Indy. Poe, so he could see how she was doing, and Pete, so he could give her the much needed lecture on firework safety.

Leaving his wife and dog behind, Pete asked Poe to take the long way to Grind Me along the beach road, instead of Highway 101. Pete needed to stop by his insurance agent's office to get the form Plink needed to sign, not that Pete thought it would do any good at the moment. Clearly flustered that Plink was going to drag the process out as long as he could, he eventually told Poe to keep going. Poe, however, stopped anyway and promised Pete they'd figure something out.

The long route also allowed Poe to fill Pete in on the day's events before the lighthouse. Beginning and ending with his certainty that the rockfall was the second attempt on his life in two days, neither of them could figure out what possible motive the man in the video might have, or why he looked so familiar to Poe.

Parking in front of Grind Me Hard Coffee, Poe was reminded of what a much better physical location Bendovren was. Here the windows were tiny, the space dark, (Poe forcing himself to remember that for Indy that was a good thing). Spying her through the window, Poe could see her just above the shoulders, clearly smiling as she talked to someone. And just as quickly he could see her frown, the word on her lips unmistakable: "Plink." Opening the door with his normal insult of Surfland's apparently universal irritant, it gave Poe added pleasure to remind the man that he owed his life to Poe. Not that Plink seemed to be considering that at the moment.

"You asshole! You told the cops I was parked in a handicapped space and they gave me a $300 ticket!"

"Now," Poe said, making no real attempt to be coy, "What makes you think that was me?"

"The cop told me it was you! What was the point in that?!"

"The point was you're a jerk and now you're out $300. Do I really need more than that?" Poe said, now smiling ear-to-ear as Indy brought him the best drink she could make without his beans. "Now, if I'm not mistaken, we have a whale to blow up tomorrow. And since I've had a very long day of people trying to kill me, I'd really like to get started..."

On that matter, even Plink had to agree, and they all got down to business. Once again going over the plan for the next day, the meeting took about an hour, until there were just a few details remaining. Those, largely a result of the afternoon's chaos, seemed at first a rerun of Pete and Plink's earlier discussion.

"It was an act of God," Plink said. "I'm not paying."

"First of all, unless God wears Birkenstocks, it was not," Pete said. "The police told you themselves about the jack and the suspect who ran back into the trees."

"That has not been proven yet, and until it is, I'm not paying." Finishing his sentence with a "Hmmff!," Plink crossed his arms like a five-year-old, and just stared at Pete.

Seeing that Pete was getting nowhere, Poe tried his own tack: "First of all, Plink, when you stare at people, it helps if one eye doesn't vibrate. Very distracting.

"Second, if you won't replace Pete's stuff, I'm sure the Tandys will. Without knowing the insurance money's coming, he can't possibly have those cameras in time for Friday. You have them on speed dial, don't you Pete?"

"Why, yes I do!" Pete said, his face now showing that he understood Poe had planned this all along. "I bet they'd even pay to have two cameras delivered to me first thing tomorrow morning from Portland!"

"Wait!" Plink said, fully aware that interrupting the Tandys was not in his best interests. "I'll sign your damn form..."

"And the cameras brought out from Portland tomorrow...?"

"Yes, dammit! You just be sure they're ready to film by 10 a.m., got it?"

"Of course," Pete said, now fully enjoying Plink's misery. "It's not like you blow up a whale twice, is it? Although I guess in your case, that's not really true, either..."

Furious, Plink grabbed his things and stormed out the door. Poe, waving as obnoxiously as he could, made sure Plink saw him as he backed out of the parking lot.

"See," Poe said to Pete, "I told you being a jerk around him would pay off. And you thought I was just doing it to be mean."

"And you wonder why people want to kill you..." Pete said. "Hey, before we go, I need to go talk to Indy. A little fireworks 101, if you will."

"Be nice; she's had to spend time with Plink," Poe said, knowing Pete would be. He was just worried about her.

Starting to pack up his own things, Poe watched as Pete walked over to Indy. Xander, who had clearly been involved in some mutual flirting, stepped back to give them some space. From the look on both Pete and Indy's faces, he could tell the conversation was serious, but amicable.

Kind of like Dick's face, only without the amicable part. Constipated seemed more like it, it seemed to Poe as Dick walked towards him. Immediately Poe felt terrible and began to apologize for not returning Dick's call.

"Ooh beh beh-Z," Dick said.

"I suppose I have been busy, but I still should have called you back," Poe said with all sincerity. "What can I do for you?"

"Ih ah-bow Pleen..."

Chapter 36
Indy & Coffee

Being chewed out by Pete was not the best time she'd ever had, but since Ryan had warned her about it this morning, she knew full well it was coming. More, she deserved it, and that somehow made it a little bit easier to take.

After finishing his lecture, she could see he was ready to call it a night; any paragraph with the word "maimed" used more than once was no fun for anyone. But upon seeing Poe and Dick sitting in a corner in intense conversation, he grabbed Xander instead. Apparently deciding one could never talk too much about explosives and whales, they sat down in the corner to go over the details one more time. As Xander would be setting everything up tonight, it seemed a prudent idea.

It was well after closing time at this point, but Indy was in no rush to see them leave. Scrote had a tendency to drop by around closing time, and though she was enjoying his increasing physical discomfort, that didn't mean she would ever enjoy being around him. Besides, having Poe and Pete in here reminded her of better times. And Xander? Well, maybe that was a better future.

These were the moments Indy enjoyed working in a coffee shop, a non-pornographic one, anyway. Nice people having nice conversations about nice things. Every person in this room a local, they were what made her long days worth it. Resting her head in her hands for a moment, she allowed herself a moment of peace — just in time for it to be interrupted from the drive-thru: "Hey, sweet cheeks, I'd like a half one-and-a-half percent milk, half soy, half caf/decaf, no foam, sugar-free vanilla latte, with one Splenda, one sugar and served at 165 degrees."

Sighing, she turned back to the window: "Another pig, another dollar..."

Life's circumstances had changed Indy's view of what had been her favorite beverage in the world: coffee.

Long before Starbucks and family-owned coffee shops began sprouting up everywhere, she'd been drinking coffee. From an early age, her dad had let her sip from his cup on the various locations where he was working. Usually more creamer than coffee, she loved it nonetheless, mainly because it was one more thing to do with her dad. As she got older, her drinks got bolder, usually shared with her dad in a small coffee shop they'd discovered off of Sunset. A cup a day, here or there, and life was perfect.

That was then, as the saying goes. When she'd moved to coastal Oregon her coffee consumption had gone through the ceiling. Maybe it was the constant rain and clouds, or maybe it was just the fact that she was cold all the time. Whatever, she quickly found herself ramping up with the most caffeine-sodden, latte-laden, Frappuccino-fraught people on Earth. She'd read once that the average American adult consumes 26.7 gallons of coffee a year, and she assumed in the Pacific Northwest it was even higher. (Hell, she'd poured half that on her toes trying to stay warm the first summer she spent in Surfland.)

Like so many things since Indy came to Surfland, coffee now represented what she felt she had lost: The power to choose. For one thing, she was clearly a caffeine addict. Knowing this, she'd tried to cut back; the fact that she often got a headache when she drank less than four cups a day worried her. But after a week of abstinence, she gave up.

Surfland was to coffee addicts what Las Vegas was to gambling addicts (and alcohol addicts, and sex addicts, and …) What's the use of a 12-step program when the coffee shops are just 10 steps apart? Hell, even the culinary program at Harrison High School ran an espresso machine at lunch so they could teach students how to make coffee drinks.

The only thing that had made it passable was working with Ryan and his family. A constant barrage of jokes, movie lines and the feeling of family she'd lost, it was her day's greatest pleasure. Once, they all looked up as many Latin prefixes as they could, just to see how many shots of espresso they could identify. "Triple" coming from the Latin "tri," "quad" meaning four, and so on, they gotten all the way to the dodeca-shot latte — meaning 12 — before they fell apart laughing, (and wondering if that might be fatal). Even the rain had a sort of value to it. Every so often, she and the Nordins would sit down in the lobby after closing all with their hands wrapped around hot mochas. Talking about the day's events, it reminded her of doing the same thing with her dad on chilly mornings in the San Bernadino Mountains.

That was over now, one more choice taken away from her by life. These days, she had no reason to giggle about six shots of espresso in a drink; too many men liked to leer when they ordered a "sex-shot." The second most annoying thing about being a barista in an occupation that had dozens, she simply had to roll her eyes when they thought they were being funny or original.

The honor of most annoying thing, however, she reserved for the type of person at her window right now: A pretentious coffee lover, who thought that the more they modified their drink, the more cultured a human being they were. Usually from Seattle, they were the bane of her existence, if not her tip jar. Indeed, she didn't know what bothered her more about the whole thing: that they honestly thought they could taste the difference or that she honestly had learned to remember all that verbiage when it came out of their mouths.

Returning to the window, she looked out, batted her eyes, glanced at their license plate, and got to work: "Washington tags? Welcome to Surfland! Thank you for ordering a half one-and-a-half percent milk, half soy, half caf/decaf, no foam, sugar-free vanilla latte, with one Splenda, one sugar and served at 165 degrees. Can I grind you anything else?"

She was disgusted, he was disgusting, and she didn't have a choice.

Chapter 37
Scrote

Parking in front of Grind Me Hard Coffee, Scrote was surprised to see Poe, Pete and the others just now pulling out of the parking lot. Figuring they would have least been maimed by today's events, he had a bad feeling Ian's plan had not worked as well as he'd hoped. As always with Ian, there was another plan, but it would have been nice to get the guy out of the way. He and Ian would talk about that tonight, he supposed.

Walking into the shop, he opened the door as quietly as he could. Lifting his feet as slowly as possible from the sticky floor, he hoped not to make noise. Talking on her cell phone, Indy was distracted enough that he just might surprise her.

"Yeah, Dad, Mom's fine... and thanks for that extra tube of adhesive. Let's just say I've decided to go for a 'full body of work,'" she said, laughing. "The UPS guy said it was the biggest yet lightest box he'd ever delivered— Jesus!"

Now right behind Indy, Scrote's appearance had the desired effect; she was surprised: "What the hell are you doing here? How long have you been standing there?!"

"What's in the box?" Scrote asked.

"Huh? 'What's in the box'? Nothing Brad Pitt couldn't handle in *Seven*. You'd like that movie; it's got a creepy, disgusting guy in it."

"When are you going to stop talking to me like I'm a high school fanboy?"

"Seriously? That would be an improvement... Dad, I gotta go. Love you, bye."

"Sorry, I thought you'd be happy to see me."

"The only time I'm happy to see you, Scrote, is in my rearview mirror," Indy said, now grabbing her things. "Kind of like now." Having changed out of her uniform before he arrived, she stormed out the door, making sure it slammed hard in Scrote's face.

Perhaps sneaking up on her wasn't such a good idea.

Heading to his office, Scrote once again lamented that it could have gone better. For one thing, she was running out of time to start falling for him — but it still wasn't too late. Closing his eyes and picturing her peeling off her green sunglasses — and nearly everything else — he sighed once again with the genius of the plan.

This was not Scrote's first plan, of course, although when it came to fruition, it would be the first one to actually work out. From the Pom-a-louge in Fresno, to the incognito lesbian at To St. Helens and Back, something — or someone — had always messed up his plan. He'd succeed once, of course, but there was no woman involved, and only Ian and Billboard magazine actually knew it had been a success.

It came during and following his time with Sheep Pimpage, the country/screamo band he'd managed for years. Their first album, "I'll Do No Farm (I'd Rather Do You)" had been a big hit all over the Pacific Northwest and Kansas. One hit after another kept the money rolling in, and after a year or so of concerts at county fairs and slaughterhouses, the band got to work on their next album: "The Pendle-Thong Round-Up."

Seeking the maximum free media exposure they could get, they planned to debut the album in Pendleton, Oregon at a live concert right before the rodeo. Press releases went out; YouTube videos were made. Just in time for the lawyers from the Pendleton Wool company to sweep in and sue the crap out of them, or at least threaten to. Within weeks the band was broken up completely. Nearly broke from the cost of producing the now-defunct album and everything connected to it — and terrified by the fear of being forever indebted to a company that made sweaters — the band members mutually agreed to take their farm animal fetishes somewhere else.

Scrote had seen this coming. For while copyright law was not his specialty, accidentally pissing people off was, and he had a bad feeling they were going to cross Pendelton Wool at some point. That's why he'd been embezzling money for months — and why the band went broke so quickly. He'd made some mistakes, of course; perhaps it hadn't been the smartest thing to invent a $12,000 expense to Melbourne, Australia, for the purposes of researching sheep shearing. And claiming a $56,000 write-down for a semi-truck with a waterbed large enough for free-range buffalo massages was really pushing it. But he'd gotten away with both — sheep, buffalo and massage therapists were all over their videos — and Scrote learned his lessons for the future.

Lessons that were now paying off handsomely, he thought, as he walked back to his office. The money he he'd helped his boss embezzle from his last job was supporting he and Ian nicely. For Ian, it meant a freedom to live where he wanted, how he wanted. And for Scrote, it meant the ability to survive the collapse of the economy. Soon, he'd be beyond just surviving, and he'd be back to building a business, one he knew Indy was going to at some point appreciate being a part of. She'd come on board... eventually.

Staring once again in the mirror, he did have one cause for lament: His attempt to surprise her having gone disastrously wrong, he'd missed the chance to get her opinion. The weird ailments that had been dogging him for days were getting worse, and he was beginning to genuinely think he had a virus or something. He skin was continuing to get pinker on his face, and even his butt. His nose itched nearly all the time, and worse, it seemed to actually be getting bigger.

Scratching all of them, he resolved to ask Ian about it when he got to his house.

Chapter 38
Scrote

"Get your ass out of my face," Ian told Scrote as he faced his partner's backside across the coffee table. "Why don't you ask that sassy friend of yours at the coffee shop. Seems if she's going to marry you, your ass is going to be a big part of her future."

"She's kind of not talking to me at the moment..." Scrote said, now pulling his pants back up.

Here, Ian paused before going on: "Please tell me this isn't like the flaming lesbian."

"You're only saying that because she was in a volcano."

"No, I'm saying that because she was flaming," Ian said, "and you never noticed. You're not exactly the most gifted at picking up on women's cues."

"I didn't know you cared," Scrote said, clearly surprised.

"I don't, but if you screw this up, it hurts me, too," Ian said, now sounding more like business. "That building is important to me, and you've made it clear your plan is going to get it for me."

"And I am. Haven't I done everything I could to make that happen?" Scrote asked. "I went in, I hired away their best employee, I stalled the driver here while you poisoned the coffee. Trust me, they'll be out of that place by the end of the week. Besides, you're the one that wouldn't let me beat them up and run them out of town."

"That would be too obvious," Ian said, trying to enjoy the dramatic nature in which things were playing out.

"And it also would have worked," Scrote said, now somewhat frustrated himself. "Just like whacking that guy with the folder like I suggested, instead of burying him under a ton of rocks. I saw them all at the coffee shop just now, you know..."

"Yes, that clearly did not turn out as I expected," Ian said, now somewhat lost in thought. "Someone screamed and warned them the rocks were coming."

"Who? I thought that end of the park was empty."

"It was, unless dogs have suddenly started learning to speak..."

Chapter 39

Ian

Sending Scrote on his way, Ian needed time to think.

He had to admit his repeated inability to kill his target was somewhat frustrating. Not for the first time, he found himself admitting it would have been easier to just off the guy in the traditional way. Indeed, it had been Scrote's desire just to kill people the easy way from minute one. A gun, a knife, something basic.

But that's not how The Captain would have done it; he had taught Ian to dispose of their enemies with flair, panache, leaving no evidence behind. Clearly that wasn't possible now; the police had the jack. But Ian was sure there was no way to trace it back to him, and so he went on planning.

None of this would have been necessary, of course, had the city not been so intent on reopening Hope Falls Park. When he picked the storage space under the podium for a hiding place, he knew it had been abandoned for more than 80 years, and assumed it would remain that way. Scrote, of course, had never understood why they couldn't just burn the records, and keep a digital copy somewhere. But that's not what The Captain would have done, Ian was sure, and as it was his grandfather who showed him the park in the first place, it seemed a rather fitting tribute.

And it had been, until Scrote had been once again scouting Bendovren Coffee's location and just happened to see a man waving the one of their leather folders in the air. Clearly, it was destined for the garbage; everyone within a two-block radius could have heard that. But Ian couldn't take the chance that the man had seen what was inside. That would ruin everything, and why he now returned his thoughts to his latest ancillary target: tomorrow's exploding whale.

Once again taking cues from the schedule Scrote had stolen from the Jeep, Ian knew the explosion was to take place precisely at 1 p.m. That's why his would take place at 12:45, just as their target was making a final inspection of the whale. As was Ian's preference, however, he'd be miles away when his victim died. Placing his explosives tonight, it was all a matter of timing.

This time he was sure: 24 hours from now, it would be over. The only man to have seen his folder would be dead, he would be on his way back to Southeast Asia, and the property deed to Bendovren Coffee would be well on its way, if Scrote were to be believed.

And if not? Well, he could always make other plans.

Chapter 40
The Home of Martin and Sylvia Niemen

The newer, more massive ocean front homes in Surfland all had a similar design. The walls that did not face the ocean were largely featureless slabs without anything larger than a tiny bathroom window, usually made of frosted glass. The giant homes built so close together, anything more than that would have meant privacy for none.

Those walls that faced the ocean, however, more than made up for it. Made up largely of giant windows and sliding glass doors that faced the sea, they were usually a terrace of one deck atop another. Like a giant ladder, they were easily to climb, and just as they had at The Inn at Roca de la Muerte Dolorosa, owners were known to spend considerable energy keeping drunken idiots off of them.

But no one had been seen climbing the decks at the house on Anchor Avenue for a very long time. Indeed, the owner had been dead for more than a quarter-century, and short of a property management company maintaining the property, no one had stayed there in that same amount of time.

Except for the past year. For the past year someone else had been living there, a local business owner the neighbors said. But since they only lived in coastal homes a few weeks a year themselves, they really didn't know what was going on next door. And really didn't care.

That's why, on a night with a full moon, nobody noticed that just a few minutes after midnight, someone scampered up all three terraces and slipped in the unlocked sliding glass door. It was not their first visit, nor would it be their last.

Chapter 41

Poe

THURSDAY

Thursday morning for Poe consisted of many of the activities the last 24 hours had: Coffee at Bendovren, discussions about Plink's latest insanity, and telling Pete, "Hell, no!"

"Please, Poe: She won't let him stay in the house, and I'm worried if he gets out of the backyard bad things will happen."

"How is it possible that many bad things can happen with a dog that never does anything?"

"You know how it is: He gets out, he finds a place to sleep, it's on top of something expensive that doesn't belong to me, the police get called..."

"I thought your wife liked him again," Poe said, desperately looking for a way out.

"She did, and then he farted in her face last night," Pete said, mournfully, "I'm telling you, he's very stressed out."

"You want me to carry a farting dog in my car? Have you lost your mind?"

"No, just my olfactory senses... just kidding, sort of..." Pete said, trying to turn the conversation around. "Look the point is, I have to drive my wife's car with all the filming equipment in it and there's just no room for Buffett..."

"She drives an Explorer."

"... and she won't let him in the car. Please! Look, what if I promised to get your car totally detailed when we're done with this project?"

"Fine..." Poe said, wanting to end the whining as much as anything. "And I want a trip to the dentist, too."

"What the hell for?"

"To get the damn dog hair out of my teeth; God that dog sheds a lot."

Walking out the door of the coffee shop, Poe once again decided to put off discussing with Ryan the subject of poisoned coffee. For one thing, people didn't seem to be getting sick anymore. That Kinkel wasn't working there anymore Poe thought an unlikely coincidence. But still absolutely convinced Kinkel wasn't trying to kill him, Poe really didn't know what it meant. That seemed reason enough to put off talking to Ryan.

More though, Ryan was busy this morning. Not so busy he couldn't keep up, but busy enough that Poe didn't want to interrupt the best cash flow he'd had in days. Indeed, so many cars were lined up in the drive-thru that Pete found he couldn't get his wife's car out of the lot. Instead, he hitched a ride with Poe, whose sole point in heading north was to get Buffett. Planning to pick Pete's car back up on their return trip south to where they'd be filming the whale, it seemed a good time to talk about their plan for the day.

"We're really going to blow up a whale today?" Poe asked.

"Yep! Xander got all the explosives planted last night, security's been on station ever since to keep the crowds back, and Dick has got a media circus already up and running in Bo's Crab and Anvil."

"I still think this is the stupidest thing Plink's ever done," Poe said.

"That's quite a statement for a man who had his ragtop pierced by projectile seagull poop," Pete said. "I'd have thought this car could outrun a seagull."

"It can, when it's not stuck in a traffic jam Plink created," Poe grumbled, still pissed about it. "I should have known then he was a menace to this town."

"You still having Rip look into his background?"

"You better believe it; there's something fishy about that guy. Besides blowing them up," Poe said, now pulling up to the red light at the GO River Wayside. Already packed by tourists, it was clearly going to be a busy summer day all over town.

"Whales are mammals you know," Pete said. "They breathe air out of their lungs and everything."

"Yeah, well, so's that homeless guy over there on the corner, from what Rip tells me," Poe said, still not believing Rip had given the guy $100. "But if it comes down to death or CPR, promise me you'll find another mammal first."

"How convenient that Buffett is in your backseat."

"Just make sure he blows from the right end..."

Chapter 42
The GO River

A river distinct enough to at one time be listed in the Guinness Book of World records, Surfland visitors and locals have been asking one thing about the GO as long as anyone can remember: Is it actually a river?

It was first called "chwa chan'-'an'" by the Native Athabaskan peoples who first settled the area hundreds of years ago. The name literally meaning "large opening," they were convinced it was not so much a river, but an opening between a nearby lake and ocean. When the Tandys and the Greys first crossed the river in 1847, they didn't even notice it. Logs having fallen across the river, when they walked over them in the fog, they couldn't hear the gurgling water below over the roar of the nearby surf. Even the first car to cross through what was then the town of Whig City just drove right through it getting only its tires wet.

Their confusion was understandable: At high tide the distance from Nelta Lake, from which the river flows, to the Pacific is only 120 feet. In times of extreme flooding, the river can be almost as wide as it is long. In times of low precipitation it's barely a river at all. Indeed, during the Great Surfland Rubber Duck Race of 2005, team members had to all pick up their ducks and run down the channel — and not one of them got their feet wet.

This is not to say the river doesn't instill passion. From the time of the Athabaskans, the river has been a source of controversy and, indeed, bloodshed.

In 1833 two neighboring tribes fighting to control the coast drew the river as their figurative line in the sand. When one tribe crossed over, it was said the river ran red with blood for a day. That this turned out to just be one guy who fell in the river after he cut his foot matters little to those who document the history of the river; it was a very big foot.

In 1926 two construction workers on The Roosevelt Highway got into a fight about which of their children should be able to sell lemonade to the workers in the summer heat. Coming to fisticuffs, both of the kids' lemonade ended up in the river. Though there was no blood spilled, the lemonade did completely immerse a small frog that died of citrus poisoning.

In 1952 the residents of surrounding Whig City held an open vote to name the river. They believed that giving it a name might give it actual status beyond just a "Great Orifice," as its detractors liked to call it. That the winning name was "Great Orifice," made residents irate. Thought to be from ballot box stuffing by residents from nearby Duver and Harrison, compromise came in form of an acronym: GO River.

With that, the spot became one of the most popular places in Whig City and eventually Surfland. A pavilion was built in the parking lot to host picnics and other events. It became the site of annual kite flying festivals, co-ed naked beach runs and crab juggling demonstrations (and subsequent first aid demonstrations). Drawn by that, and the ocean itself, thousands of tourists came to visit every year. By 1990 the river and the attached GO River Wayside were the most popular tourist destination in Oregon.

That status changed in 1994, when a new tribal casino opened outside of Portland. Attracted by gaming, shows by musical celebrities not-quite dead, and crabs that didn't fight back, it soon took the title of most popular tourist spot in Oregon. In the beginning, local businesses took this change in status lying down — literally.

Looking to market the GO River as a great place to relax and lie in the sun, the executive director of the Surfland Tourism Advisory Board spent thousands on marketing efforts throughout the west. It failed miserably when after a year of spending it was very clear that no amount of money would change the fact that in Surfland it rained nearly 100 inches a year. What tourists did come felt misled and lied to, and they let local businesses know it. And while local business leaders quickly dispensed with the campaign — and the executive director — it was too late.

For one of those angry tourists turned out to be the executive director of the Jackson Falls, Montana, Chamber of Commerce. Drawn to Surfland by the marketing campaign for spring break, he was irate when the weather was so cold that his entire family, save one, refused to leave the room. And the one that would leave, his teenage daughter, only chose to do so because the cold weather made her nipples particularly perky under her bikini top.

Upon returning home, he spent three months vowing to do something to avenge his now pregnant teenage daughter and his wife, who remained hypothermic in a variety of ways. And then he found it: The Roe River, a nearby river he knew had to be shorter than the GO — and he made sure the Guinness Book of World Records knew it. When they verified his claim, the town of Jackson Falls hosted a very public parade with Girl Scouts, busses and a variety of floatation devices. More, they loaded the entire bunch on busses, drove to Surfland, and held their own mini-sit-in on the sand at the GO River Wayside.

It would become a very ugly affair, with girl scouts screaming, crabs flying and not near enough first aid for anyone, forcing Guinness to eventually cancel the category altogether. Dick Yelpers' first public event as President of the Surfland Tourism Advisory Board, the whole incident was a complete disaster, splayed across front pages all over Oregon. Amazed not to find himself fired, Dick found himself particularly indebted to Plink Blayton. On the job just a few months, it was his idea to apply to the Tandy Family for a grant to replace the aging pavilion.

That grant was, of course, granted. What would become the GO River Wayside had been one of the places the Tandy family had relaxed in the sand during their honeymoon all those decades ago — and had ever since. The pavilion they funded was remarkable: Hexagon in shape, it had windows all the way around, with a sliding glass door in front and back. Of use in any season, the Tandys could see it from their beach house, and used it whenever they visited Surfland.

Such as today, when the entire family had come down to the beach. Already 60 degrees it promised to be a spectacular day, and the kids couldn't wait to put on their wetsuits and play in the sand and surf.

Rolling his mother's wheelchair into the Tandy Pavilion, Evan told Fuzznut/Bekk to keep an eye on his mother while he stepped outside to make a phone call. Waiting for the treasurer from Star Trek in the Park to pick up, Evan couldn't help but think again what a beautiful place Surfland was. The lighthouse to the north, the unusually blue ocean to the west, the beautiful homes climbing the ridge to the south, and the mountains to the east. Smiling at his family's role in putting aside the ugliness that had been here just a few years ago, Evan considered the entire GO River Wayside perfect and unblemished... save for the homeless guy standing on the corner.

So much for no ugliness, he thought, cutting himself off as the other end of the phone picked up. "Hey, T'Pau! That's how you say it, right? This is Evan Tandy. Listen, I was wondering if you might explain this extraterrestrial exchange student program to me ..."

The explanation proved fascinating and long, so much so that as Evan wandered about the wayside, he never noticed that the homeless man was opening the back door of the Tandy Pavilion.

Chapter 43
Fuzznut

Staring out the window at Evan Tandy as he wandered about the wayside, Fuzznut thought the whole thing kind of funny. Here he was a fake dog, left in charge of a centenarian while her family played about outside. To anyone looking in, it would have seemed ridiculous; Giant English Sheep Dogs weren't exactly known for inciting terror in the hearts of men.

Placing his front legs up on the windowsill so he might get a better idea of just where Evan had gone, Fuzznut started to speak: "Well, Margaret, let's see where your son's wandered off to this time."

"Holy crap! You're not a real dog!"

Whirling around on his two real legs, Fuzznut was stunned to see that while he was looking out the front, a homeless man had walked in the back door. Looking back and forth between the bum and Mrs. Margaret, he had to admit for the first time in his life as a mascot he wasn't speechless: "So, Margaret, now what?" Fuzznut said, clearly knowing he was in trouble. "She knows I'm not a real dog."

"It's OK," Mrs. Margaret said. "She's not a real homeless guy."

Once again, the bum seemed stunned. And with a voice that was rising quickly by the octave, said: "Holy crap! You're not a real vegetable!"

"You were expecting a carrot?" Mrs. Margaret said.

"Holy crap!" the bum repeated.

"Well, since you seem to know such much about what I'm not, I think it's only fair you share the same," Mrs. Margaret said, the vacant look having completely left her eyes. "Now, what's your name young lady?"

"Indy, Indy Monroe."

"Well, of course you are."

Chapter 44
Indy

It had all started one day when she was walking from Bendovren Coffee to her hated job at Grind Me Hard Coffee.

She'd been stopping to tie her shoes while she waited for the WALK signal at the GO River Wayside, when she noticed a rather wispy looking man in a suit trying to offer one of the homeless guys food for work. Not finding anyone interested in actually working — she'd suspected as much — the man in the suit hopped back into the ugliest car she'd ever seen and left. But on her walk the next day she saw him again trying with another homeless man and the next day another. Curious, she vowed to leave a little bit earlier for work the next day and see if she could see what he wanted.

Eavesdropping from nearby as he offered work, she discovered he was the executive director of the local tourism bureau and he was looking for homeless people to spy for him. Offering them food in exchange for just standing there, he'd simply strap a parabolic microphone to them under their jackets and, using a digital tape recorder, record everything they heard. But just as the first three men had, the fourth one said, "No."

Indy would say yes.

Going home that night, she applied every trick her father had ever taught her to turn her beautiful feminine face into the scraggly visage of a homeless man. Topping it off with an old wig from Halloween and clothes she'd bought at Goodwill (then frayed, nicked holes in and rolled in anchovy paste), she headed for the office of one Plink Blayton. His reaction was immediate:

"Get out, you smell like dead fish."

"I'm a homeless guy," she said in the deepest, gravelliest voice she could muster. "Just when do you think I shower?"

"I assume you do it when all the other people you hang out with do it: When you go back to your condo at the end of your shift," Plink said, now clearly ready for her to be out of his office. "I'll find someone else."

"No you won't," she said. "I've watched you for four days..." and running down a list of every last man she'd talked to, her descriptions of their clothing, their hair, their look, she made it very clear she indeed knew he hadn't found any takers. "You need me. You want information, and I can give you a hell of a lot more than a parabolic mike."

"I don't need you..." Plink said, his twinge of curiosity once again giving way to arrogance. "I can learn exactly what I need to know just by watching down there. Might be kind of nice to just to go hang out on the beach. Now get out."

"Fine! But before I go, answer me this: If you're so damn smart," she said, ripping off her wig and bushy eyebrows, "Why didn't you notice I'm a girl?"

Plink's only answer was to hire her.

At first, he almost threw her out again when she said she would not work for food, only money. Just as quickly he realized Indy offered some major advantages. For one thing, he wouldn't have to deal with actual homeless people; they creeped him out. More, however, with her observational skills, she could give him insights into not only what was being said, but who was saying it.

And so it was that every busy day Indy the Bum went down to the GO River Wayside and spied on tourists. Sometimes, she was close enough to barely hear what was being said herself, other times they were people on the other side of the parking lot. With her parabolic microphone strapped to her arm, it didn't matter. Just point it at them, and they'd be recorded. Meanwhile, using a toggle switch to go back and forth between the parabolic and a lapel microphone, she could record as much demographic data as she could observe about who was speaking.

Working most mornings, Indy would go to city hall in her costume, stop off at the tourism office to give her recorder to Plink's assistant to download, and then go back down to the wayside. Some days she spent four to five hours, others not so much, depending on her work schedule at Grind Me Hard Coffee. Always showering when she was done being the bum, she found it remarkable that it was still working with Scrote that left her feeling truly dirty.

Not that Plink counted as an actual human, himself. Not as outright perverted and clueless as Scrote, he was still charmless and a butthole in his own way. And just like Scrote, if she wanted to keep the bills paid, she didn't really have a choice but to work with his constant diminution of her. Not that she expected to be treated like royalty, but for all the information she'd brought him, she expected better. He'd be nowhere without her.

His idea to call Surfland "Water-ful"? He'd gotten than when she recorded a toddler who couldn't properly say "waterfall" every time he splashed his hands in the water fountain. The idea to blow up the whale? He'd gotten that when she heard a bunch of college kids saying it was coolest thing they'd ever seen, but wouldn't it be cool if they could see it again without the crappy video? Bringing the Tandys back to Surfland to reopen Hope Falls Park? She'd inspired that when she recorded two trust-fund kids loaded with REI gear saying they wished there was a good lake to camp next to.

Knowing her value to him, she even went in last week and asked for a raise. Knowing his contempt for her — indeed everyone — she should have known it would go as it did:

"I'd like a raise."

"No," Plink said, never looking up from the cruise brochure he was reading on his desk.

"If it wasn't for me," she said calmly, "you wouldn't know half the things you do."

"If it wasn't for you, I wouldn't know I could go to The Valley and hire a sophomore theatre major from Portland State to do the same thing you do."

Getting nowhere, she tried a different tack. "If it wasn't for me hooking you up with my dad, you never would have been able to buy that whale from Monterrey Bay."

"True, but now that I have the whale, that's really pretty useless information," he said, now clearly staring at photo of a chocolate fountain.

"What about all the other connections I could hook you up with?"

Plink, seeming to ponder for a moment, allowed Indy got her hopes up. She shouldn't have.

"Honey, I'm so ironclad in this job, I don't need you or anyone else," he said, finally looking at her. "So if it's hooking your interested in, by all means, quit."

Stunned motionless by what she'd just heard, she watched as Plink opened up his desk, took out a tape, spun around his chair laughing, and then placed it back inside. "Are you still here?" he said to her, now looking back down at his desk. "I assume that means you'll be back on shift tomorrow. See ya..."

Thinking back on it now made her even angrier than when it had first happened. Because as she walked out of the office, she promised herself she would never work for him again. And yet here she was — talking to a dog who wasn't and a dementia-ridden woman who wasn't, all the while dressed as the man she wasn't. Amazed that both had never wavered in their interest in her story, she now suddenly felt embarrassed by what her life had come to. Shedding a tear for the first time since she'd moved to Surfland, she simply looked at them both and said, "I just don't have a choice..."

Sitting in a silence that seemed like eternity, Indy finally walked to the window and let the tears clear from her eyes. Her makeup running, Indy said out loud, "I must look like crap."

"Well, yes, but since that's your job at the moment..." Mrs. Margaret said with humor in her voice, "...you should be very proud of what you've done."

Laughing now, Indy began looking around. "If no one's coming in here, do you mind if I take this microphone out of my sleeve? It's so long my arm won't bend; it starts to go numb after a while."

"Of course, dear," said Mrs. Margaret. "And trust me, if I know my family — and I do — you don't have to worry about anyone coming in here for a long time."

Setting the microphone on the windowsill next to the door, Indy was finally beginning to relax, maybe for the first time in days. Telling someone else her secret seemed to lift a weight off her. She'd thought about telling Ryan, or course, but he had enough concerns, and she knew he'd do nothing but worry. Besides, if anyone understood secrets, it was clearly these two. The dog fascinated her most.

"You'll forgive me, but even as I listen to you I have very hard time believing you're not a real dog. Now that you're sitting there next to her again, I feel like I'm in a very bizarre Disney film. You're not a D.A., are you?"

Laughing, Fuzznut said, "No, just a guy dressing up and making a killer paycheck."

"Well, at least one of us is," she said, once again reminded of how cheap Plink was. "Don't you get hot in that thing?"

"Yeah, but it's not as bad as you think. I've been a mascot everywhere from Phoenix to Florence. Trust me, Surfland's weather is about as mascot-friendly as it gets. I lost 14 pounds in an hour in

St. Louis once..." Fuzznut recalled, remembering also that he couldn't walk straight for two days. "That's why I always keep a camelback under here."

"Never thought of that... But, seriously, you HAVE to smell."

"You're one to talk."

"Good point, but that's my job," she said. "You're supposed to smell like... whatever it is a dog smells like. After two hours in that thing, you have to smell like a middle school hallway."

"As I say, Surfland's pretty friendly to not perspiring profusely," he said. "That, and they wash the suit every day in one of the super-sized washers and dryers at a hotel they own. They take very good care of me."

"As they should, dear," said Mrs. Margaret, "as they should. Speaking of which," she said, now returning her attention to Indy. "What can I get you? My family's left more supplies in here than my grandmother carried with her 165 years ago."

"Yeah, I read about that and the rest of your family in my history class," Indy said. "Although I must admit, you're clearly no vege— Oh, sorry. That's not very nice..."

"No! That's a compliment! It means my acting skills are every bit as good as yours!" Mrs. Margaret said, clearly delighted to talk to someone other than her dog. "I've been working for more than five years to perfect this act, and clearly I have."

"Mrs. Margaret — can I call you that? Mrs. Margaret, why are you doing this?" Indy asked, now clearly returning to her normal self. "I mean sitting here, doing nothing all the time. It just seems like real life is so much more interesting."

"You have no idea, my dear, you have no idea..."

Chapter 45
Maggie

Rebekkah Talmedge was 15 when she boarded the *Magna Vomere* for the trip to her new home in the Oregon Territory. Accompanied by her friend from church, Adeline Rogers, it was June 1836 — and both were virtual slaves to their soon-to-be husband's families. Neither of them wanting to leave their homes, family politics and debts to the church were forcing both women to marry men they did not love, nor even like.

Setting sail from Boston, they were on their way to Fort Vancouver in the Oregon Territory to begin their lives of virtual servitude and forced parenthood as missionary wives. The families of their husbands-to-be as cheap as they were cruel, the women were being forced to set sail on a ship whose name meant "Great Vomit," and it earned every ounce of that name. A packet ship, its job was to deliver mail and keep disciplined schedules. This often involved harsh treatment of seamen, earning the ships the nickname "bloodboat."

The passengers didn't fare much better and the months-long journey to Honolulu was a nightmare. To begin with, the waters around Cape Horn lived up to their reputation as almost homicidally hazardous, owing to strong winds, large waves, strong currents and icebergs. Even in the best of times it was a sailors' graveyard. Sailing with a drunken captain who often abused his men and passengers, both women felt particularly helpless.

Upon arrival in Honolulu, both women were prevented from leaving the ship, per the orders of their husband's families. Fearful that they would flee the vessel while in port, both were kept under lock and key in a vomit-encrusted room in the ship's hold. Their only view of the tropics out a porthole, it would be 80 years before Rebekkah would see the island again. Adeline never would.

Sailing from Honolulu, they crossed the Columbia River Bar on March 20, 1837, arriving in Ft. Vancouver not long after. Walked literally from the ship to the church, both women were married off in morning ceremonies immediately, Adeline vomiting on her wedding dress in the bathroom after the wedding. Both of them in fear of their wedding night, they were actually relieved when they immediately mounted horses and began the long journey out to the coast.

The ride was much as history recorded: They took two days to reach the summit of the Coast Range and reached the Pacific on March 28, 1837. In an area that would become known worldwide for tourism, Josiah and Rebekkah Tandy had become the first tourists on the central Oregon coast — save for the fact that one of them was a virtual prisoner. Nevertheless, during that week they did travel to all the places history said they had. The rest of it — the romance, the journeys of personal discovery, the harmony with nature — was an utter and complete historical fraud, proffered by a church and state that had everything to lose.

One anecdote, however, was word-for-word as history suggested. On Ageya Head, the two young couples did pull out a small bottle of wine they had managed to carry all the way from Ft. Vancouver for the purposes of toasting the virgin spaces they'd been allowed to cross. And indeed, sitting in a circle, all of them could see the ocean to the west, save for one: Josiah. But as he looked east and pondered the virgin spaces, he was thinking not of the trees, but his innocent wife just five feet away. Shortly thereafter, what both women had avoided on their wedding night, they could avoid no longer.

When they returned to The Valley, Josiah did not stay a missionary long; he'd never really planned to. Leaving the church, he immediately began exploiting Native Americans, unwary settlers and anyone else he could make a buck off of. For her part, Rebekkah played the part of the wife, having kids and staying quiet in public about her husband's abuses and the lie he'd passed off to everyone who would listen. These were dark times for her, but she handled them far better than Adeline, who took her own life in 1862.

But if she was staying quiet in public life, she was not at home. Certainly, she never told Josiah what to do; he was too arrogant and abusive for that. But through careful appeals to his ego, she learned to manipulate her husband into thinking things were his ideas, and therefore good ones. Investing in logging, shipping and railroads were all her idea — as was Rebekkah writing his will. Upon his death in 1900, she took over the company. The age of 79, herself, she considered it her job to hold the company together until the right heir came along.

Immediately, she knew this was not to be her children; while never truly knowing their father, they were too much like him for her tastes. Instead, she looked to her grandchildren, hoping that one would be able to carry the torch. The last one, Maggie, did, and Rebekkah taught her everything she could about running the family business and life itself. Some things, however, she kept private, including the true story of how her life in Oregon began. It wasn't that she never planned to tell Maggie, but the time just never seemed right — until Honolulu.

The result of a surprise family trip, all of them were anxious to give Rebekkah a triumphant return to the geographic beginning of her life-long adventure on the Pacific. A well-intended gesture, timed to end back in Oregon with the dedication of Tandy Park, it served only to make her sad. Her hotel room looking down on the very port dock where she had been kept a virtual prisoner, she could not help but think of how Adeline had never recovered from those horrific days.

But if it depressed her, it also steeled her resolve to not let her or Adeline's story go without being told. Sending messages back to Portland on express mail ships, she had the workers at one of her metal foundries make some changes to the plaque that would be mounted in the park upon her return. To begin with, she wanted her and her husband's name removed and the entire thing renamed, at least in part, Hope Falls Park, and there were other changes, as well.

Thinking about it on the return trip to Portland, she felt more of a sense of purpose than she had in years. The truth would no longer be hidden. It wasn't much, but it was a beginning, and the park dedication would be the ending.

The middle came in Whig City, the night before the park dedication. Asking Maggie to join her alone on the deck overlooking the ocean, Rebekkah told her everything, starting with the trip from Boston right up until that moment. Grandma Bekk, as Maggie called her, left no mysteries for her heir-apparent. Talking late into the night so that Maggie might have every question answered, Rebekkah went to sleep content as she never had been. Perhaps that's why, other than uttering a few words to her family, she never truly awoke again, the park dedication still waiting to be the end of the story.

Chapter 46
Mrs. Margaret

"It's been 85 years since that story's been told," Mrs. Margaret said, looking out the window wistfully. "You can see the deck on my house from here where I heard it from my Grandma Bekk. When we expanded the house, I made sure to leave the original deck there." Without even realizing it, she began to scratch Fuzznut on top of his furry head.

"Whatever happened to the plaque?" Indy asked as she opened up a bottle of Fuzznut's water.

Focusing again on Indy, Mrs. Margaret said, "It's still sitting in the garage wrapped in the paper put on by the foundry in 1927. It will be at the park re-dedication tomorrow. Seems time..."

"Why didn't they ever come get the plaque? Didn't they want it in the park?"

"I don't even think they wanted the park at that point," she said. "My Grandma Bekk's death really shook the town, and I think that was just their way of trying to forget about it. Still would be, I guess, if they weren't reopening the park. I suppose I have you to thank for that, don't I?"

"I just delivered the information; it was Mr. Blayton that came up with the idea," Indy said.

"The fact that you still call him 'Mr. Blayton,' after the way he's treated you," she said. "It says a lot about your character."

"I learned it from my parents."

"Perhaps, but if you'll forgive an old lady for saying so, I think Mr. Blayton's a douche."

"Ppppphhhhhttttttt! Oh my God?!" Indy said, clearly shocked at what she'd just heard. "I'm sorry, I just wasn't expecting..."

"Don't apologize to me dear, it's Fuzznut you just sprayed in the face."

"Yeah, sorry about that," Indy said, now brushing off the part of the costume that Fuzznut saw through. "I notice you don't call him 'Bekk'? Isn't that his name?"

"That was my dog's name, Indy. He's been dead for seven years, and last I checked the man inside this costume has a name — albeit a strange one."

"Then why go along with pretending he's a real dog? Heck, why the whole act in the first place?" Indy asked, now getting clearly revved up — before she remembered who she was talking to. "If you don't mind me asking..."

"Not at all dear," Mrs. Margaret now clearly getting a twinkle in her eye. "Let's just say I wish my kids and grandkids were just a little bit more douchey."

"Ppppphhhhhttttttt!"

Her entire life, Margaret Tandy had considered herself a nice person. Yes, she was a business person, and a good one. But she never considered herself ruthless. Certainly there were times when she wished she had been, like the time she saw Matti Niemen at a society function during her senior year in college. Still irritated that he'd blown her off after that magical summer of '26, she thought about crossing the room and giving him a piece of her mind. Certainly the punch would have left some terrific stains on his linen shirt — and the cup would have made some equally great marks on his forehead.

But she didn't; what good would it do? She was happy now, so clearly her life wasn't meant to include him. Good enough.

Margaret considered this kind of reasoning to be one of her greatest virtues: The ability to think of a really crappy, cold thing to do, and then not have to do it. Grandma Bekk would have called it a bit of a mean streak, while her great-grandkids were known to say someone could be a douche. (She had to admit, it was a fun word to say at times.) In her mind, however, she just thought of it as being a bit bitchy. Not that she took kindly when people called her one; she did not. (That was often known to be their last conversation with her.)

But for that part of her personality, the part that had to kick in to get things done, she had to admit bitch was as good a name as any. It was this hard-edged part of her that enabled her to lay people off when she had to, fire people when she needed to, and make hard decisions when they were necessary. Business wasn't always pretty.

And if, on occasion, someone who knew her well enough remarked that she was acting way, that was certainly all right, like the night she found out she'd lost nearly $750,000 in the To St. Helens and Back fiasco. Taking her CFO out to dinner, she described with great anatomic detail what she'd like to do the embezzler. Sitting quietly through the whole thing, her CFO simply knocked back another drink and said, "For a 95-year-old, you can be one scary bitch," to which she had just one response: "Damn right, sweetie."

Which was why she was so frustrated that not a single of her offspring understood that. Not a single one had a mean streak, a bitchy edge, a certain "douchey-ness." Maybe it was their wealth that left them wanting for nothing. Maybe it was they'd seen the joy of giving so many times, they couldn't imagine not doing it. Or maybe they were just insipidly nice, somewhat-spineless twits. Whatever the case, her family had spent millions in the last few years, on what? A waterproof book section at the library? A science fiction museum for people that didn't even ask for it? And now an Aveda spa at the hospital? The more she thought about it, the angrier she got — now, and for the past decade.

""They couldn't even tell me my dog died!" she said, now standing up in her chair. "They've been paying some circus performer $2,500 a day for seven years because they couldn't even tell me my dog died!"

"Mrs. Margaret, I know I'm just the hired dog, and one you clearly have given a very large raise," Fuzznut said. "But you are 102 years old. Perhaps you should calm down a bit..."

"Perhaps you're right," she said, once again lowering herself into her chair. "I wish all my dogs had given me this good of advice. Maybe then I wouldn't need to worry about my offspring..."

Filling the silence, Indy still had more questions: "OK, I get that, but what does pretending you're a veg— a senile person accomplish? Aren't you afraid they'll run the company into the ground without you?"

"First of all, they only think they're running the company; I still control every last thing that matters, even if they don't know it," she said, making it clear she wouldn't discuss that any further. "Second, I was hoping that with me out of the picture, one of them might step up," she said. "I knew Evan and his sisters were too far gone, just as my Grandma Bekk knew that about her kids. But the grandkids, I was hoping one of them might."

"Nothing, I take it?" Indy asked, sadly knowing where this story was going.

"Worse than nothing: In just the last two weeks one of my granddaughters told Plink to completely redo the menu at tomorrow's event because she heard me once say I liked Benihana."

"You don't?"

"I like the razor sharp knives; I took my CFO there once because it was the closest I could come to stabbing the S.O.B that had ripped us both off."

"Does your family really have that little conviction?"

"Indy, I faked a heart attack two days ago just to see if any of them would overcome being too scared to do anything and save me," she said. "The DOG had to do it," she said, pointing to Fuzznut.

"Yeah," Fuzznut said, suddenly, "I meant to talk to you about that: Thanks a lot! You scared the hell out of me! You know how hard it is to control 30 pounds of legs as you push them into someone's body? I could have broken your ribs," Fuzznut said, seeming to actually shudder in the dog costume. "And good Lord! What if I'd forgotten to take off the outdoor feet again? I could have sliced 10 holes right in—"

"OK! OK!" she said, patting Fuzznut on the head one more time as she started to glance out the window. "As someone recently reminded me, I am 102. And now, if you'll forgive me, I think I may need to slide back into nothingness soon."

"I knew it!" Fuzznut said. "You're—"

"Relax, Fuzznut. I just meant Evan's probably coming back any minute."

Starting to gather her things, including putting the microphone back in her sleeve, Indy couldn't help but look out the window. "How do you know?"

"How I always know: He's walking this way looking guilty and his lips aren't moving."

Chapter 47
Indy

Getting ready to leave the pavilion, Indy could see Evan approaching outside the door, and thanks to the microphone now literally back up her sleeve, she could hear him, too. Surprised to find she'd never turned it off, she learned three things: That Mrs. Margaret's minister was coming to visit that afternoon, that another call was coming in about the hospital spa, and that Evan was easily distracted. This last piece of information mattered to her most: focused on his call again, Evan began walking away from the pavilion. Grateful that she didn't just have to bolt out the door, she began to say her farewells to Mrs. Margaret and Fuzznut.

"Well, I certainly understand now why all the good movies about history are rated 'R.' History — the real thing — isn't exactly pretty all the time," she said. "You're nothing like in the books."

"That's because I didn't write them," Mrs. Margaret said. "Although I can't imagine even if the truth was told it would be the most interesting thing in school."

"Hate to say it, but no; history's more my friend Ryan's thing," she said, laughing. "I'm more into science and numbers. My dad's job had so many technical aspects growing up that I guess they just stuck..."

"You sound like that makes you sad," Mrs. Margaret said, clearly wondering why.

"Let's just say my life hasn't exactly been a storybook, either," she said, and seeing that Evan was now on the other side of the parking lot Indy began to tell her story.

"...And it never seems to get better; just yesterday he found out he didn't get the job on *Grimm*. That would have been so perfect! Makeup, Portland, weird Hollywood-type people to hang out with," she said, now once again starting to gaze out the window. "Which means here I am again, never getting to business school, never getting out of these crappy jobs, and no choice in the matter whatsoever."

"I don't know, seems like you've made some very difficult choices," Mrs. Margaret said. "You don't HAVE to help your mother; you choose to."

"Who wouldn't?"

"My kids left a dog to save me," she said.

"Good point."

"Indy, I'd like you to come to the park dedication tomorrow, if you can."

"I'm supposed to work, and when I miss a day, it's a lot of money."

"That's true, and commendable," she said. "But to quote a great philosopher: 'Life moves pretty fast. If you don't stop and look around once in awhile, you could miss it.' Consider that, and I'll have my minister drop some money in your tip jar to cover your losses."

"You don't have— Hold on," she said incredulously, "Did you just quote Ferris Bueller?"

"You get parked in front of a lot of movies when you fake senility, sweetie."

"Well, who am I to say no to Ferris? He's a righteous dude," she said, excited at just the mere thought of having a day off from Scrote and Plink. "But I do need to ask you one more thing, if that's OK?"

"Go ahead; Evan's lips have stopped moving, but he's still on the other side of the wayside."

"You haven't told a soul any of this in 85 years. Why me? Why now?"

"Well, for one thing, it's nice to know when I do keel over, there's someone other than my dog who will give me CPR. Yes, dear, I heard about what you did; my grandkids read about it on Facebook," she said, clearly loving Indy's surprised face before she got serious again.

"More importantly, however: when you've been waiting 85 years to do something, it makes sense to practice it at least once."

Chapter 48
Scrote

Sitting in Ian's Bug in the GO River Wayside parking lot for the past two hours hadn't been Scrote's first choice. With Indy not scheduled until this afternoon and him out of the shop, it was left to one of his other girls to keep things moving. She was new, and while she seemed to be working out, she was no Indy — and she only wore a B cup.

It had been a good talk, however. Sitting with the windows open and the cool sea air wafting through the car, they'd discussed Ian's success last night with the whale — and gone over what had gone wrong at the lighthouse. Here, Ian was clearly still frustrated that he had no idea how his prey had gotten an early warning. But with today's success at Bo's Beach that was about to be relegated to a regrettable detail. They'd discussed both of their final plans for the Bendovren Coffee building and how Indy fit into it — whether she liked it or not. They'd even discussed what to do with the remaining folders Scrote had collected from the park. He'd spent more than two hours crawling through the overgrowth that covered the stone podium that originally held the folders, and collected all of them. Each one of them numbered, he knew only one was still missing, and even that one he was sure wound up in a dumpster somewhere.

What remained unclear after all this time was what became of all the printed spreadsheets inside. Again, probably nothing. But both of them had seen the man who'd found their folder in action: clearly he was a bastard, capable of just about anything. If anyone would use the information in that folder against them, it would be him. He was too much of an unknown, though one that in less than an hour would be completely removed — though Scrote had to admit there seemed to be far simpler ways to do it.

Other than taking the lead in desperately wanting the Bendovren Coffee building, Scrote's only role in everything else was to be Ian's lackey, just as he always had been. Everything stemmed from Ian's ideas. Which was why Scrote could only sit by and watch (figuratively) as their target dodged the rocks that were supposed to crush him, and narrowly missed being killed by his own poisoned beans. And now the whale. Certainly, this would do it; a blast powerful enough to vaporize a whale — even a model one — would easily do the same to a man standing next to it.

But Scrote had his doubts, and calmly explaining these to Ian, he was thrilled when he thought his partner was beginning to see the wisdom in just burning the remaining folders, as opposed to storing them somewhere novel and unique. As he'd tried to point out more than once, if they'd just done that back in 2006, they wouldn't be in the mess they were in now.

Cautiously optimistic that his partner was finally coming around to his way of thinking, Scrote got excited: "Finally! I'm telling you, if you put that brain of yours to work making money instead of plans, there's no end to what we could do! This is what I've been waiting for, I—"

"STOP!" Ian yelled. "I told you to never call me that! That man is dead! If I hear you speak it again, I'll kill you myself."

And with that, the conversation ended.

Both of them sat there for a while, neither saying anything, Scrote's comment having sent Ian's mind seemingly a thousand miles away. Bored, but afraid to break the silence, Scrote popped one of his tapes into the car's cassette player:

"Cow many ways can I love you?
Cow many ways to say you so fine?
Udderly wonderful you're my woman,
There never been someone bovine."

His favorite music filling the silence, Scrote began to relax and look around the wayside. Always looking to upgrade his staff from B cups, he was hoping to find someone in a bikini top. True, it was only 61 degrees, but teenagers were known to do stupid things, and his hopes were high.

What he got instead was a street bum coming out of the pavilion about 50 feet to his left. Pathetic, he thought: If I had that much hair coming out of that many orifices I'd kill myself. Suddenly self-conscious, however, he grabbed the rearview mirror and tilted it towards himself. "Ian," he said very careful to use his partner's name, "I need you to look up my nostrils. See anything up there? I swear to God, all my hairs are gone."

Still clearly pissed, Ian ejected the tape and jerked the mirror back towards him. Staring at Scrote, he spoke only after another 10 seconds of uncomfortable silence. "Seriously? It's 12:44, my plan is about to solve our problems, are you're asking about nose hairs?" he said, contempt oozing from every word. "I don't even know why I let you call me partner. Now shut up."

Less than a minute later, every head at the GO River Wayside turned to the south as a mighty 'BOOM' drowned out every other noise. It wasn't enough to set off car alarms, but it was close. And definitely distracting enough to drown out Scrote saying some words out loud that he'd been told not to say, followed by "...you are such an asshole."

"What was that?" Ian snapped as he put the car into gear and backed out of the space. "Don't tell me my plans don't work..."

Chapter 49
Plink

It was not yet nine in the morning, and Plink Blayton was already being bombarded with things that pissed him off. In his driveway, his car had once again locked him out. Pounding on all five doors, it was only hitting the last one that had finally released the driver's lock. The hatchback, it was the hardest of all of them and his hand still hurt like hell. Even now, standing outside his office, he found himself cursing his car.

Next, Poe and Pete texted him to tell him they were running late to Bo's Beach, site of this morning's whale explosion. Something about traffic and picking up a dog. In and of itself this wouldn't have bothered him; this morning was just about details. But Poe had to include on the end: "And don't park in the handicapped spaces. Karma's a bitch, and so am I."

God, how he hated that man.

And finally, he'd once again locked himself out of his office. The locksmith was on his way, but Plink wanted in NOW. Pacing, he walked back down to his aide's desk, intending to ask her where the locksmith was — only to find the guy flirting with his aide. "Is this what I pay either of you for?"

"Actually, it might be," said his aide, "since you don't let me do anything else."

"Get back here," he said to the locksmith, ignoring her. "And stop waving at her; you're on my dime."

Within minutes, Plink was back in his office, still cursing the morning, while simultaneously running to grab his now ringing phone. It was Rip, and he had no good news whatsoever about the nudist video still running all over YouTube. Damn...

As he often did, however, he once again opened the drawer to see the tape. Always serving to mollify him when he was angry, it even mellowed him on the subject of his car. If it weren't for the Aztek's bizarre doors and locks, he never would have known how to get into the one owned by the "news photographer" and wouldn't have Dick Yelpers by the balls.

Plink knew that Dick considered his hiring a horrible mistake, and indeed a lot of people would like to see him gone. But despite his dismal failures in Surfland, none of them were enough to get him fired, at least not when he had the President of the Surfland Tourism Advisory Board in his back pocket. Coupled with an officially unblemished work history — PETA had never been able to make anything stick — his background was impeccable.

Except for one thing.

As he fled from Ocean Springs in the spring of 2006, Plink returned to the only part of the world where he'd found any success: The Midwest. Still being chased by PETA for the tranquilized rodent incident at the Indiana golf course, however, he knew the name Plink Blayton would not be conducive to professional success nor staying out of perpetual litigation. So he invented P.K. Barker: A first name that was close to his tongue, and a last name close his mother's heart. (She never did warm to Drew Carey.)

Using a variety of vaguely legal internet services to disguise his identity, Plink — P.K. Barker — went out and got himself a job in marketing at a small zoo outside of Columbus. Once again hoping to make a name for himself with original thinking, he was trying to get a leg up on the other people in his department. All of them asking, "What do people want?" "P.K." knew that the first one to answer the question would be the next one in for a promotion, possibly to corporate. But how?

The answer came as he drove home in the car one day. His car radio limited to one station, Plink found himself in the deathly throes of NPR. Worse, the signal would cut in and out, no matter how many times he pounded on the dashboard. In between the static however, Plink heard one thing: "Guerilla marketing," and about numerous success stories across the country. He knew he had to try it.

What he did not hear was that it was advertising strategy using non-traditional and low-cost means of communication, like graffiti and stickers. And what he did not understand — as always — was how it was spelled. Which was how upon his return to the zoo, Plink began instigating a "Gorilla Marketing" program. And once again, Plink told no one, lest they steal his idea.

Taking advantage of the primate department's annual convention in Orlando, Plink found an out-of-work circus performer to dress as a gorilla and put him in a separate cage next to the zoo's real gorilla. Just a man in a suit, he moved and behaved exactly like a gorilla. It hadn't been cheap hiring the understudy from the latest King Kong film, but it was worth it.

By using many of the same techniques he would have Indy replicate a half-decade later, Plink learned more about zoo patrons needs and wants in a week, than anyone else had all year. Cheaper popcorn, more interactive exhibits, better scheduled feeding times so people could watch the animals tear apart flesh and fruitcakes. (Christmas: always a big time at the zoo.) These were the things people wanted.

Eventually, "P.K." did tell his bosses what he'd been up to, if for no other reason that the primate convention in Orlando ended. At first they were horrified; this was a zoo, not Disneyland. But upon seeing P.K.'s ideas they demurred a bit; perhaps this was something they could use. Asking Plink if he and his performer could be ready the next day before the corporate president, Plink quickly agreed — and quickly regretted it.

For that was the day his performer decided to leave town. Something about a job as a dog paying ten times as much out on the west coast. Calling up the talent agency where he'd hired the first one, Plink discovered it would be another week before they could get him someone to perform. But Plink needed to act now; the president was only in town one day, and he had lots of other zoos to visit. That's why when Plink walked into the president's office the next morning he brought with him the zoo's real gorilla, heavily drugged.

And that's why to this day there was still a warrant out for the arrest of "P.K. Barker." on charges of assault by proxy, abuse of animals, public vandalism and contributing to unlawful fecal distribution in a community water supply. Indeed, it was a miracle no one was killed as the gorilla rampaged through the office, destroyed the lobby, and pooped in the neighboring water treatment facility when he briefly escaped, gorilla tranquilizers being quite the laxative. The assault charge, however, derived solely from Plink's own actions, stepping on the president's face — twice — as he fled from the scene.

That was what had brought Plink to Surfland, and while he occasionally feared that someone would connect the lives of Plink Blayton and P.K. Barker, time and distance seemed to make that less likely every day, especially on a day like today.

For today was the day when so many of his plans would start to pay dividends. Today was the day they would blow up the whale.

As Pete had snidely commented so many times, he would not be the first. But as Indy's observations had shown him, he didn't need to be. He just needed to be the best, and after this afternoon, he would be. No longer would people have watch grainy footage from 40 years ago and wonder, "Where is that?" Now they would watch it all in HD, and say, "Hey! That's Surfland!" As always, when the battle came down to fake versus real, Plink knew what people really wanted.

Not that finding a whale had been easy. Indeed, when Indy first told him she'd heard people talking about it, Plink dismissed his own idea out of hand. But when Indy mentioned her dad had worked on Star Trek IV, and knew the model-makers that had created the whales at the Monterey Bay Aquarium, he asked her to put him in touch with them. His hope had been to use the whales from the actual movie; that would have been double the news coverage. Sadly, those were actually just tiny whale models. Instead, however, he managed to get one of the life-sized sperm whale models that hung from the ceiling in the aquarium, the staff there happy to let him overpay for it.

That was six months ago, and today Plink was going to blow it up. Well, it was actually Xander that was going to do it; the ceremonial red button being set up in Bo's was just a stage prop. Whatever; people thought it was real — just like the whale. Having filled it with desiccated fish parts and the blubber from a bunch of sea lions the bureau of wildlife was killing off for menacing area salmon runs, it smelled absolutely vile. He had no doubt it would provide lasting memories for all.

Chapter 50
Whales & Other Exploding Things

When the Oregon Highway Division blew up a whale on the coast of Oregon in 1970, it was not the area's first grim experience with either whales or exploding things.

In 1947, a Japanese mine left over from World War II drifted near the shoreline about 10 miles south of Surfland. The Coast Guard was sent to blow it up and did so — along with enormous pieces of Nadine Jeffers' house and two neighbors on either side of her. The beginning of Oregon's history with the government blowing aquatic things up and then having to pay people when it went horribly wrong had begun.

A year later, more mines from the war washed up, three 500-pounders coming to rest only the length of a football field away from Highway 101. Once again, the government came in to detonate them, and once again, windows were rattled and broken, this time along a five-mile stretch of beach near Newport.

So it was in 1970 that the road department was called in to blow up a dead sperm whale. On the theory that when it came to blowing things up — like cliffs and hillsides and other impediments to road construction — no one knew more than the Oregon Highway Division. Given the government's dubious history with exploding things on the beach, one might have thought concern was in order. Not that it should have ever come to that.

The area's equally poor history of dealing with dead whales and other aquatic creatures should have been more than enough to scare the hell out of everyone.

Dead whales, of course, have been washing up on the beaches of Oregon as long as there have been both whales and sand. Indeed, Whale Cove south of Surfland, not too far from where Miss Nadine Jeffers would eventually build and rebuild her house — was named when white travelers found Indians working on the carcass of a dead whale. One presumes they did not call the government, if only because there was none to call.

By 1912, however, there was a government, and other signs of human stupidity. Case in point: This was the year a government survey expedition spotted a dead whale they wanted to tow into Lenobar Bay as a tourist attraction. It is not known if they planned to blow it up, as the other item they'd dragged in was a 5,000-pound shark that was very much not dead. A fact made painfully clear when it broke loose from the rope around its tail and terrorized the bay.

In 1924, having learned nothing about tying things up, a dead whale broke loose from its moorings below the Ageya Head lighthouse. Not needing to be alive to incite terror, the rotting corpse drifted in the sun off the coast for days. Described in the Surfland Siren as "stronger by several hundred percent than Limburger Cheese," this account was described as wholly accurate even three days later — at the writer's funeral.

In 1938, when a whale washed up at the yet-to-be-named GO River Wayside, attempts were made to cremate the carcass. Unfortunately, there was little blubber left to burn, and instead the meat began to slowly roast, not smelling anything like chicken. Later, switching winds blew the smell over all five of the towns. On the upside, the bones did eventually become a coastal exhibit on Highway 101, until confused black-market scrimshaw artists stole all the bones in the late 1970s.

In 1970, then, the karma was perfect for a perfect convergence of dead whales and human stupidity. An eight-ton, 45-foot sperm whale having washed up on the beach outside of Florence, the Oregon Highway Division was called in to dispose of it. A half-ton of dynamite seeming just the right amount to do the trick.

On its surface, the decision alone to forcibly remove a dead whale seems ridiculous; again, they'd been washing up for a long time. But as the people of Surfland discovered in 1924, a rotting whale smells God-awful, and that's bad for tourism, along with not being terribly hygienic. In a day and age when tourists have been known to pick up dead crabs and seaweed off the beaches to take home as souvenirs, it was horrifying to Oregon State Parks personnel to imagine what they might do with a whale and its various parts.

Dead whales can also be hazardous. Not enough that humans keep trying to blow them up, dead whales have been known to do it themselves. In Taiwan in 2004, a decomposing sperm whale exploded in the middle of the city. The buildup of gas finally too much for the corpse to handle, the explosion, according to Wikipedia, "splattered blood and whale entrails over surrounding shop-fronts, bystanders, and cars."

Perhaps this type of disaster was on the minds of Oregon state officials in the fall of 1970 when they pondered what to do with the carcass. Nature taking its course was obviously a bad thing — so the government did it for them.

What transpired was legendary, so much so that even today a website called TheExplodingWhale.com is dedicated solely to the event. Captured by news crews on site in 1970, the half ton of dynamite vaporizes parts of the whale, as workers intended — but not nearly all of it. Random pieces, some of them weighing pounds, come crashing down all around: on dunes, in the surf, on cars, and even a few people. Horrified, all of the people survived intact. The cars were not so lucky, their roofs having been crushed by falling chunks of blubber. Possibly the single most spectacular thing to ever be captured on film on the Oregon Coast, the reporter on site is still invited to speak about it 40 years later.

But what was well-known throughout Oregon was largely considered an urban myth outside the Pacific Northwest. Only when humorist Dave Barry wrote about seeing the video in 1990 did the rest of America know about Oregon's tragic history with exploding things and whales. Calling it the "the most wonderful event in the history of the universe," Barry put the exploding whale on the global map.

What his story did not do, however, was tell people the incident had happened 20 years earlier, just as it did not tell them where it happened. For readers, it had just happened, and as they called tourism boards up and down the coast, they wanted to know where. In the beginning, the people manning the phones, usually volunteer senior citizens, had no idea what people were talking about. In Surfland, volunteer Edna Krebbs got so confused by the questioning about what had happened 20 years earlier outside of Florence — she'd been living in Topeka at the time — that when she met All-Star Florence Henderson at the Joan of Arc Memorial Horse Race and Bonfire, she remarked she was surprised to see her alive; Edna had been telling callers she'd been eaten by a whale.

Even 25 years after Dave Barry's article, and all the websites and all the stories, some newspapers across the country continue to rediscover the incident, even telling people that it just happened. To them, it's not history and it's not Florence: It's here and now, and they want to see it.

Plink Blayton was going to give it to them.

Chapter 51
Poe

"This is the stupidest thing ever."

Watching as Pete pulled his camera gear out of the Explorer, Poe talked as he pulled his Jag in next to Pete. Making sure to take the space furthest from the whale — he'd seen the video — Pete thought his fears were ridiculous.

"Poe, trust me, there's not enough explosives in that thing to send a pound of sea lion blubber over the driftwood, much less the bluff. This is a lot of very visual smoke and pyrotechnics, and that's it — just the way Plink wants it."

"Perhaps," Poe said, putting up the top as he prodded Buffett out of the backseat. "But I also have a rule: Never park next to a car whose value is less than that of fixing a door-ding."

Poe now pointing to Plink's Aztec, Pete could see what he meant. On the other hand, at least it seemed like Plink was finally listening. His car was nowhere near a handicapped space even though all of them were empty. Indeed, Plink having closed this parking lot to the public, too, the only vehicles to be seen were media trucks and Ryan's van.

Gathering up the cameras before walking across the parking lot to Bo's Beach, Poe had to complain again: "Let me get this straight: Where even the government has learned it's better to bury whales than blow them up, we're about to unleash an explosion in a town full of retired people with leaky bladders. Who the hell is sponsoring this, Depends?"

"Nope, just the town of Surfland — as you can plainly see."

And see they could: There behind the whale, in full view of all the cameras, was a giant sign hanging on the bluff: "Surfland! A Water-ful Place To Be!"

Poe was stunned: "I think I should have brought my own Depends."

At this point the three of them went their separate ways. Pete went to talk to Xander, who was double-checking his work from last night, slowly marking items off his two-hour to zero checklist. Buffett wandered inside Bo's Crab and Anvil, looking to score a booth to sleep in. Poe, meanwhile, began grabbing cameras both new and old and placing them in various locations along the 150-yard square perimeter. It took him close to an hour to make sure everything was just right, each camera angle perfect. Like before, he'd eventually just leave all of them running and have Pete edit everything later.

Finally completing the cameras' placements, he walked back to each of them again to turn them on. A mindless task this time, it gave him a chance to see all the hundreds of gathered onlookers kept back from the whale by a small rise of sand and what seemed like a half-mile of caution tape. Hired security guards were everywhere keeping people back from the whale and behind the tape. Their dozens of dark blue jackets and pants ubiquitous, they stood out easily against the more brightly dressed crowd.

None of them, however, were dressed brighter than Raina Bowe, Surfland's resident drag queen. Decked out in her prism-grabbing finest, Poe was surprised to see her here. "Raina! What are you doing here? This hardly seems like your thing."

"They're about to blow up a white-bellied whale on the beach," he said. "You never know; if I came down here in my street clothes I could be next."

"Uh-huh... Let me guess, Plink asked you come."

"Honey, he does volunteer work for me, remember?"

"I do, but I also know you're just the kind of colorful person he wants in all his videos. Plink does nothing without a reason."

"And neither do I; he's going to put a link to the Big Whig City Drag Queen Festival on the exploding whale web page," she said, starting to sway a bit on her feet.

"You OK?" Poe asked, wondering if the heat was getting to him in the makeup and the multi-layered dress.

"No, just these damn heels; four-inch stilettos were not made for sand."

Starting to laugh, Poe was cut off by a call from Rip. Waving a small good-bye to Raina, he made his way back up the beach, anxious to hear what his friend had to say.

Chapter 52
Rip

Talking to his friend over the phone, Rip started to harass Poe: "You are not a very graceful person in the sand... How would I know? Well, I'm standing about 20 feet from you. If you'd stop staring at your damn feet, you'd know that."

Watching his friend look up, Rip could see a momentary flash of irritation cross his face, then disappear just as quickly. Feeling bad for not a moment, Rip owed Poe some grief. Rip had been up all night checking out Poe's myriad conspiracy theories, naked friends and other weirdnesses. It would have been irritating — if it hadn't been so rewarding.

Still panting from his walk up the beach, Poe let Rip speak first: "You owe me, big."

"And you still have five of my shirts; we're even," Poe said.

"And you have two of mine, that's even?" Rip asked.

"Sure; you still have three more shirts," Poe said, now starting to get his breath back.

"Yours come from Goodwill, mine come from Tommy Bahama. How is that possibly even?"

"You're right; mine are better," Poe said, now clearly back to his normal self. "Stop whining; what did you find out?"

"That you're a bastard; but I already knew that, so let's talk new stuff," Rip said. "I think your naked friend on the beach is OK. I told Plink it was a random nudist, a drunk kid out of the U of O."

"Did he believe you?"

"I think so, especially since the video will be down in a few days."

"How'd you pull that off?"

"Let's just say the head of security at the The Inn at Roca de la Muerte Dolorosa had no idea his teenage son was playing with camera, and he'd rather people not know," Rip said. "I don't think you or your friend need to worry about that particular camera again."

"And speaking of our friend Plink, what's up with that?"

"Well, at first glance, everything in his background is just as he claims, although there are some holes."

"Like what?" Poe asked, now starting to speed things up; Plink was coming out of Bo's and walking towards them.

"Well, for some reason the fans of the bands Smashmouth and Katrina and the Waves both have him listed as a 'lying, cheating, misspelling bastard' on their Facebook pages. No idea what that's about, and every time I contact someone on the Gulf they just hang up the phone."

Poe looking perplexed, Rip paused to ask why: "What's got you confused? Bands who sing songs with words? People who use Facebook? How a drag queen can walk in the sand and you can't?"

"No," Poe said, ignoring him. "I'm wondering why what it is that the crown jewel in Plink's résumé is something no one will talk about. It's like they just want his time there to disappear."

"Interesting that you put it that way, because for about six months, he did."

"What do you mean?"

"I mean after he left the Gulf, there's no sign of the guy until he popped up in Surfland."

"Maybe he was just taking time off..." Poe speculated, not really believing it himself.

"Maybe, but there would still be credit cards, tax records, something," Rip said. "I don't know; there's just something fishy about it. I'm having my guys check it out."

"Good deal, and thanks" Poe said, genuinely meaning it. "So, you going to stick around for another hour or so? We got a whale of a show!"

"Now who's the kitschy one?"

Chapter 53
Xander

With just a bit over half-an-hour until the scheduled blast, Xander was as sure as he could be that everything was ready. Everything around the whale was exactly as he had left it the night before, all the flaps tied down that could be, all the safety measures in place that should be.

All that was left for him to do now was return to his spot in Bo's, twist on a few last wires, and wait for Plink to press the big, red — and fake — button next to him. Walking past Plink and Pete, he could hear once again his boss was wearing out his welcome: "Now you sure you and Poe placed all the cameras right? If you can't see the words — all the words — through the smoke and fire it's pointless."

"I thought the point was to see that this was Surfland," Pete said wearily.

"Well, yes," Plink said, "But without my new tourism slogan what's the point?"

What Pete said next, Xander missed as Poe and Rip were rapidly drowning out everything around them as they walked towards the whale: "You paid how much for an Atari 2600?"

"It was autographed by Cee Lo Green," he said, trying to explain himself. "He even dedicated it to me: 'F-You, Rip.' Except he didn't put 'F,' he put the real thing, like in the song..."

Here, too, the rest of the conversation was lost, as Xander was going one way, his eavesdropping subjects the other.

Walking in the VIP entrance at the back of Bo's Crab and Anvil — otherwise known as the loading dock — Xander went right to his seat next to the giant bay windows. Before sitting, he could see that behind his chair were numerous faces he recognized, like Dick Yelpers, the mayor, anchors and reporters from the Portland news. The rest were all kinds of other people he'd never seen nor met in his life. All he knew was they had a lot of cameras.

Focusing once again on his own work, Xander settled in and prepared one last visual check of the explosion site. Pulling out another checklist, he noticed there was now 20 minutes to go, just as he'd planned. Pulling out a pair of high-powered binoculars, he began once again going over every seam, every tie-down, every last thing that he'd done yesterday evening before sunset. Talking through his radio, he had it wired to a loudspeaker outside, and he let Plink, Pete and everyone else gathered know just where they were in the process.

"Ladies and gentlemen, we will start the 15-minute countdown shortly," he said, his voice booming across the beach. "Please, prepare your cameras, tie down the children, and if you haven't already, empty your bladders. Thank you!" He could see by Plink's reaction his boss did not appreciate Xander's sense of humor, but Poe and Pete clearly did, and that was good enough for him. Taking one last glance through the binoculars, he knew they were ready to go.

Except for one spot that caught his eye: A piece of "Whale skin" was flapping in the wind.

Their model whale actually a giant wooden frame covered with carefully painted canvas, Xander knew this meant there was somehow a hole in the model. Indeed, knowing the fragile nature of the model, Xander had made sure not to accidentally split any of the seams when he was inside the whale placing the explosives. The only external evidence he'd even been inside was a series of tie downs across the mouth of whale. Carefully disguised to blend in with the teeth, they wouldn't be seen on film.

But here was a piece of canvas, just behind the dorsal flipper, clearly flapping in the wind. Grabbing the radio and holding down the button, he opened his mouth so he could tell Pete to somehow put the flap back in place. Indeed, he could see now it was almost completely off the whale, almost like it had been pulled off and then unsuccessfully stuck back on. Really focusing on the hole now, Xander saw something inside he never expected to see: bright red numbers ticking down, every number zero save for the last one...

"GET DOWN! GET DOWN! GET DOW—"

And then everything went black.

Chapter 54
Buffett

In the seconds following 12:44 p.m. Buffett did not see every last head at the GO River Wayside, and most every other head in Surfland, turn due south to see a pillar of black smoke rise above the southern cliffs of the Harrison District.

He did not see every window in every business up and down SW 51st Street crack and collapse.

He did not see hundreds of pounds of sea lion blubber and desiccated fish parts rain down in neighboring parking lots and on top of Bo's Crab & Anvil.

He did not see the men and women gathered on the beach as they dove behind the sandy rise in front of them at the sound of Xander's warning, nor did he see them scream as they were splattered with smaller parts of aquatic life.

He did not see his bipedal mammal, his bipedal mammal's friends — and one enemy — dive into the sand, cover their heads and ears and hope that the blast wouldn't tear out their spines, eardrums and (in one case) hair transplants.

He did not see the windows in Bo's Crab and Anvil explode inward, just missing the hundreds of people gathered inside as they dove under benches and tables.

He did not see the bipedal mammal that yelled at everyone to get down, suddenly draped in a velour painting of Bo that had fallen from the ceiling.

Some of these things he did not see because he was not there to see them.

But mostly he did not see them because he never bothered to wake up from his nap.

Chapter 55
Xander

Though Buffett would never understand the irony of such things, what finally woke him up was Plink screaming at Xander in the shattered remains of Bo's Crab and Anvil: "What the hell did you do? Do you know what you've done?" he yelled, grabbing a dozen strands of his own hair. "Do you honestly think Hair Club for men covers this under their warranty?"

Having already thought his immediate post-blast blackness was death — instead of rotting thumbtacks, gravity and a disturbing amount of velour — Xander really didn't care what Plink thought at this point. Xander knew he hadn't placed that digital timer in there and, if what he thought he saw was accurate, he sure as hell knew he didn't go to Cambodia to get it.

But who did?

Leaving Plink behind to be screamed at by Dick, he couldn't help but notice that his Plink didn't seem particularly concerned about it. Indeed, the last thing he heard Plink say was, "Is this that 'BEE ih BAH' nonsense again?" After that... well, he knew where Yelling Yelpers had got his name.

Grabbing his backpack and walking back outside the restaurant, Xander once again thanked the powers that be that no one had been killed or even seriously injured. He'd seen enough of that overseas. Feeling only a sense of relief that he'd probably saved lives with his warning, he still couldn't quite reconcile the place he'd called home his entire life with the scene before him. One of broken buildings and windows, all of them covered with mammal parts real and otherwise.

Not surprisingly, a little more than an hour after the blast, there weren't too many people around that weren't cops, firefighters or people that otherwise belonged there. One exception: Raina Bowe, who had Poe's full attention.

"Poe, do you know how hard it is to find a rainbow-feathered tiara?"

"Well, look at the bright side," he told her, walking her back slowly through the sand. "Now you can write off another trip to Miami..."

Having already talked to the cops inside for close to an hour, Xander figured there just couldn't be anything else to ask him about. Pete, he knew, would be another story, but strangely he was nowhere to be seen, which was frustrating to Xander. Even after being quizzed and even interrogated, Xander still wanted to talk to him — but only him. He and Pete had talked through every second of today's display. What had just happened, what he thought he saw before the blast, just made no sense. Somehow, he hoped, Pete might be able to help him make sense of everything.

Now mindlessly picking his way around the debris field near the base of the cliff, Ryan stopped as he came upon an overgrown path that he vaguely remembered using as a kid. Completely overgrown now, it never ceased to amaze him how quickly Oregon's moisture and vegetation could make something disappear like it never was. Looking up the cliff one last time, Xander started to turn back towards Poe when something completely foreign — and all too familiar — caught his eye: A package with Cambodian writing.

Chapter 56
Poe

Sending Raina on her way with a promise to go out clubbing with her soon, Poe had to admit he wasn't entirely focused on her problems. Being nearly killed three times in less than 48 hours will do that to a person.

The police and fire department, of course, had no idea what had happened yet. All they knew was a small, carefully controlled pyrotechnic explosion had turned into a very large, out-of-control blast. Certainly foul play was suspected, but how, why and what were involved were still complete unknowns. Honestly, he was beginning to think about taking Raina up on her invitation to Miami. South Florida was nothing compared to this.

Just as quickly, though, he dismissed the idea; something weird was going on and he wanted to know what the hell it was — that, and he'd rather not end up dead. Looking around the scene one last time before heading home for a much-needed shower, he saw Xander walking away from the cliff, a backpack slung over his shoulder and a cross look on his face. Clearly, Poe wasn't the only one trying to work things out. For a lot of reasons, Poe felt like he should be the one to start.

"Have I said thanks for saving my life yet?"

"No problem; all in a days work," Xander said, trying to sound casual.

"Maybe, but I heard Plink in there; he didn't sound very appreciative of your work."

"Never does, though I can't say that I blame him," Ryan said, now starting to walk towards his van in the parking lot. "He hired me to do one thing: blow up a whale, and instead I took out the southern half of Surfland."

"Half?" Poe said with a smile. "More like a quarter, I think. Seriously, though, do you have any idea what might have happened?"

Here, Xander seemed to pause before talking again. "You ever heard of Tannerite?"

"No, should I? Let me guess: It blows things up."

"Well, not exactly, it's an explosive, but more importantly it's a catalyst. It makes things burn hotter and explode bigger than they ever would without it."

"And you think that's what happened here?" Poe asked.

Again, Xander seemed to pause before continuing. "Maybe... just a lot of similarities to something I saw in Cambodia when I worked for the NGO."

"Tell you what, I'll have Rip look into it," Poe said, beginning to understand why Xander seemed so distracted. "Anything else?"

"Yeah, I think I'm going to keep poking around a bit, if the police don't mind," Xander said. "If I wanted to look at the evidence they've found, maybe drop off something I find, do you know where I'd do that?"

"Yeah, right over there in the pink 'Hello Kitty' van."

"You have got to be kidding."

Chapter 57
Dick

Dick had been on the phone when the blast came.

Ill-timed, as always, it was his Aunt Desdemona, who was once again having issues with having gotten discount sex-reassignment surgery. Both of them maintaining a curious bond — each had all of Elton John's albums — he once again was trying to talk her off the figurative cliff: "Yes, the surgeries were a lot different then... No, no one thinks you're less of a lady because you have hair on your chest. It's kind of —"

"BOOM!"

That's when the glass came in, the tourists dived down, and velour rained like manna from the ceiling. Like Xander, he momentarily took the blackness for death instead of No. 6 in a series of 11 velour artworks.

At least, he thought, I can die without regrets.

When Poe had gotten up to leave their meeting at Grind Me Hard Coffee yesterday afternoon, Dick almost didn't tell Poe anything. Indeed, when he'd approached him, it was to tell him to forget the phone call, not feel bad about it. But when Dick saw how genuinely bad Poe felt about forgetting to call him back, Dick was once again reminded that Poe was a man he could trust — and probably the only one could help.

It had begun at the debacle at the GO River Wayside: Seemingly half the population of Jackson Falls, Montana, was chanting on the beach:

"Hell, No, The GO's a No-Go!

"Hell, No, The GO's a No-Go!"

Not for the first time, Dick was stunned: fifty years of protest chants, and that's the best they could come up with? Sweet Jesus, everyone in the '60s had been stoned out of their minds, and that's the best they could do?

Keeping his thoughts to himself, however, Dick went down to the head of the Jackson Falls Chamber of Commerce and tried to talk about things calmly: "Cah we juh tah a-bow dih?"

Clearly taken aback by Dick's speech impediment, the response was not positive: "What the hell did you say to me?"

"Cah we juh tah a-bow dih?!"

"Dear God, man, what's wrong with you?"

By now, a crowd had gathered, the Montanans seeming to move closer and closer. Immediately surrounding Dick were five bus drivers from the Great Falls local of the Teamsters and the 208 Girl Scouts they'd driven west. All of the murmuring and rustling making it harder than ever to hear, Dick tried one more time, this time earning every bit of his unfortunate nickname: "CAH WE JUH TAH A-BOW DIH?!"

Immediately, girls began to cry and scream, while Teamsters began to yell and threaten. Within seconds, people began running from Dick, who wasn't improving things in his attempts to keep people calm: "CAH DOW! CAH DOW!"

It was, to put it mildly, one ugly scene.

On the edge of it all was Plink Blayton, who'd actually encouraged Dick to go down onto the beach in the first place. Struggling back up to Plink's car, Dick found him just sitting there with his arms crossed.

Waiting for a moment for Plink to speak, Dick finally gave up and started the conversation.

"Weh, tha dih go weh."

"No, it didn't go well at all," Plink said. "And in fact, it went even worse than you think."

"Thah nah pah-sah-bah."

"It's very possible," he said pointing to a man just locking his backpack up in a car like Plink's. "See that guy? He's Jack Donlow, KPRO undercover news. He just got that whole thing on videotape, especially that part where you were terrifying the girls."

"No..."

"Yes."

"I'm deh."

"Yes, you are dead," Plink said, now clearly enjoying himself. "Unless you could somehow get that tape back..."

And so it began. Plink walked over to the Aztec, pounded on three doors, and popped open the hatchback. Taking the tape from backpack, he had Dick join him in his office where they watched the tape together. Plink was right: It was not good. He looked like a psychotic, screaming crazy person, definitely not the kind of person that any city, or company, would want representing it.

Plink had Dick by the balls — and he had ever since.

Every stupid idea got green-lit, every budget request filled, every mistake glossed over, all because Dick didn't dare say, "No." Not because Dick cared about losing his job with the advisory board, but because he and his family's life would be ruined. His wife's faith in him all those years ago? Destroyed because of one video tape. (A tape he was reasonably sure was shot not by Jack Donlow, but just by some random guy who happened to be filming at the time. Who the hell drives an Aztek if they don't have to?)

In recent months, however, something had changed. No, it wasn't Dick; he was still scared to death. But Plink had; his arrogance was becoming dangerous, clearly in many ways. Today's whale incident made that much clear. Certainly, he didn't think Plink had planned this fiasco, but it could never have happened in the first place if Dick had been able to control Plink, hell, fire him, the way he should have so many times before.

So he talked to Poe. And now, as he pulled the velour away from what he thought was a death shroud, he was content he had done the right thing. There were a lot worse things than being embarrassed.

For instance, velour painting No. 6 in a series of 11: Who the hell wants to be seen on the deck of a neon pink fishing boat?

Chapter 58
Poe

Watching Xander go, Poe couldn't help but think something was still bothering the young man. Couldn't say that he blamed him, though he hoped a guilty conscience wasn't it. There was so much more going on here than Xander understood... and one more time, Poe's cell phone brought him back to the here and now.

"Dr. Bracewell! How nice to hear from you," Poe said. "I'm surprised your ER's not full."

"It is, but I had to pee," he said, sounding very much like he was talking from an echo chamber. "Your results are in from Atlanta. You've been poisoned with hot pink cyanide from a dragon millipede."

"Shut up."

"Seriously, it's a centipede they recently discovered in the Mekong Delta region. Totally true; I just got a link to the story on CNN."

"And they knew this in Atlanta, how?"

"Well, that's sort of what they do — and the guy on your case golfs with Sanjay Gupta."

"Of course he does."

"Yeah? Isn't life funny?"

"Hilarious," Poe said, beginning to wish the doctor would get back to his E.R. "Did they tell you how the hell it got in my coffee?"

"Their guess was whoever it was that poisoned you got this stuff from an actual centipede, likely in liquid form, and laced your beans with it. That, or they put a centipede on your cup and you just missed it," he said, chuckling.

Poe, starting to get the annoying feeling that this is what it must be like to talk to him sometimes, was starting to develop a theory: "Dr. Bracewell, did that story on CNN tell you where the Mekong Delta was?"

"Yeah, Southeast Asia, mainly Vietnam and Cambodia," he said. "That mean anything to you?"

"It's beginning to... Hey, was there anything else in the coffee I should know about?" Poe asked.

"Nothing major: Sucralose, but that's just— Hey! Get out of here! Can't a man relax just for second in peace? I swear to God, I can't wait to get that Aveda Spa... Poe, I gotta run; there's a drag queen who needs to use the bathroom. Honest to God, he can get away with using either one and he has to walk into mine..."

Laughing for just a moment — he really did need to go clubbing with Raina — there was just too much random crap going on all of a sudden for there not to be a connection. He needed to just sit down and talk with his friends; that somehow always made things better.

Texting Pete first, wherever he was, Poe called Rip next and gave him the same message: "You, me, Pete, Bendovren, 90 minutes, and no kitschy crap, unless you're dropping it off for the auction." And without waiting for an answer, he hung up.

Finally starting to walk back to his Jag again, Poe saw Plink, Dick and Buffett walking out of the restaurant and across the parking lot themselves. As always, Plink was yelling at Dick, but this time Dick seemed to be yelling back. Not that Plink was listening, but it was a good sign — he hoped. If Poe couldn't figure out where that tape was and how to get it back, Dick's liberation would be a short and pyrrhic one.

Frowning at the thought, Poe felt his mood starting to darken, only to have it deepened by Plink screaming at him at the top of his lungs: "Poe! You did this! This is your fault! You son-of-a-bitch!" Not even beginning to be able to imagine what Plink was talking about now, Poe barely had the energy to look Plink's way and try to understand what he was complaining about this time.

The effort was definitely worth it.

Plink's car was covered with sea lion blubber and what Poe took to be the small intestines of at least 14 cod and halibut. Certainly not the only car with debris on it in the parking lot, Plink's Aztec had definitely gotten the worst of it. Even better, not a single micron of debris had fallen in any of the handicapped spaces, nor on Poe's car. Pondering for a moment that perhaps life was just, Poe was even happy to let Buffett in the backseat. There were a lot worse things than dog hair, he thought.

Pressing the button to put the top down, Poe backed out of his space, cranked the theme to Pirates of the Caribbean 3 to full volume, and headed out of the parking lot, making sure to pass Plink as he went. Tossing him a jaunty wave, Poe made sure to only use one finger.

Chapter 59
Mrs. Margaret

Even though it was only a few blocks from the GO River Wayside to the Tandy house overlooking the beach, the trip took quite a bit longer than usual. Evan and the other family members had tried to get Mrs. Margaret and their entourage of vehicles out of the parking lot immediately after hearing the blast and seeing the black pillar of smoke to the south. But it was already too late, and the city was in gridlock within minutes.

Sitting in traffic, Evan couldn't help but notice that even the homeless man now walking up the hill was moving faster than they were. Indeed, within minutes he was out of sight, likely on to more lucrative places to panhandle — which meant nowhere in Harrison. Listening to his police band radio, it was obvious that though there'd been thankfully no fatalities, there was still a lot of destruction. Finally rolling in the driveway, he instructed his sister to let the corporate offices know to expect a lot of grant requests.

Pushing his mother into the house, he could see the minister was already waiting for them in the library. How he missed the traffic, Evan could only guess. Not for the first time, he wondered if he had a direct line to God. Pondering this as he rolled Mrs. Margaret into the room with him, he allowed Bekk to follow, as always, before he left and closed the doors behind him. Quietly, the minister made sure they were locked as well.

"Father, how good to see you," Margaret said.

"Uh-huh; I'm about as much a holy man as that guy is a dog."

Fuzznut pretended to take umbrage: "As an attorney you should try it sometime; it would be a step up for you."

All of them laughing sincerely, albeit quietly, for a moment, Mrs. Margaret was ready to get down to business. "I assume you have the monthly reports?"

"As always; the trusts are doing just as you planned," he said, showing her a spreadsheet on his iPad."

"And the kids? They still have no idea?"

"No, as per your instructions, I show them data, they say 'wonderful,' and we move on."

"I knew you were right for this job the moment your father introduced you at Benihana," she said.

The "minister," recalling the night, laughed. "I must admit, you seemed pretty angry that night..."

"Not at you, dear, nor your father," she said, once again getting angry. "We were all duped. But that's neither here nor there; let's get down to business..."

Mrs. Margaret's "minister" was in fact the son of her long-time CFO, and when she'd decided to take a very long winter's (and spring's, and summer's, and fall's) nap, she knew he was just the man to help her maintain the ruse. Her Life Alert bracelet programmed to call his office instead of emergency services, he was always there when she needed him.

Today's meeting was no different, although this time she did have one more request of him.

"I'd like you to run a complete background check on these names," she said, handing him a piece of paper. "As always, use that local fellow, Rip Rockford."

"I must admit, I've never quite understood why you use a man who looks likes a beach bum for this type of work..."

"Well, for one thing, he's a high-class beach bum; Tommy Bahama runs $110 a shirt," she said, seeing he still clearly wasn't convinced. "And besides, who do you think background checked you?"

Chapter 60
Ian

The Captain would have been proud — but just a little bit.

Ian had completely blown a fake whale and Bo's Crab and Anvil from here to hell. Yet the man he needed dead still lived, and that had been the point. Worse, Ian had even failed at something simple: burning down another theme restaurant.

It had started last night when, as Ian planned, he was working his way down the path on the Harrison cliffs. The old trail almost invisible to the naked eye, he knew it was still there from his days as a youth. What he had not planned on was slipping, falling, and almost tumbling to the bottom when it was a lot more overgrown than he'd supposed it would be.

On the upside, it validated his decision to use Tannerite as a catalyst. For even though he had already mixed the two component powders that would explode when detonated, they were still incredibly stable; a fall or hard bump wasn't going to set them off. He was living proof (literally) of that. Given the number of times he'd dropped the bag, if Tannerite was unstable, Ian would have been vaporized on the side of the cliff.

Stunned that no one had heard him as he stumbled his way down the path, Ian once again found his first plan frustrated. He'd wanted to simply enter the whale through the mouth and place the Tannerite and timer. But finding that the ropework tying the mouth closed was far too ornate to be undone and redone in a short amount of time, he went to his backup plan. Indeed, if Ian had learned anything from The Captain, it was not just to have a plan — but another one, and another one, if necessary.

That's why he moved quickly to the shadow behind the dorsal fin and cut out a flap large enough to slide his backpack through. Then, after activating the timer and a small triggering explosive strapped to the outside of the bag, he shoved them both inside the whale. To stick the flap back down and cover the hole, he simply put tiny rolls of duct tape along edge of the canvas he'd cut out, and stuck the edges back to the frame. Largely hidden by the dorsal fin, it was virtually impossible to see what he'd done.

Not the most elegant plan; in fact, it was his third one. His second would have been to perform the same operation on the side of the whale facing the hill, so there would be no chance of being seen. But that side of the whale was basically pressed up against the bluff, making it impossible to get to. Nevertheless, standing in the shadows, wearing the same dark-colored jacket as the security crews, he slipped in and out in less than five minutes without being noticed. Less than ten minutes later he was back up the hill, a journey far easier without the heavy backpack.

It was a flawless plan, or rather, three plans. And when he heard the blast go off at 12:44 p.m., he was so supremely convinced of its success, that when he dropped off Scrote at Grind Me Hard Coffee, they didn't even bother discussing what came next.

That's why when he left Scrote, he'd already planned to take more of the Tannerite and pay what he planned would be humanity's final visit to Penny's Parrots. Despite being one of the older places in town, it's cacophony of parrots and macaws were certainly never meant to be on the central Oregon coast, or any North American coast, for that matter. Although he and The Captain had never actually discussed it, Ian was sure the old man would agree the place had to go.

And today it would, as located just a few blocks away from Bo's, it was about to be one more casualty of whale. Walking into the edge of the blast zone, Ian stuffed several pounds of blasted blubber into a trash bag, and made his way back towards Penny's. Taking advantage of the craziness and the empty streets, he tied the Tannerite onto the gas line, and placed the blubber underneath. Lighting the blubber on fire, he knew it would smolder awhile then ignite, giving him more than enough time to get away. Aside from using blubber instead of a dead fatty fish from the IGA— a nice touch he thought The Captain would have appreciated — it was exactly what he'd done at Mermaid in Oregon.

What he had not counted on was the arrival of a volunteer fireman, the photographer whose Jeep Ian had destroyed a day earlier. Once again surprised he wasn't dead as collateral damage, Ian could do nothing but watch as the fireman walked the perimeter of the building, found the still smoldering blubber, and doused it with a simple garden hose.

Frustrated, doubt began to creep into Ian mind for the first time: If the fireman was alive, who might also be? Returning to his car, Ian decided to drive to the top of the bluff overlooking Bo's Beach to see the actual scene of the crime. Parking in the same place he had the previous night, he was out of his car only two minutes before he saw his target was, once again, not dead. Ian couldn't believe it; what was it going to take to kill this man?

Everything The Captain had ever taught him about killing people — and nothing. He'd used the poison of a dragon centipede, not easy to get, considering all those legs — and the guy didn't even drink his coffee! He'd unleashed a giant rock avalanche tumbling down a mountainside, and he was saved by someone who hated him almost as much as Ian did! And today? He had no idea what had happened today. But the man lived; although it seemed once again his boss was yelling at him. (Truly, the way this man made enemies, Ian was surprised someone hadn't already done the job for him.)

Up until now, he'd always thought The Captain would have been proud of him. The first time he'd killed someone it had been so simple: a sliced brake line and his parents were gone. The second time was equally simple: just a pile of Tannerite under the snow and — POOF! — no more CFO. But not this latest man, the man who knew his secrets, this man who would not die.

Wondering again briefly if Scrote might be right — just shoot him — Ian quickly discarded that idea; he just needed another plan. And, as always, he would start with the fireman/photographer's plan, which Ian still had neatly folded in his back pocket. Looking at it, Ian saw with frustration where he'd already crossed out the Wednesday and Thursday items and written "DEAD." Quickly, he put them out of his mind.

For as The Captain would have reminded him, there was no time for regret, just more planning. Secure in that, Ian ran down the list to Friday's first item: "Noon: Re-dedication of Hope Falls Park."

Chapter 61
Indy

It had not been the afternoon as Indy Monroe had planned it, either. Which dovetailed perfectly with her morning. Walking out of The Tandy Pavilion after nearly an hour with Mrs. Margaret and Fuzznut, Indy was still having a hard time believing everything that had just happened.

When her morning began she was miserable and confused, as always, and certainly her conversations hadn't left her feeling less of the latter. She'd never really seen her actions as her choices; maybe that made her feel better for choosing some of the mortifying ones she had. But the truth was, she'd always known this was rationalization. Indeed, if someone had told her two years ago the degrading things she'd be doing now, she wouldn't have believed it herself. In high school, she'd been the one with the occasional mean streak, the one that got bitchy once in awhile. Not that she was mean or a bitch, but everyone understood you didn't mess with her. (That's how she first met Ryan: Seeing her after school at an auto parts store, he'd intimated she didn't know anything about cars and she'd clamped an oil filter wrench around his groin.)

What had happened to that Indy?

Pondering this, Indy still had to admit Mrs. Margaret had her feeling better about herself. After hearing the icon's true story, how could she not? Indy had been through nothing like that. Pondering Mrs. Margaret's invitation to the dedication tomorrow, Indy had no idea what was going to happen there, but she also knew she wouldn't miss it for the world. That thought alone put a long too unfamiliar bounce in her step; she couldn't wait to tell Scrote she was blowing him off tomorrow.

But that was later, this was now, and she realized very quickly that neither the smile on her face nor the bounce in her step looked anything like a homeless guy. Mentally returning herself to the task at hand, she was surprised to find she'd never turned the recorder or the microphone off. Promising herself to wipe it of anything it might have picked up in the pavilion, she literally stopped in her tracks when a giant BOOM erupted from the cliffs several miles behind her. Spinning to face south along with everyone else at the wayside, Indy nevertheless gazed that way just a bit less time than everyone else. Instead, her attention was caught by a very familiar looking Volkswagen Bug backing out of a parking space and heading out of the parking lot.

Recognizing Scrote in the passenger seat, it somehow gave her the heebies that this entire time he'd been less than 50 feet away. She didn't know what bothered her more: that once again he was near her life, or that she hadn't realized it until this very moment. Deciding neither was worth wasting her time with — she had to work with the guy in 90 minutes anyway — she walked out of the park and began making her way back up the hill towards her house.

As she feared, Scrote was there when she got to work. As she changed in the bathroom, she could hear him talking to his latest B-cup beauty, obviously standing before the full-length mirror in his office as he did so. "Do you think my eyebrows are getting blonder? And I feel like my butt is getting pinker... Can you see that?"

Clearly she could not, nor would she ever. Throwing her tool belt onto his desk, she screamed, "I'm out of here!" and was gone. Sympathetic — and jealous — Indy couldn't help but harass Scrote: "Another one bites the dust?"

"Is that a movie line?"

"Sorry, no; song title."

"Why can't you just talk to me like you like me?"

"Because I don't; you're a pig."

"Couldn't you like a pig someday?" Scrote asked, now seeming to genuinely want to know.

"Not even tomorrow, Scrote, not even tomorrow..."

Clearly having no idea what she was talking about, she watched Scrote close his eyes, smile and then mumble something about her green sunglasses. Disturbed to know what he might be thinking about, she said nothing and let him retreat to his office.

Business quiet for the moment, Indy busied herself with stuffing used coffee grounds into bags that people could take home for compost. Drilling them directly into a small basket from across the store, Indy used the time to ponder again what Mrs. Margaret had said about choices, bitchy-ness, the wisdom of talking dogs, etc. Her overhand as lightening fast as ever, her train of thought was broken when she noticed Scrote watching her out of the corner of his eye. He said nothing, so she didn't. But as he left the shop mumbling and scratching both his butt and his head, she couldn't help but remark under her breath, "I had no idea a pig could scratch two asses at the same time..."

The only sound now in the shop was once again the horrific sounds of "Sheep Pimpage."

"Oh my baby, now's the time,
You my Pegasus, you my dove.
It's time to mount you, equine,
And set a horse for love."

Wondering how many songs could possibly be on one CD, Indy bound up 10 Splenda packets with rubber bands and drilled the stop button on the player in Scrote's office through the open door. Pleased that she did it on the first try, she almost missed the congratulatory voice behind her:

"I hope you didn't turn that off on my account," Xander said. "I rather like horse movies."

"Xander!" Running to the door, Indy gave him a giant hug. The act seemed to surprise both of them. "Sorry," she said now stepping back. "I just heard what happened at Bo's Beach. I'm just glad you're OK. You know, you and everyone..."

"Of course..."

"So, do you know what happened yet?"

"Well, I have an idea..." and with a story of binoculars, breezes and errant flaps, Tannerite and Cambodia, the truth began to spill out of him like water. When he was done, Indy was stunned, and Xander seemed so, himself.

"I don't know why I told you all that; I guess I just needed to talk to someone," Xander said, now staring at the floor. "I guess it just brought back a lot of bad memories..."

"Totally get it, but I really think you should tell Pete."

"Yeah, there's a little problem with that... I kind of stole evidence from the scene."

"You what?!"

I kept the Tannerite; it's in my van," he said, sounding very certain of his cargo — if not himself. "Don't worry; it's stable. I just couldn't turn it over to a bunch of guys in a 'Hello Kitty' van. Now I don't know what to do; as mad as Pete got at you about the fireworks, he could have me arrested. I can't get a police record; my job with the NGO would be over."

"Shit!" Indy exclaimed.

"You see my point, then," Xander said.

"No, well, yes, well... crap," Indy said. "It's not you, but you saying 'record': It just reminded me that I have a bunch of recordings that I need to erase. I brought the recorder to work with me so I could get it done, and I completely forgot."

"And I thought my story was confusing: recordings?"

"Look, I can't explain it; let's just say it's something I don't want Plink Blayton to hear."

Now even more confused, Xander simply nodded and said: "That, I understand. Tell you what, I'll keep an eye on the drive-thru while you go into your boss's office and listen to whatever it is you don't want me hearing."

Not the best plan she'd ever heard — Xander's breasts were not going to get her many tips — she had to concede it was the best one at the moment. She was scared to death if she didn't erase the recording now she'd forget — and Plink would know everything. Taking a moment to write Scrote an official note saying she wouldn't be in tomorrow afternoon because she'd been invited to the event at Hope Falls Park, she knew he'd start harassing her about it even before he had time to gaze at himself in his office mirror.

That made it even better.

For the next hour, no one pulled through the drive-thru, as Indy hit the fast-forward button again and again, trying to find the moment when she'd entered the pavilion. But when she got to that point what she heard was not what she expected at all. Instead of just random snippets of people passing by, she had Scrote and the Bug's driver's full conversations, as well. Almost as if she'd planned it, the parabolic microphone had been aimed straight into the open window of the Bug. Realizing she was about to hear Scrote's uncensored thoughts, she had one thought: "Ick," and almost hit the delete button anyway.

But curiosity getting the best of her, she listened on. Coinciding with the longest period of quiet in Indy's time at Grind Me Hard Coffee, it was also the most well-timed. For what she heard on the recording explained much of what had gone wrong in her life — and maybe everyone else's. Eventually, she had to stop listening. Hearing this alone, sitting in Scrote's very office, was just too hard. She'd finish listening to it when she was with friends, friends who could do something about it.

"Xander! We have got to find Poe, NOW; he needs to hear this recording," she said, grabbing his arm frantically. "You have a car?"

"I have a van."

"Tell me it's not down by the river...," she said almost reflexively in spite of herself.

"And no government cheese, either," Xander said, now returning a smile that seemed much more than friendly. "That's cheating; that's not a movie line."

"So sue me," she said, grabbing his hand as they ran out the door.

Chapter 62
Fuzznut

Fuzznut's house was well-hidden at the end of a dead-end street along the beach in the Harrison District. One part house, one part gourmet kitchen and four parts costume closet, Fuzznut had spent virtually no time here in the last few days. Being a full-time dog kept him far busier than his preference, though for five-large a day, he was happy to have the problem.

Happy to be home, he was as he always was: naked save for an apron, his hands working a dish made from fresh crab meat over the open flame of a gas stove. The last of the crab he'd retrieved a few days ago, his dog job had kept him off the rocks for a few days. Frustrated, he had to admit it was probably a good thing; until the The Inn at Roca de la Muerte Dolorosa turned off its damned cameras he was at risk of being exposed.

Well, more exposed.

From the minute Poe had called him and told him about the video, Fuzznut knew he had a problem. An ample supply of crab and his massive hours as Bekk the Dog had allowed him to push it out of his mind. Both would be ending tomorrow, however, and soon he'd have to deal with his problem.

Lost in thought, he suddenly heard a voice behind him: "Nice ass. Your dog days are clearly a wonderful workout."

"Don't you knock anymore?" Fuzznut said, without even turning his head. He knew who it was; only one man in town knew where he lived.

"Only when you don't answer," Poe said. "I came by to get the eagle costume," he said, seeing it hanging next to the door. "You sure you just want to give this to the coffee shop?"

"I don't wear other people's costumes," he said, now dumping a crab alfredo dish onto two plates. "Besides, they can keep using it for promotions later on. Maybe they can hire someone to do backflips."

"What would be the point in that?" Poe asked, dreading the answer.

"Mascots don't have middle fingers; that's the only way they can flip someone the bird."

"Uhhh... it's a good thing your food isn't as nauseating as your jokes," Poe said, diving into what was a very late lunch. "Seriously, though. I know how attached you are to your costumes. You sure this is OK?"

"Yep, I know how hard they're working to keep that place open, and this is my way of helping. I still feel bad that I had to cancel on them because of this dog thing," he said. "Besides, at what the Tandys are paying me, I can buy a whole flock of 'em."

"Do eagles actually flock?" Poe asked.

"No idea," Fuzznut said, stuffing another wad of crab into his mouth. "I hate to think seagulls are the only ones that get all flocked up."

"You're killing me..."

"And apparently I'm not the only one trying," Fuzznut said, now getting quite a bit more serious. "Any idea who?"

"No, but I do have a few theories; I'm meeting with the guys here in a few minutes. And by the way, thanks for saving our lives at the lighthouse the other day," Poe said, worried that this was becoming an ongoing theme.

"Sorry I couldn't do more," Fuzznut said. "But as soon as I jumped up and screamed I had to lay right back down. Between the high grass and the sightlines in the costume, I have no idea where that guy went after he tipped the rock."

"No worries. Just glad you were there," Poe said, now using his finger to clean the rim on his plate. "When someone wants you dead, it's nice to have a stealth dog around. How much longer you in this job anyway? Kind of miss 'U. Otter B.' at the aquarium. That clown they hired: His balloon animals suck."

"Those aren't balloon animals; they're small intestines with feet..."

From the moment he was hired by the Tandys, Fuzznut had been upfront with Poe about what he was doing and whom he was doing it for. Fuzznut's only real friend in town, the Tandy job had started with virtually no notice and no free time, so he'd asked Poe to cancel and reschedule his various appointments and events for him. Telling Poe completely violated his agreement with the Tandys, of course, but he knew he could trust Poe, and considering everything that had gone down at the hospital that night, the decision had been a good one.

What Poe did not know was Mrs. Tandy's very live status. Indeed, until the night she "keeled over," neither did Fuzznut. He discovered her secret when he went to give her CPR. Clearly unprepared, he could see complete surprise register in her eyes are she stared right through the screen in his costume.

And then she smiled.

Deciding right then that he wasn't the only one trying to keep a secret, Fuzznut waited until the next day when the minister came and they were once again all three alone. Within minutes it was very clear that none of them were who they pretended to be — and that nothing needed to change. In all the years the previous "Bekk" had been with her, he'd never once stepped out of character, never done anything but respond to the wishes of the family. Giving her no reason to trust him, she never did. Unlike Fuzznut, who was clearly willing to walk away from the money and everything else to save her life. There had been nothing but honesty from that moment on. Certainly, he'd given her a hard time about making him think she was dying — and would continue to do so. But he understood her reasons for doing everything she had done, and he would respect them.

As he would her secrets, even if that meant keeping them from the only real friend Fuzznut had.

"So," Poe asked. "What's it like spending countless hours as a dog? Do you get to drink from the toilet whenever you want?" Poe asked, thoroughly enjoying himself. "What if they leave the lid down? Do you get dehydrated?"

"Has no one ever heard of a Camelback?" Fuzznut asked with exasperation. "And no, you're not funny."

"Seriously, though," Poe said. "Don't you get bored spending all day at the side of someone who does absolutely nothing? I have to imagine that's kind of hard; she seemed to deserve an end better than that."

"You have no idea..." Fuzznut said, stuffing more crab in his mouth to try and cover up his misdirection.

"In fact, how did you manage to get back here now?" Poe asked. "Aren't you her 'constant companion'?"

"Even companions have to sleep, and when she does they strip me down, run the costume off to one of their hotels to be washed, and I walk down the beach home."

"When you say, 'stripped down,' you do realize what that brings to mind," Poe said. "Never mind the hotel cameras; you are one ugly naked guy. If that's not a crime against Surfland code, it's certainly one against humanity."

"I keep a shark suit there; it's fun to tease the tourists with on my walks," he said, now turning serious. "Speaking of those cameras: What's the deal? I'm almost out of crab."

"Relax, my friend got them turned off, you're free to dive freely again, let us say," Poe said. "I'll tell you though, with everyone and their brother having a camera these days, you're going to have to think more about covering your ass when you're not covering your ass, if you know what I mean."

Before Fuzznut could respond, however, Poe's phone rang, and from the look on his face it wasn't who he was expecting. As Poe took the call, Fuzznut could see his friend's eyebrows seemingly rise to his hairline. Handing Fuzznut his plate, he headed out, grabbing the eagle costume along the way. Before heading completely out the door, he held his hand over the microphone and turned back to Fuzznut: "I'll see you tomorrow at the park; I think it's going to be a pretty interesting day."

Watching the door slam behind him, Fuzznut turned and walked into the kitchen, still talking to Poe even though he was no longer there. "You have no idea, my friend, no idea..."

Chapter 63
Poe

Rolling up to Bendovren Coffee in the Jag, Poe was surprised to find Rip, Indy and Xander all in the parking lot. All of their attention focused on Ryan, Poe suddenly understood why.

Standing at the rear of his car, Ryan's front was covered virtually head-to-toe in what looked like motor oil and black soot. Ryan seemed frustrated beyond words: "When I re-routed the compression system pressure release through the oil pan and exhaust, it wasn't supposed to have that much force..."

"Nor, I assume," Indy said, trying to be kind, "was it meant to go off before you hit the switch."

Absent-mindedly rubbing his jaw that was still sore from Tuesday, Ryan just kept staring at the car. "Uh, no... I've now gotten to learn that lesson twice."

"Is there time for Lesson No. 3?" Indy asked him, a smile now playing at the corners of her mouth.

"Lesson number...?" Ryan asked quizzically — before a knowing smile began to make its way across his face as well. "Certainly," he said, now grinning ear-to-ear in spite of himself. "There's no point going off half-cocked."

Now thoroughly mystified, Poe tried to get everyone focused again on why they were all here. "Look, I have no idea what you're talking about," Poe said, trying to keep it light. "But I think 'Lesson No. 3' should be Ryan going home and learning how to wash all that crap off."

"Who will watch the shop?" he asked, hoping he already knew the answer.

"I got it," Indy said.

"Won't Scrote get mad?"

"He always did have an inflated opinion of himself..."

With that, Ryan smiled again, hopped in his car and drove himself home, promising to be back as quickly as possible. Watching him go, Poe still had no idea what he and Indy had been talking about, or why he had suddenly seemed so relaxed after seeming so disappointed just moments earlier.

"Do you two always speak in code?" Poe asked Indy as he opened the door for her to go inside.

"James Bond movie lines; it's our thing," Indy said. "*Live and Let Die*, Roger Moore, 1973. Not the best Bond, but a pretty good movie."

"Whatever works," he said. "And speaking of such things, you said you had a recording that explained the last few days. As someone who's very much interested in living and not letting die — including myself — you mind explaining to me what's going on?"

When Indy had gone into Scrote's office to listen to her recordings, she found herself fast-forwarding and stopping a lot. She didn't want to go too far into the recording and have to rewind. As a result, she got to hear a rerun of her morning at the Wayside: "... I hate parking up the road; you can never find a crosswalk... the worst thing about this ocean is peeling off the wetsuit when you're done; it's how it must feel to be inside a condom... I want to see the whale blow up; I heard Florence Henderson will be there... That guy we walked by smells like anchovies and now I want a pizza..."

It was nothing she hadn't heard before, but she had to admit sometimes it got old. Indeed, the comment that she stunk was what had driven her toward the pavilion in the first place. She needed a break, and with the pavilion marked "Closed" for the Tandys' private use, she figured she might as well use it, since no one seemed to be in there, anyway.

Listening to her actions now several hours later, she could still visualize every step in her head. First, slinking in through the back door of the pavilion backwards. Second, the door clicking shut in front of the microphone. Third, a string of muffled and heavily echoed conversations about mistaken identity, the parabolic microphone clearly not designed to gather conversations that loud and that close. And finally, fourth, the sounds ending when Indy pulled the microphone out of her sleeve and set it on the open windowsill.

Finally hearing the "thud" she was waiting for as the mike hit the surface, Indy moved her finger to hit the delete key — and then froze at the sound of Scrote and another man's voice on the recording. She listened to all of it, speechless, growing angry and scared all at the same time. Grabbing it and her clothes, she sprinted from the office: "Xander!"

Still clearly agitated as she retold the story, Poe told her to calm down, that they would just listen to the tape together to see what it all meant. Honestly, he had a hard time believing that just one tape could explain the insanity of the last 72 hours. Not that Poe was the only one having a hard time believing things.

"You're the bum?" Rip asked, incredulously. "You're the one I gave $100?"

Indy seemed pleased she could so thoroughly fool even someone as astute as a P.I. "Guilty as charged. And thanks for the $100, by the way. My Mom and I really appreciate it."

Just as she finished, a bell rang, indicating that there was a car in the drive-thru. As Indy walked from the back corner where they were sitting to the window, Poe and Rip couldn't help but watch her go; they still couldn't believe the beautiful young woman they were looking at now was the street bum they'd seen face-to-face just yesterday morning. Just as they couldn't believe the $300 she now held in her hand.

"That was quick," Rip said. "Do you always get a $300 tip for not making anything? Let me guess, you pulled all of his kids out of a riptide."

"Just a friend," Indy said, now waving at the driver of the SUV as it pulled away.

Both Poe and Rip suspected there was more to it, but Rip's phone rang, forcing him to walk across the room to take the call. For Poe's part, the realization that Indy worked for Plink suddenly gave him the solution to a problem that had been dogging him all day. Promising himself he'd talk to Indy about that later, Poe now just wanted to get down to what was on the recording.

"So, let's hear it."

Pete's timing perfect, he got to Bendovren just Indy was preparing to press "Play." Poe, glad to have his friend back, said simply: "Glad you're here. You can catch up as we go along." Watching Pete's reaction, Poe thought he might want to say something. But Pete waved him off and Indy finally got to press "Play."

The beginning of the conversation didn't have many small details, but it did answer one major question: Who was responsible for the attempts on Poe's life at Bo's Beach and the lighthouse. Sometimes, Pete shot him quizzical looks, as he hadn't heard the story of how this recording had fallen into their hands. But when Scrote's unidentified partner wondered out loud who had warned them at the lighthouse, both of them shot each other a knowing look.

After that it was harder to hear; words like "jack" and "crushed" mixed randomly with the sounds of other people. Eventually, the recording became completely unintelligible as two surfers coming out of the ocean had stopped between the microphone and the Bug. Trying to pull her 280-pound boyfriend out a wetsuit, a much smaller woman was doing a lot of grunting, while he and his suit made groaning and stretching sounds. Ultimately, there was a scream as the suit pulled off of him and snapped her in the face. Thinking that a good place to stop, Poe said simply: "That's why I don't surf."

"That, and you're terrible at it," Pete said.

"OK," Poe said, tossing Pete a look, "You've had your knickers in a twist since you got here. What's up?"

"Someone tried to burn down Penny's Parrots," he said. "That's why I bolted out of Bo's Beach so quick. We got a 911 call from someone who thought it odd that someone was running towards the destruction instead of running away from it."

"I'm hanging on the word, 'tried'" Poe said, hoping that meant what he thought it did for one of his favorite breakfast spots.

"It's still there; your morning Explosiladas are safe; God I don't know how you eat those things," he said. The reason I bring it up is because whoever did it is the same one that burned down Mermaid in Oregon."

"And you think it's linked to this?"

"Maybe, maybe not, but everything that's happened to us in the last 48 hours has been incredibly peculiar, don't you think?" Pete asked. "And now this," he said pulling a white piece of paper from his pocket. Clearly at one time it had been wrapped around something. Now it was just a mostly-charred piece of paper with strange writing on it. "I found this on the outside of some kind of explosive that had been wrapped around the gas line at Penny's. But I have no idea what the explosive was, nor even the vaguest clue about the writing."

"It's Cambodian..." Poe said, only to have Rip finish his sentence: "...wrapped around Tannerite."

Rip had now returned from across the room having finished his phone call, trying quickly to help Pete through total confusion. "After poking around the beach, Xander told Poe he suspected Tannerite, and he had me check it out. While I can't be certain that's what that is, I think lab testing will prove that out. Interestingly, one of the few sources for Tannerite on the international black market is Cambodia. How did you know that?" he asked, now looking at Poe.

"A centipede told me," he said.

"Whatever," Rip said, knowing Poe would eventually explain himself. "It's pretty rare stuff, actually. A little of it goes a long way, if you know what I mean. In fact, the only domestic use I could find of the stuff, besides legal, was an arson fire at a Chinese restaurant in Portland six or seven years ago."

Poe, now anxious to get back to listening to the recording, asked rhetorically, "Is that a little too much a coincidence for anyone but me?" With a simple glance at Indy, he indicated she should restart the recording.

"Hold on," she said, "I see Ryan pulling up to the shop — he's going to want to hear this."

Coming in, Poe gave him a quick rundown on what they'd already learned. Still trying to figure out the Reader's Digest edition himself, he was able to explain it fairly quickly.

Why Indy wanted Ryan to hear the next section was clear to Poe the moment it began. Scrote had been after both Indy and the shop the moment he discovered both. The shop for its enormous windows fronting the road, and Indy for the way she would look inside it. Poe, who could sense she was growing angrier by the minute, wasn't surprised when she hit the "Stop" button and stalked across the shop.

Placing her hands on the counter and lowering her head to calm herself and catch her breath, she stood alone for a full minute before returning to the group in the back corner. Clearly, hearing it the second time hadn't made it easier.

Looking up the highway in the direction of Grind Me Hard Coffee, she simply stared out the window and said, "My vengeance will be sweeter for I have already planned its course."

"Bond again?" Poe asked.

"Nope," she, said turning to look at him. "India Marion Monroe. It's my legal name. My dad used to use it when he got really pissed, and that's how I'm feeling right about now."

"Indy," Poe said, now concerned. "As twisted as this is going to sound, it almost sounds like he's in love with you..."

"You noticed that, too, huh?" she said, though oddly not too concerned about it. "I've always wondered why he put up with so much of my crap. Don't worry, it's nothing I can't handle; once a pig, always a pig..." she said, her thoughts clearly elsewhere for a moment.

"Ryan," she said now turning to look at her friend, "I am so sorry you got caught up in this."

"Indy, this isn't your fault," he said, genuinely meaning it. "Besides, I don't see what your creepy boss has to do with Kinkel poisoning my customers." Trying to cheer her up, he said, "Let's keep listening; maybe there's something in here that will help." The look on her face saying she'd like to believe it, Indy pressed "Play" again. The discussion now turned to one of the folders, and it became very clear that the leather folder from To St. Helens and Back that Buffett had dragged back from his scrounging in the park was at the heart of all of this. Ryan grabbing it from the among the other auction items in back, he returned with it just as Indy hit the "Stop" button one more time. Handing the folder to Poe, Ryan sat back down next to Indy.

Opening the folder, and actually looking at the inside for the first time, Poe found several dozen spreadsheets. Each one was numbered, as was the folder. Not even close to an accountant, none of them made any sense to him. What he did recognize were numbers, from some type of account, and two names, though neither of them meant anything to him: "Who the hell are Kirby Ionescro and Ian? Who does this guy think he is, Cher?"

Indy spoke up first: "I have no idea who the second guy is, but the first one is my boss; his real name is Kirby Ionescro."

"And he goes by 'Scrote?'" Poe asked. "My God, he is deranged. Well, here's the good news, our mystery man has a name: 'Ian.' But the question remains: Why is this worth killing for?" Handing the folder off to Rip, he hoped his friend could make some sense of it. As a P.I., he'd spent a lot of time investigating the things — the not-so-legal things — that people did. And he did not disappoint.

"Well, I'd need to take this to my forensic accountant to be sure, but this looks to me like our friend Mr. Ionescro was embezzling like mad from To St. Helens and Back," Rip said, now pulling up Poe's old editorial on his iPad. "Yeah, this is what you and I were talking about the other day, Poe, remember? The son and the CFO were out scattering the kid's parents' ashes when they both died in that avalanche near Mt. St. Helens. Only to find out later the CFO had been robbing the company blind. Guess he wasn't the only one."

"Are you telling me that Scrote and this 'Ian' want me dead because they think I know what this folder means?" Poe asked, finding it nearly impossible to believe. "I'd never even seen this thing until two days ago, and clearly these little homicidal stage plays have been in the works for weeks."

"I don't know," Rip said, clearly trying to make sense of it himself. "You did write about the whole thing in the New York Times. Maybe he's pissed."

"That, and he reads slow," Poe said, clearly frustrated. "I wrote that nearly six years ago. Indy, you've heard the recording all the way through. Does this make any sense?"

"Actually, I haven't," she said. "This is right about where I stopped listening. I'm as lost as you are... No offense."

"No offense taken; I reserve that for nameless people who try to kill me for no apparent reason," he said, trying to return a little levity to the room. "Miss, if you don't mind, enlightenment awaits your delicate finger."

"Can I save the middle one for Scrote?" she asked, now smiling again.

"You may save all 10 for him," Poe replied. "Ideally in a curled position headed straight into his apparently favorite body part."

"Oh, my 10 fingers have far better plans than that for Mr. Ionescro..." Indy said. And leaving that hanging in the air again, she pressed "Play."

At first there was more discussion of folders; there were apparently lots of them. At the moment they were in Scrote's garage. Here, again, the recording got interrupted by someone who had stopped in between the microphone and the Bug. This time it went by quicker; a tourist who'd been feeding an already engorged seagull Wonder Bread seemed stunned that it had pooped in his hair: "Honey! Is this covered by the warranty?!"

Now the recording moved on to the poisoning. Here, Poe focused in one phrase: "Killed by his own poisoned beans." He'd been meaning to broach this subject with Ryan for more than a day, and he'd been avoiding it. That was no longer an option.

"Ryan, is that even possible? Could someone poison my beans? I mean other than Kinkel."

"I suppose. The delivery truck that brings the beans that I grind stops all over town," he said, understanding now beginning to dawn. "In fact, Grind Me Hard is the last place before it stops here! Son of a bitch!"

"OK, but why would that make everyone else sick?" Poe asked.

"Well, Kinkel always did grind too many beans per drink, and sometimes he didn't wash his hands after making a drink," Ryan said. "Maybe some of your leftover ground coffee got into other people's drinks."

"Great plan," Poe said, shooting it down even as he said it. "But I'm the only one that uses those particular beans. I pay extra for it, just like Plink and a bunch of other people."

"Heh, heh," Ryan began to snicker. "About that: The company that roasts our beans stopped making Plink's beans right after my parents left. Said he was the only one buying it. He's been drinking the same stuff as everyone else does for days. I just had them keep sending it in the same old bag so he wouldn't give me grief about it."

"He never tasted that you switched it?" Poe asked, "He's such an ass about that."

"Oh, please, he puts so much Splenda and crap in it anyway, he can't tell the difference. I could serve him Liquid Gold and he wouldn't know."

"Didn't he wonder why you lowered the price?"

"I didn't," he said, sheepishly. "I see the way he treats people. I call it a butthead tax. That, and it helps pay for all the Splenda he steals. He puts it in his pockets from the bar and takes it with him. My Mom was spending like an extra two bucks a day just to cover him."

"Stealing Splenda," Poe said, "Is there nothing... Ryan! What's the generic name for Splenda?!"

"White, fake, powdery crap?"

"No! No! The name on the ingredients," Poe said, now finally beginning to understand. "It's 'Sucralose,' isn't it?"

"I suppose so, why?"

"That's it! Dr. Bracewell told me that in my system they found both poison and sucralose!" Poe said excitedly. "At the moment it didn't really mean anything; a rare hot pink poison from a Cambodian river will do that to you, you know?"

Pete was now looking at him like he was crazy: "What are you talking about?"

"Don't you see? The coffee wasn't mine; it was Plink's! This whole time, they've been trying to kill Plink!"

Chapter 64
Pete

Pete had to admit it made sense: Every time disaster befell them, Plink was there, too.

And when he suddenly began to rebuild the events of the last several weeks, it was obvious: Plink was the one who had been waving the folder right here in this very shop all those weeks ago. If Scrote and his partner had been in here and seen that, they might have assumed he not only had the folder, but also was interested in what it held.

"Well, that's great, problem solved," Pete said. "We can call the police and go home now."

"No, that is not great," Poe said. "Because guess who's hanging out with Plink again tomorrow? There is no way the cops or anyone else are going to be able to make sense of this by the time of the park dedication."

"I'm still not sure *I* can, and I'm here," Pete said. "One thing I still don't understand: If all this Ian had to do was kill Plink, why not just shoot him, stab him, throw him off a bridge? Everyone in the city has thought about it. These guys were actually motivated and homicidal enough to do it. Why didn't they?"

"I think I can answer that," Ryan said, much to everyone's surprise.

Sitting quietly since discovering what had happened at his coffee shop, Indy and Xander had been getting him water, talking to him quietly and just genuinely trying to help him process it all. Clearly, on top of his parents' absence and his sister's accident, it was all a little much.

"Don't shoot me when I say this, but he's like a villain in a James Bond movie. It's not enough that he just kill Plink, he has to do it with a certain style, a certain flair," Ryan said. "The man clearly has certain passions, or shall we say, anti-passions: He's burned down one theme restaurant, tried to burn another, obliterated a fake whale, and whatever his link is to To St. Helens and Back, you don't get more kitschy than that. They had a woman being sacrificed every night at 7 and 9, for God sakes."

"Hey," Rip said, "I really liked her."

"Rip," Poe said, "don't start..."

"The point is, he doesn't just want to kill Plink, he wants to do it his way. You heard Scrote say to Ian on the tape, 'If you put that brain of yours to work making money instead of plans, there's no end to what we could do!' Clearly Ian is about the plan, and if you're not expecting something similarly big tomorrow, you're missing the point, I think.

"He's going to keep doing it until he gets it right."

After a long silence, Poe finally spoke: "Well, we know the what, how and when, at least the past whens. And thanks to Ryan we understand the why," he said, now smiling at the young man. "But we still don't know the who."

Clearly hitting his stride now that he was finding more answers instead of questions, he was anxious to get started.

"Indy, what do you say you press 'Play' again, and we'll see what other surprises lie in store?"

Chapter 65
Rip

Thirty minutes later and four times through the tape, they had no more answers than they had before. Looking across the room at Poe, It seemed to Rip that whatever burst of insight and energy he'd had earlier was clearly petering out.

Rip once again removed himself to take a phone call. During the last phone call, he'd had one of his employees do an Oregon plate search on vintage Bugs registered in Surfland, but that was a broad target, and even if they found something, it might be hours. His employee calling to let him know the bad news, Rip took the chance to give him the bank account numbers he'd found in the folder, in the hopes that those might lead somewhere. Walking back across the room towards his friend, Poe looked as still and lifeless as the people in the historical photos hanging on the wall.

"OK, one more time," Poe said. "Play the last part." Indy dutifully pressing the button, Rip could tell her heart wasn't in it, either. But she did it anyway, hoping the fifth time was a charm.

"STOP! I told you to never call me that! That man is dead! If I hear you speak it again, I'll kill you myself."

"Ian, I need you to look up my nostrils. See anything up there? I swear to God, all my hairs are gone."

BOOM.

"I—- An— —en you are such an asshole."

"Well, I think we all agree that whatever Scrote's talking about in the middle there, that clearly he has some kind of medical condition," Poe said. "Given the incredible asshole he is, I think we all agree we hope it's quite painful and permanent."

"Ppppphhhhhttttttt!"

"Indy?" Poe asked as she wiped water off of her chin. "Are you OK?"

"Yeah, just wishful thinking, I guess."

"I get that," Poe said, now getting back on topic. "It seems to me that whoever Ian is, that's not his real name, and had that blast not gone off precisely at that moment, we'd actually be able to hear a name."

Rip, appreciating the process Poe was leading them through, said, "So what else do we know about him? We know his first name starts with an 'I,' whatever it is. From the tape shot at the lighthouse and Indy's description we know that he looks like a generic Scandinavian guy. And from the brass tag on the jack, we know that he buys his hardware at a place that's been closed for nearly two decades."

"Maybe he has a Delorean and a Bug," Ryan said, trying to lighten the mood.

Now it was Indy's turn: "No way. He'd never be able to get it up to 88 miles per hour in Surfland traffic."

And finally Xander: "Sorry, but if I was going to go 'Back To The Future,' I sure as hell wouldn't do it just to steal a car jack. There's a lot better stuff than that to steal from this town's history."

Slowly, Poe began to sit up, and as he did so, he looked at Xander: "What did you say?"

Xander, not quite sure of why Poe was asking, talked slowly: "There's a lot better stuff in Surfland's history to steal. Like the Spanish treasure that's supposedly under Bo's, or the mobster that's supposedly buried under the pool at the The Inn at Roca de la Muerte Dolorosa, or..."

"That's it: History," and now rising from his chair, Poe began to look closer at the close to two-dozen historical photos on the wall. "I knew I'd seen him somewhere before!"

Only Pete dared to speak. "OK, you lost me again. What the hell are you talking about?"

But Rip knew Poe was onto something, and when Poe stopped and grabbed a photo off the wall, he was more anxious than anyone to see what his friend had found. "That's him," Poe said, now pointing to the photo. "That's Ian," and he tossed the photo to Indy.

Taking a long look, she agreed — sort of. "Maybe, except each of these guys are like a different Ian, one 20 years younger and one 40 years older — at the same time," she said, now obviously confused. "How is that possible?"

Now handing the photo to him, Rip could see she was right: It was two men sitting on the porch in rocking chairs, a grandson and his grandfather, the younger clearly the spitting image of the older. "You think Ian is the kid in this photo?"

"I know it," Poe said. "Take the photo out of the frame and read what's written on the back; there's usually a caption or something."

Flipping the photo over, Rip was careful as he bent back the tabs that held the cardboard backing in. Pulling it out, he could see Poe was right; there was writing. But the name wasn't Ian, or anything else like it.

"Sorry, buddy, no go," Rip said, as sorry as anyone to be back to square one. "The name says Isaac Andrew Niemen and The Captain, Matti Niemen."

"It says WHAT?"

"Isaac Andrew... Niemen... Oh my God..."

Without even looking up, he knew Poe was scrambling to look at the papers inside the folder again. Holding them up, Poe began tapping them with his fingers with a vengeance. "These don't say Kirby Ionescro and *Ian*! They're initials: 'I,' 'A,' 'N:' Isaac Andrew Niemen! Tell me I'm wrong!"

Rip, however, could not. Looking once again at his iPad, there was Isaac Andrew Niemen's obituary in The Oregonian: Isaac Andrew Niemen, son of the late Martin and Sylvia Niemen, killed in a snowslide in the Mt. St. Helens National Monument, December 2006. The sole owner of To St. Helens and Back, the last heir of a fishing and restaurant family that went back more than a century in Portland and on the Oregon Coast. There was even a link to a YouTube video of the slide sweeping him down the mountain into the lake to his death. No body was ever found, no service ever held, per Niemen's will.

Poe could barely contain his glee: "You were right, Ryan, Ian is an amazing planner, right down to faking his own death — until today. Isaac Andrew Niemen is alive — and we're going to catch him."

Chapter 66
Ian, a.k.a. Isaac Andrew Niemen

Embedded in every plan Ian made there was one constant: The Captain. What would the captain do?

That's why he always stayed here, in the old house south of Surfland; it had been their home. Never once did he consider staying at the family mansion on Anchor Avenue. Even when Scrote invited him over to talk about plans or finances, Ian preferred to do it in the car somewhere. The title on the house still bore the names of his parents, Martin and Sylvia Niemen, and since they and the family name had long since stopped having any meaning for him, he preferred to stay away from it altogether.

His new name, Ian Matthews, was a tribute to The Captain: Matti Niemen. That was the only name he answered to now. He'd chosen it nearly a decade-and-a-half before he became it, that's how long he'd had the plan. But now, sitting here on the deck in the same rocking chair as he had so often with The Captain, he had to admit it had only been a chance meeting that had allowed him to put the plan into motion at all.

It was shortly after Isaac had completed his studies at OSU, about 15 years after his parents had sold Niemen Salmon to a conglomerate and started their disgusting theme restaurants, To St Helens and Back. He was in the human resources department at his parent's corporate headquarters in some faceless building in downtown Portland, mindlessly wondering which nine-month-old culinary magazines to steal. His parents under the fanciful illusion that he actually wanted to work for them, he was waiting in the lobby to have his photo for his I.D. badge taken.

Sitting next to him was a man he would come to learn was Kirby Ionescro. Fired for sexual harassment of a co-worker and inappropriate use of a corporate bikini, he was waiting for his exit interview. Curious about who might be so morally bankrupt as to get fired from what Isaac considered the most morally bankrupt company on Earth, Isaac began a conversation, which Kirby was happy to continue. His friends called him "Scrote," he said, and before Isaac knew what was happening, the strange accountant with the funny name was going into exquisite detail about all the financially lucrative things he could have done for the company had he not been unfairly fired. ("I wouldn't have even talked to her if I knew she was lesbian," Scrote said. "I thought they had to wear jackets or something.")

But Isaac listened, a long-dormant plan once again beginning to bloom in his mind. And as he listened to Scrote's financial wizardry and total immorality, Isaac knew what he had to do. Inviting Scrote out for a drink, the night became a non-stop party, as did the next day and the next. Soon, Isaac confirmed what he suspected and hoped: That both of them had an equal penchant for greed, hating people, and doing whatever was necessary to accomplish their goals.

The two of them were quite the scene. Planning in the dark corners of LuLu's Tech-yes, Tit-yes Pleasure Palace — the only nudie bar in Portland with Wi-Fi — by day, they began to create the financial framework of their plan. And by night, they simply went out, got drunk and harassed women, half of whom Scrote seemed to fall in love with. They were, in their own way, legendary.

One particularly fun morning, Isaac just back from a trip to Vietnam, he and Scrote were still out boozing at sunrise. Whipping out his wallet, Isaac left the waitress a quarter-of-a-million in foreign bills on a $1,000 tab. Following her to the bank, both of them laughed as she tried to exchange her bills of Vietnamese Dong. She found them worth less than $50, and by the time she got done paying the bank, it was worth less than $20. She screamed at both of them; after having had put up with an entire night of them naming her breasts, "Frank" and "Creamy," it hadn't been even remotely worth it. Hurt, Scrote asked her if that meant the engagement was off.

By this time, Scrote was basically working for Isaac, though they were the only two who knew it. Sending Scrote ever more financial reports from the company — his parents thought he was taking an actual interest in what was going on — Isaac did his thing overseas while his partner figured out how to rob the company blind. When he came home from Cambodia in the winter of 2006, they were finally ready to put their plan in motion.

First was disposing of Isaac's parents. Expressing to a sudden desire to spend time with them on the mountain that had defined their existence the past 20 years, Isaac paid the money to have the road plowed and The Coldwater Ridge Visitor's Center opened just for them. Treating them to a gourmet dinner he catered himself, he told them both how much he loved them — and then cut the brake lines on their car. Watching them drive off down the road, it was last time he or anyone would see them alive. Their speed carried them through two guardrails and off one 200-foot cliff into a river. The coroner pronounced cause of death as "becoming paste," with only one notation at the bottom: Both of their stomachs were filled solely with faux crab meat and what looked to be 13 ounces of Filet O' Fish from McDonalds. The car was never recovered, just as Isaac had planned.

Next was killing off their company.

On the pretext of scattering their ashes, Isaac and the company CFO returned to Coldwater Ridge. Putting their ashes in a large backpack, they cross-country skied down to the shore of the lake. There, Ian killed him in a very ornate way involving fishing line, a frozen halibut and a halter-top with volcanic cones where the breasts would be. Then, Isaac pulled an inflatable dummy out of his backpack, and dressed it in the clothes he'd been wearing. Scampering back up the ridge now in white, he went unseen, even as he buried a small batch of Tannerite and an even larger pile of dynamite near the summit. Now returning to the visitors' center, he pressed a button — right on schedule — and set off a rock and snow avalanche down the mountainside. The rocks and snow crushed and pushed the bodies — both real and now un-inflated — to the bottom of the 200-foot deep lake. No attempt was ever made to recover them, just as Isaac had planned.

Meanwhile, on an opposite ridge to the south, an amateur videographer in a tour group recorded the whole thing and posted it YouTube. Though the grainy video gained thousands of hits, no record of who downloaded it could ever be found, though some vaguely remembered him as being a Romanian exchange student. Any doubt about the cause and finality of Isaac and his company's CFO had been removed, just as Isaac had planned.

And, just as Isaac had planned, in the coming days and weeks evidence would be found on the CFOs computer implicating him in embezzling virtually every dollar the Niemen family had made in the last century. (That and dozens of horrifying photos of several members of the wait staff doing something inappropriate in the volcano with the dishwasher — a Maytag.) The restaurant chain soon as lost to history as the fishing company Matti Niemen had founded, investors all over the Pacific Northwest could only wonder what foreign bank the late-CFO might have stashed their cash in.

That's where Ian Matthews was born, on the shores of a frozen lake, spawned by three murders — Just as he'd been planning for more than two decades. A cynical birth, or an idealistic one, from Ian's point of view, it freed him from ever having to deal with his parents and their legacy again. Giving Scrote a chain of coffee shops, a virtual never-ending supply of capital, and dozens of tool belts leftover from the restaurant chain, (they'd held ketchup and A-1) Ian headed back to Cambodia. There, he ran a backpacker bar and donated lots of T-shirts to the local orphanage. Grateful to keep the children clothed they never asked why all the girls' shirts had volcanoes over their breasts.

He laid low and kept to himself. Sometimes, people would wander in from Oregon and start asking questions, making comments. "You know, you look just like...," "Hey, anyone ever tell you that you bear a striking resemblance to..." Most of the time, they went away, casually dismissed as most drunk people are in a bar late at night. Sometimes, though, they persisted. Then, Ian would simply make a trip to the ammunitions market in Phnom Penh, buy some Tannerite or other creative means of killing someone, and execute a plan, execute being the operative word.

And so it was until the spring of 2012. That's when a dog pried open a podium he and his grandfather assumed would never be found, and a man found it, one who could never seem to be quiet.

That was not part of the plan.

So he returned to coastal Oregon, and when he discovered that his plans and Scrote's could still work together, they sat down and figured out what they would do. All along the way Scrote told him to keep it simple, and all along the way Ian would not, just as The Captain would not have. Sometimes Scrote would even complain, until Ian would remind him to relax, that he had Scrote covered. For one thing, The Captain had helped build the Bendovren Coffee building as part of the WPA and Ian wanted to own it. That, and that Ian still controlled the money.

Ever since then, however, the plans had not gone as planned. And as Ian sat in his small cottage south of town, he had to admit he was feeling increasingly pressured to come up with one. He'd been fortunate to have a copy of Plink Blayton's every scheduled move, but that ended tomorrow. And while he should have been comforted by the fact that he and The Captain had explored every inch of Hope Falls Park in his youth, he also knew the park had been massively cleaned up and changed. That's why the dog had been there in the first place. He was lost at the moment — never as he had planned.

And that's when his phone rang, the answer coming just as it had nearly a decade ago.

Chapter 67
Poe

Now listening to Indy's recording of Scrote and Ian/Isaac for a sixth time, everything became clear, and confirmed what they already knew to be true. "I— An— —en" was clearly Scrote saying "Isaac Andrew Niemen." And Ian saying, "That man is dead!' well, that spoke for itself.

What they needed now was a trap. Something to bring Ian in from the cold, so to speak.

"He wants that folder, right? Let's give it to him," Poe said.

"I have to be honest, Poe, of all the things I'd like to give him, a folder is not among them." Ryan said, clearly angry at what he'd been put through.

"Very true, and you'll have your justice — caffeinated," he said, not even really sure what that meant. "But right now, we know if we don't catch him first, he's going to raise hell tomorrow at the park. You said it yourself."

Ryan nodding, it was nevertheless Indy who pushed Poe to get to the point: "True, so what's the plan?"

"You are."

Twenty minutes later, everyone had to admit what Poe had come up with was a perfectly good plan. What still remained, however, was what to do with Isaac once they caught him. Here, Pete spoke up first: "Uh, isn't that the point where we call the cops?"

"Not yet!"

"How did I know you were going to say that?" Pete asked. "Why can't we just get rid of the guy? Seriously, are you this angry that he ruined your coffee?"

"No, but I am still pissed that your damn dog continues to have to sleep in the back of my car."

"Really, I am sorry about that." Pete said, now glancing out the window towards Pete's Jag. "But seriously..."

"And seriously," Poe said, now pulling it back a notch. "We still have nothing on this guy, not really. All I want to do is take him back to my house, sit on him a while and let Rip work a little bit of his magic. Lay a paper trail that a lawyer can't just make go away overnight. Ian's got the money to do it, you know. This man's nearly ended the livelihood or lives of everyone in this room, and a few other innocent people. He needs to answer for that."

"And don't forget about Plink," Pete said.

"You're right," Poe said. "I guess Ian isn't all bad."

Laughing, Pete asked, "No waterboarding?"

"None, though there is the little problem of how we convince him to come with us, and stay once we have him," Poe said. "As much as I dislike this guy, I'd rather not have to hit him with a rock every 10 minutes."

"I don't know, seems fair to my Jeep." Pete said. "And another thing: All of your plan is directed at Indy talking to Scrote. How do you know Scrote won't just show up himself?"

"You're a lot of fun, you know that?" Poe said. "Here's—"

But here, before Poe could go any further, Indy stepped in to talk: "Trust me, Ian will be here; he won't have a choice, if he wants his folder back. Scrote, I assure you, will be quite busy."

Saying it with a finality that brokered no further discussion, even Poe was done. Pete, however, couldn't resist: "I'm assuming you're planning to use your feminine wiles on him."

"What else would it be?" she asked, a steel edge still lining her voice.

"Oh, nothing," he said, trying to keep it light. "But if that's the plan, you might want to go chill a bit. Because, no offense, right now you are one scary bitch."

For a moment, Poe thought she might tear his head off. But then, much to his surprise, she started laughing, and after glancing at Ryan, went right back to talking to Pete: "The job is done, and the bitch is dead."

"Huh?" Pete said, now seeing a smile creep across Poe's face.

"Bond, James Bond, I presume?" he said.

"Very good, Poe!" Indy said. "I was beginning to think you were completely clueless when it came to Bond."

Pete, however, was clearly was still in the dark: "OK, one more time tonight: What the hell are you two talking about?"

Taking a cue from Poe, Indy simply said, "'Casino Royale,' Daniel Craig, 2006. Great Bond, great film."

Deciding at this point to leave well enough alone, Pete simply threw up his hands and started to sag at his knees. He wasn't alone; all of them agreed it had been a very long day and that tomorrow was likely to be one, too. Between the charity auction and fundraiser here tomorrow morning, the rededication in the afternoon, and catching a non-dead homicidal creativity junkie in the middle, everyone was looking forward to getting a good night's sleep, although one person's would be starting a little bit later than everyone else's.

"Indy, can I talk to you for a minute?" Poe asked her as they walked out to the parking lot. "If you need a lift home, we could talk on the way."

"No, I think I got that covered..."

Seeing her glance over towards Xander and his van, Poe understood — and promised her he'd make it quick. "Look first, thanks for be willing to go back over and talk to Scrote; I can't imagine how hard that must be for you. The guy really is a pig."

"Soon enough, yeah," Indy said.

"Huh? Let me guess: another Bond thing. Whatever; I clearly need to start watching more than just 'Bullitt' on DVD...," Poe said, trying to get back on track. "Anyway, I was wondering if I could ask you for one more favor before you go home. There's something I need over at city hall, and I think you can help me get it..."

Chapter 68
Indy

Driving up to her and her mom's house to pick up her boxes and supplies, Indy was grateful that Xander had been kind enough to let her borrow his van for the evening. Certainly, she could have walked, as she did everywhere else. But there was a lot to bring along tonight, and given all the other things that had been added to her list, it would help to move faster from place to place. Loading the boxes in the back with a dolly that was already in Xander's van, she was surprised to see Xander's backpack — and the Tannerite — still there. This worried her. Not because she was afraid it would go off; he'd told her how stable it was. But rather, the longer Xander held onto it, the worse it was going to be for him. Indeed, now thinking about it, she recalled she'd never once seen Xander make any attempt to talk to Pete the whole time they'd been together at the coffee shop. Indeed, it had almost been like Xander wasn't there at all.

Perhaps that was partly her fault, she thought as she started the drive to city hall.

Headed there to help Poe and his friend, Indy had time to reflect on how she'd acted at the coffee shop: She was going to tear Pete's head off there at the end. Only her almost reflexive ability to draw on a corny movie quote saved her, as it had many times in the past. Another thing her dad taught her.

Still, though, it bothered her that she'd reacted that way. Ryan had teased her about being a bitch before and she hadn't reacted that way, and so had others. Indeed, she used to be proud that she had a bit of a mean streak, as Mrs. Margaret would have called it. (Indy would never be "douchey.") It gave her an edge, in its own weird way — something else she'd lost in the last few months.

Parking now at city hall, Indy cleared her head as she hopped in the elevator and rose to the fourth floor. Certainly it was well after 5 o'clock, but Indy had a feeling Plink's assistant would still be at work. Which she was — and she was not alone.

"Hey, Pam," Indy said as she exited the elevator. "How's the Plink business?"

"Still crappy."

"I'm sure," she said, now turning to Pam's friend: "Hey, Donald, how's the locksmith business?"

"Still great; I get probably four hours a week overtime just in this office."

"Listen, Donald, I was wondering if you might do me a favor..."

And he did, though finding him there had never been part of Indy's plan. She was just going to use the key to Plink's office that Pam had Donald make for her. Until Pam and Donald had started dating, the repeated demands from Plink to be let into his locked office had been making both assistant and locksmith nuts — so he made her a key. That way, whenever Plink locked himself out, she would lie to Plink and say Donald was on his way, wait five minutes, walk the key back herself, and explain that Donald was still at the front counter, respecting his privacy. Playing to Plink's love of secrecy, this worked perfectly — and for Indy, too.

Slipping into Plink's office, the item in question was just where she knew it would be. Indeed, when Poe found out that she knew exactly what he was looking for, he could barely contain himself. Nor could she. For as she slid open his top desk drawer and pulled out the tape, one thought ran through her mind: One down, one to go.

Chapter 69
Scrote

Staring once again in his mirror, Scrote had shifted his focus from his nostrils to his eyebrows: They had gone almost completely blonde. He'd heard of people's hair bleaching in the sun, but this was ridiculous. Looking at the rest of his dark hair still atop his head, he wondered if Hair Club For Men had something just for eyebrows.

Sighing and returning to his desk, he once again started going through the day's receipts. Not only had Indy had closed the shop early, she'd just disappeared, leaving nothing but a note saying she wouldn't be in tomorrow. Amazingly, he found he was actually mad at her. As nice as he'd been, all the kindnesses he'd showed her, and she did this to him? He knew she was tired from working, and he had promised her to get more help at the shop. But it just hadn't worked out — for either of them. He'd tried to hire new employees, he'd even lowered his standards a bit — how could someone be a B and C cup? — but he still couldn't keep enough women working. And now this? Resenting the bind she'd put him in, he knew it would be a long time before he saw her again on Satur—

"Scrote! I'm back!"

Never mind.

"I am so sorry I had to go; my mom called, and there's the fundraiser tomorrow, and the auction... It all just got to be a little too much."

"That's not a movie line is it?"

"No, why?"

"No reason," Scrote said, thrilled that she finally seemed to be coming around. "You know, you could have held your auction here."

"You know, I thought about that," she said, wandering into his office to look in the mirror. "But you don't want that here. All it is is a bunch of old junk and kitschy crap: a T-shirt from an old horse race, a photo of some old famous drag queen juggling crabs — the edible kind — a beaten up leather folder from some old volcano restaurant in Portland, my old softball uni—"

"What?! What did you say?!"

"Yeah, my old softball uniform will be there," she said as she walked out of the office. "I don't know who'd want that old thing. Smells just like me."

Scrote didn't know which excited him more: the folder or the softball uniform. Both were a dream come true, but only one truly held his interest right now: "This old folder: where did it come from?"

"No idea," she said. "Some smelly thing some fireman was going to throw in the garbage. There were a bunch of papers inside, but they all got wet. I don't know, seems like crap to me. But, hey, it's all money for my mom, you know?"

"I do... What time is the auction?"

"9 a.m. Why?" she asked, now nicer than she'd ever been to him. "Do you want to help my Mom? That would be great! I want you to be there! See ya!" And with that she ran out the door.

Scrote couldn't believe it. Pulling out his phone, his fingers mindlessly began scrolling down to Ian's number. Through his mind ran three concurrent thoughts: He'd found the folder, her softball uniform was for sale, and she'd said, "I want you." When Ian picked up, Scrote said just one thing: "Get your ass ready for the nudie bar, it's time to go find Frank and Creamy."

Chapter 70
The Home of Martin and Sylvia Niemen

Indy climbed up the three decks of the monstrous beach house just as she had last night and the night before. Wearing all black, including her standard windbreaker, she did the same thing each night: Slink in the open sliding glass door into Scrote's bedroom, slowly pour a Dixie Cup of water and ground-up Temazepam down his throat, wait 20 minutes, and get to work. Honestly, as soundly as Scrote slept, the Temazepam was probably overkill in the beginning. But for the later part of her plan she knew it would be necessary, so she tried the very first night to see if she could get him to swallow it and not wake up. And he did not.

Just as he hadn't when he fell asleep in his office about a month ago. Staring at himself in his office mirror, he'd fallen asleep with his hair dryer still in his hand — while it was still on. Ryan, who was visiting her at the time, commented that she could do just about anything she wanted to him, and encouraged her to try. Curious herself, she wrung out a dishrag into a Dixie Cup and poured it down his gaping maw of a mouth, which was now pointing directly at the ceiling.

Nothing.

It was quite the discovery, and remembering a conversation she'd recently had with her father, made a decision. That's why almost every night for three weeks she'd been scaling the decks and sneaking inside, no one ever seeing a thing. This time, however, as she waited for the Temazepam to take effect, she returned to the deck to use ropes to pull up the box and supplies she'd brought from home.

Carrying them inside, she couldn't help but think back to the last thing she'd said to Scrote: "Do you want to help my Mom? That would be great! I want you to be there! See ya!" Ugh. Saying it almost made her throw up in her mouth, as did thinking about it again.

In truth, she hadn't gone very far when she left the shop. Returning to Xander's van, she simply drove across the street and waited. Seeing him leave, she returned to the shop, snuck back in — he never locked the drive-thru window — grabbed something from his office, and returned to the van. From there, she drove to Scrote's house on Anchor Avenue and simply waited to see all the lights go out. He had the same routine every night, and tonight she assumed would be pretty much the same.

Naturally, it was not.

Tonight, she arrived in time to see Scrote heading back out the door, hop into his testosterone-powered muscle car, drive south to pick someone up, and then head for the local nudie bar. Following him and now parking outside Boobkini's Tiki and Titty Hut, she saw that riding shotgun and now entering the bar with Scrote was Ian. Slipping in the back — she had gone on a blind date with the bouncer in high school — she saw both of them getting quite rowdy. Surprising, considering Surfland city code prevented anyone from actually stripping down to more than a bikini. Maybe that's why Ian had to get himself absolutely hammered — or why Scrote chose to drink very little. Curious about that, she had the bouncer ask the bartender if she knew why her customer wasn't drinking. Her answer: "He's getting married next week, to some local girl. And he doesn't want to get drunk and touch something that might get him punched in the balls."

Ick, ick, ick...

The truth was, however, Scrote's sobriety worked for Indy. If he'd had more than just a drink or two, she'd have been afraid of what the combination of Temazepam and alcohol might do to him, as tonight she needed to double his dose. She didn't want to kill the guy. What she had in mind was far worse. So she waited, until 2 a.m., when Scrote put his friend Ian in a cab and finally headed home himself.

Finally having pulled the box and supplies over the railing, Indy looked again at her watch: 2:45 a.m. She'd never gotten started this late before, nor had she ever had this much to do. But calculating it out, she knew she could still be done before the sun rose.

Her father had taught her well.

Chapter 71
Scrote

THURSDAY

Waking up well after the sun rose, Scrote couldn't believe how hung over he felt; he'd only had one drink for God sakes. Going to rub his eyes, he felt extraordinary pain as he almost stabbed himself him eye.

"Ow! What the hell?" Now actually opening his eyes, Scrote could see that where his fingers and thumb had been there were now black pieces of plastic that looked very much like hooves. Immediately, he tried to pull them off, but they were not only glued on, they were so slick that he couldn't use any part of his now three "fingers" to get a grip on anything else.

Now thoroughly confused, Scrote began to look at the rest of his body as he lay on his back. On his feet were similar plastic hooves, and atop that were what looked to be giant pink legs. He couldn't be sure, however, as he had a giant pink belly sticking out so far that it seemed to block his view. Noticing now that his feet were higher than his head, he began to realize that his butt was so big, it was actually pointing his legs in the air.

Struggling to roll over onto his stomach, Scrote finally did so and pushed himself to where he was sitting on his knees. At this point,

Scrote's attention began to focus on more than just his attire, as he began to realize where he wasn't: in his bedroom. Indeed, he wasn't in any room, as he was completely surrounded by trees.

Wondering now how the hell he ended up in the forest, Scrote began to turn slowly to look at his surroundings. He stopped when he suddenly saw something he did recognize: the mirror from his office. Again, talking to no one, Scrote began to speak: "How the hell did that get..." But then he stopped, as he stopped noticing the mirror and paid more attention to what he saw inside it.

He was a pig.

Encased in a pink foam rubber body-suit from head to toe, he was positively huge. Looking more like a bright pink pear than a person, he turned slowly from side to side, barely able to see that not only was his ass heavily padded, it also had a spiral tail attached.

Looking now to his face, he could see he was completely bald, but not shaved. His hair was just gone. Like it was never even there, save for his eyebrows, which were now completely white. His facial skin, now almost as pink as the suit he wore, seemed to just be an extension of the suit. Glued on the side of his head and covering mainly the tops of his ears, were two giant pig ears the same vibrant shade of pink.

What horrified him most, however, was his nose. It seemed to point almost directly out. Yes, there were some small prosthetics glued there to round out the shape, but the almost horizontal nostrils that made his snout were absolutely his.

"AAAAUUUUUUGGGGGGHHHHHHHHH!!!!"

Screaming for as long and as loud as he could, Scrote finally began trying to tear at his nose with his plastic hoof hands. It was no use; even if he'd had fingers they wouldn't have come off. Whatever they were attached with, it wasn't anything that wasn't coming off without taking his skin with it. Tugging on his ears, he found them similarly attached. Worse, as he struggled, he could feel the costume tearing at his skin inside, where the same adhesive had obviously been used. Some of it even appeared to be glued to his—

"AAAAUUUUUUGGGGGHHHHHHHHH!!!!"

Stopping now to catch his breath, he found he was incredibly hot and panting like a dog. Starting to feel dehydrated, he found himself wishing for a glass of water, and then immediately changing his mind; how would he pee in this thing?

Suddenly, the ailments he'd been experiencing over the last few days made perfect sense: his nose itching and its hairs falling out, his eyebrows going blonde.

Taking stock of his situation, he began look around the forest where he'd obviously been left. Most immediate was his full-length office mirror, nailed to a tree by whoever brought him here. Off in the distance, however, there seemed to be a dirt road of some sort. Accepting he was out of options, he began making his way to it along a small path that was likely created when he was dragged out here. Watching his feet carefully as he shuffled forward on his pig feet, he'd gone about 10 feet when he was surprised to see a pair of sunglasses lying on the ground. Picking them up, he knew immediately who they belonged to: Indy.

Indy had done this to him? But why? He thought she loved him. He thought...

He thought wrong, as always. Whatever she'd said to him last night, it was obviously just another damn movie game or some other thing. She'd told him her father was a makeup artist. Well here he was, her best joke ever. Crushing the sunglasses in his hand, he decided he had to find her. For revenge, for the hurt she'd caused him, for the chemical compound that would dissolve the glue all over his body. He had to find her, and though he suspected he was far too late to find her at the coffee shop, he knew exactly where she'd be this afternoon. She'd left him a note.

Finally at the dirt road, Scrote began walking downhill and what he assumed was west. Clearly a logging road, he knew it could be hours before someone came by, and even if they did, who the hell would pick him up? Hoping dehydration wouldn't become a problem before he got out of the costume, he couldn't believe his luck when a logging truck came down the road behind him just 10 minutes later. Sticking his thumb out — or what passed for a thumb out — Scrote felt his chances improving when the truck pulled over and the two men inside asked him to hop inside.

"Hey guys," Scrote said, Thanks! I wasn't sure anyone would—"

"I told you, Buford, this hear's a man-pig, from that SyFy movie," the driver said.

"Yep, I believe you're right," Buford said. "Him's special."

"Uh, guys," Scrote said, now starting to grow a bit nervous. "I just need a ride back to town."

"No problem," Buford said. "We'll get you there... eventually."

"Oh, no..." Scrote said, now genuinely worried. "Maybe you guys could just let me out here. I think I'll walk instead. Beautiful day, you know."

"Hey, boy," Buford said. "You got a real pretty mouth ain't ya?"

"Wait! Wait! I get it! This is that movie game!" Scrote said, now starting to get it. "OK, tell me: What movie is it?"

"What the hell you talkin' about, boy," Buford said. "This ain't no movie."

"Oh, no..."

Chapter 72
Poe

Poe's day started off as it had the previous one: Stopping at Pete's to pick up Buffett. Thinking he should be angry that he was still on dog duty, he now found that since Buffett had stopped farting all the time, he really wasn't that bad. There was still the dog hair issue, but since Poe didn't listen to music you could sing to in the car, his mouth was rarely open to actually inhale it.

Choosing the soundtrack from "Eternal Sunshine of the Spotless Mind" as a tribute to the beautiful day that lay before him, he was surprised to find Pete's wife and Buffett waiting out front for him. Seeing the Explorer nowhere in the driveway, Poe assumed Pete had already gone to Hope Falls Park, getting ready for the event. Pete's wife did not seem happy, and muttering something about a chiropractor's appointment, she simply waved at Poe before walking back in the house.

Loading Buffett in the backseat and heading back to the shop, he was glad he'd remembered to leave the eagle costume at the coffee shop yesterday afternoon. Having to pick dog hair off it once was enough. Arriving at the shop just a bit after 9 a.m. he was thrilled to see that Paxton was already in the costume, waving at everything that moved.

Walking inside, Poe was thrilled to see that the shop was full of people, all of them buying, either auction goods or coffee. Indy was greeting everyone who came in the door, and though she looked a little bit more tired than usual, she was clearly thrilled to be among friends. Even her Mom was there, sitting in a high-back plush chair next to her daughter.

Dick and Kinkel — he still wouldn't get near the Espresso machine — were running the auction for the 25 or so people gathered for that purpose. Kinkel would describe the auction item, while Dick would actually conduct it. His speech impediment not a problem, as no one understood auctioneers anyway, he could work a crowd like no one else in town, getting bids out of people that didn't even know they had money.

Poe flashing Dick a huge smile as he walked in, Dick cocked his head slightly and mouthed, "OK?" at Poe. Returning with a thumbs-up — Indy had texted Poe this morning that it was mission accomplished — Dick suddenly seemed instantly more energized.

"Fif-EE Dol-AH! Fif-EE Dol-AH?"

"Fifty!" Rip yelled, as he thrust his numbered card in the air.

Poe, walking over, couldn't help but ask: "Fifty dollars? For what?"

"It's awesome! It's a commemorative T-shirt from the All-Star Joan of Arc Memorial Horse Race and Bonfire," Rip said, never taking his eyes off it. "It's got Florence Henderson on it, and when you get her hair wet it turns orange and looks like it bursts into flames!"

"Never give me grief about my car again..." Poe said, still not believing that anyone would spend $50 on the thing.

"Sih-EE Dol-AH! Sih-EE Dol-AH?"

Once again, Rip thrust his card into the air, although this time he did stop to look at Poe. "You should be nice to me, I learned a few more things about our friend 'Ian.'"

"Do tell."

"Well, all those account numbers were from a Cambodian bank, and there must be millions and millions in there, though it's hard to say how much."

"Then, how do you know?" Poe asked.

"In Cambodia, you can bribe everyone to tell you everything—"

"And you suddenly went cheap?"

"Seh-Uh-EE Dol-AH! Seh-Uh-EE Dol-AH?"

Giving Poe a dirty look, he thrust his card into the air again, this time as much to answer Poe's question as to raise his bid. "No, that's my point — if you'd let me finish — however much money is in there, Ian made sure he's paid off anyone I could bribe. I may have $70 dollars—"

"Ay-EE Dol-AH! Ay-EE Dol-AH?"

"...Eighty dollars for a T-shirt," Rip said, thrusting his card in the air again, "But I don't have that."

"Good enough," Poe agreed. "Anything else?"

"Yeah, I did find an Ian Matthews on record as a property owner of a small backpacker bar in Siem Reap, Cambodia," Rip said. "I called, but the manager said no one's seen the guy in weeks."

"Ny-EE Dol-AH! Ny-EE Dol-AH?"

Pausing before thrusting his card in the air again, Rip turned his attention back to the auction. Smiling, he rose as Dick closed out the bidding: "SO! Fah Ay-EE Dol-AH!" Poe could only shake his head in disbelief: "You paid $80, for THAT?"

"I would have gone as high as $100."

"Oh my Lord," Poe said. "Well, if you don't mind, I'm going to grab a cup of coffee. Watching you is making my stomach ache."

"I'll come with you," Rip said, now rising to walk with him.

"What, no other crap to buy?"

"No, there are other things, but those come up later," he said, checking his list of items. "Right now it's just a donated DVD of 'Famous Rodent Sports Videos.' Who the hell wants that?"

Rolling his eyes, Poe headed over to see Ryan at the coffee counter. Waiting at the counter with him was Aly Oliviera: editor and ex.

"Well," Poe said, "Fancy meeting you here."

"You invited me to come," she said. "Promised me a big story."

"Yes I did, but you know me and my coffee," Poe said, handing Ryan a five dollar bill. "Keep the change."

Saying thank you as always, Ryan this time handed Poe something more than his cup: three small bags of ground coffee and an individual-sized French press. "What's this?" Poe asked.

"Well, it occurred to me that with 17 other coffee shops in town, you might occasionally be forced to go somewhere else, and I know how cranky you get without the right coffee," he said, Aly and Rip's eyes both rolling in response. "So I made you these little individual sized bags, and that way you can always have them and the press in your car."

"You didn't have to do that..." Poe said, genuinely appreciating the heartfelt gesture.

"And you didn't have to do what you did either," he said. "But it says something that Indy knew who we both could trust."

Truly speechless for one of the only times in his life, Poe put the small bags of coffee grounds in his breast pocket. Promising to grab the press before he left, we went with Rip to sit down with Aly. Kindly, she allowed Poe another minute before going on.

"You mentioned a story..."

"Indeed I did..." Poe said, and over the next hour, he told her about pretty much everything that had happened over the last three days, and indeed weeks. There were still some loose ends, of course, but he'd wanted to talk to her now. Ryan needed to get the word out about what had happened at Bendovren Coffee ASAP, and Poe wanted to ensure today was Plink Blayton's last day, assuming Rip had found something.

Waving the P.I. over on a hope, Poe could clearly see Rip didn't want to leave the auction. His whining when he arrived confirmed it: "Seriously? There's an autographed picture of Raina Bowe juggling crabs, the edible kind."

"Shut up," Poe said, patting a seat next to him and Aly. "I'll have her come by The Seabiscuit and juggle some. You can take as many pictures as you want and have her autograph those."

"Well, OK... What's up?"

"Did you ever fill in that gap in Plink's life?"

"Did I not mention that? I got the info back last night." Poe's furrowed brow answering Rip's question, the P.I. got started: "Well, there was this gorilla, see..."

Within 20 minutes, Poe — and the editor of the local newspaper — knew everything. Indeed, Rip planned to make a call shortly to the Columbus, Ohio, police department, so that the Surfland PD might get a warrant for his arrest. All of them agreed, however, that it would be best to let him finish out the day's events at Hope Falls Park. Given the special efforts it had taken to get Mrs. Margaret to the event, they didn't want to do anything that might upset her delicate condition.

One more bad person about to take the fall for their own misdeeds, Poe saw it was coming up on 11 a.m., the end of the auction. Looking over at Indy, she returned his smile and flashed four fingers on her left hand, and pretended to pull a slot machine with her right. Meaning $4,000, he assumed, it had been a better fundraiser than anyone could have imagined.

Only one thing remained, however, but it was huge. The last item was coming up for bid, the leather folder from To St. Helens and Back, and Ian was nowhere to be seen. Looking around the shop, and into the parking lot, Poe saw neither their prey nor his vintage Volkswagen Bug. Poe began to worry that their day at Hope Falls Park might not go so smoothly after all.

Chapter 73
Ian

Where the hell was Scrote?

Sitting in the parking lot down at the GO River Wayside, Ian's partner was supposed to have been here an hour ago. Hell, he was the one who had drunk like a fish, not Scrote. Rubbing his temple once again, he began to remember why even owning a backpacker bar, he choose not to drink much anymore.

When Scrote called him last night saying he had a plan, Ian's initial reaction was dubious. Scrote did not usually have the kind of plans Ian liked. But the more Scrote explained it, the better Ian liked it: Forget killing Plink; they didn't need to, anymore. And the folder and spreadsheets? How daring was it to walk right into a crowd, in a city he once called his own, and get what he wanted? Right under everyone's noses! Perfect!

It did, of course, occur to Ian that it might be a trap; Scrote's belief that suddenly Indy was actually in love with him seemed just too good to be true; impossible, really. But given Scrote's complete inability to read women, he could have said she hated him, and he'd still take that as a good sign; at least she was talking to him. That, and the fact that the auction had been scheduled for weeks, led him to believe that this might in fact be the real deal.

To assuage his fears, however, Scrote promised him he'd walk up from the wayside first, just to make sure it wasn't a set-up. If anything were amiss, he'd call Ian off; they'd get the folder another way. Maybe just follow the buyer home. Not elegant or daring, but one way or another, Ian had to admit he was ready to get back to his quiet life in Cambodia.

Content that there was finally a plan, and even a backup, Ian knew The Captain would be proud of what he'd come up with. As Scrote had suggested in his phone call, it did seem like a good time to go out. They hadn't done it in years, and even if his face did register with anyone after 20 years, Ian would be out of the country by this time tomorrow.

Still staring out the window looking for Scrote, Ian pondered the last loose end: The folders in Scrote's garage. Even last night, Scrote had been willing to go home and just burn them, and Ian almost let him. But once again, The Captain held him back. Maybe he could sneak them into a construction site and hide them in an unfinished wall, or lock them in some type of waterproof crab trap and then hide them on the bottom of Lenobar Bay, or...

KNOCK! KNOCK!

Turning suddenly to the left, Ian was surprised to see a woman standing next to his Bug. Having his attention, she shouted through the closed window: "Excuse me! My husband is stuck in his wetsuit and needs help getting out. I think it's become wedged in his colon!"

Tossing her a dirty look and his middle finger, she stomped off as Ian turned his attention back up the hill towards Bendovren Coffee. Looking at his watch, Ian could see it was almost 11 a.m., and wherever Scrote was, it obviously wasn't here. Stay or go? Stay or go? This was not part of the plan.

Finally, Ian decided to walk up the hill to Bendovren Coffee. He'd go slowly, checking the place out through the windows to see if it was a trap. Again, that seemed unlikely; no one even knew who he was. But if he'd learned anything this week, it was that plans often go awry. Stopping to pat his ankle just to be sure before he got out of the car, he started making his way up the hill. He thought Scrote would be proud of him, even if The Captain wasn't.

Walking into Bendovren Coffee, Ian felt like he was walking into the lions' den; he'd almost killed the man standing by the barista — three times. He even recognized Indy from his trips through the drive-thru at Grind Me Hard Coffee. Even more beautiful now that he could see her from the waist down, she was walking around the room with a giant jar of coins taking donations. The man behind the counter, the one he'd tried to run out of business, busied himself with making a cup of coffee and opening a bottle of water.

The lions had no idea who he was.

Looking around, still a bit wary, all continued to seem in order as he took a seat near the auction table. He jumped a bit when an eagle mascot came back inside and two children screamed, but soon everything was calm again, and Ian began to relax once more. The bidding just having finished on a gift basket of Crisco and vice-grips donated by a local wetsuit shop, Ian saw he was just in time for the auction of the folder. At first, this made him nervous; he didn't like the timing. But when the young man announced it was the last item because no one had made a bid when it was up earlier, that made sense to him.

Showing the folder to the crowd, the young man explained its history, where it was found, and what was inside. As he opened it up, he could see that the papers inside were indeed wet and smeared by their short time outside. (None of the ones in Scrote's garage bore such marks.) More certain than ever that nothing had been learned from the spreadsheets in the folder, Ian knew his problems were over once he got the world's last piece of To St. Helens and Back, back.

"Wuh-Huh-Neh Dol-AH! Wuh-Huh-Neh Dol-AH?!"

"One hundred dollars?" Ian asked out loud.

"I hah Wuh-Huh-Neh Dol-AH!"

"What?" Ian said. Clearly, Ian would pay whatever he needed to, but he was simply stunned that it had begun so high — and that he'd just made a bid.

"Tuh-Huh-Neh Dol-AH! Tuh-Huh-Neh Dol-AH?!"

Before Ian could even process that — it was going up $100 a bid? — Ian was surprised to find someone else bidding on it: "Two hundred!" said a man wearing a hideous aloha shirt.

But now it was Ian's turn, and this time he didn't delay, "Three hundred!"

The man with the ugly shirt now stood up and raised his card again: "Four Hundred!" — and this time he spoke to Ian: "This was my favorite place growing up," he said, "And I just really want one of these old menu covers, you know? That place was just so real; everything really taught me something about life, about nature."

Too offended to give him a response, Ian yelled, "$700!"

At this point, everyone in the room seemed stunned. Even the barista, who was holding a cup of coffee out in his hand seemed speechless, if just for a moment: "Excuse me sir, would you like a free cup of coffee? As a thank you?"

"No, thanks," Ian said, wanting to get back to auction.

"How about some water, then? It's bott—"

"NO!" Ian yelled, now turning his attention back to Dick and Kinkel. "I'll give you $1,000 right now for the folder!" Staring over at the man in the ugly shirt, Ian was daring him to outbid him. At his mention of Ian's parents and their abomination of a restaurant, this had become personal. Seeming to realize that, he simply held up his hands and began to sit back down.

Finally beginning to calm back down, Ian was taken aback when the man in the ugly shirt said: "I assume you have that on you? It's yours, certainly. But as this is all for charity, I'm sure everyone would like to make sure you have it. That's quite a bit of money."

"Well, of course I have it," Ian said, now happier than he had been since he returned to Oregon. "It's right here..." and opening his wallet, he began to pull out a pile of $100 bills. Counting out 10, he was just beginning to look up when Indy began to approach him with her jar of coins.

He started to speak to her, saying, "I don't have any coins, I'm afraid this is—" But before he could finish, she suddenly tripped and sent the jar flying straight towards his head. Trying to get out of the way, it was no use; it was like she'd thrown it right at him.

And that's when he realized she had.

Slipping into to darkness, the last thing he remembered was her grabbing the bills out of his hand, before whispering one word in his ear: "Douche."

Chapter 74

Poe

"Douche?" Poe asked, as he grabbed Ian's hands and started to move the unconscious man into the back storage room. "That doesn't really seem like your kind of word."

"Got it from a friend of mine," she said, holding Ian's feet by his boots and struggling to get him through the door.

"I can't see James Bond saying that, so I'll take you at your word," Poe said, now finally letting Ian drop on the floor of the storage room. Breathing heavily, he paused for a minute — gotta stop eating those cheesy sticks, he thought. Stopping to pick over a small manila envelope that had fallen out if Ian's left pocket, he glanced inside it briefly before putting it in his own pocket.

"More money?" Indy asked hopefully. "No, passports, quite a few of them. I have a feeling our friend here was getting ready to leave town."

"He does like to plan ahead, doesn't he?" she asked.

"Unlike some people, apparently..." he said, now looking at Indy. "Knocking him out with a change jar? Please tell me that wasn't your original plan. For one thing, Ryan's going to be picking change out of the planters for weeks."

"No, my original plan was to drug him," she said. "But when he wouldn't take the water or the coffee from Ryan, I had to come up with a backup plan."

As if on cue, Ryan suddenly appeared with a small, slightly milky cup of water. Taking it from him, Indy kneeled down, and poured it down Ian's throat. "That should do it, for quite a few hours, I should think," she said.

Poe continued to just stand there, not quite sure of what he was seeing. "Why do I get the feeling you've done this before? And what did you just give him?"

"Temazepam," she said. "It's what all the stars use in Hollywood."

"You mean all the dead ones who O.D. on crap?" Poe asked.

"Don't worry; he'll be fine," I didn't give him that much. "The knot on his head going to hurt him more than the drug."

"Remind me never to piss you off," Poe said, now starting to laugh.

Laughing a bit herself now, Indy turned to Ryan, pulled $2,300 out of her pocket, and gave it to her friend. "Here, that's for the shop; it's all the money in Ian's wallet."

"I can't take this; this was for you."

"No," she said, now placing her hands on both his shoulders. "This man tried to destroy what you and your family have built. This will help put it back together."

"I don't know what to say..."

"Promise me you won't do anymore crazy shit with your car," she said. "That's gonna get you killed."

Leaving Indy, Ryan and Ian in the storage room, Poe had to admit it hadn't gone down as planned. But Ian was down — and that was all that mattered.

It had been Indy who'd seen Ian coming up the hill; she wondered if he hadn't parked at the GO River Wayside. With ample warning, they all got into their assigned places, even though Rip, Ryan and Indy were the only ones who had any idea something more than just an auction was afoot. Only Kinkel's statement about the folder's place in the auction was a lie, and even he didn't know it. He was told they'd tried to sell it before he arrived.

There was one other problem now, however: How to get Ian out of the shop? To keep anyone in the gathered crowd from calling 911, Rip had told everyone the injured man was now doing just fine in back; he merely needed some air. That in mind, they certainly couldn't just carry Ian's insensate body back through the lobby.

They couldn't just leave him back there, either. All of them were scheduled to attend the park dedication; Ryan was even going to close down the shop early. A special request from Indy earlier in the morning, he told her he wasn't sure he could. Now he had 2,300 reasons to say yes, and Poe was certain he would. Indeed, with the folder auction going down after 11 a.m., they were running late as it was.

Rip now coming over to Poe near the counter, Poe simply handed him Ian's envelope full of passports. Looking inside much as Poe had done, Rip quickly reached the same conclusion Poe and Indy had: "Someone was looking to get of here in a hurry..." Rip said, now sticking the envelope in his pants pocket. "I'll have my guys add this to the increasingly large file we have on Isaac, Ian, and whatever other names we find on those."

Now glancing into the storage room at Indy, Ryan, and a prone Ian, Rip couldn't help but smile as he patted Poe on the back. "Well, not exactly textbook, but, hey, we figured it out along the way."

Returning the compliment, Poe said, "Hey, all that stuff about To St Helens and Back being 'so real,' and how it 'taught you something about life,' that was good. You really egged him on. Gotta admit, I didn't quite know what you were going for there, but it worked."

"Actually, I meant all of that," Rip said, "though it did seem to get us done faster..."

For a moment, Poe could do little more than just stare at his friend. Deciding, though, that there were just some things he would never understand, Poe let it go and moved on to more important things.

"You're sure you have copies of those papers from the leather folder?" Poe asked. "I'd hate to think we ruined our only evidence."

"Nope, scanned 'em in myself," Rip said. "Besides, Indy told me this morning that all the other folders truly are in Scrote's garage and waiting. I sent my forensic accountant over there this morning."

"How did Indy know they were actually there?"

"No idea," Rip said. "She just found me this morning before the auction, told me where they were, and said that the garage door was unlocked. You wanted rock-hard evidence, and now you're going to have it."

Poe was curious as to how Indy would know where the folders were, but thankful that another loose end was being tied off. He now turned his attention back to the problem at hand: How to get Ian out of here and into Poe's car. Almost as if he read Poe's mind, Rip jabbed him in the ribs and said: "So, Poe, have a plan for getting our unconscious friend out of here?"

"I suppose throwing out a whole bunch of people that are giving you money is kind of tacky, isn't it?" Poe asked, already knowing the answer.

"Yep, especially when they're still all scrounging for change to give back to Indy," Rip said, gesturing out at the lobby. "You know, they've picked nearly $4.50 in dimes out of the eagle's beak alone. I don't think they're going to be flying out of here anytime soon, if you know what I mean."

"That was terrible," Poe said.

"Yep, I know, that's why I said it."

"And it was genius..." Poe said, now starting to walk towards Paxton in his eagle costume.

"Yes it was," Rip said, now starting to follow him. "Why?"

"Because Ian IS going to fly right out of here."

Five minutes later, Poe's solution seemed a good one.

Paxton had taken off the eagle suit and laid it on the floor. It was the kind with two zippers, one running from each wrist, through each neighboring armpit, and to the ankle immediately below. Not the most popular kind of suit among performers — it was a pain in the ass to get in and out of — but it allowed the illusion of an unbroken front and back, as the seams were hidden in the folds of the costume on each side. Even the wings seemed perfect, as the four-fingered mitts were sewn into the end of the wing tips.

Today, however, the design would serve another purpose. Lifting Ian in the same way they carried him into the back, they laid him on top of the back of the costume. Then, laying the front piece on top of him and stuffing his hands into the wing-tips, they'd zipped him into it. Encasing each of his Birkenstock-covered feet in a giant yellow foot, they then strapped the fake head onto Ian's with the chin strap.

"Voila!" Poe said triumphantly. "Ian Eagle Flight 1, non-stop to my trunk."

Paxton, ever the mascot, spoke up. "Aren't you worried that the kids out there are going to see you carrying the eagle costume out of here and freak?" he asked. "They're either going to think you killed me or skinned me."

"Good point... Ryan, can you go out there and manage to get all the kids in the back corner? Then we can go out the front door unseen."

"No problem," he said, "I'll just drop more change on the floor back there. They seem to like that."

Watching Ryan head out, he waited a few minutes before he tossed Ian the Eagle over his right shoulder and headed out of the storage room. Not exactly flying out of here, he had to admit, but good enough.

Having Rip scout his way and make sure there were no unforeseen obstacles or kids, Poe walked quickly to the door, making sure to grab his French press on the way out. As he planned, he was out to his car in the parking lot behind Bendovren in less than three minutes. Indy followed right after him, preparing to ride shotgun with him. Pressing the trunk button on his remote, the lid rose to meet him, and he tossed Ian into the 18-square foot trunk. Noticing the chin strap had come loose, as had the head, Poe pushed the fake head back onto Ian's real one and closed the lid.

"Well," Poe said, "let's go to the park."

"You're just going to leave him in there?" Rip said incredulously. "What if he wakes up?"

Indy answered for Poe: "Trust me, he won't."

Rip once again looked at Poe: "You're really just going to leave him in there all afternoon? He could get hurt."

"Yes." Poe said simply. "Besides, both Indy and I need to be at Hope Falls by noon, and I don't intend to be late because of this A-hole — and you shouldn't be either."

"Why?" Rip asked.

"They're giving away commemorative T-shirts and limited edition pet rocks they found during the clean up." Poe said.

"Let's go."

Chapter 75
Indy

Riding with Poe out to Hope Falls Park, they were on track to be on time, until traffic started picking up on the road. Worried they would be late, they shouldn't have been; it was Plink's fault, and everything had been pushed back an hour. The line to get in was nearly half-a-mile long, and realizing this, Indy took advantage of the long wait to take a much needed catnap. Finally reaching the entrance to the park, Indy could see Plink had his staff checking every car coming in, segregating them by importance, and relegating anyone who wasn't working or media to the outer regions. Waking from her slumber, Indy saw a face she recognized as Poe rolled up to the checkpoint.

"Hey, Pam," Indy said, grateful now for the convertible top. "Nice to see Plink's finally letting you do something."

"Yeah, stand out on a damn road and piss people off when I tell them they can't park here because they're not on the list," she said bitterly. "Kind of like you're friend, here. I don't see a Jag listed anywhere on my clipboard."

"Look under Jackson Poe," Indy suggested.

"Nope, nothing," Pam said, as Poe started to grumble.

"What an asshole!" Poe said.

"Oh, you must know him," Pam said. "Never mind, go right in."

Laughing, Indy told her thanks and asked her for one more favor: To look out for Ryan in his Alpine Sunbeam. As late as he might be getting here, she didn't want him to have to walk too far. Promising to let him in, Pam waved them forward. Still, Indy could hear Pam talking to the next car in line as they drove off: "Yes, I know you're the mayor, but…"

Parking on the far side of the parking lot near Xander and Pete's cars, Poe let Buffett out of the backseat, not really worried about where he was going. He'd been willing to let the dog sleep in the back with the windows cracked at Bendovren, but that was a friendly spot to Poe. Here, there were too many unknowns, and he turned on the alarm as he locked to the car up.

"Are you going to check on Ian?" Indy asked.

"Certainly," Poe said, as he walked over to the trunk, pounded on it with his flat hand a few times, and walked away. "He's good."

Heading with Poe into the park, Indy had to admit, for the first time in quite some time, she was having a very good day.

She was also having a long day, starting at 2:30 a.m. when she'd first gotten on to Scrote's deck. She'd worked quickly, as she knew she'd have to, but she'd been planning this for weeks, and now it was about to happen.

After discovering that Scrote could sleep through anything, an earlier conversation she and her father had had about the movie *Farmagddon* crept into her mind. If he could turn a sexy Hollywood actress into a farm animal, why could she not do the same with a coffee-shop owning scumbag? Running the idea by her dad — he'd been hearing her Scrote stories for months — he thought it was a great idea and over a period of weeks sent her nearly everything he'd created for the move. (*Farmageddon II: Sheepocalypse* having been yanked from the production schedule, the costume was on the way to the dumpster, anyway.) The last item, the body suit, had arrived just a few days ago, and Indy was delighted to see the bodysuit and the pigment colors she'd been injecting into Scrote's skin matched.

Some things, of course, she'd done before tonight, like slowly turning all of Scrote's facial skin bright pink. It had itched tremendously, of course — which was why she also injected it into his ass just for fun. Bleaching his eyebrows, making his nose hair fall out, that was all done on earlier nights, too. Part of it was that some things took time to develop, like the skin color, and part of it was that she wanted to get done what she could early, as she new the last night would be a lot of work.

That, and it was making Scrote crazy.

Every day she watched as he tried to ignore what he saw happening to his body. The hours he spent looking in that mirror in his office trying to make sense of it: often, that was the only thing that got her through the day. The majority of the work, however, had to be done the last night, and given that she had to start two hours later than she expected, she was glad she had gotten so much done earlier.

The first thing she did was cover his head and ears with Nair. Letting it stay there for a while, she sliced all his clothes off him — even his undies — and covered his body with a kind of skin-safe Super Glue. It would come off with a dissolving compound made by the same company, but without it, it would stick to anything, damn near forever. Designed even for underwater use — her dad had worked with it on "Mermaids Do Manhattan," when he'd had to glue a fake dolphin tail to a prostitute — she might as well have been preparing to weld the prosthetics on.

Covering his body with the glue — all of his body — she was committed to making Scrote as miserable as possible. Rolling him over from his stomach to get the glue on his front, she felt herself starting throwing up in her mouth for the third time tonight. So much for two layers of gloves doing the trick. That done, she pushed, pulled and manhandled his body into the costume. Coating his hands and feet in the glue next, she then put on the hooves.

All that remained now was his face and head. A suitable period having gone by now, she took a rag and water and wiped the Nair from his head. All his hair coming off with it, he was now bald as a cue ball, save for his eye brows. Now using the glue one last time, she attached the pig ears to his real ones, and used more padding to round out his nose.

But it was his nostrils sticking almost straight out that Indy was the most proud of, because it was her father who invented the technique. Acquiring defective heart-stints from surgical supply companies, he'd reasoned that while they might not suitable for holding life-giving arteries and valves wide open, they might work quite nicely for holding open noses. And they did; wonderfully, in fact. Using them on werewolves, cat people and other mammalian-human hybrids in the movies, he'd scored their maximum effect when he'd created, "Ursinia: Queen of the Man Pigs," and her man-pig slave, "Wilbabe."

And now Scrote.

Looking at her watch, Indy realized it was only half an hour or so until sunrise. She'd originally planned to use a rope and belay system to pull him off the bed, onto the deck, and then into a position where she could lower him to the ground below. From there, she planned to simply roll him onto the beach. Having Ryan's van, however, had given her the option of leaving him ditched in the forest, so she'd opted to do that instead. That did not, however, solve the problem of getting him out of the house and into the van, and all in under 30 minutes.

Gathering up all of her things into her backpack, save for one thing she intentionally left on the bed, Indy then ran downstairs and into the garage, where she turned on the light and looked for something that might help her out. The first thing she saw did, but not in the way she needed it; they were the folders that Scrote and Ian had talked so much about. She still needed a way to move Scrote, and quickly. Certainly, she could leave him in his bedroom; he'd still freak out. But she'd been dreaming for the last two days about abandoning him in the woods, and she didn't want to give up just yet.

And then she saw it: An elevator in the corner of the garage. And while she couldn't believe anyone was rich enough to have a personal elevator, she'd heard some beach houses had them, and now here one was. Climbing in and taking the elevator to the third floor, she found it opened around the corner from Scrote's bedroom. That's why she'd never seen it. Taking it back down, she'd solved the problem of the stairs, but not how to move him all the way down the hall and into the van.

Returning to the garage, she looked for anything that would roll, anything she could move him with. Other than Scrote's car, there was nothing. And then she remembered: the dolly in Xander's van! Turning the light off in the garage again, Indy opened the garage door and ran to get Xander's van to back it inside. From there it was easy: She took the dolly up the stairs, strapped Scrote to it, took him back downstairs, rolled him into the back of the van, and took off, the garage door closing just as the first rays of light were beginning to break over the city.

Heading east, out past Hope Falls Park onto one of the logging roads, Indy had to admit she kind of felt stupid. Knowing the elevator was there earlier would have made things a lot easier. Whatever; soon she came to a spot she knew well, about 10 miles up an old logging road. (Again: the blind date with the bouncer.) Rolling the dolly and Scrote back out of the van, she dragged him through the forest, about 300 feet from the road. It would have been perfect had she not tripped and accidentally rolled the dolly over. Temazepam aside, God the man could sleep...

Deciding here was as good a place as any, she unstrapped him from the dolly and dragged him another ten feet or so in front of the biggest tree anywhere around. Then, running back to the van, she pulled out Scrote's mirror from his office and nailed it to a tree.

Her mission done, Indy returned to Surfland and parked Xander's locked van outside his place as she promised. Once again thankful she'd had the van, she hoped when this whole thing was over, the consequences from the past few days and surely what was to come would still allow them to spend time with one another. She had a feeling that between Pete, Scrote, Plink and perhaps even PETA, neither of them was just walking away from this easily.

Tempted to see if Xander would like to grab a cup coffee, she decided not to; they both had a long day coming up. Shoving the keys through his mail slot, she couldn't help but notice his apartment overlooked the GO River Wayside. Laughing to herself as she walked home, she mused that he really did live down by the river. Idly wondering if that meant he lived next to Matt Foley, she decided to take him at his word that he did not eat government cheese.

Lost in thought as she relived the night's adventures, she suddenly found herself blinded by the sun as she came into the clearing that was Hope Falls Park. There, she stopped and blinked a bit to let her eyes adjust from her shady walk along the edges of the parking lot. Tossing Poe a smile as he kept walking into the park, she let him know it was OK to keep going. Following and then leading him was Buffett, who was now bounding — bounding for him, anyway — into the park as well.

Still waiting for her eyes to adjust, it certainly didn't help that she'd slept only three hours of the last 24. But it did give her a chance to see a car backing out of a nearby parallel parking space immediately next to the park. Quickly grabbing two nearby road cones, she put them on the edge of the space and blocked it off. There was nothing to keep someone else from moving them, of course. But hoping would people just accept it and look elsewhere for a place to park, she texted Ryan that he should look for the space with the cones right up front.

Standing now on the south edge of the park, she began looking for Mrs. Margaret. Quickly, she found her on the stage behind a podium, both of which had been brought in for the occasion. The lake and falls serving as a backdrop, "Bekk" sitting by her side, Mrs. Margaret still looked as blank as ever — but Indy knew better. Her family seated next to her on both sides, there must have been two dozen people on the stage, all Tandys. Only one chair was still empty. Not surprisingly it was marked: "P. Blayton."

Now curiously wondering where the soon-to-be ex-Executive Director of Surfland Tourism was, she visually swept the area in front of her. The large grassy area at her feet was what made the place a park. About 75 wide and at least a football field long, it was now ringed with giant speakers and elevator platforms for camera shots above the crowd. She looked for Plink there first, and then among the hundreds of chairs set up on the grass. Doing so, she noticed on the opposite side of the grass the original stone podium. Mrs. Margaret's plaque setting on top of it, still wrapped in its original paper. Assuming she would see a newer plaque wrapped as well, Indy was surprised she didn't see anything near the podium. Along with rededication of the park, she knew the Tandys had also been given the honor of finally naming the lake today. Indy assumed there would be a new plaque to go with it nearby. Deciding it was either elsewhere, or just not finished, she continued to sweep her eyes to the west.

There she saw the biggest buffet table she had ever seen in her life, backdropped completely by giant Sitka Spruce trees and bracketed at both ends by a hibachi table, three Japanese chefs working each one. Their razor-sharp blades whirling like propellers, Indy couldn't help but laugh at the effort and money Plink had gone through for something that made no damn difference whatsoever to Mrs. Margaret.

Served him right.

As she continued to sweep her eyes west, she could see the table with "A Water-ful Place to Be" T-shirts and the pet rock adoption center. At the former, Dick Yelpers was gesturing wildly at the T-shirts, saying what appeared to be "No, no, no!" Rip sympathetically nodding at the table next to him, Indy didn't think Rip was actually paying attention to Dick at all. Instead, he seemed focused on his wallet as he brought out two bills to buy a bright blue pair of rocks on leashes. Ignoring them both was Raina Bowe, who was juggling crabs — definitely not the edible kind.

Smiling at what seemed like a perfect scene on a perfect day, she suddenly heard what she'd been looking for — and was reminded of why she hated her soon-to-be ex-boss so much. He was once again screaming, this time at Xander and Pete. What about she had no idea. It couldn't possibly be cameras; there were hundreds of them everywhere. Maybe it was the fireworks: Although it had been a minor job compared to blowing up the whale, Xander's last official task for Plink was setting off a small, low-altitude fireworks display right after sunset. Wondering if Xander was regretting his decision not to just quit and go back to his NGO job early after the whale incident, Indy began to walk over to see what she could do to help.

Before she began, however, she had to do something about her eyes. Amazing, she thought to herself: I've lived in the rain and murk so long, my eyes are now actually allergic to the sun. Wondering again when she might get to visit her dad in Hollywood, she reached for her windbreaker pocket to grab her sunglasses. Figuring she'd lost them when she tripped and launched the coins, she resolved to ask Ryan later if he'd found them at the coffee shop.

Chapter 76
Buffett

As soon as he realized where he was, Buffett knew where he wanted to be next.

Making a beeline for the old podium, he hoped he would find more of the soft things to lie on. Having spent two days now in the bipedal mammal's roofless car, Buffett liked the idea of lying on the nice-smelling things while still lying out in the sun.

When he got to the podium, however, there were no nice-smelling things to lie on. Just like last time they were all gone. Now looking around for something else soft to lie on, he eventually found a very large, white something behind the table. Sticking his nose into it, however, he found it was even better: It was hundreds of smaller square things! And as he thought, when he laid down on them, each one sort of moved apart from the other ones, so it conformed perfectly to his body. He could not believe how lucky he was!

Planning for a long nap, Buffett was awakened by a very loud bipedal mammal coming towards him. Usually, yelling meant he was in trouble; he was in trouble a lot. But this time was different; the bipedal mammal was actually yelling his name! That was good!

And with that happy thought in his head, he went back to sleep.

Chapter 77
Plink

"The buffet napkins!" Plink screamed as he stomped towards the table. "The buffet napkins!

"Why won't that damn dog move?!" he asked Pete, who was following closely behind him.

"You're calling his name," Pete said, as if that explained it all.

"His name? Usually that makes a dog do something!"

"Not Buffett: He pretty much only hears his name when he's being good."

"Well then, what do you say when he's being bad?" Plink demanded, now finally standing behind the buffet table.

"My wife's more the expert on that," Pete said sheepishly. "But I'm pretty sure there's nothing you can use with kids around..." And with that, Pete went to push Buffett off the giant pile of folded linen napkins the dog had found for a bed.

Not that Plink was done screaming, now turning his attention the Japanese chefs. Virtually paused in mid-chop with their knives, they looked like someone had hit pause on the DVR during a Benihana commercial.

"Why in God's name are you letting a dog sleep on your napkins?" Plink demanded.

"You told us to let the dog do whatever he wanted...," the lead chef said.

"Not THAT dog," he said, pointing after Buffett. "THAT dog!" he screamed, now pointing at the stage and Bekk. To further make his point, Plink yanked the giant knife right out of the chef's hand and pointed back towards the stage. "THAT! BIG! GIANT! DOG! Am I the only one with any brains around here?" he asked. Seeking to emphasize his point, he drove the knife straight into a tree about two feet above his head and stomped off towards the stage.

"ARGH!"

Now walking furiously, Plink once again could not believe how incompetent the people around him were. He'd been here since 5 a.m., making sure everything was perfect — and save for a dumb dog and a few audio glitches, it was.

Every media outlet in Oregon was here, or at the very least a media-type from every town that had ever benefitted from the Tandys. (Which is to say, nearly all of them.) He didn't fool himself; their interest was a morose one: Seeing Mrs. Margaret in a public venue for the first time in more than five years; indeed, no member of the family was going to even speak at the event. After what had happened on "Good Day Portland," Evan was terrified of public speaking, to say nothing of Bernese Mountain Dogs.

This suited Plink just fine: Once again he would be in the limelight, he would be the one to move Surfland forward. Knowing "A Water-ful Place to Be" was marketing gold, he even hoped to bring cruise lines back to Surfland 32 years after the "Great Triple Dysentery Incident," as it had come to be known. To that end, he'd even hired Raina Bowe to juggle crabs with the logo of a different cruise line painted on every shell. Pete now capturing all of it on HD, he'd send it off to them next month as part of a complete marketing package.

Everything was perfect — except for one thing, who just kept popping up.

"What do YOU want?" Plink said to Poe, who was now virtually at his side.

"Actually, I think it's what you want," Poe said, now grabbing him by the arm.

"What are you talking about? I don't have time for this," he said, looking down at his watch. "I have a speech to give in five minutes."

"You have plenty of time actually," Poe said, now smiling larger than Plink had ever seen him. "Seeing as you're about to be unemployed and rotting in a Columbus, Ohio, jail cell."

Feeling his stomach sink, Plink thought it couldn't get any worse — until it did. Now holding a very familiar video tape between his fingers, Poe let Plink stare at it for a moment before he dropped it on the ground and crushed it with his foot.

Still speechless — How? When? — he could only stand with his mouth open as Poe gave him one last pat on the back and pushed him towards the stage and taunted him one more time: "The cops will be waiting for you after the event," he said. "And don't you even think about doing anything that will upset Mrs. Margaret..."

Now walking like a robot towards the stage, Plink couldn't even begin to think about doing anything that would upset Mrs. Margaret — he could barely even think. Finally reaching the podium he grabbed the microphone and pulled it down to his height, the screech across the speakers letting the crowd know he was ready to begin. Deciding not to pull out his speech notes, he was relieved he'd decided to have it memorized. He was pretty sure he was starting to go blind in his right eye.

Chapter 78
Poe

Once again feeling a sense of vindication, Poe started to walk back over to the other side of the park where Pete was filming with his hand-held camera. He'd liked the fact that he'd kept his explanation to Plink minimalist; it was fun watching his face collapse. He hadn't even thought about explaining to Plink he was Ian's target all along; the guy's head was already inflated enough.

Now arriving next to Pete, Poe stayed standing as he leaned up against the scaffolding holding up one of the camera platforms. Still waiting for Plink to start — he seemed to be having a problem with his microphone — Poe could see the park was absolutely packed. For everything that had gone on, the only thing that seemed out of place was the giant knife still sticking out of the tree, its upturned blade sparkling in the sun. Laughing as the Japanese chefs simply walked under it, he figured they didn't want the knife having anything to do with food once it had been in Plink's hands.

Plink now finally starting, Poe could see that his right eye was twitching so fast it could have been sending out Morse code from a sinking ship. Only half listening, Poe heard Plink began to speak: "Today, ladies and gentlemen, we come to pay tribute to Mrs. Margaret Tandy," Plink said, his voice getting slightly more even as it went on.

"One of the driving forces in Surfland and Oregon tourism until she left this world for her own mental holiday..."

Not able to stomach anymore — Poe had read the speech after all — his attention began to drift. He'd edited Plink's speech five times before it became even palatable, and it still was absolutely terrible. Turning back to the stage to see what Fuzznut might be doing, he was silently hoping his friend might bite Plink's leg and cut him off.

No such luck.

"... She gave her life for tourism, so that others might frolic..."

Oh my God, thought Poe: Plink was pulling it from his memory instead of reading the speech he'd promised Poe and Dick he would. Poe now speaking out loud, but still just to himself, he slumped back against the scaffolding and said, "Oh my God, this can't get any worse."

And that's when Mrs. Margaret rose from her chair, pulled Plink away from the microphone, and began to speak.

Poe was almost speechless himself. Almost. "Oh my God, this can't get any better..."

Chapter 79
Fuzznut

Fuzznut, of course, knew this was going to happen. This had been her plan all along, from the minute she'd had her "minister" manipulate the family into saying "Yes" to Plink's incredibly crass idea. Mrs. Margaret was back — and with that his job was done.

Slinking backwards off the stage — walking down the hard metal stairs was nearly impossible in his spiked feet — Fuzznut knew he had to stay in the dog costume. Even if the entire Tandy family was now aware the ruse was up, all the people gathered in the park were not. He had a feeling just taking off his head and walking across the grass might distract from Mrs. Margaret.

Instead, he decided to stay on all fours and walk over to where his friend Poe was standing. At least then he'd be near someone who might have the decency to talk to him, even if he couldn't talk back. That, and he'd be able to see Mrs. Margaret deliver her speech.

Starting to walk, Fuzznut barely missed Plink's body falling off the stage behind him. Apparently he'd stumbled through the gap left when Fuzznut and his giant dog suit left the row of chairs. Checking to see if Plink was OK, the only sign of injury Fuzznut could find was that his right eye was completely swollen shut and that his left eye was starting to twitch uncontrollably. "I can't see," Plink moaned quietly. "I can't see..."

"Good," Fuzznut said, now very much out of character. And with that he started walking over to Poe.

Chapter 80
Mrs. Margaret

Mrs. Margaret Tandy's first public words in more than five years were directed at Plink, but they were meant for everyone there, especially her family: "I'll take over from here."

It took several minutes for everyone to calm down, none more so than Evan, who had what seemed to be gallons of tears running down his face. Mrs. Margaret had worried he might be angry, but he was not, which was honestly what she thought would happen. Still waiting for the crowd to get quiet, she dispatched her "minister" — she'd explain that to the family later — to complete the assignment she'd started him on yesterday afternoon. This also gave her time to make sure Plink was OK. He was a terrible person, but she still asked her family to make sure he was OK after he stumbled off the stage. He was, and as she curiously saw what seemed like every gathered cop in Surfland and one paramedic make their way to back of the stage, she assumed he'd be at least medically fine.

Now starting to speak again, she spoke first to Evan: "My son, I am so sorry for what you went through this all of these years," she said. "I have never been sick, even for a day, and I hope to make it clear to you why I did what I did in the coming days."

"But Mother, you've been so pale..."

"It's Oregon, honey, everyone is." And with that, Evan laughed, as did the rest of the crowd. The tension broken, she once again turned her attention to the hundreds of people who had come to see her, even if for all the wrong reasons.

"More than 150 years ago, my story began with a lie," she said, the audience now thoroughly confused. "And 85 years ago, my Grandma Bekk tried to fix it, but she died before that could happen. But on that day, she asked one thing of me: 'Remember' — and I did. Vowing to one day tell the true story of Rebekkah Talmedge and Adeline Grey, I remembered every word she told me. Today is that day..."

Over the next hour, Mrs. Margaret told a story that she'd only told once in 85 years, and even then only on the previous day. Tears and shock running through the crowd, more than one Oregon book publisher could take some solace in the fact that they were about to make a lot of money selling new versions of history books.

The "minister" now returning, he and Indy jointly carried the original plaque onto the stage. Setting it in front of Mrs. Margaret, she unwrapped the paper and began to read what it said, just as her Grandmother had planned to do 85 years earlier:

"Adeline Rogers Grey Park"
"Where Hope Falls into The Lake of Broken Dreams"
"On this spot in 1847 two women realized that life does not always unfold fairly, and that history will not always treat them with honesty and respect. But from that, greatness may still rise and give words to the true dignity of the past. One last attempt to make sure that those who paid the ultimate price will not be forgotten."
"In Memory of Adeline Rogers Grey, 1832 - 1862"

The tears now running down her face, Mrs. Margaret knew what she had done would not be popular with some; the truth never is. And as she guessed, over the years, it would occasionally be suggested that the city change the name of the park; not exactly the best marketing tool for a tourist town, they argued. But out of a respect for history — and a fear the Tandys would never donate another dime — it never was.

Today, however, the task her Grandma Bekk had given 17-year-old Maggie Tandy was complete — which left only Mrs. Margaret's. She would take care of that now: "Indy, could you come here please."

Surprised, Indy rose from where she'd been sitting — Plink's chair being empty, and all — and walked slowly to Mrs. Margaret's side. From the look on her face, Mrs. Margaret knew she was completely baffled.

"When I began, I promised that I would make it clear to you all why I chose to be absent in all the ways that matter from my family, my company, my world, for so long. And so I shall, starting now," she said.

"For years, I have worried for my family. Not because they were bad, but because they were good, perhaps too good. And because of that, I could never put the pressures of maintaining what my Grandma Bekk and I had built, upon them. Not just because it might destroy our company, but because it might destroy them. It was a problem that vexed me so much, I had to spend six years of virtual solitude to find an answer.

"Today, I have," and looking at her family and then back at Indy, she looked simply into the young woman's eyes and said three words: "She is me."

Chapter 81
Indy

When Indy heard the three words that were to change her life, she had no idea what they meant. Waiting for Mrs. Margaret to finish her speech, Indy sat in a daze. Even when she was done, Indy barely noticed. The minister then taking Mrs. Margaret and Indy both by the arm, he led them from the stage. Handing Mrs. Margaret a large envelope, he then turned and left them alone.

"I want you to take over the Tandy Family businesses," she said to Indy.

"You can't be serious, I'm a barista in a bikini."

"I don't mean now," she said. "Later, after I send you to business school, and have you intern in the various departments of the company, under my direct supervision, of course."

"You can't be serious," Indy said again. "You don't even know me."

"Actually, I do," she said, now patting the folder she held in her arms. "I know where you went to school, your grades, and every last detail of your life that can be pulled from public — and some not-so-public — records. Based on that, and our conversation yesterday, I think I do know you."

"You background checked me?" Indy said stunned, and even a bit angry.

"You, and your family," she said. "I like to know who I'm dealing with; family matters to me."

Still a bit irritated, but understanding her point, Indy found her voice becoming barely above a whisper. "Then you know how messed up my family life is."

"I already knew that, for the same reason I know what you've done to help them: You told me."

"Then, you know I can't just leave my mom in Surfland," she said.

"Oh, sweetie, those days are over. Your mother already has an appointment with the best diagnostician in Portland set for next week, and your father can take her," she said, now thoroughly enjoying the smile of wonder spreading across Indy's face. "He'll be starting as the head of the Extraterrestrial Student Exchange program at the Science Fiction Museum on Monday. Maybe once he starts he can tell me what the hell it is..."

And with that, Indy realized that whatever problems she'd had, they were over. After all she'd been through she still wasn't entirely sure Mrs. Margaret had the right person, but she sure as hell wasn't going to debate that right now. She'd figure it out — hopefully.

Hugging Mrs. Margaret, she asked if it would be all right if she went to call her mom. As her fingers went for her phone, however, she noticed the first person she really wanted to tell was Xander. "Xander..." she said out loud. "I just realized, he has to go back to work soon." And even though she was as excited as she had ever been, she did find that thought making her sadder than she would have thought possible.

"Indy..." Mrs. Margaret said, "I wouldn't worry about him."

"I know, I know," she said. "I have a lot to do, best not get sidetracked by a guy."

"Well, that's certainly true," she said, remembering her own history. "But my point was to genuinely say don't worry about missing him — because you won't. I own the NGO he works for. I have a feeling you'll be seeing him a lot."

Once again riding on top of the world, Indy now put Xander's number into the phone and started walking towards the parking lot. Holy surprises, Batman, did she have one for him.

Chapter 82
Ryan

Ryan, too, was feeling pretty good. Even though it had taken him hours to get everyone out of the shop and all the change out of the espresso machine, for the first time in weeks he wasn't worried about him and his parents having a job. Even his sister was doing better, now due to be discharged from the hospital in Canada tomorrow.

Thrilled to find the parallel parking spot Indy had left him still blocked by cones, Ryan slid his tiny car in between them and turned off the ignition switch. Looking around the interior, he felt a little sad that he'd be giving up his James Bond project with the car. But Indy was right; he was going to end up hurting himself, or worse. More, she knew that only something as sincere as a promise to her would make him stop. And she was right; despite what he told her Wednesday, he'd already re-wired the switch to the ejection sheet. No explosives mind you, but he still had those in his garage...

No. He would keep his promise; Indy didn't need anymore visits to the hospital. If he'd only gotten one of his contraptions to work even once...

Almost as if on cue, Indy came walking towards him, not even waiting until she got to him to start the conversation, one-sided though it was. Half babbling, half talking, Ryan made sense of most of what

Indy said: "Tandys... paying for college... mom's going to be alright... dad moving to Portland for a job..."

Ryan now seeing Poe walking into the parking lot as well, Ryan looked at him, the unspoken look on his face saying: "Do you have any idea what she's talking about?" Simply shrugging back and smiling, Poe kept walking — and very quickly Indy was following him. Calling back to Ryan, she yelled, "I'll promise I'll explain it more later! I gotta meet Xander!"

As she ran off, Ryan simply tossed her a small wave and watched her go. Still thoroughly confused, but happy for his friend, Ryan decided it didn't really matter. Wandering into the park, he wondered if it was still too late to adopt a rock.

Chapter 83
Poe

Seeing Ryan look quizzically at him as Indy went on with her story, Poe shrugged not so much because he didn't know what she was talking about, but because it was her story to tell. Certainly, Poe didn't know all the details, but given what Mrs. Margaret had said on the podium — and a strictly off-the-record conversation with Rip — Poe had some idea.

Poe was now heading back to his car; he'd had a long enough day. Pondering his responsibilities at this point, he thought of the two dogs in his life. He decided both of them were fine: Bekk, a.k.a. Fuzznut, was sleeping in grass under the shade of the viewing platform, while Buffett was going to be catching a ride home with Xander.

Next he moved onto Plink, whom Poe was happy to recall was now safely in the hands of the Surfland PD. Virtually every last cop in attendance at the event had been happy to help bring Plink back to the jail. Apparently, they were still smarting from when he'd told them at the "Cops for Tots" clam and clothing drive that they were bad for business because they smelled like pork and donuts. That, or because he had treated them like crap just as he had everyone else. Whatever, they all agreed that arresting him and parading him back to town all lights flashing was a lot more fun than just giving him parking tickets.

Poe's last thought was of Ian, still safely in his trunk. Honestly, he was ready to be rid of the guy. Had all the cops not have left, Poe would have given Ian to them right here. OK, change in plan: Next stop Surfland PD. Besides, Ian and Plink in adjoining cells might prove to be seriously entertaining.

Indy now catching up with him, she told him she just needed a second. "Thanks," she said pecking him on the cheek. "You saved everyone."

Blushing a bit, Poe teased her to try and cover it up. "Be careful; what would Xander say about us making out in the parking lot?"

"I don't know, you should ask him," she said pointing over to his van. "Gotta go!"

And with that she was gone towards the van herself.

Still somewhat amazed that everything had turned out the way it had, Poe kept walking towards the Jag. Once there, Poe couldn't resist making sure Ian was still comfy as Poe one more time pounded on the trunk with his flat hand, and yelled "You good?!" and kept walking around to the driver's side door — his back now facing the rising trunk lid.

"No, asshole, I'm not good at all," Ian said. "And you're not going to be either if you don't turn around really, really slow."

Surprised, Poe did as he was told, now seeing an eagle's head and wing rising slowly out of his trunk. Obviously, not only had Ian woken up, he'd been able to pop the trunk's interior emergency release handle, despite the costume. Watching as Ian worked to extricate himself from the trunk, Poe almost laughed at the comical sight. With Ian's limited sight in the mascot head, as well as what must be horribly cramped muscles, Poe couldn't help but laugh.

"You realize one swift kick in the balls and you're down again?" Poe said to Ian, actually looking forward to it after all Ian had put him through. "I guess just a change jar wasn't enough."

Ian seemed completely unfazed: "You realize one bullet between the eyes and you're down for good."

And that's when Poe saw it: a gun barrel sticking out of the tip of Ian's right "wing." How the hell had they missed that? Still trying to keep some control of things, Poe prayed Ryan was right: "Seriously, you're going to just shoot me?" Poe said. "Don't you have to have some master plan?"

"If you'd asked me that at breakfast, I would have said yes," Ian said, a very audible click now coming from inside his right glove. "But at this point, let's just say I'm trying to simplify my life."

And with that, he pulled the trigger.

Chapter 84

Ian

It was hours earlier when Ian had started to wake up to a pounding hand and a screaming voice: "He's good!"

Remembering the voice from the coffee shop as someone named "Poe," Ian was perfectly content with Poe leaving and it growing quiet again. His head pounded at both the front and back, the front likely from the flying jar of change he was fully beginning to remember. He also understood immediately the pain at the back of his skull: he'd been drugged. With what, he had no idea, but living in Cambodia, someone was always slipping something into someone else's drinks. Another reason he didn't drink so much.

But if living in Cambodia had given him anything, it was a cast-iron stomach. Coupled with a system that had been witness to more than a few altered substances in his time overseas, he wasn't surprised that he'd come around so completely, so fast.

What did surprise him was where he was: in the trunk of a car. How the hell he got here, he had no idea, but the good news was he could get out. Every car sold in the United States in the last several years had an interior emergency trunk release. Put there to prevent kids from being locked in the trunk, he was happy to put it to anterior uses.

Getting to it, however, was another matter. He was completely wrapped in some kind of suit. What kind he had no idea, but it covered him head to toe, making it damn near impossible to move or manipulate anything in the trunk. His hands, what little he could move them, were basically encased in giant furry gloves, and he couldn't feel anything. Trying for an hour, he damn near exhausted himself — and got absolutely nowhere.

This was going to be harder than he thought.

He did find something else, however, something he'd forgotten: a small pistol. It had been Scrote's idea. And even though Ian knew The Captain would not have approved of such a pedestrian plan as shooting someone in a coffee shop, Ian had brought it along just it case the auction was a trap. It had been, of course, but by the time he'd found that out it had been too late. (Honestly, Ian was somewhat impressed.)

Now remembering again that the gun was taped to his leg, Ian knew he needed to get it. Able to pull his arm up through the wing of the giant costume, he was able to take his hand, run it down his body and leg, and retrieve the tiny Sig Sauer P238. (He'd bought it at the local gun store/Radio Shack) Now, pushing the barrel of it back down into the eagle's "fingers," he was able to press the fabric-covered barrel up against the wall of the trunk and begin twisting. After what he guessed to be two or three hours, he'd actually made a hole in the finger tip. Pushing the entire barrel though the hole, it was wide enough for him to actually get two fingers through. Able to now feel his way around the trunk, he was lucky enough to find the trunk release within reach.

Preparing to pull it, Ian stopped when he heard voices approaching to car. One was Poe. Eventually, though the pair stopped talking, he could hear one of them approaching the car. Hoping it was still Poe, he wrapped his fingers around the trunk release and waited. When Poe's voice then yelled, "You good?" and slapped the trunk, Ian made his move.

Moving slowly at first, he popped the trunk and prayed it would open quietly. When it did, he made sure to stick the barrel of the gun back through the hole in the finger. Working quickly, he wasn't sure it was even in there until he saw the barrel poking out of the fingertip. Now sticking his head and wing out, he could honestly say that freedom was the third best thing he'd ever felt since killing his parents. It immediately preceded the second best thing, which was uttering, "No, asshole, I'm not good at all."

The best was pulling the trigger.

After all the time he'd spent concocting how to kill people, he was stunned at how good it felt to do something with no pretense, no complications, nothing. Simply decide to kill someone and just do it. Suddenly, he wanted a Nike T-shirt.

Like his recent plans, however, pulling the trigger did achieve what he'd planned. The damn fabric from the gloves was wedged in between the trigger and the rest of gun and despite the telltale click, nothing fired, no bullet came out.

"Shit!" Ian yelled. "Why does nothing go as planned?" Now throwing off the eagle head, Ian could get a better look at his glove. Trying to work the gun around inside it, Ian made sure to never move the barrel from Poe's direction. Not that it mattered; Poe seemed to be frozen in place, although finally he did say something.

"You don't want to kill me," Poe said.

"I just pulled the trigger, and I will again here soon," Ian said. "Trust me, I do want to kill you."

"How are you going to get back to Cambodia? Your passports are gone."

Stopping, Ian felt down to his left front pocket. Even through the costume, Ian could indeed feel they were not there. "Give them to me."

"I don't have them," Poe said. "Let me drive you out of here, and we'll go get them."

"Hell, no. No more plans," Ian said. "Why don't I just shoot you and then go looking for them? Every damn person you know hangs out in the coffee shop. I'll just start grabbing people there until I get them back."

"No! Wait! My friend has them over in the park," Poe said. "Go over there with me, I'll find him, and you can get the hell out of here."

"Now that sounds like a plan I can live with," Ian said. "Who knows about you, though..."

Chapter 85

Xander

Wrapping his arms around Indy, Xander mentally went back in time to high school, looked at her, and then returned to the present. Yep, he thought to himself, this is as awesome as I thought it would be.

Standing behind his van, she said seductively, "You and I have the same boss."

"You have a very strange way to begin a romance," Xander said. "I— Oh, shit..."

"Your way's not exactly normal itself," Indy said, as much confused as she was perturbed.

"No! Shhh!" he said, now pushing her up against the van. "Look over there at Poe's car: It's Ian!"

"What?!"

Both of them only peeking their heads out from beyond the van, they could see that Ian was indeed out of the trunk and very much conscious. Too far away to hear anything being said, what their body language said was obvious: Ian was pissed, and Poe was in trouble.

"I thought you said he'd be unconscious for hours!" Xander said.

"He should have been, Scrote always was."

"What? Scrote?"

"Never mind, we have to do something for Poe," Indy said, clearly trying to change the subject.

"Well, it had better include following him, because they're going back to the park," Xander said.

"What? Why the hell would Ian do that?"

That Xander had no idea how to answer that question just made it one of many: Why had Ian put the eagle head back on? Why was Poe looking so relaxed and casual, and why did it look like the eagle had a gun? He'd spent enough time in war zones to recognize when people were armed. What didn't make sense was why Poe looked so relaxed.

"Xander!" Indy said, interrupting his thoughts. "You still have the Tannerite in the van?"

"Yeah... No, no, Indy," Xander said, now beginning to see where her mind was going. "That man has a gun."

"So did Ernst Stavro Blofeld," she said. "And what about the fireworks, have you put those out yet?"

"Indy, this isn't a damn Bond movie!" Xander said, though she was already too far across the parking lot to hear him. Damn! The girl of his dreams finally falls for him, and now she's going to get herself killed! Climbing into van, Xander found his backpack still containing the Tannerite and stuffed as many fireworks in as he could. Making his way as stealthily as he could muster, he virtually crawled the last 50 feet up to Ryan's car.

Mere yards from the park, Xander could see that the Tandy Family was almost to the parking lot themselves. At 102, even as happy as she was to have the truth finally out, Mrs. Margaret was a very old woman. Seemingly ready for some rest, she was moving slowly. Not so much because of her age, however, but because of all the people who wanted to talk to her. Surprisingly, her dog was not by her side, but rather 15 feet away, sleeping under some scaffolding.

Briefly noticing now that Ian and Poe were standing next to that same scaffold platform, Xander decided he'd ponder the mystery of Mrs.

Margaret's dog later. Returning his attention to Indy, he could see that she, too, had been careful, and was now already in the car. Everyone oblivious to her presence, he could hear now talking to herself: "Ryan, you delightful S.O.B..."

Letting her leave the thought incomplete, Xander had to admit he had no idea what she was talking about. Still doing something under the front seat, she stopped just for a moment to smile and acknowledge he was there: "About time you showed up," she said. "What changed your mind?"

"You're kinda hot when you're bitchy," he said.

"You have no idea," she said sticking her head back down below the seat. "You have no idea..."

Chapter 86

Fuzznut

Still dozing comfortably under the scaffolding, Fuzznut awoke when he heard Poe's voice. This surprised him, as Poe had told him earlier he was going home.

Opening his eyes, he could see Poe was trying to get Dick's attention. At first ignoring Poe, Dick was completely focused on talking to Raina Bowe: "Doe yuh thee gay pee-puh wuhd lie 'Tah BEE ih BAH'?" And while agreeing she thought that both gay people and cross-dressers would like his tourism slogan, Fuzznut could tell by the look on her face that she needed someone to get her away from Dick; she had crabs to juggle.

Not surprisingly, Poe did, but in a harsh manner that Fuzznut had never seen him take with Dick — or anyone else for that matter: "Dick! If you say that tourism slogan one more time, I will kill you myself! Now, go get Rip!"

Watching Dick move off, Fuzznut turned his attention back to Poe. He was definitely not himself, though, seeing how other people were now staring at him, Poe seemed to suddenly relax, almost as if on cue. Perhaps that's why Fuzznut suddenly noticed the eagle standing next to Poe. He was the worst mascot Fuzznut had ever seen. He was just standing there, one arm at his side, the other just sticking out from the elbow. He wasn't doing anything.

This was more than Fuzznut could handle; he'd given that costume to Ryan at the coffee shop. And now he was letting Paxton treat it like this? Walking out on all fours from underneath the scaffolding, Fuzznut got right in the eagle's line of sight and began swaying back and forth. Having seen Paxton as a mascot before, Fuzznut was trying to remind him of one of the basics: never stop moving.

Nothing.

Turning around, Fuzznut then wagged his tail at him, followed by spinning around and rolling over. Looking every bit a real dog, Fuzznut was hoping to remind him: "Be the bird. Be the bird."

Nothing.

At this point, Fuzznut decided he just needed to get Paxton away from everyone and talk to him, dog to bird, mascot to mascot. This was not mascot behavior. Fuzznut had been doing it for 40 years now, and if he — going on his early '50s — could get it in gear, a teenager certainly could. Intending to push Paxton off behind the cars in the parking lot, Fuzznut started to head-butt him in the groin.

Which was when the eagle kicked him right in the head.

"What the hell?!" Fuzznut yelled, surprised. What was Paxton thinking?

Which was when the eagle yelled, too: "What the hell?!" before ripping off his head and pointing what Fuzznut could see was a very heavily armed eagle finger at him. Recognizing him as the man that had tried to kill Poe at the lighthouse, Fuzznut couldn't help but think: Hmm, that's not mascot behavior at all.

Chapter 87
Poe

Walking across the parking lot with Ian at his back, Poe had to force himself to relax. Poe's only hope of not getting anyone killed — including himself — hinged on getting Ian out of here as quickly as possible. Quite frankly, it had terrified Poe that Ian had been perfectly willing to shoot him. Any reserve of patience or humor that Poe might normally have was gone.

He'd realized that when he'd almost torn Dick's head off sending him to get Rip. Honestly, he liked the slogan and he liked Dick, and later he would apologize. But right now he was worried about his friends, including Dick, and that took precedence over everything.

Gazing around the park, the armed and eagled Ian still at his back, Poe was actually glad there weren't any cops around. The last thing hundreds of innocent people needed was a gun fight. If Rip could just get here with those passports still in his pocket, everything would be fine. But where was he? He could see everyone else he knew; hell Pete was blindly setting his camera up next to him, like there was nothing wrong in the world. Which there wouldn't be, if Dick could just get back here with Rip. And suddenly, there Rip was, walking towards Poe with a confused look on his face, but coming nonetheless. Fishing through his pockets, Poe pulled out his car keys to give them to Ian.

Which is when he saw Bekk the dog — Fuzznut — start to headbutt Ian in the groin. Within seconds, Ian had his eagle head off, his gun out, and everyone suddenly very nervous. Accidentally dropping his keys in the grass, Poe made no effort to retrieve them. Silence over all of them, Poe waited for Ian to speak first.

"Isaac Andrew Niemen: You lying little piece of shit!" said Mrs. Margaret. "Where is my money?"

"Mother!" said Evan. "Such language!"

"Oh, my dear sweet boy," she said, never taking her eyes of Isaac. "You spend a lifetime on the coast, things are going to get a little bit salty sometimes."

For a moment, Ian couldn't believe what he was seeing; he'd thought Mrs. Margaret was a vegetable. But soon, he gathered his thoughts, now seemingly angrier than ever, the gun pointed at a new target: "You! You gave my parents the money they needed to destroy The Captain's legacy!" Ian screamed. "You don't deserve my grandfather's money!"

"And you do?" she asked. "Although it seems fitting, he was an asshole, too."

"Mother!"

"Fuzznut?" she said, now totally ignoring Ian/Isaac. "Are you OK? You can talk; I'm paying your bill."

"Yeah," said a voice coming from inside the Giant English Sheep Dog. "I'm fine. My jaw hurts like hell, though."

Now sweeping his gun across the crowd, Ian demanded that Rip bring him his passports. Seeing Rip glance at him, Poe simply nodded, whereupon Rip went over and placed them in Ian's left hand. Once again focused on Poe, he said, "Alright, smart guy, you and me are getting out of here. Get your keys out."

"I don't have them," Poe said genuinely, now pulling his pockets inside out. "If you'll give—"

"No more tricks! No more talking dogs! No more!" he screamed. "All I want to know is who the hell is going to get me out of here?!"

"I am."

Almost as if from nowhere, Indy suddenly seemed to have materialized right at the edge of the park. From the look on Ian's face, Poe could tell he was trying to determine if she was part of everything else crazy that had happened in the last 10 minutes: "Why the hell would I want you?"

"Simple: I've got the keys to a car, and I'm about to become the leader of one of the biggest companies in Oregon," she said. "Who the hell wouldn't want me?"

"OK," he said, "But before we go, I want you to check something. After today, I don't trust anything anymore."

"Indy..." Poe said, as she walked by him.

"Trust me," she quietly. "I have a plan. I know what I'm doing."

Watching her go off towards Ian, Poe could see that he was having her go through the envelope at gunpoint. Apparently, it was more than just passports, as he had her unfold a myriad of papers and check them one by one.

Pete, now standing next to Poe, was simply leaving his camera running sitting on the tripod. Managing a small smile, Poe could only imagine what footage he'd have when he got home. Taking advantage of the lull, Pete started speaking quietly to Poe: "Let me get this straight...

"Ian is Isaac who has not been dead for seven years. Mrs. Tandy is not a senile incoherent mess, but rather a corporate titan who is still sharp as a tack. Bekk is not a Giant English Sheep Dog, but a guy in a costume. And the disgusting bum in the park is in fact Indy, who is now also about to become a corporate titan of her own. Do I have that right?"

"Yeah, pretty much—"

"AAAAUUUUUUGGGGGGHHHHHHHHHH!!!!"

Like everyone in the park, Poe and Pete's conversation stopped as if robbed of oxygen. Suddenly worried that Ian might just start shooting, Poe immediately looked to make sure Indy was OK. He needn't have worried, however, as even Ian's attention was frozen on the horrible pink creature that now came running out of the woods from behind the T-shirt table.

"AAAAUUUUUUGGGGGHHHHHHHHH!!!!"

Still screaming, it ran straight through the crowd and onto the stage. Clearly exhausted from the effort it had made to get here, it had finally stopped screaming. Now watching it just huffing and puffing, Poe once again looked to make sure Indy was OK. She was not, but this time, neither was Ian. Both of their eyes were as wide as saucers. Returning his gaze to the thing on the stage, Poe suddenly understood why: "Sweet Jesus, that's Scrote..."

Pete, for his part seemed to take it in stride: "...And the coffee shop owner is a pig."

Chapter 88
Scrote

From the moment Scrote had climbed into the truck, his life had been a horror. Not that the loggers had actually been able to do anything to him — the costume prevented that — but they had tried. Indeed, for the first 30 minutes they tried to accomplish it while one kept driving. But after about 10 miles and three near accidents, they finally stopped the truck, deciding that maybe there was a better way to become part of Ursinia's minions. Locking him in the sleeper capsule behind the cab, they got out and argued for what must have been hours. In the end, scared that he didn't seem to have any actual bodily openings, they decided to take him to a born-again preacher they'd heard about. Worried their pink and mutated find was possibly the spawn of the devil, they made a follow-up appointment with a butcher they knew out in Hebo, just in case.

Recognizing that this might be his only chance to get away, Scrote waited for them to get into the truck in the hopes that they would unlock the sleeper cab. Wanting to check one more time if their man-pig had any orifices from the neck down, they did, and Scrote literally bowled his way out of the truck. Crashing to the ground outside the cab, he bounced three times before landing in a ditch. Getting to his feet he just started running as fast he could. Afraid they were still behind him as he came to what looked to be a gathering of people up ahead, he began screaming: "AAAAUUUUUUGGGGGHHHHHHHHH!!!!" Even when he realized he was finally in the middle of hundreds of people, he could not stop screaming. Seeing an elevated stage where he could check if he was still being followed, he ran up the stairs and began scanning the trees from where he'd come. Finally feeling he was safe, he stopped, now just huffing and puffing, on the verge of passing out right there on the stage.

And in fact he might have, had not one person caught his eye: Indy. Standing there with Ian, who for some reason was dressed as an eagle, he could not believe she was here. But he was very glad she was. Lumbering now down the steps from the stage he waddled past the gathered crowd and stood in front of the woman he thought he loved — and he thought loved him.

"Why, Indy? Why?"

"Scrote," she said, her voice as nice as could be. ""What makes you think I—"

"This!" he screamed, her crushed green sunglasses still jammed in his right hoof. "This!"

Now suddenly knowing where her sunglasses had gone, Indy's mood changed — and not for the better.

"You were a pig to me, Scrote," she said angrily. "It seemed fitting."

"Indy," he said now hoping for her sympathy. "Two loggers found me. They called me 'Wilbabe.' They... they did things to me."

"Scrote, a real 500-pound pig couldn't have sex with you in that costume," she said. "That was the point. How's the peeing thing going, by the way?"

"I haven't, and it hurts," he said. "Do you know you glued this thing to my... thing?"

Fighting her own stomach, Indy said, "Well, that was the fourth time... Don't worry, the solvent to get you out should be here next week."

"Next week?!"

"I'm kidding, Scrote, I left the stuff at your house," she said. "Besides, I think you've learned your lesson. I truly believe you're going to be a better person for this. Or at the very least not eat bacon anymore."

"Indy," Scrote said, once again hoping her tiny bit of kindness might mean something. "Seriously, what are my chances with you? Like one in a hundred?"

"I'd say more like one out of a million," she parroted back to him, a small smile creeping across her face.

"Those aren't even real odds for pe—" he said, stopping as his face become suddenly more twisted and angry. "God dammit! That's another movie line, isn't it?" Enraged, he began to step towards her, and for the first time, he didn't care if she was afraid of him — and from the look on her face she was. Indeed, only Ian prevented him from taking his revenge right here in the park.

"Jesus, Scrote!" Ian said. "Even I've seen 'Dumb and Dumber.' Honest to God, I don't care anymore about you, your stupid company or your stupid life. I want to take my passports, my account numbers and disappear! I did it once, I can do it again, and if you don't shut the hell up, I'm leaving you with nothing!"

Seeing the truth of what Ian was saying — for once — Scrote simply said, "Fine, I'll catch up with you later, but leave me the girl and the gun. You owe me that much."

"Anything, if it gets me the hell out of here," he said, telling Indy to tear open the eagle glove so he could finally get the gun out. "So, the original question remains: Who the hell is going to get me out of here?"

"He will," Indy said. And as Scrote and everyone looked on, all of them were surprised to follow the direction of her finger to oldest friend she'd ever had. None more surprised than the friend himself.

Chapter 89
Ryan

"Me," Ryan asked? "Why me?"

Standing just a few feet from Scrote and Ian, Indy tried to sound as natural as possible. "Because I trust you to do the right thing," she said, slowly. "You just get in your car and don't worry about any promises you've ever made me."

Raising his eyebrows a bit at that, he asked her, "What about you?" Watching as Ian wedged the gun into Scrote's right hoof in a way that would still allow him to pull the trigger, he noticed the barrel never left Indy — nor did Scrote's eyes. "He's got a gun, you know."

"James Bond didn't always need one..." she said, her voice suddenly dropping in volume, as she gave him once last set of directions.

"Hey!" Ian yelled at Ryan. Get over here, I don't trust you even for a minute, he said now looking back to Indy. "I'm still not sure why the hell I should trust anything you say."

"You want out, and we want you gone," she said. "And he's got a car parked 30 feet away."

"How do you know I won't kill him anyway?"

"Well, for one thing, you don't have the gun anymore. And while I suppose you could come up with some grand scheme to go off a cliff, have him eaten by sharks, smothered by sting rays, or some other nonsense, the simple truth is, you want to get the hell out of here," she said. "And while I'm being honest, I'd still rather you take me. But you've already made it clear you're going to leave me to your pig friend, so the longer you stand here, the greater chance someone could hurt."

"Now are you leaving or not?"

Chapter 90
Indy

Even though Ian no longer had a gun, he still insisted Ryan walk in front of him. Taking Ryan's cellphone, and wedging it into Scrote's left hoof, he once again scanned the crowd.

"Now remember," he said to Indy and everyone else. "No one calls the cops on me, or anything else. If I so much as see anything I don't like: I may not kill your friend, but I will make him wish he'd never been born."

"And Scrote," he said now pointing to Ryan's cellphone. "If this thing rings in anything less than three hours and you see it's from me, shoot her."

As Ian hustled Ryan to the car, Indy could only watch him go. After making Ryan get seated first, she could see Ian getting his still-furry and -feathered body into the seat next to him. Now looking around at her friends, she could tell they'd all thought she'd lost her mind.

"Indy!" Poe exclaimed. "What the hell are doing? That's your best friend!"

"I know that..."

"And you're just going to have him drive off with that lunatic?" he asked, incredulous.

"I've had a few optional extras installed," she said, a favorite smile once again creeping across her face. And even as she turned to face Scrote, she could see recognition dawning on Poe's face. With Poe hopefully on board, only one thing remained — but the clock was ticking, and she knew it.

"Well, Scrote," Indy said. "What's your plan?"

She knew now that he hated her, but she also desperately hoped that a tiny shred of what he called affection was still hidden in that pink suit somewhere. Not for a minute did she regret what she'd done to Scrote; he was a pig always, now, and — thanks to what she was sure would be the miracle of YouTube — forever. But she had to admit this wasn't exactly how she'd planned this coming to an end. He was supposed to have found his way back to Surfland, his perverted business and his comfy bed, where a tube of glue solvent awaited him.

The fact that it was now ending with a gun here at the park had never entered her mind. Indeed, she hoped when this was all over Mrs. Margaret was still speaking to her; endangering someone's family was not easily forgiven. On the other hand, she couldn't wait to tell her dad that someone had actually seen *Farmageddon* and remembered it. Even if it was two pervert loggers, he'd appreciate the story. Assuming she lived to tell it.

"You think you're so smart!" he said to her, now returning her mind to the present. "You don't think I know what you said to him was a movie line?"

"Who?" Indy asked, "When?" Even as Scrote held the gun, Indy noticed that he would back up every time she took a small step forward. Taking advantage of that, she began to back him into a corner, literally.

"Everything you just said!" he replied angrily. "I'm not that stupid."

"OK," she said. "How about I tell you something you'll know isn't a movie line."

"What the hell will that prove?" he said, now taking another step backwards.

"I don't want to end up dead, and I want you to know you can believe what I say," she said, now seeing out of the corner of her eye that Ryan was beginning to look down in his car. Looking at Scrote, she was barely a foot from his face when she spoke: "The eagle has landed."

"Well, duh," he said, not quite understanding what Indy was getting at. "That's history."

Now following her last advice to Ryan — "Dive! — Indy said what she hoped would be the last words she ever said to Scrote, very much hoping they wouldn't be the last she said to anyone. "Wrong again, pig; it's not history.

"It's now."

Chapter 91

Ian

Still not quite trusting Ryan, Ian had to admit there didn't seem to be anything amiss as Ryan started up the car. Watching him as he went to shift, however, he could see Ryan's hand suddenly flip up a hidden panel and flick a switch. Still wondering what the hell was going on with that, he was stunned to see Ryan throw open his car door and roll into the parking lot.

"You stupid kid," Ian yelled, "Do you honestly think you can get away?! You're dead! Your friend? She's d—"

But even as the words came out, Ian could feel a massive source of heat building underneath his legs. Desperately trying to find the door handle, Ian's giant furry hands once again prevented him from grabbing anything. Struggling to push his right hand out of the suit through the hole where he'd removed the gun, he felt his fingers just begin to tickle his target when suddenly the seat under him began to move.

"Oooooooooooohhhhhhhhhhhhhhhhhhhh..."

Chapter 92
Buffett

"...SSSSSSSSSSHHHHHHHHHHIIIIIIIIIITTTTTTTTTTTT..."

Still shaking off the rude awakening from his nap, Buffett was having an even harder time than usual making sense of a very confusing thing.

He'd just been roused minutes earlier by bipedal mammals that did not appreciate piles of dog hair on their T-shirts. Why this was suddenly a problem now — he'd been sleeping on them under the table all afternoon — he did not know. But as a result, he was now standing at the edge of the big grassy area looking for another place to sleep when he suddenly saw a giant roar of smoke and flames on the right side of the park. This excited him, as smoke and flames meant his bipedal mammal would once again be busy and he could sleep some more.

The smoke, however, was then followed by something very different: The biggest bird he had ever seen came shooting out of the smoke. Watching the bird as it flew through the sky, Buffett watched as it flew in a giant flaming arc over the park, the flames going away just before it started coming down on the opposite side. Continuing to watch it, Buffett decided it was not only the biggest bird he had ever seen, but the loudest. Which was surprising, as it had a really tiny head.

Watching it continue to fly and scream as it prepared to land on the other side, Buffett was happy for the bird. He was about to land in the pile of white things — napkins, he heard them called — which Buffett knew to be very soft. He hoped the bird would not get in as much trouble as he did.

Buffett, however, was suddenly very happy. The people that had made him stop sleeping on the shirts were now leaving, starting to run over to the bird. Taking this as a sign it was OK to sleep on the T-shirts again, Buffett laid down as the noises from people in the park grew louder and louder. Dozing off, Buffett began to think that maybe the bird was in trouble, after all.

Chapter 93
Pete

Looking through his camera at Ryan's car, Pete wasn't even sure why he was filming anymore. But Poe had insisted, simply telling Pete that he should keep filming — even as he told him he might want to seriously start backing up. Indeed, Poe seemed to be moving everyone back as quickly — and as subtly — as he could.

Maybe that's why Pete wasn't particularly surprised when suddenly Ian was surrounded by a bloom of smoke and flame and his seat came roaring out of the car like a rocket. Indy from minute one had seemed to be up to something, although she clearly had not listened to any of Pete's talks about fire safety. Thankful to see Ryan now tumbling away from his car through the parking lot, Pete realized he was going to need to talk to Ryan again, too.

But even as he thought this, Pete's experience as a cameraman had his hands and camera reflexively following the action, in this case a literal screaming eagle moving in a bright orange arc right above his head. Almost bending over backwards before he pivoted and kept following the action downward, Pete marveled again at the amazing clarity of HD. Able to actually see Ian's screaming face as he began to crash into the trees, Pete had a virtual front-row seat for Ian's final moments — which were not pretty at all.

Turning off the camera, Pete knew he had to go get Poe. But looking back to where he'd left his friend, Pete couldn't believe what was happening. Another plan shot to hell, Pete dropped the camera and started to run.

Chapter 94
Fuzznut

Fuzznut watched as Indy dove to the ground, much as her friend Ryan was doing out in the parking lot as he tumbled from his soon-to-be flaming car.

Figuring he should do the same, Fuzznut pressed himself into the grass, where he could now see that Poe had gotten everyone else to do so, as well. When Ian launched out of the car, only Scrote remained standing, and as the blast wave rolled across the grass and slammed him in the back, Fuzznut simply waited for him to be knocked to the ground.

Except he wasn't.

The enormous padding cushioning Scrote from the blast waves coming from under Ian's seat, Scrote not only stayed upright, but he began to walk forward. Once again realizing Indy had gotten the best of him, he was enraged and began making his way towards her as she still lay on the ground.

It was Poe, as always, to the rescue.

First, he pulled a small bag of something out of his shirt pocket, and with that firmly in hand he charged towards Scrote. At first, Fuzznut thought Poe might be crazy enough to try and tackle Scrote. But flying fists had never been Poe's thing, and they weren't today either. Stopping just shy of the pink foam behemoth, Poe threw what appeared to be coffee grounds in his eyes. Musing that only Poe would carry coffee as a concealed weapon, Fuzznut then watched as Poe took advantage of Scrote's blindness and kicked the pig as hard as he could in the groin.

Not the most honorable fight, Fuzznut had to admit, but a usually effective one.

Usually.

Scrote ignored Poe's kick like he would ignore being hit with a toothpick. The massive amounts of foam rubber covering every inch of his body, Poe's kick simply bounced away. This in turn threw Poe off balance and onto the ground, where Scrote, now in even more of a rage for having been partially blinded, began kicking Poe with his giant hooves. Even though they were only plastic, they were hard plastic, and Poe was very quickly losing the fight. As Poe curled into a fetal position trying to protect his head and face, Fuzznut could hear Pete running up from behind him, yelling "HOLD ON, POE! HOLD ON!"

Hearing this, Scrote's vision had obviously begun to clear, and with that he began to look around, intending to take on Pete, as well. Indy, who was now starting to pick herself up from the ground, also drew his attention. Scrote just stared at her, maintaining his gaze even as she slowly started to walk towards him. Fuzznut couldn't believe Scrote would hurt her, but as Fuzznut looked at Poe still lying on the ground, he realized he wasn't really sure what Scrote was capable of anymore.

Almost as if on cue, Scrote suddenly stood up as fully as he could and yelled, "C'MON!"

Fuzznut would never read "Charlotte's Web" again without having nightmares.

Scrote now laughing hysterically, he was still wielding the phone and gun wedged tightly in his hooves. Once again looking to see who would come next, Pete or Indy, Scrote was clearly awaiting his next challenge.

Fuzznut decided it should be him.

Now standing up on his real legs, Fuzznut charged Scrote from about 25 feet away. Scrote, watching him come, simply stood there facing him, his arms tensed but hanging at the ready by his sides. But instead of tackling Scrote, Fuzznut put his two fake front legs together and twisted his arms as he made impact.

Scrote wasn't laughing anymore.

As Scrote slammed backwards against the scaffolding, the five small spikes on each of Fuzznut's outdoor feet acted as tiny daggers, slicing clean through the foam rubber. Genuinely hoping he wasn't carving up anything inside, Poe twisted one more time, the look of Scrote's face letting Fuzznut know that he had at least made very painful contact.

Pulling back, Scrote reacted as all men — even Wilbabe the Man-pig — do when they've been kicked in the groin: he threw his arms down over it and howled. Taking advantage of this, Fuzznut stepped back, pirouetted on his right foot and spun around as hard as he could, throwing his front legs out as he went. Striking Scrote square in the face, thirty pounds of crutches and shock absorbers did the job nicely, as Scrote dropped like a sack of hams.

Now sitting back down on his haunches like a real dog, Fuzznut looked once again at Scrote, just to be sure he was down for good. Seeing his giant pink form lying on his stomach, his arms pinned beneath his own mass, Fuzznut was still hoping he hadn't drawn blood. No man deserved that.

But then neither did Poe, who Fuzznut was happy to see wasn't nearly the bloody pulp Fuzznut feared he would be. Watching Indy and Pete running over to help him, Fuzznut was more than willing to let them take care of it. Pete was medically trained, and at least Indy had actual hands. Even as Fuzznut watched, however, Poe was starting to wave them off.

Looking away from them, Fuzznut realized he'd attracted a crowd, none more immediate — and shocked — than the Tandy family. The littler ones still thought he was a real dog, even after all that had happened. Some of them now crying, Fuzznut looked over himself in costume, made sure he was still all together, and walked slowly over to them. Praying that they would just pet him and not ride him, he tried to get them to scratch the back of his neck where it was the sorest.

Finding their scratches remarkably well placed, the last thing Fuzznut heard before he lay down on the ground were two teenage boys. Always on the listen for praises of his mascot performance, Fuzznut couldn't help but smile as he fell asleep to one last comment: "When the hell did Chuck Norris start training dogs?"

Chapter 95
Poe

Staring at Scrote's still unconscious form lying in the grass, Poe was happy to know it wasn't his job to decide what to do with this bad guy. Sirens in the background, a fire truck was on its way to extinguish the remains of Ryan's car. The police, too, were on their way — back — to lock up another member of Surfland's non-finest.

Still staring at him, Poe was happy to see Fuzznut walking towards him, still on all fours. The Tandy kids now making their way home, Mrs. Margaret had told them the doggie needed a break. Mrs. Margaret, however, remained in the park with Indy, and he could see they were having a stern, but mutually respectful, talk. Indy's hands now wrapped around a steaming mug of coffee, the smile on her face told Poe everything was going to be OK.

Returning his attention to Fuzznut, Poe found himself thanking someone for saving his life for the third time in just as many days. With Fuzznut, though, it was getting to be a habit, which naturally meant that Poe needed to give him a hard time.

"So..." Poe said, "running across the ground on your back legs. Isn't that breaking some kind of mascot code?"

"Sometimes," he said, now poking his head around Scrote's fallen form, "rules were made to be broken. Either that, or your face was going to be."

"Good point," Poe said, laughing. Now watching Fuzznut turn his rear to Scrote's body, he watched as Fuzznut lifted his leg on Scrote and let a stream of liquid run down a tube along his dog leg and out onto the body. Laughing once again, Poe couldn't help but ask: "Camelback?"

"Nope."

With the fire department finally on site, Pete felt safe leaving Ryan's still smoldering car. With everything that had gone down, he should probably be having Indy, Ryan and Xander arrested. His heart wasn't in that, though, and in the coming days he promised them he would talk to the police about not pressing charges. But having done that, he made them swear they'd never do anything like it again — again. That and commit to volunteering at the next Joan of Arc Memorial Horse Race and Bonfire. Planning to bring it back next summer as a Surfland Fire & Rescue fundraiser, Pete promised to let them be in charge. Pete was hoping to get Florence Henderson to attend, or at the very least toast the marshmallows over a flaming Chia Head that looked like her.

Now walking across the grass to where Ian had landed, Poe felt sorry for his friend. "I know you're still going to get paid and all," Poe said. "But the last few days have been pretty much a bust for you, haven't they? Not a lot there to bring in the tourists, if you know what I mean."

"You know, I've been thinking about that," he said. "And I'm wondering if this might be a good thing. I mean, I've got avalanches, crushed cars, exploding whales, blown out restaurants, flying eagle people, screaming man-pigs and a now a Kung Fu dog. Forget the X Games; we got excitement right here."

"You really think you can sell that?" Poe asked, knowing that Pete could.

"Well," Pete pondered, "it would still need the right message, you know something kind of edgy, yet friendly. Whatever it is, you have to admit, it would be a helluva lot better than a 'Water-ful Place to Be.'"

Laughing even harder now, Poe said, "You let me know how that turns out," he said. "Just try not to scare off all the tourists over 35."

"That," Pete said as they approached the buffet table, "is why we're going to skip this part."

When Ian came down crashing into the pile of napkins, it was not the first thing he had made contact with. That distinction went to the giant knife still sticking out of the tree. Far from gleaming in the sun, however, it was now a dark shade of red, just like the napkins below it. All of it still there untouched as evidence, Poe couldn't help but muse that it wasn't exactly going to take CSI: Surfland to figure it out. Flying body, gravity, really sharp knife sticking upside down out of a tree: Not exactly a normal combination Poe had to admit, but a predictable one. He had no problem believing that the whipsaw investigators in their Kittymobile could figure it out.

Morosely, however, Poe wondered just what part of Ian had come down on the knife. Looking over at Ian's body he could see it was crumpled over on itself, almost in a fetal position.

Seeing the bald eagle costume once again without the part that made it bald, Poe idly wondered what had become of the actual costume's head. Maybe he'd been hanging out with Fuzznut too long, but Mrs. Margaret's great-grandkids had experienced a hard enough day as it was. They didn't need to see a charred eagle head rolling around in the parking lot.

"Hey, Pete," Poe asked. "What ever happened to the head?"

"Oh, they already put that in a Hefty bag," Pete said. "It was attracting a lot of flies."

"No, I meant the..." Poe said, suddenly realizing exactly what Pete meant.

"Well, that's gross."

Now walking back across the grass with Pete, Poe could see that pretty much everyone who'd played a part in the drama of the last several days were all gathered together. (Save for Buffett, who was thought to be sleeping on the laps of a freakishly large set of twins.) Scrote's unconscious body still the main attraction in the center of the semicircle they were standing in, he could see even Mrs. Margaret remained. Indy was on one side of her, still sipping coffee from her mug as she looked out over the lake. While on the other side of Oregon's most famous centenarian was Dick, no doubt trying to sell her on his marketing slogan.

Thrilled to see all of them, Poe was reminded he had amends to make when he saw Dick suddenly stare at him and immediately quiet down. Leaning in to whisper to Mrs. Margaret, Dick still kept a leery eye on Poe.

"Well," she said, "I think that's a wonderful idea!"

Starting to apologize to Dick, Poe never got the chance.

"INDY!"

It was Scrote, yelling as he suddenly sat up in the middle of the circle. Stopping everyone where they stood, all eyes were on him. His gun still hoof-in-hand, he stared at no one but her. Not knowing if he was the object of her affection or his aggression, everyone except Indy and Mrs. Margaret began diving for the ground. Asking simply, "A one in a million chance?" before he began walking towards both women, all Poe could do was wonder how they were possibly going to take Scrote down this time.

Indy, however, had no such concerns, and in less than a second, her coffee mug had shot from her hand like a laser beam and nailed Scrote square in the forehead. Dropping him once again like a sack, Indy went back to simply looking out over the lake.

With everyone picking themselves up off of the ground one last time, only Mrs. Margaret seemed unfazed by the incident. Clearly more than a little water under the bridge in her 102 years, she patted Dick on the knee and began to speak. "You know, I think Dick's right.," she said, as she looked at Indy and laughed. "The beach IS back."

And still without turning to look away from the lake, Indy found her answer, and the truth, simple:

"Yeah... I guess she is.""

Epilogue

Plink Blayton was returned in handcuffs to Columbus, Ohio, where his trial was carried on CourtTV. Asked to interview with Ann Curry on *Today*, he went blind for two days. Found guilty, he was sentenced to two years in jail and 2,000 hours of community service. Half his hours were to be served cleaning out the waste ponds at the city water treatment plant. The other half was to be served concurrently volunteering at the local petting zoo — as a sheep.

Mrs. Margaret Tandy returned to publicly running her company's daily affairs, starting with tracking down her and the other investors' money that had been embezzled by Ian and Scrote. Cambodian bankers, agreeing that bribes from a very live person were better than past ones from a very dead one, turned over all of the money. The money finally deposited in Tandy corporate accounts, Mrs. Margaret took Indy and Xander out to dinner at Benihana, where she made sure the knives had never been anywhere near a Surfland buffet table.

Rip Rockford returned to the The Inn at Roca de la Muerte Dolorosa to learn more about their infrared camera technology — and then immediately went and bought the same equipment. He overpaid by a factor of three as it had been used once by Sylvester Stallone in

"The Expendables." He also spent six months trying to convince Dick Yelpers that Surfland's new tourism marketing strategy should be "The Kitch is Back," with Florence Henderson singing the vocals. He did not succeed.

Dick Yelpers dream finally came true: He convinced the Surfland Tourism Advisory Board to use "The Beach is Back" as a tourism slogan. Following Poe's advice to embrace the city's more recent history of avalanches, crushed cars, exploding whales, blown out restaurants, flying eagle people, screaming man-pigs, Kung Fu dogs and a highly caffeinated — and attractive — version of Nolan Ryan, Dick saw to it that Pacific Northwest residents knew Surfland was a place anything could happen — and probably would. He was less successful, however, at getting the board to change their name to a simple acronym, although they did agree to let him use it on marketing materials sent to shish-kabob culinary competitions and vampire slayer conventions.

Pete Polanski sold most of his footage for a hefty fee to the Surfland Tourism Advisory Board, with the exception of anything including Plink Blayton — which he sent anonymously to the *Today Show*. Still planning to return the All-Star Joan of Arc Memorial Horse Race and Bonfire to its former glory, he plans to invite Jimmy Buffett, the guy from *Jackass* and the entire cast of *Backdraft*. Randy Newman has already agreed to appear on the condition that he not be asked to sing the city's new theme song — ever.

Buffett the Slumber Dog slept.

Ryan Nordin and his family continue to run Bendovren Coffee in Surfland, where there is now one less historical photo on the wall. As a thanks for sacrificing his car for the greater good, Mrs. Margaret gave him the title to her 1963 Jaguar E-Type convertible on two conditions.

One: He must never remove the "Bonded in Crap" bumper sticker. Two: The bumper sticker must be the only thing related to Bond he ever does again with the car. He happily agreed.

Kirby "Scrote" Ionescro was arrested and taken to Portland, where he was held all weekend in county lock-up in his pig suit. It is not known how he went to the bathroom. Sentenced to six months in prison for his role in embezzling from To St. Helens and Back, he was kept from the general population and several goats that were there to keep the grass short. While incarcerated, bootleg video of his porcine escapades were spliced in with cow videos from the California Dairy Board to create "Farmageddon 2: Aporkalypse Cow." Upon release from prison, he immediately found himself with three job offers from various farm animal-related enterprises, including a theatre group. Currently on a four-month tour of the Midwest, "Farmesan Cheese" has been held over by popular demand in southeast Kansas 14 times.

Ryan "Xander" Reynolds received pyrotechnics-related job offers from Universal Studios, The Army Corps of Engineers, PETA and several militia groups with no return address in Wyoming and Idaho. He turned all of them down, choosing instead to return to his NGO job. There, he maintains a long distance relationship with Indy while working on his latest project: getting Internet access via laptops and exercycles to the Rebekkah Talmedge Tandy Memorial orphanage in Siem Reap, Cambodia.

Indy Monroe's family was finally reunited. Her mother, finally diagnosed with something very long and Latin, is expected to make a full recovery. Her father, now the executive director of the PDX-Treme Sci-Fi Museum, took over the Extraterrestrial Student Exchange program. A program that gives poor children the greatest Halloween make-up jobs and costumes ever created, it allows them to be the coolest kid in the universe one day a year. Indy sees her parents as often as she can, when she is not studying as a full-time student under the personal tutelage of Mrs. Margaret. This, while also being voted Seventh-Sexiest Woman on the Internet, after she re-enacted her mug-throwing moment for Dick and Pete in a Surfland promotional video.

Jackson Poe returned to a life of freelance writing, driving with the top down on all but the rainiest days and relaxing with the perfect cup of coffee at Bendovren. His last story, on hotel balcony safety, made the cover of Sunwest Magazine when he caught a photo of a rainbow-attired drag queen doing a swan dive off the ninth floor into the pool at The Inn at Roca de la Muerte Dolorosa.

Author's Notes

The quad-suit of Bekk the Dog actually exists and functions entirely as described, although the virtual life-like resemblance has been overstated, just a bit. All the injuries suffered by Bekk — and even a few of the ones he inflicts — are entirely true (as the author can testify).

The chapter on Oregon's history with exploding things and dead whales is largely true — including the website www.theexplodingwhale. com — although the locations have been changed in some cases. It is also true that Oregon coast chambers of commerce continue to get calls to this day wondering where it just happened.

Although the ensuing chaos at the GO River Wayside is entirely fictional, there were two communities that feuded over the title of "World's Shortest River." Also, one was in Montana and the other the coast of Oregon — and in the end the Guinness Book of World Records did find the whole thing to be so ridiculous that they pulled the entire category.

About the Author

Barton Grover Howe is an Amazon.com best-selling author, humor columnist and high school teacher who has spent most of the last 10 years teaching, being a mascot and generally not being near as funny as he thinks he is. He currently resides in a small town on the Oregon coast within shouting distance of Surfland. For more of his writing, including his weekly humor column, go to www.BartonGroverHowe.com.

If you liked *The Beach is Back*, check out Barton Grover Howe's other books:

The Surfland Novels:
Beach Slapped

Surfland Day Trips (Short Novels):
Parrot Eyes Lost

Humor Column Collections:
Flying Starfish of Death: A Beach Slapped Humor Collection, 2008
Addicted to Foo-Foos: A Beach Slapped Humor Collection, 2009
Cats with Thumbs: A Beach Slapped Humor Collection, 2010
Mermaid—The Other White Meat: A Beach Slapped Humor Collection, 2011

Proof

Made in the USA
Charleston, SC
21 May 2012